THE
HUNTERS
CALL

William Scott

I realized fear one morning, when the blare of the fox hunters sound.

When they are all chasing after the poor bloody fox, 'tis safer to be dressed like a hound.

-Liam   Devlin

***

Chapter 1

1971. The Summer of Love was over, but free spirited youth continued to arrive in California year after year. Leaving their homes of suburban conformity, they aimlessly rolled westward like tumbleweeds. For most the journey was the focal point; what they saw, who they met, and what they learned. Some had a vague notion of heading to California; of getting rich, getting famous, or a combination of both. But the majority had no real plans and eventually found themselves beached along the California coastline with no food, money, or prospects.

Sitting in a small café along Venice Beach, Leon White had to smile at his luck for finding a place such as this. Unlike the desperate creatures he observed walking along Ocean Front Walk, he had not been disappointed when he arrived.

Relaxing in a pair of crumpled cotton pants, floral shirt and buckskin vest; most would have been surprised by his past. Originally from Chicago Leon had been a beat cop on the payroll of the Syndicate, which was the more polite name used by the mob. He'd happily accepted his first bribe a few weeks on the job, having hoped it would come when he joined the force. Unlike some of his fellow recruits at the academy, he knew that money brought power as much as a gun and a badge. So he figured he might as well have all three.

He'd straddled the line between good and evil for many years, before a storm of justice descended on his shady city. Finding himself under investigation, Leon had jumped at the first opportunity toescape that came his way. The skills he'd learned on the force and on the take had made him a dangerous man and had led directly to his new employment.

Soaking up the sun by the ocean, Leon felt as though things had turned out alright. He'd always tried to live in the moment, and right now the moment was very good indeed. Taking a sip of cold beer, he watched the arrival of a young girl on the boardwalk across from him.

Each day for the past two weeks she showed up around noon with a small beat up guitar. Today was no different as she shuffled over to a spot of grass and sat down, laying her wide brimmed hat out in front of her. Taking the guitar out of the case, she began strumming it and humming along to a nameless tune.

Without the hat, her long auburn hair seemed to glow in the autumn sun. A small braid ran across the top of her head and then ran down the side. Chuckling to himself, Leon thought he could even see the odd flower woven into the long braid.

He'd seen girls like her before and after watching her for two weeks, he felt confident enough to make his approach. He waved the café owner over, a middle aged hippie the patrons called Walrus.

"Hey Wally, how about a pair of Cokes," he ordered after the Walrus eventually sauntered over to his table.

"Sure man," came the slow monotonous reply. Leon could smell the reefer on him and figured it would be even odds if his order ever showed up.

Looking back at the girl playing the guitar, he got the feeling again. It was the same kind of feeling he used to get before approaching an informant, a combination of excitement, doubt, and hope. Embracing the feeling, he took out a pack of cigarettes from his vest pocket and lit one with a match struck on the battered table.

The boardwalk was a flurry of activity with bicycles criss-crossing as they dodged sandaled beach goers and side walk vendors trying to sell their cheap goods. Leon calmly walked through the circus, expertly avoiding those flying past him without hesitating. He ignored an old woman offering to read his fortune and was amazed at a pair of young men trying to sell their finger paintings. In this case it was actually foot paintings, as their feet were stretched out and still awash in blues and greens.

"How's business?" Leon asked after exhaling a puff of smoke and flipping a quarter into the girl's hat.

"Swell," she retorted scornfully, shooting him a dark glance.

"Usually you say thank you when someone actually gives you change," he countered with a smile.

"Thank you so much," she mockingly replied while continuing to play. "Now I'll be able to eat for another day."

"How about you save that for tomorrow and let me buy you a meal today?" Leon asked with a sly grin, offering her a cigarette as additional enticement.

She took it without hesitating, shoving it behind her uncovered ear between strums on the guitar. But she seemed to give his actual proposal more thought.

"If I go eat with you, I'll miss out an all the business out here," she finally pointed out as a kind soul passing by dropped a nickel into her hat.

"Suit yourself; I wouldn't want to interrupt your thriving music business," accepted Leon sarcastically. When she didn't budge he simply shrugged and turned to leave. "If you change your mind I'll be across the way."

Leon dodged his way back across the boardwalk without looking back, arriving at his table as the Walrus deposited the two drinks.

"You guys want anything to eat?" the Walrus asked after setting the drinks down.

Initially confused by the plurality of the request, Leon quickly realized the reason as the girl's guitar case whacked his left leg as she squeezed past. Without a word she plopped down across from him on a rickety metal chair.

"Two burgers, plus another two Cokes," he ordered as he joined her at the table. "By the time he finally brings them we'll be finished these ones."

The girl looked at the two bottles Leon pointed to on the table and took one, unceremoniously gulping it down. Before finishing it completely she set it back down on the table and shot him a piercing stare.

"I'm not going to sleep with you," she announced simply, crossing her arms across her chest.

"What?" Leon asked, slightly surprised by the statement. He knew that it wasn't a stretch for her to assume this, but most of the girls weren't this aware. Most were just happy for the food and attention. But this one was different and more wary. However, the fact that sex wasn't his ultimate goal made his surprised response seem more genuine.

"Just because you buy me food doesn't mean I'm going to have sex with you, just keep that in mind," she repeated, although seemingly satisfied with his initial confused response.

"Hey, I'm just trying to do my good deed for the day," Leon replied with upraised hands, displaying his good intentions.

"What are you, a Boy Scout?" she scoffed as she finished off her coke.

"Something like that," Leon laughed as they both relaxed into their seats. The shade provided by a pair of nearby palm trees made their spot very comfortable in the afternoon sun. Without another word they turned to watch the myriad of characters passing along the boardwalk, the constant action seemingly miles away.

They sat in silence, the music from a nearby radio and the din of the boardwalk ensuring it wasn't too awkward. Leon didn't want to force any conversation and the girl seemed content to remain quiet. He was having a hard time figuring this girl out; she seemed both suspicious and at ease with him at the same time. Then there was her accent, hardly noticeable at first but more pronounced as they had been speaking. Her accent seemed English, but her manner of speaking didn't seem to match.

"So where are you from?" he finally asked, his curiosity overcoming his patience.

"Nowhere."

"Fair enough," he allowed easily, understanding the need to ignore the past. "What's your name then?"

"Some of them have started calling me Duchess," she replied, nodding towards the buskers and vendors lining the boardwalk across from them.

"Because of your accent?" Leon observed after finishing off his own drink.

"No because my husband's a Duke," she replied sarcastically, rolling her eyes.

Leon almost coughed up his Coke at her quick retort, barely keeping it down. He smiled and chuckled to himself as the Walrus brought them two more bottles. The girl's strong spirit and quick wit was a nice change to the others he'd recently recruited. They were mostly simple pretty girls from Midwest shitholes. But he could tell this one was different, she'd probably need more than simple words to convince. She might need something stronger.

"I'll be back in a second, I've got to make a phone call," Leon informed her as he stood up from the table. With another drink in her hand, the girl barely acknowledged his departure. He squeezed past another table on the patio before walking through the small doorway into the café. The eclectic mix of furniture within matched the customers who frequented the spot; hippies, surfers, tourists, students, and even the odd square. With only a scattering of customers, the Walrus was leaning against the front counter by the register, listening to a small radio tuned to the local university station.

"Hey Wally, can I use your phone?" Leon asked as he walked over to the counter and reached for it.

"Local call?" the Walrus asked through the bushy handle bar moustache that gave him his name. When Leon nodded, a smile broke through the hairy mess. "Fine, just be careful man. The government's probably listening in."

Leon simply winked at him and started dialling the memorised number. A gruff voice on the other end answered after the first ring with a simple *ya?*.

"I saw Mary this morning and she looked good," he said casually, meaning that he'd found another girl.

"You going to ask her to the movies?" asked the voice on the other end.

"Yeah."

"That's pretty fast work," replied the voice with admiration. "You just went out with Janet. What's she like?"

"Beautiful face, gorgeous ass, and flowing brownish reddish hair," Leon rhymed off as he looked at the girl through the café window. "Plus she's got some real spirit to her."

"Sounds good to me, but those ones can be hard to convince."

"And harder to break," Leon agreed, a wolfish grin breaking out on his face. Breaking them was always the best part of his job. So the longer they took, the happier he'd be.

*

"The Walrus says your name is Leon and that you work for a cult," the girl said nonchalantly between bites of her burger as Leon returned to their table.

"Why'd he say that?"

"Because I asked him," she replied simply. "How does somebody work for a cult?"

"I don't work for a cult, he's just being paranoid," Leon countered calmly. "I work for a youth shelter. Some rich guy back East donated a ton of money to set it up years ago after his son died out here."

"So what do you do there?" she asked, genuinely curious.

"I hang out along the boardwalk on the look out for kids that might need some help," he explained after biting into his own meal. "Sometimes they need a meal, a place to stay, or help getting a job. So which one are you?"

A shrug was all that she could muster while she continued to eat, enjoying every bite of her burger.

"Well the food seems to agree with you, how about a place to stay?" Leon offered with practiced sincerity. "Don't trust me? Hey Wally, remember those two brothers I helped out last month?"

The Walrus looked up from the table he was clearing and sauntered over to them, happy to be avoiding any kind of work.

"Sure, but I haven't seen them since then. Did you sacrifice them to some crazy god?"

"They got cleaned up and went home to Indianapolis," Leon explained to the girl, ignoring the implication.

"So you say," uttered the Walrus doubtfully.

"How about that blond girl, Shirley?" Leon continued undeterred. "She's working at the gift shop three doors down."

"Oh that's right."

"See, this paranoid hippie doesn't know what he's talking about," Leon smiled, gesturing to the Walrus amiably. "No offense."

"None taken," he allowed before heading back into the café, the dirty tables forgotten.

"So you want a place to stay, or are you content staying at the Ritz?" Leon asked before switching to a snooty accent. "Your Highness."

"Very funny," she scowled, slightly scrunching her face. But the look was instantly replaced by her practiced indifference. "But next time you should say, *Your Grace.* That's how you address a Duchess."

"So how'd you know that?"

"I read." She answered quickly, finishing off the last of her second Coke.

"Well I can see you're still not sure, so take this if you change your mind," Leon pulled out a business card along with the cash to pay for the meal. He put it on the table across from her, and watched as she eyed it carefully.

He knew he had to be careful to not come on too strong. Kids her age were predisposed to distrust adult figures and kids on the street even more so. Run-ins with authority figures were normal and usually did not end in their favour. Leon had to suppress a smile as memories of his run-ins with kids like her sprang to mind. Without another look at her he walked out onto the still busy boardwalk.

Leon shoved a pair of cheap aviator sunglasses on as he started walking down the street, the bright sun no longer stymied by nearby palm trees. He resisted the urge to knock a pair of skateboarders over as they rolled past him. The new fad had broken out along the boardwalk a few years ago, adding another hazard to an already chaotic environment.

At the gift store he'd mentioned earlier, Leon stopped and looked at the window display. A cheap collection of souvenirs were spread out over some blue cloth, doubling as the nearby ocean. In the reflection of the window, he watched as the girl casually sidled up to him.

"So where is this place?" she asked brusquely after a short pause, her worn guitar case banging against her leg in the breeze.

Despite her bedraggled appearance and clear need for assistance, Leon knew success was still not assured. There was something more to her, just below the surface that only seemed to appear for seconds. Seeing her now in the window reflection, he realized it was probably the obstinate nature of a young girl rather than strength he sensed. Her decisions would not be based on what she wanted to achieve, but contrary to what others wanted her to do. Knowing he could use this new insight to his advantage, he moulded his answer accordingly.

"It's just east of here, near UCLA," he pointed with his head, keeping his hands in his vest pockets. "It's about a ten minute drive. My car's just around the corner if you want to go. Unless you don't feel comfortable driving with a strange man. Nice girls aren't supposed to jump in with just anyone. Some people might get the wrong idea."

"Which people? I don't know anyone around here, so why should I care," she huffed in response, indirectly agreeing to join him.

Taking her cue, Leon led her along the street towards the alley where he had parked his car. They walked silently across cracked and uneven sidewalks, leaving the bustling boardwalk behind them. The neighbourhood turned into a ragtag collection of beach houses and businesses in varying states of disrepair.

"Wait a second," the girl uttered breathlessly after walking a few blocks. "I'm feeling a little weak and tired."

"Come on, my car is just around the corner," Leon encouraged, watching her sway slightly before straightening herself.

"Here, take my guitar," she said, shoving the case into his hands while she blinked away her short bout of fatigue. After composing herself, she slowly followed Leon around the next corner.

A large beige sedan sat in the alley, wedged between the back of a private garage and the wall of a run down two-story apartment block.

"I'm feeling really strange," the girl admitted dazedly as she leaned against the wall of the garage. She tried to focus on her tingling hands as she raised them to her face, but no amount of blinking seemed to help. "I think there's something wrong, I think I need to go to the hospital or something."

"Don't worry, you're fine," Leon assured her as he walked over to the back of the car and opened the trunk. Watching her determined struggle to regain control of her body, he hoped the Walrus hadn't dosed her food too much. Sure it would be easier to simply put a passed out body into a trunk. But where was the fun in that?

"No I don't think so," she said, shaking her head slightly as she slid down along the wall onto the dirty alley floor.

"No you're right, you're not fine," Leon smiled, finally revealing the predatory face he'd been hiding all day. Instead of putting the guitar case into the trunk, he flung it behind him carelessly. As it thumped to the ground, he watched with delight as her confused face turned into one of fear. "And you're not going to get better anytime soon."

"Wait, I..." She mumbled in horror as she tried to vainly stand up.

"Not so pompous now, are you *Your Grace*?" He taunted icily as he slowly walked towards her, relishing every step. "You look scared now, and you should be. No one's going to come looking for you, because nobody's going to miss you. You belong to my master now. Would you like to meet him?"

Without waiting for a reply he reached down and pulled her back towards the opened car trunk.

*

Leon leaned against the closed trunk, a well earned smoke dangling from his mouth. He'd forgotten the pure pleasure of abductions, especially the surprise ones. Taking another drag, he smiled slightly as she banged weakly against the trunk lid. Her continued fight only made it better, so he didn't even try and threaten her into silence.

"Everything alright?" called a voice from the alley entrance.

Shocked by the sudden interruption, Leon spun around and peered over the car. A young man in ripped combat fatigues and a Hawaiian shirt was standing at the edge of the alley. He had long wavy brown hair and a few weeks worth of stubble. When Leon didn't answer, the man took a step closer displaying a limp and a small cane he hadn't observed before.

"I thought I heard some banging from your car," he continued, peering over the hood of Leon's car into the front seat.

"You didn't hear anything," Leon answered, slowly walking around the car with quiet menace.

"But I'm sure I…"

"Listen, I would have thought you were done playing hero," Leon challenged as he walked up to him, standing a full head higher. He could tell this was just another beat up vet, wasting away in drugs, booze, and memories of the jungle. But that also meant he might also be unstable, so he didn't want to be too threatening. "Listen, here's a couple bucks, why don't you go climb back into your bottle."

He shoved the notes into the man's good hand and watched him eventually turn away and continue his rambling journey down the street. A part of him had wished that the vet had tried something; he had a new knife he was dying to try out. But it was probably for the best, since he had enough to do without disposing of a body.

Content once more he lit another cigarette and climbed into his car. He hated the car and its blandness, but for this work he had to keep a low profile. Thinking about other cars he'd rather have, Leon turned the ignition, ready to be on the road.

But nothing happened, not even a chug or a click came from under the hood. He tried again and got the same response. He rolled the window down, put his head out and tried a third time, hoping to hear something.

"Maybe you should have kept your money and bought a better car," mocked a familiar voice as the vet limped around the corner and back into the alley.

"Sunovabitch!" swore Leon to himself as he reached down and popped the hood. While he was down there he grabbed his pistol, shoving it into his waistband as he got out of the car. He desperately wanted to shoot this loud mouth, but he needed to get his car running first. After all, he still had a girl in the trunk.

Ignoring the smirking cripple leaning against the alley wall, Leon lifted the car's hood and started looking in the engine compartment. He wasn't a real mechanical guy and didn't really know what he was looking for.

"Kinda hard to start a car without a battery, eh?"

Leon immediately stopped his inspection upon hearing these words. He'd ignored the man's accent at their first meeting. Just like the street kids, many vets from across the country also found their way to California's sunny shores. But this time the voice brought him back to his time in Chicago and dealings with those from across the border to the North.

"What the hell is this?" Leon demanded as he turned from the car and faced the vet once more. Better with people than with cars, he could immediately tell his initial appraisal of the man had not been correct. The bleary eyes and slack face were a well constructed façade. "Did you take it?!"

"A man's got to eat," the vet shrugged, despite the growing anger of the man opposite him.

"You've got three seconds to give it back," Leon ordered as he pulled the pistol from his waistband. "Or I finish the job those slanty eyed bastards started."

With shocking speed, the vet's cane swung up and knocked the pistol out of Leon's hand before he could cock it and start counting.

Rather than lunging for the gun, Leon merely smiled wider and pulled a switchblade from his pocket. He liked blades better anyway.

Leon shot a few quick jabs towards the injured vet, only to discover the limp had suddenly vanished. Ignoring a small sense of unease at the back of his mind, Leon continued to make probing attacks.

"You're good," Leon allowed after the vet had easily evaded his few stabbing attempts. "So what, you just hang out on the boardwalk and pan handle? Pretend to be another poor soldier?"

"Beats kidnapping innocent girls," the vet replied with a smile, rapping Leon's knife hand with his cane.

"You little…!" Leon growled in anger, taking a step back and tightening the grip on his knife. "I'm going to gut you and spread your intestines from here to Sacramento!"

But rather than shock or scare his opponent, the vet calmly maintained his smile and took his own step back.

"Not with that you won't," he goaded the larger man as he transferred his cane to his left hand. With a wink, his right hand grasped the cane's handle and smoothly pulled out a long glinting blade. "You need a longer sharper blade to gut someone properly. Want me to show you?"

Leon's eyes widened upon the appearance of the small sword and he began to feel the sense of danger more strongly now. But his primal nature was one of fight rather than flight, and he was not used to being beaten.

"What the hell is this all about?!" He shouted, circling his opponent and looking for an opening. Sensing one, he attacked from the side with a sweeping blow. But the opening closed as quickly as it had appeared and he received a cut on the forearm in return.

"Is it about the girl?" Leon asked after receiving another gash, this time across his chest. He knew he couldn't keep this up, so he hoped to trade the girl for an escape.

"It's not about the girl, well not entirely," the man replied easily, nicking Leon's ear with a quick flick. "It's not even about all the other girls and boys you've taken."

"What?!" Leon yelled in confusion. He'd been so careful all this time that the shock of being discovered almost took his breath away. But this quickly led to rage at being stopped and he charged towards his enemy, slashing as he went.

Ready for this last surge, his opponent backed away and dodged the first attacks. When his back touched the alley wall, he decided to fight back. With lightning speed he blocked Leon's next sweeping slash with the cane in his left hand, knocking the knife to the ground. He then stepped forward, pointing the blade in his right hand against Leon's throat.

"What's this all about?" he repeated with a whisper. Leon finally realized he was the prey, and for the first time in ages he felt fear. But his pride was too great to show it, so he just stared back angrily.

"You haven't figured it out yet, you fucking sadist?" asked the man incredulously. His steely eyes didn't depart from Leon's as he swiftly shifted the blade tip from his throat to his crotch. "You don't recognize me?"

"No! Jesus Christ!"

"Close lad, but not quite," chuckled a familiar Scottish voice from behind, though Leon was too scared to turn his head to verify it. "Although I agree the hair and beard make the resemblance uncanny."

"Shit... Lord Pierce... I didn't..." Leon mumbled as the full impact of his situation dawned on him. But before he could offer a pitiful excuse everything went blank as the full impact of Patrick Pierce's ebony swordstick crashed across his face.

Chapter 2

The wind blew through his hair as he climbed the steps up to the bridge, the boat gently plowing through the waves. The afternoon sun was almost as warm as it had been at noon, lazily descending westward. He slipped on a pair of sunglasses as their boat passed a buoy and turned out to sea. They had just left Long Beach, so there was plenty of traffic to keep everyone on the bridge alert.

"How's she doing, sir?" Sean asked from the helm, confidently steering the cruiser. He nodded down to the girl sunbathing on the deck below them.

"You know Kat, tough as nails," Pierce replied truthfully. He hoped the sunglasses would keep her from noticing a lingering stare he might unconsciously make. She was laid out on a towel and expertly filling out a red bikini; something she'd never imagined existed before leaving the Manor with them.

She'd leapt at the chance of accompanying Patrick Pierce and his men on their manhunt and even stayed excited when she discovered she'd be acting as bait. Initially uncertain about having her join them, Pierce was glad he'd agreed. Her enthusiasm and positive attitude had helped keep his team focused during their long search.

It was almost six months ago that Lord Pierce and his team had exited an old church in San Diego. Though the church itself was very ordinary, one of the doors in the crypt was not. The door was in fact a portal that crossed time and space, connecting to Ravenwood Manor. This portal was like many others spread throughout the world and history alike, all connecting to the Manor.

Pierce had yet to find anybody that could explain how the portals worked or why they were created. But the lack of knowledge concerning the source of the power did not stop the struggle to control it. As a result a secret civil war was now raging across history.

Ravenwood Manor had until recently housed a secret society, the Black Tower Hunt Club. The Hunt was divided into twenty packs, each with its own colour, emblem, and leader. The Hunt travelled through the portals in the Manor to different times to hunt down predetermined targets, usually criminals. But a foiled coup by the second in command had led to the disappearance of almost half of the club's packs through various portals.

Lord Lodge, the Master of the Manor, had immediately ordered the portals closed and shut the Hunt down. Lord Pierce and a few of the loyal packs were then charged with tracking down the escapees, lest they wreak havoc with history.

"Well the bar's fully stocked," Liam exclaimed as he joined the pair on the bridge, pulling cans of beer from his pocket like a magician. "This American stuff is like piss, but at least its cold."

Pierce gladly accepted his and smiled when it cracked open. He enjoyed the refreshing coolness as he took a big gulp, slowly relaxing from his earlier altercation with

Leon. It had been his plan and his team had carried it out perfectly. He knew it had been a risk to fight him alone, but Pierce felt as though it would yield the best result.

Leon was the first target they'd tracked down after six months of hunting. Once they confirmed it was him, MacDuff filled in the blanks on their target from the file; Leon was a bully, a sadist, and overconfident in his abilities. So Pierce decided that they needed to shock him during his apprehension. That would make the next step much easier.

Looking down at their captive from the bridge, Pierce was confident things were unfolding as planned. He wanted to break Leon and he knew there was no better way than to shatter his confidence and then scare him. So he had beaten the big tough guy in a street fight, in the guise of a run down cripple. He'd seen the uncertainty in Leon's eyes when the tip of his sword touched the man's throat. Now it was time for the second stage.

"Liam, you want to wake up our passenger," Pierce ordered as he gestured towards the ladder.

"The full treatment?" Liam acknowledged with a wicked grin as he descended the few steps to the main deck.

"The messier the better," Pierce confirmed as he followed him down.

Without setting down his drink, Liam walked over to a large white bucket and removed the lid. He shoved his hand in and then pulled out a handful of chum, better known as fish parts. Savouring the moment, he wound up like a pitcher and whipped the oozing ball of fish at Leon's incapacitated body. As soon as it landed he pulled out another handful and continued the bloody barrage.

"...and here's the pitch," Liam intoned in his best baseball announcer's voice as he threw yet another large piece. It covered the distance quickly, exploding as it impacted against Leon's head. "Strike! Now that's as pretty a pitch as you're ever going to see."

Laughing inwardly at his subordinate's twisted sense of humour, Pierce poked his head into the main cabin to find his trusty aide poring over items on the galley table.

"Is that rascal torturing the prisoner again?" MacDuff asked without raising his head, rolling his R's in his highland accent.

"What can I say, he's got a gift," Pierce shrugged, sensing the buoyant tone of his companion's voice. MacDuff was his closest friend at the Manor, though he usually acted more like a father or mentor to the younger man. "Find anything in his possessions?"

"Maybe," MacDuff allowed calmly, lifting up a matchbook from the table. "It's from a diner, though well outside the city. It might be a meeting place, or it might just have good pancakes."

"Well we'll ask him. Anything else?"

"Cheap fake id and some cash in his wallet, but nothing insightful," MacDuff continued clinically as he moved items around the table. "And nothing really from the car. It wasn't stolen, but the address on the ownership listed the hotel as his residence."

"Which we've already been through," Pierce concluded as a shout echoed from behind him. "Looks like our prisoner is awake. You want to join in?"

"I wouldn't miss this for the world."

Pierce waited for MacDuff to clear the table and put the contents into a plastic bag. They then exited the cabin together and stepped onto a now messy deck at the stern of the boat.

"What the fuck is this!" Leon screamed as he struggled against his bindings. They'd tied him to a chair and placed him on a bench that ran along the stern of the boat. The only thing keeping it from toppling backwards into the ocean was a single cable attached at the back that ran to a small crane used for pulling large fish out of the water.

"Apparently he's not a fan of fish," Liam smiled as he hefted another handful of the chum. "Or baseball."

Leon's shouting had turned incoherent and an innocent bystander would have thought he was seriously wounded. He had splotches of fish blood and guts from head to toe. Chunks were now matted in his hair and beard, lending to his desperate appearance.

"You ever see Jaws?" Pierce asked calmly, ignoring the prisoner's wild state. He sat down on one of the deck chairs by the cabin door and opened another beer, staring at Leon the entire time. "It won't come out here for another few years yet, but chances are you might have seen it at some point."

"What are you doing with me?!" Leon yelled back in concern as Sean slowed the cruiser.

"The best thing about that movie was that you never see the shark at the beginning," Pierce continued after taking a drink from his beer. "All you saw was a giant fin sticking up from the water, and then BAM! Fish food."

"Fuck you!" Leon sneered in reply, trying to regain his composure. "And fuck you too, you Irish bog bastard!"

This was directed to Liam who had stopped flinging the chum directly at Leon. Instead he started to lob the pieces over the stern like grenades, watching them plop into the small wake of the boat.

"Now there are some people who say that Jaws was unrealistic in its portrayal of sharks," Pierce carried on after a short pause, leaning back into his chair and paying no attention to the captive's cries. "Before that time the number of shark attacks on humans was very minimal. Apparently we don't appear very palatable to the creatures, at least not as much as other fish. So they'll only attack if provoked or we're the only thing around to eat."

"My Lord, is it true that sharks have no known natural predators?" MacDuff asked innocently, joining the conversation for the first time. He was standing by the winch that controlled the cable attached to Leon's chair.

"That's right MacDuff," Pierce answered happily, releasing his inner documentary filmmaker. "So that means they're at the top of the food chain, so everything in the water is free game."

"Nice try assholes!" Leon sneered at them. "You're not going to feed me to any shar..."

Leon went deathly pale as he heard a loud splash behind him. He then froze in place as a second splash soon followed. His hands were clamped onto the arms of the chair and his eyes widened in disbelief as MacDuff cranked the winch. Just a few turns of the handle made the chair angle backwards slightly.

"No, no, no," Leon whispered as he shook his head from side to side.

"Don't worry, Sharks won't ordinarily attack a human," Pierce offered with mock reassurance. "Especially little guys like those."

"But what if a human landed in the water with blood and fish guts all over him?" Liam asked innocently after lobbing another handful of chum into the water.

"Oh, well in that case they'd tear him to pieces. But it would be slow and painful, what with the multiple wounds in the salt water," Pierce replied quickly, trying to contain the smile that was desperately trying to escape. There were no sharks trailing the boat. The sounds Leon believed to be sharks were in fact a collection of dolphins and sea birds.

Just like the movie, Pierce knew that Leon would be more scared if he couldn't see the sharks, but thought they were there. So with a little inference and the timely appearance of some nautical friends, Leon could only imagine a mouthful of teeth waiting to tear him apart as MacDuff continued to lower the chair backwards.

"Pull me back up, for Christ's sake!" Leon screamed after one of the dolphins came close to brushing him.

"Where's Grigori! Where's the rest of your traitorous crew!" Pierce yelled back, jumping up and throwing his beer can at the tied man. They had reached the breaking point and Pierce knew that it if he didn't talk now, they might not get anything from him later.

"I don't know!" Leon whimpered miserably as he tried to peer behind him as the splashing continued.

"Fine, you want to be a hero?!" Pierce countered venomously as he marched to the stern and grabbed one of the front chair legs hovering in mid-air. "MacDuff, lift him up a bit so I can push the legs out. We'll let them nibble on his feet first. See if that jogs his memory."

"Nooo! I don't know!" he cried as the chair slowly started to rise. "I swear I'm just the first part of the chain!"

"Ok I believe you," Pierce calmly accepted, signalling MacDuff to stop cranking.

"But I don't! I think he's lying and I'm going to gut him with his own knife."

Everyone turned in surprise as Kat walked through the cabin door, like a devil's dream in her red bikini and auburn hair. She seemed on fire as she stormed onto the deck, Leon's switchblade in her hand.

"Well I've learned to never doubt a woman's intuition," Pierce shrugged in condolence.

"And I've learned to always heed a woman carrying a knife," Liam chimed in, washing the chum off his hands with a towel.

"Both are good lessons," MacDuff agreed with a nod. "Looks like you've got more to tell us lad, or the lass here will gut you. And when that happens we'll have no choice but to drop you over the side. Can't be messing up this fine boat after all."

*

Despite Lord Lodge's ambivalent attitude towards the means of retrieving the rogue Packs, Pierce wanted no part of perpetuating the violent nature of the Manor. His pack had agreed, partly due to their continued shame from some of the acts they'd committed while employed at the Manor. But mostly they'd agreed because they were good men and it was the right thing to do.

So they had ventured into the San Diego sun almost six months ago with the goal of retrieving some of the deserters without bloodshed or unnecessary violence. Pierce still had nightmares from the last excursions with his men. He'd killed for the first time in his life, two retched soldiers in a bombed out warehouse in 1930's Spain. It had been in the middle of a firefight and they'd suddenly appeared, causing Pierce's deadly reaction. But he'd had little time to fully process it, as they were on the heels of a violent madman bent on changing the world's history. Pierce had killed this man himself when they caught him, up close and with the swordstick he still carried with him.

But unlike those first two, killing Colonel Bufford had been a deliberate act; not an accident, not in self defence, and not to save another. He'd felt justified at the time and received no criticism from anyone who heard the news. By all accounts Bufford had only got what he had coming. However, that did not stop Pierce from waking up in a cold sweat some nights with the Colonel's crazed eyes staring at him through the dark.

Thus, the trickery and rehearsed script used on Leon after his capture. Pierce figured some might call what they did mental torture, but he thought it was better than pulling out his toenails or shooting him in the kneecaps.

"So where were you going to take me?" Kat continued the interrogation, sitting down on the deck chair Pierce had vacated. "Clearly not a youth shelter."

Leon looked from one captor to the other, their hard faces staring right back at him. He involuntarily gulped as he watched the girl play with his switchblade. "No I wasn't."

"That wasn't so hard, now was it?" Pierce observed, signalling to MacDuff to crank the handle a couple times and raise Leon's chair slightly. "So where is Grigori?"

"I don't know," he repeated slowly, his eyes locked on the winch.

"Wrong answer!"

"I'm not sure exactly but I know some things!" Leon pleaded before MacDuff could grab the winch handle and send him back down.

"Go on," Pierce ordered, staring into Leon's eyes in search of deception.

"He's got some kind of retreat out in the country, like a commune or something. It's remote and off the grid."

"Where?"

"I'm not sure, somewhere north of L.A. maybe?" he guessed desperately. "He was supposed to tell me where after this last package so that I could join him."

"Package!" Kat snarled, jumping up from the chair with the knife still in her hand. "I'm not a package. Human beings are not packages!"

"Sorry, that's just the word he used," Leon apologized quickly.

"Fine. Liam, can you take Kat back inside before she knifes our prisoner," Pierce suggested over his shoulder, his eyes never leaving Leon.

Liam nodded with disappointment before leading Kat towards the cabin door, gently taking the switchblade from her.

"Thanks," Leon breathed as they disappeared through the door.

"Shut up," Pierce replied coldly.

"So how many packages have you sent him?" MacDuff asked, refocusing everyone.

"One every couple weeks," Leon replied nervously with deliberate vagueness. When MacDuff raised an eyebrow he quickly turned more helpful. "Ok, thirteen. Thirteen so far, and she was going to be fourteen."

"Well you've been a busy lad, haven't you," accepted MacDuff with obvious contempt.

"So how does it work?" Pierce inquired with genuine curiosity. "What was the next step?"

"I pick them up along the boardwalk, where all the street kids hang out," Leon began, clearly not caring about holding out any longer. He'd crossed the line of trust with his master and divulging more info wouldn't change that. "You can tell the desperate and weak ones. I offer them a meal and then tell them about the youth shelter, which is real by the way."

"Of course it is," MacDuff grinned dangerously. "It's a good cover. Well almost, since that's how we found you."

"You offer a ride, slip them something into their meal and throw them into the back of your car when they pass out," Pierce rhymed off the routine they'd watched during their surveillance. "Then what?"

"I don't drug them, the Walrus does," he countered righteously, trying to save face.

"Which he probably gets from you and gives under your order," Pierce waved Leon's attempt at integrity aside. But then he looked over to his comrade. "MacDuff, we need this Walrus character for anything?"

"No."

"Then he gets a bullet in the kneecap for his trouble if we see him again."

"Yes sir."

"How does he know to drug the meal," Pierce suddenly reversed, feeling as though something was missed.

"What?" Leon asked, caught off guard before realizing the meaning of the question. "Oh, when I have one on the hook, I go make a phone call before the food shows up. That's his cue."

"You didn't say anything about a phone call before," MacDuff observed, leaving the winch and crowding over Leon.

"Sorry, I'm having a hard time thinking straight with all this crap on me."

"You'll get cleaned up when we're done," MacDuff allowed coldly. "With a hose if we're happy, or in the ocean if we're not."

"Ok, Ok! I get it."

"Who do you call?" Pierce questioned simply.

"My contact. I let him know I've got another package and then hang up. I assume he contacts Grigori."

"Who is he?"

"I don't know it's just a voice on the other line, I've never met him."

"Go on," Pierce ordered, trusting what he'd just heard. This was one of his first interrogations, but he thought he could tell when Leon was evading, lying, or being honest. It was a feeling he got looking into the man's eyes, and he finally understood how someone could get turned on by the power of it.

"There's nothing else to tell about him," Leon repeated in confusion.

"Not about the contact," MacDuff corrected impatiently. "You've got the girl in your trunk, then what?"

"Oh, well I have to wait for instructions," Leon continued slowly, his eyes lowering. "So I take them to one of my places and wait."

"And you have a little bit of fun with them while you wait, don't you?" MacDuff spat in disgust, easily filling in the blanks Leon wanted to omit. "My Lord, I'm going to kill this piece of filth. Lord Lodge gave us permission and I'm going to use it."

"But I'm telling you everything!" Leon pleaded loudly, his eyes once more wide with fear.

"You'd better!" MacDuff threatened as his hand slammed down on the bench beside Leon, causing the man to jump despite being bound.

"Focus Leon," Pierce calmly continued, naturally becoming the good cop. "When do you get the instructions? How do you get them?"

"Usually within a day or two of the phone call," Leon answered after a deep breath, his eyes still on MacDuff's grim face. "I find a matchbook on the passenger seat of my car with a date and time written inside the cover. That's the meeting place, usually a diner or bar outside of town. I drive out there, leave the keys on the floor and go have some food. When I come out, the car is gone and I get in the replacement."

"And then you drive back home like nothing ever happened," Pierce concluded, inwardly upset with himself for appreciating the effectiveness of the plan. "The car we found was registered in your name, what about the other one?"

"It's the same make, model and colour as mine," Leon admitted with renewed satisfaction. "It's registered to John Smith."

"One last question and then we'll wash you off," Pierce promised despite the sharp look from MacDuff. "Where were you going to take her while you waited for instructions? What's the address?"

After a moments hesitation Leon rhymed it off before deflating in the chair, exhausted from the continued stress and fear of the interrogation.

"Have Liam hose the bastard down," Pierce ordered as he turned to leave the deck. The chum had dried onto his body and the stink was starting to attract gulls. They had been circling overhead during the interrogation and were starting to get closer.

Climbing up the stairs to the bridge once more, Pierce noticed that the sun had lowered considerably. The intense yellow rays had transformed to a red glow as it reached for the horizon. The sea had calmed and the peaceful feeling that enveloped Pierce at that moment was welcome after the intensity on the deck below. For a minute he just stood soaking up the sun and wind, a smile creeping across his face.

"We're heading home Sean," Pierce observed after deciding to rejoin the world. "Back to the Manor."

"I'll plot a course back to San Diego then," Sean acknowledged without requiring the direct order. "I take it he talked then sir?"

"Like his life depended on it," Pierce chuckled as he looked back down on the deck below. Liam had finally hooked up the hose and was enjoying himself as he cleaned up their prisoner. The force of it had almost knocked Leon and the chair backwards into the water, eliciting more screams and shouts.

"Are you going to tell him about the dolphins?" Sean asked with a grin as he followed Pierce's gaze below.

"No, I want the threat of violence to remain real to him. That wasn't the last interrogation he's going to face, and if he finds out he was tricked he's likely to close up like a clam."

"Wait till Tiberius gets a hold of him," Sean whistled, thinking about what awaited them at the Manor.

"Yeah, he'll be begging for fish guts and sharks then," Pierce concurred with a quiet shudder. If Lord Lodge had been angry by the exodus of the disloyal, his trusty lieutenant had been furious. For days a black cloud followed him as he stormed around the Manor searching for clues.

Pierce knew it was a real possibility that they were bringing Leon back to face pain and death. He hoped it wouldn't come to that and was prepared to try and stop the cycle of violence. But not everyone shared his sense of justice.

"That's Catalina in the distance, so it will be a couple hours before we reach San Diego," Sean offered as he turned the boat south and pulled down on the throttle. The powerful engines sprang to life and they were skimming across the water in seconds. "If it stays calm like this we should make good time."

"Sounds good, I'll send up someone to relieve you in a little bit."

Sean nodded and checked the chart on the table behind him, plotting the most direct course. Pierce had discovered that Sean was a skilled seaman and navigator, having picked up many skills during his service at the Manor.

Stepping back down to the main deck, Pierce noticed that the chair Leon had been strapped to was empty and back in place. So he decided to follow the sound of voices into the main cabin, ducking as he walked through the door.

"That was some act lass," laughed MacDuff from the other side of the galley table. "For a second I thought you just might stick him with that knife."

"I thought she was going to stick me when I tried to take it from here," Liam joined in as he sat down beside him.

"You're too kind," Kat smiled with satisfaction as she approached with a platter of sandwiches. "Sir, I've made some food if you'd like."

"Looks delicious, thanks," Pierce accepted readily, suddenly realizing he hadn't eaten since the morning. "Where's our buddy Leon?"

"Drugged and in the forward stateroom," MacDuff answered before taking a bite of his sandwich. "He'll be under for a couple hours. We don't want him wandering off or causing trouble when we reach port."

"Good thinking. He'll have a nice shock when he wakes up. We're heading to San Diego and then back through the portal to the Manor."

Everyone seemed to brighten at the prospect of returning home. Pierce himself felt eager to be back walking the halls of the large labyrinthine building. There was a power that seemed to flow through the place, described as magic by some, energy by others, and consciously ignored by a few. Whatever it was, Pierce had been feeling its absence the longer they'd been away.

"How long will we be staying?" Kat asked as innocently as she could, hoping it would be more than a day.

"I'm sure it will be long enough for you and Tiberius to get reacquainted," Liam commented brightly, but with a hint of jealousy.

"I'm sure I don't know what you mean," she replied with batting eyes. Her relationship with Tiberius, the new Master of the Hunt, was the worst kept secret at the Manor.

"So once we dock we do the drunken tourist routine?" MacDuff asked, recalling a ploy they'd used in Dublin. "We all stumble to the road, with Leon supported by a pair of us, the drunkest of the bunch?"

"Yeah, that's probably the best play," Pierce agreed thinking it over. "We take a cab to the church and then bing, bang, boom, back to the Manor. Except for Liam and Sean."

"Why is it always us with the extra duties?" Liam mumbled skyward.

"Because you're the best," Pierce offered with mock flattery. "And because you two are still the junior associates in this enterprise."

"What about her?" Liam pointed his half eaten sandwich at Kat. "She's the newest member of the Pack."

"Yes that's true," Pierce conceded quickly. "But I'm not going to be the one to tell Tiberius that she's delayed because of some silly errand."

"Fair enough, what's the job?"

"Leon told us that he gets instructions on the meeting place from a matchbook placed in his car," Pierce began, shifting his plate to the side as he got back to business. "But we left his car in the alley. So in order for us to follow the trail to Grigori, we need to reach that meeting."

"Which means we have to travel back to L.A., get his car and take it to his hide out," Liam concluded gravely, having switched to business himself.

"Precisely, but you don't have to wait for the matchbook to appear. You can head back to the Manor after you park the car."

"Sounds easy enough," Liam shrugged in acceptance. "Plus who doesn't enjoy a road trip."

Chapter 3

1988. Due to its strategic geographical location and its impressive combination of natural and manmade defences, the French military engineer Lazare Carnot described Luxembourg as the Gibraltar of the North. Sitting on a plateau where two rivers met, the cliffs that surrounded the majority of the city dominated the surrounding countryside. But unlike the real Gibraltar, Luxembourg had been conquered and occupied multiple times. However this had only contributed to continuous upgrades to the imposing fortifications.

Walking up a steep street from a lower section of the city, known as the Grund, Tiberius appreciated what was left of the fortified city. Some enterprising engineers of the past had tunnelled into the cliffs and created multiple openings in which to place cannons. From below, the imposing rock walls threatened those approaching like an ancient warship bristling with open gun ports.

Having fought in castle warfare and charged cannon loaded with grapeshot, he shivered at the prospect of attacking the city in its heyday. Imagining the carnage

William Scott

such an attempt would create, Tiberius hoped such activities were well behind him.

Despite his youthful appearance and powerful physique, Tiberius was much older than the thirty odd years a casual observer would guess his age to be. His dark hair remained untouched by grey and only the hint of a scar above his left eye showed the impact of time upon his body. But he was in fact significantly older than he looked. Tiberius himself regularly admitted that he didn't know how old he was, having given up counting after decades at Ravenwood Manor. It could have been centuries since Lord Lodge had recruited him, being one of the longest serving members of the Manor.

He'd begun as an employee at the Manor, eventually acting as Lord Lodge's faithful right hand. But after the disappearance of the rogue packs, he'd taken over the duties of the traitorous Dr. Cleaver. So now his position, Master of the Hunt, properly reflected his innate authority and dominating presence. It was these qualities, along with his powerful but sorrowful gaze that truly showed his considerable age.

The island where the Manor was located was a strange place, where time seemed to stand still. And though the passing of years had little effect on the bodies of the inhabitants, the same could not be said for their minds or souls. It was worse for the members of the Hunt, who regularly passed through the mysterious portals of the North Tower. The portals led to a multitude of eras throughout time; places of danger, intrigue, and opportunities for corruption.

He'd just passed through one of these portals, the exit being in the upstairs of a narrow cottage wedged between a shop and a pub. Like most of the buildings in the Grund, the cottage seemed to be jockeying for the

35

limited space available. This part of the city was its own little village, sitting isolated in the steep river valley below the cliffs.

He walked alone as the steep street finally began to level out, leading him to the heart of the old city. His men would have just left the cottage, keeping their distance to avoid unwanted attention. The instructions for the meeting were for Tiberius to appear alone; however he wasn't foolish enough to follow them to the letter.

As the Master of the Hunt he was currently coordinating the efforts to track down the rogue members that had fled the Manor. They had dispersed through the various portals of the North Tower, making it a daunting and difficult task. The fact he had few reliable resources to conduct the search was making things even more difficult. Currently there were only two packs actively pursuing leads beyond the portals; Lord Pierce's Brown Pack in 1970's America and Lord Schell's Red Pack in 1600's Germany. The remaining members of his Black Pack continued their sweep of the island itself. But the fact that some of them might still be in league with their old master, Doctor Cleaver, kept him from sending them through the portals.

The leads Pierce and Schell were following were long shots, provided by Lord Lodge who had isolated himself in his office. Day and night he pored over an endless stream of documents in search of clues, making Tiberius worry for his health. Three of Lodges most trusted servants were working their way through the myriad of portal doors, obtaining newspapers and documents from the other side. These were then brought directly to the Master of the Manor for his review. No one knew what he was looking for and Tiberius had the feeling his master didn't either. But the elder statesman kept trolling patiently for clues.

His patience had paid off a few days ago when one of Lodges old valets had walked through the very same portal Tiberius had just passed. Before he could head to the shop next door for a collection of newspapers, he spotted a letter on a chair in the middle of the hallway. It was addressed to *Victor Lodge*.

Tiberius felt the short note in his pocket as he continued past the Grand Duke's majestic palace. Like most of the Manor's correspondence it was both succinct and vague. A typewritten note with a location, time and date was ominously followed by *come alone*. He didn't know what to expect from the meeting and hoped that his presence, rather than Lord Lodge's, would not alter things. But what he did know was that he'd made such little progress to this point, that he would welcome any potential help.

Turning into the Place Guillaume II, a large square in the heart of the city, he walked around groups of camera laden tourists eagerly drinking up the history. Tiberius hoped his circuitous route towards the meeting spot would allow his men time to get into place first. Since they might potentially be recognized by their unknown host, Morgan and Dufresne would take up distant positions in order to observe the meeting. Despite his objections, Morgan had been strictly instructed to keep his sniper rifle behind.

Continuing towards the meeting place provided in the letter, Tiberius took a few random turns and made sudden stops to check for a tail. But none of those actions elicited a feeling of danger or unease. He didn't observe anyone stop when he stopped or trying to look inconspicuous. Feeling confident he crossed a wide street towards the meeting place, the Gëlle Fra monument.

Also known as the Monument of Remembrance, it was a towering obelisk with a bronze lady on the top. With a breathtaking view of the Petrusse Valley below, it was another favourite tourist spot.

Tiberius crossed the road and joined a group of British tourists in front of the monument. A local guide tried in vain to enlighten them on the monument's history, but most were too busy snapping photos to listen. Tiberius was similarly ignoring the guide, instead using the group as cover as he looked around the site, hoping to see a familiar face.

"In place?" Tiberius whispered as he pointed his own camera at the top of the monument. He spoke into a small microphone clipped to the inside of his jacket cuff. He heard a pair of quick affirmative responses in a nearly invisible earpiece. "Anyone see anything?"

"Negative sir."

"Fine I'm going to move to the walkway on the other side. Make sure you can see me from there." Putting the camera down, Tiberius separated from the group and walked around the large base of the monument. A small parking lot was on the other side, crammed with small tour vans and taxis. He weaved through the vehicles, carefully checking their occupants as he moved past. But nothing seemed out of place or threatening.

Past the parking lot, a wide walkway provided a magnificent view of the Petrusse Valley. Tiberius whistled appreciatively as he looked at the Aldophe Bridge in front of him. It was a majestic combination of engineering and art gracefully spanning the distance of the wide gorge.

"You got eyes on me?" he whispered as he once again lifted the camera towards the bridge. Once again two affirmative replies crackled over the radio. Feeling as confident as he could under the situation, Tiberius turned from the impressive view and scanned the walkway. Nothing seemed out of place or suspicious; tourists took pictures, vendors sold trinkets, and children were running happily between everyone.

"Monsieur?" intoned a young boy who had stopped running right in front of Tiberius, stretching his neck upwards in order to look up at the imposing man.

"Oui?" Tiberius replied in confusion by the appearance of the boy.

"Pour vous," was all he replied, handing over a newspaper before running off down the walkway. Tiberius watched as the boy joined a group of similarly aged children, quickly losing track of him in the throng of the noisy class.

Initially shaking his head at the strange occurrence, Tiberius quickly reprimanded himself for missing the seamless tradecraft employed. This realization was proven correct as he unfolded the newspaper and a small paper note fell to the ground.

"Bistro Le Paris, 5 minutes," he read into the microphone as he bent down and picked up the note.

*

"Master of the Hunt I see," mused a handsome man over a raised cup of coffee. "How very progressive of Lord Lodge to hand the title over to a member of the staff."

Tiberuis had approached the new meeting spot feeling prepared for anything. However this feeling evaporated as soon as he reached the bistro and saw the familiar face sitting on the patio.

The shock was enough to make him momentarily wonder how news of his promotion had reached the man in Luxembourg, before realizing he was wearing his black hunt jacket. The new metal symbols on the collar of his jacket displayed his new position to anyone with knowledge of the Manor, such as the man before him.

"Herr Zeidt, what a pleasant surprise," Tiberius replied, gracefully acknowledging the Leader of the Gold Pack as he sat on the offered chair. After the portals had been closed, Tiberius had been surprised that Zeidt's name was alongside those who had fled the Manor. He had not been one of Cleaver's cronies, generally staying neutral in the affairs of the Manor.

"And for myself as well," Zeidt replied, slowly setting his cup down and motioning a waiter over. "I wasn't sure if Lord Lodge would accept my invitation, but I'm pleased that he sent you as a replacement. If he had sent Drummond, I doubt I would have kept the meeting. The man's a pompous bore."

"Drummond's dead," Tiberius offered simply before casually accepting his own coffee from the returning waiter. They were the only ones sitting on the patio outside the bistro, the crisp autumn air keeping the other patrons indoors. As such Tiberius felt able to speak more freely with his companion. "He committed suicide the day Cleaver vanished."

"Did he really?" Zeidt replied with little remorse. "I wouldn't have thought he had it in him. I don't suppose your men gave him a helpful nudge?"

"Of course not," Tiberius replied with feigned indignation. "We wouldn't have acted so quickly. He would have spent months being interrogated first."

"Just so," smiled the former Swiss Banker, recognizing the cold practicality of Tiberius' reasoning.

Before being recruited by the Manor, Josef Zeidt had been an influential yet shadowy Swiss banker. Born to a rich banking family in Zurich during the First World War, Zeidt had quickly learned the profitability of being neutral. He then increased the family fortune by looking after the assets of anyone willing to pay his fees. He had no agenda himself, and rarely concerned himself with the activities of his clients. All he cared about was what he could see in the ledger, and the blacker it was the better. If he could make a profit he would deal with anyone from the Red Cross to the Mafia. His indiscriminate avarice soon found a complimentary partner with the growing Nazi party in neighbouring Germany.

Despite their rhetoric, there were some things the Nazi's did like about the Jewish people; their money, jewels, and art. Like vicious mockingbirds, senior Nazi's grasped at the shiny riches of people they forced from society. The private homes of Germany's wealthy Jews were confiscated and the riches within divvied up amongst the *collectors*. Those with enough foresight or those simply wishing to hedge their bets decided to hide their ill gotten gains outside of Germany. Men like Josef Zeidt accepted anything shipped their way, throwing it in secret numbered accounts and happily accepting the added fees for their discretion.

But eventually the great houses owned by enemies of the state within the Third Reich became empty. So the truly evil, corrupt, and greedy decided to turn to the people themselves in order to continue obtaining wealth. Personal items, including gold from their teeth, were taken from prisoners of the concentration camps and passed amongst the conspirators. Some of these blood spoils found their way to the opened arms of Zeidt and men like him, careless of the methods used to obtain them. After all, gold was gold to them.

Tiberius had read all of this from Zeidt's file as he researched the Hunt Member's that had fled the Manor. Like the majority of those recruited to the Manor, Zeidt had been eager for a new life as his began to crumble around him. His involvement with the Nazis was about to come to light after the war. Despite his connections and immense wealth, he knew that he would never be able to ride out the storm of public opinion as the truth of the camps came to light.

"So why did you run with the others?" Tiberius asked, knowing the banker was not one to take chances.

"I'm a tired man Tiberius," he answered without any outward signs of weariness. "I'm tired of the endless days of drinking, debauchery, and violence. I might not have lived at the Manor as long as you, but it no longer holds the same appeal as before."

"That's it then; you joined up with Cleaver in order to leave the Manor. To do what exactly?"

"I didn't join up with Dr. Cleaver," Zeidt rebuked gently. "He merely opened the door and I decided to pass through it. I've returned to my first love, banking. I've missed the simple beauty of numbers."

"Spare me the sentimentality, what was in it for you?" Tiberius challenged the perfectly tailored man across from him. His suit, watch and glasses were probably worth a combined twenty thousand dollars.

"Avoiding a bullet to the brain," Zeidt replied evenly. "Knowing I wouldn't join his plot without an incentive, Cleaver offered me the best kind. However despite the method of my departure, I would very much like to remain here."

"So you've come to make a deal in case Cleaver's side is not successful?" Tiberius observed immediately, having realized Zeidt would try and stay neutral as soon as he sat down across from him. "I'm afraid you're going to have to choose a side this time."

"Why is that?" he replied with genuine confusion, the idea being foreign to him.

"Because I've started following the rule *if you're not with us, you're against us.*"

"How very simplistic," Zeidt countered with a wave of the hand.

"You know what's also simplistic?" Tiberius asked casually as he folded his hands together. "I take the pistol out from behind my back, aim it at you under the table and put two bullets in your gut and simply walk away. My job is to bring you back, dead or alive. You want to make a deal? You can make it with Lord Lodge, back at the Manor."

"From the inside of a cell no doubt? I think not."

"Well those are the only two options."

"Tiberius, life is not black and white," Zeidt countered as the waiter returned to pick up their empty cups. Zeidt ordered an aperitif while Tiberius simply waved the waiter away, annoyed by the interruption. Zeidt continued once they were alone again. "There is a grey space between the two and I'm willing to trade some information to remain in the grey."

"If you truly have information worth trading for, what's to stop me from forcing you back to the Manor and taking it by force?" Tiberius asked pleasantly, knowing the words themselves carried enough of a threat.

"Nothing," Zeidt conceded with little concern. "However it will take some time for you to break me, time that I daresay you don't have."

"Bullshit," Tiberius challenged forcefully, tired of the conversation and for Zeidt's inner greasiness. Despite his perfectly groomed exterior and chiselled good looks, he knew Zeidt was nothing more than a shallow con man. "Give me one good reason to refrain from walking away and returning with more men and hunting you to the ground."

"I'll give you three," Zeidt countered holding up three fingers, almost catching the waiter as he approached with a small green drink on his tray. He apologized mechanically as the glass was placed on the table and the waiter hurried off. "First, I'll give up the location of my men. They left me after discovering I wanted to lead a simple life of banking. So you can bring them back as trophies and interrogate them to your hearts content."

"That's a start, but they won't know the full details of what Cleaver has planned."

"Sadly no, which is why there's a number two."

"Go on," Tiberius implored with more patience than he felt. A part of him was itching to pull out the pistol from under his jacket and finish the tiresome conversation. But he knew that at this current stage of the hunt, getting information was more important than getting kills.

"On the condition that I can provide the information here without returning to the Manor…"

Tiberius merely raised an eyebrow and signalled him to continue.

"…I'll provide everything I know about Cleaver's plan and tell you how everyone was able to escape the Manor."

"Very persuasive," Tiberius mocked when Zeidt finished, wondering what number three was. "You're going to tell me how the gate was opened, after all the horses disappeared. My job is to get them back, not figure out how they did it."

"Sometimes knowing the means can be just as useful as knowing the ends," Zeidt offered sagely as he lifted his glass from the table.

"That's it!" Tiberius growled through gritted teeth as he pulled the pistol from his back and pointed it at Zeidt from under the table. "I can deal with your fake sincerity and your second class attempts at intrigue. But when you start spouting fortune cookie proverbs at me, I'm done."

The outburst caught the banker by surprise and he almost dropped his drink, recovering in time to place it back on the table. Clearly flustered, he regained his composure by running his manicured hand through his straw coloured hair.

"What I meant is that knowing how the escape was made might be more important to you than why they escaped."

"I doubt it," Tiberius scoffed, thumbing back the hammer of his pistol loud enough for his companion to hear.

"Think about it," Zeidt implored, his smooth veneer beginning to crack. "Megalomaniacs like Cleaver are always searching for power. Who cares if he escaped in order to take over a business, a country, or even the world? But if you look at how he escaped and how he organized the others' escape, you might get a better lead to follow in order to hunt him down."

Tiberius wanted nothing better than to simply ignore the pleadings of the man at the end of the gun and pull the trigger. He knew that Zeidt was using the situation to his own means and had no intention to simply live the life of a quiet banker in Luxembourg. But the fact was that the man made some sense and he was curious as to how they had all escaped the Manor without attracting any attention.

"I can't simply leave you here, but I can promise that if you return with me you will not be imprisoned," Tiberius promised after some thought. His current task was to hunt down and return the missing Hunt Members. So he couldn't avoid bringing back the first one he'd found because he might have some useful information. "You have my word you won't be harmed."

"That's not good enough," Zeidt objected forcefully. "I'm not going back to the Manor."

"Why, you don't trust I'll keep my word? My men and I will ensure you're treated properly."

"I believe you will, but it's the others at the Manor I don't trust."

"You don't have much of a choice in the matter," he countered stonily, his gaze turning just as hard.

"Oh but I do. You forgot about number three," Zeidt replied triumphantly. Like a seasoned gambler, he'd saved his best card to play at the end. The slight lines of worry that had been slowly appearing on his face completely disappeared, making Tiberius wonder if he'd been acting the entire time. "Number three is the real reason I won't return to the Manor and it's the most useful information to you."

"Very well, what is so important that you think I'll let you remain here?" Tiberius asked gruffly, his remaining patience slowly evaporating.

"Cleaver left a mole at the Manor."

The single sentence did not have the desired effect upon Tiberius. He merely raised a condescending eyebrow in reply. The idea that not everyone associated with Cleaver had fled the Manor was an accepted fact. None of the staff was missing, providing dozens of possible agents in place. But without direction from their departed master, they could do little harm. At least that was what Tiberius and the others had reasoned.

"You don't seem shocked," Zeidt observed anxiously, worried that maybe the mole had already been discovered and thereby negating his wildcard.

"I'm not. Of course he left agents in place; anyone spending more than five minutes with Cleaver would figure that out."

"I'm not talking about the idea of a mole," he continued, regaining his confidence from Tiberius' generic response. "I'm talking about a highly placed mole at the Manor. Someone trusted by both you and Lord Lodge that remained in place to subvert your hunting of Cleaver."

"That's impossible," Tiberius muttered groggily as the full impact of the statement sank in. Between him and Lord Lodge they had compiled a list of Cleaver's possible associates. But those names all belonged to minor staff members at the Manor and the odd person from the nearby village of Rooks Bay. Who could Zeidt be referring to?

"It's a fact and I know this because I know the identity of the mole," Zeidt offered, his tone all business. "Would that information allow me to stay here?"

Suddenly Zeidt's reluctance to return to the Manor was clear and offered further proof to his assertion. If there truly was a high placed mole left at the Manor, then it stood to reason that there might be another whose name he didn't know. In that case all the minor agents they'd listed would have leadership. Zeidt had to be afraid that if he turned up at the Manor, these agents would be directed to eliminate him. Dr. Cleaver was not known for his forgiveness and he expected complete loyalty. Once

Zeidt accepted Cleaver's offer and escaped through the portal, his allegiance was determined and any overt duplicity would end with his demise.

"If you give me the name of the mole, I'll let you stay," Tiberius offered after a brief pause. "But there will be some conditions."

"It's either yes or no," Zeidt countered. "Plus I want more than your word that I can stay, Lord Lodge will have to agree as well. No offense, but I think the decision is above you."

"Now look who's dealing in absolutes," he shot back with a cold smile. But his demeanour quickly turned to barely contained anger. "Listen you slimy parasite, it's time for a quick refresher on where we all stand. You already pointed out that these badges on my jacket signify my position as Master of the Hunt. That means that I decide who gets targeted by the Hunt, not Lord Lodge and not anyone else. Even if Lord Lodge agrees to your demands, there's nothing stopping me passing your picture around the Hunt room. On a whim I could do this and they would all eagerly rush through the portal ready to make the kill. How long do you think you would last? There's only one thing that can protect you from me."

"What's that?" Zeidt gulped, intimidated by the truth of the statement.

"My word."

"But that's…"

"Shut up," Tiberius interrupted shortly, now firmly holding the upper hand of the conversation. "I will give you my word that you will be able to remain in Luxembourg if you provide me with the three pieces of information you promised. However there are some caveats that you must accept. First you will live the simple

48

life of a banker. The moment you stray from that, I call the Hunt together and pass out your file."

"And the second?"

"You will make yourself available for further visits," Tiberius smiled menacingly. "If you don't cooperate fully you get dragged back to the Manor. Do we have a deal?"

"Ja-vohl," Zeidt answered quickly, his broad businessman's smile flashing once more. He had been ready to concede much more and was surprised when Tiberius made his offer.

"So who's the mole?" Tiberius asked with urgency as he moved to place his pistol back in its holster.

"You would have never guessed," Zeidt began as he lifted his forgotten green drink from the table. He gave Tiberius a small salute before throwing it all back like a shot. But the smug smile instantly disappeared from his face as he shuddered and dropped the glass.

Chapter 4

Zeidt began to cough immediately and started grasping at his throat. Within seconds a green froth began foaming out of his mouth as he desperately tried to speak. Tiberius jumped up from the table, the gun still in his hand, and started shouting for help. A crowd of people rushed out from inside the café and nearby stores to see what the commotion was.

A man in a crumpled suit rushed down to Zeidt, who had fallen off his chair and was now writhing on the ground. When the man looked up to Tiberius, he saw the gun and shouted in alarm, quickly followed by some of the others.

"Gendarmes!" Tiberius yelled quickly to the assembled crowd, pulling out a fake police ID before things got out of hand. Despite the supposed short duration of his stay in Luxembourg, Tiberius had ensured he had a full complement of fake ID's at the ready. He knew from experience that any trip through a portal could spiral out of control if you didn't come prepared.

Tiberius had seen enough poisoned and dying men in his time that he knew Zeidt's time on earth was coming to an end. But his anger at the dying man didn't diminish with his impending demise. He'd been angry at the banker's selfish wheeling and dealing for personal safety when they'd started talking, but now he was angry at his stupid showmanship. He had to take that last celebratory shot of green booze!

Like a shot to the shoulder, Tiberius became refocused as he looked at the glass that had contained the poisonous green liquid. It still lay where Zeidt had dropped it, in the middle of their table and knocked on its side. He pushed through the crowd and was about to take it when sirens started to wail in the distance. If they were headed here, he knew he'd have to leave evidence along with the body. But not willing to leave empty handed, he grabbed a napkin that was stained with the drink. Hopefully someone at the Manor could use the lab to get some kind of clue from it.

Another thought suddenly popped into his mind as he saw one of the café waiters in the crowd surrounding Zeidt's body.

"Where's the other waiter?" Tiberius asked the man in French after flashing his badge once more. "The one who served us the drinks?"

When the waiter looked at him in confusion, Tiberius didn't wait for a reply. He realized there was no second waiter, just a guy dressed as one. He looked past the crowd into the café and saw a white shirted figure react to his stare and dart past the few patrons remaining inside. Raising his weapon up, Tiberius shoved his way through the crowd into the café as the waiter confirmed his suspicion; *Monsieur, I am the only waiter at the café.*

"Target is going out the back of the café!" Tiberius yelled into his microphone, over the screams of an old woman with a white dog as he barrelled through the front door. He received acknowledgements from his men on the other end of the radio, who had been pleading for instructions since Zeidt had fallen over in a choking mess.

The small café had a door in the back across from the kitchen which led out into a narrow alley. The uneven cobblestones of the alley were still damp from the night's rainfall, receiving very little of the days sun over the tall buildings on either side. Tiberius caught a glimpse of the fake waiter as he slipped while turning a corner at the end of the alley. He took off after him at a run, his pistol still out despite the uneven footing.

It only took him a few seconds to reach the end of the alley, making the turn onto another without the same difficulty as his quarry. This alley was a winding passage filled with boxes and with multiple doors leading off. There was no sign of the man in the white shirt or of any of the doors being used, so Tiberius continued running down its length.

Seeing a flash of white up ahead, Tiberius increased his speed, being rewarded within moments with the departing shape of his target running out of the alley and taking a left on the quiet street up ahead. Unwilling to take the time to properly conceal his pistol, Tiberius tried to hide it against his chest as he crossed the road, calling out the street name over the radio as he passed.

"I've lost him," Tiberius called out immediately afterwards, not seeing anyone in a white shirt down the street. He slowed enough to properly hide his pistol, but continued at a jogging pace. "Anyone have anything?"

"I might... wait... got him," announced Morgan breathlessly over the radio. The expert marksman was high up on the neighbouring roofs and had just jumped between buildings in order to get near the intersection

Tiberius had previously rhymed off. "He's just at the Place Des Armes. Shit, I've lost him under the trees."

Tiberius knew it was a short distance up ahead, so he didn't start sprinting again. The Place Des Arms was a large square surrounded by shops, restaurants, and historic buildings. It was a popular spot by tourists and locals alike, so he didn't want to draw unwanted attention to himself by sprinting into the area. But as he took a right into the square, he knew it no longer mattered. The place was filled with crowded pockets of people, many of them wearing white. Large leaf filled trees lined two sides of the square where most of the restaurants were located. It would be impossible to find the man in the white shirt in this mess.

"I see you sir," Morgan informed him through the earpiece seconds later. "I lost him under the trees on the North end of the square, near the MacDonald's."

Tiberius looked in that direction, the bright modern signs of the recognizable franchise clashing with the weathered grey stone of the building. Groups of students and their adult wranglers buzzed around the area, completely destroying any trail of the mysterious fake waiter. Nevertheless he walked to the north end of the square, hoping for a trace.

"You're just about where I lost him now," Morgan offered from a nearby rooftop as he watched Tiberius walk under the trees.

Snaking his way through the groups of students and tourists, Tiberius casually looked over the entire area. Nothing escaped his experienced eyes as he pretended to look around for a friend. But the trail had run cold as the large lunchtime crowd overwhelmed his team's ability to track the target.

"He's gone," Tiberius sighed over the microphone to his men. The three of them weren't enough to mount an effective surveillance screen of the area. By now he could have jumped on a bus or on the back of a bike and be heading out of the city.

"Wait a second, I might have something," Dufresne whispered in reply, entering the conversation for the first time. When Tiberius had yelled that the waiter had run out the back of the café, Dufresne had left his observation post across the street. He had run a route parallel to Tiberius, hoping to cut the target off if he turned. So he found himself one block away on the other side of the square when Morgan lost sight of the fleeing waiter.

"What is it?" Tiberius asked immediately. When no immediate response came, Tiberius anxiously repeated the question. Static was again the only response his covert earpiece yielded. "Morgan, do you have eyes on Dufresne?"

"Negative."

"Shit," he swore under breath. Though he knew Dufresne could more than look after himself, accidents could happen to anyone at anytime.

"Sorry about that," came the eventual reply over the air from Dufresne, much to the relief of his comrades. "I think there was some interference, these radios are garbage. Sir, you'd better head over two streets north of your location. I think I've found our man."

"You've got him?"

"In a matter of speaking. But you've got to see this."

Tiberius left the square as hastily as he could without appearing out of place. Survival on missions though the portals was often about blending in, rather than any martial skills one might have. So he casually walked north, appearing natural as he heard a police siren in the distance.

A crowd was gathering the next street up and Tiberius felt a hollow feeling grow in his stomach. This was confirmed as Dufresne casually sidled up beside him on the sidewalk. Through the crowd he could see a black sedan parked in the middle of the road, it's lights still on and engine running. Both men joined the crowd as they neared, acting as curious as the others.

"Is that him?" Dufresne whispered as they looked over the shoulders of a pair of fashionably dressed women. Tiberius took one look and nodded. The fake waiter from the café was pinned under the front bumper of the sedan, his body astride a mangled scooter. Despite the administrations from a pair of good samaritans, the man's head was smashed and clearly beyond help. "What do we do?"

"Well we are the police aren't we?" Tiberius offered with a raised eyebrow. "Get some statements and I'll check the body."

Dufresne simply nodded as both men removed their fake police identifications from their jacket pockets. Pushing through the crowd, a few initial dark looks immediately turned to submission as they held up the ID's and asked for calm. Dufresne had everyone move back before he started asking questions amongst the front row of the crowd. Tiberius meanwhile bent down by the pair attempting first aid.

"Was he alive when you started? Did he say anything?" he asked as they took a step back in failure. They nodded to his first question before shaking their head at the second. "What about the driver? Are they alright?"

"We didn't see the driver," came the hesitant answer. "I didn't think of it until just now, but they must have fled immediately after hitting this poor soul."

"Very well, thank you for your assistance. If you could have a seat at the curb my colleague will take your statements."

Turning from the pair, Tiberius began to look over the collision once more. The front of the sedan was a wreck; the hood was dented, the grille was cracked, and the left headlight was smashed. But the damage to the sedan was nothing compared to the unlucky man on the scooter. The machine had offered no protection, as the hit looked as though it came from the side. The small narrow street had probably meant the speed was low, but that had not made a difference in the end.

Tiberius once more lowered himself down to the body and began searching through pockets. He couldn't find a wallet, juts some scraps of paper that he inconspicuously placed in his pocket. Without finding anything else, he stood up and remembered the camera he'd used at the monument earlier in the day. Taking it out of his pocket he took a series of photos of the accident and the man's face.

Turning from the front of the car, Tiberius moved around to the open driver's side door. The sirens were now closer and almost upon them as he looked through the cabin. The car was immaculate from the inside, but he didn't go into it as two police cars screeched onto the scene. Men in uniform quickly exited and ran towards the scene. The two younger ones immediately started pushing the crowd back while the older and clearly senior one approached Tiberius. He walked with the precise cadence of a soldier, his face calm but hard as steel.

"What are you doing here?" he asked with a solid voice that matched his demeanour. Tiberius had only seconds to decide his reply. He and Dufresne could claim to be good samaritans like the others and simply vanish from the scene. But something told him that he needed more information than the pieces he now held. Plus who better than the police to do his dirty work?

"I'm Inspector Tiber and that is my associate Inspector Dufresne, INTERPOL," Tiberius offered calmly, handing over his ID. The forger at the Manor was a true master, and the ID was an example of his skill. The policeman handed it back without issue.

"I'm Sargent Lafleur. How did you come to get here so quickly?" the officer asked with honest curiosity.

"We were actually trailing this poor soul before he slipped away from us on his scooter. By the time we caught up with him, this had happened and the crowd had gathered," Tiberius explained easily, his commanding presence all the corroboration the officer needed. "Inspector Dufresne has been taking statements if you need copies for you report."

"Why were you after this man?"

"I'm afraid I can't say," Tiberius answered after hesitating a moment, hoping to show an inner conflict in the decision. "We were hoping he would lead us to someone. But sadly that won't happen now."

"An accident?" the policeman offered after taking a quick glance at the scene. An ambulance slowly pulled up, the lights still flashing but the siren thankfully quiet.

"It appears so," Tiberius concurred solemnly. "However the driver took off a little too quickly for an accident. If you have no objections I'd like to see a copy of the autopsy when it's complete, just to allay my suspicions. I'll contact my supervisors to see if I can provide you with further details on my investigation. It might be helpful to you."

"Thank you," Sargent Lafleur replied appreciatively.

Tiberius took a step back after shaking hands with the grateful officer and watched the paramedics remove the body from under the car. Dufresne walked up and stood beside him, his small black book open and filled with notes.

"I take it we now work for INTERPOL?" he asked quietly as the scooter screeched free from the car.

"Indeed. What did you find out from the witnesses?"

"Not much," Dufresene began, glancing at his notebook. "Apparently the scooter was driving down the street and was hit by the car. The driver knelt down to check the injured man and then ran off. No real description; medium height, medium build, brown hair, dark clothes. Do you think it was an accident?"

"You've listened to the witnesses, what do you think?" Tiberius asked noncommittally.

"I think it looks like an accident," Dufresne replied with obvious doubt.

"Exactly, it's just a little too convenient for my liking," he concurred gravely. "Two men just died minutes apart and I think there's a direct link between the two incidents."

"So what do we do now?"

"I've made a good impression with the lead cop over there, but pretty soon this place will be crawling with police. I think we should leave while we can," Tiberius ordered before slowly walking away from the scene. They ducked under the police tape that was slowly being put up to keep the growing crowd at a distance. "You still with us Morgan?"

"Affirmative."

"We're heading back to the Grund, let me know if anyone follows us."

*

"When do I get to flash a badge?" Morgan asked hopefully as he approached the garden patio of a small pub in the Grund. Tiberius and Dufresne were already there and had ordered him a pint, which he gladly accepted after sitting down.

"You'd never be believable as an officer of the law," Tiberius replied with a smile before taking a sip from his amber coloured beer. "So nobody followed us?"

"Not a soul, everyone's attention was on the accident," Morgan reported casually, staring at his beer after tasting it. "This stuff is good."

"Microbrewery," Dufresne explained simply, nodding towards the sign over the pub door.

"Back to business," Tiberius ordered gently, setting his drink down. His men followed suit as they began discussing the shocking events of the day. "Before his untimely death, Zeidt said there was a mole within the Manor, someone we'd never suspect."

"Which seemed pretty dubious at the time."

"Yes, until he was poisoned a few seconds later," Tiberius continued quickly. "Just before he could tell us the name or names."

"Well it was definitely the work of a hitman," Morgan observed immediately, recognizing the skill of the kill. "But the timing and method make me question the motivation."

"How so?"

"I think we can agree that the fake waiter was a pro," he elaborated logically and receiving nods from around the table. "He was able to hit to his target in a public place, with multiple escape routes planned, and with almost nothing to tie him to it. He drops the poisoned glass off at the table, goes back inside the café and waits to be sure the target drinks it and goes down. Then he nonchalantly exits through the back door. No one pays attention to waiters, so no one would have remembered his face."

"I didn't even look at his face," Tiberius grumbled in agreement, having concentrated too much on reading Zeidt during their brief meeting.

"Exactly, but what was the motivation for the hit?"

"Surely to stop us from learning the identity of the mole," Dufresne offered confidently.

"I'm not so sure," Morgan replied shaking his head slightly.

"Why is that?" Tiberius challenged, pleased that his men were working through the problem.

"If the hit was planned to keep him from telling us the name of the mole it would be much easier to kill him before the meeting. Then there's the method employed. The poison was definitely potent and fast acting, but the hitter loses control as soon as he delivers it. What if Zeidt decides not to drink it, what if he tells his whole story before drinking it? There are just too many things that could go wrong."

"How would you have done it," Tiberius asked quietly, trusting the knowledge and skill of his subordinate. Lord Lodge had been sceptical when Tiberius had suggested recruiting Morgan to the Manor, but had trusted him with the decision in the end. Tiberius was still glad that he'd followed his instinct on the reformed hooligan sitting across from him.

Supposedly a bastard son of the famous Captain Morgan, he was born in a small English fishing village on the Cornish coast. He joined a crew of privateers as soon as he was able, leaving behind a desolate life on shore. The young Morgan grew up amidst the brutal, violent, and dangerous world of the privateers, travelling from the Caribbean to the Mediterranean and countless places in between. His skills with blades and firearms were so impressive that he jumped ship in Italy to become the bodyguard of a minor noble. But his abilities were insufficient when he and his charge were accosted one dark night in Milan.

Confronted with five masked men, Morgan was able to fight them all off as he protected the noble. However a sixth attacker seemingly appeared out of thin air, quickly dispatching the noble and disarming Morgan. Impressed with the bodyguard's skill, the sixth attacker invited Morgan to join an assassin's guild. With death being the other option, Morgan readily accepted, learning the tools of the trade of a professional killer.

"Like I said, I would have killed him before he ever sat down at the café," Morgan repeated confidently. "But if I wanted to take him out at the meeting, which doesn't make much sense by the way, I would have used a rifle from a rooftop."

"That's a little noisy," Dufresne observed as he took a drink of his beer.

"But it's effective," he countered immediately. "That way I can read his lips and take him out before he gives up any information. I would have more control. Waiting to give him the poison at the meeting and hoping he drinks it in time doesn't make sense."

"You're right," Tiberius agreed thoughtfully. "Everything was too organized for the most important part to be left to chance. What's to keep Zeidt from blurting out the name of the mole as soon as I sit down?"

"Nothing, except we all know Zeidt would never do that," Dufresne countered, reminding them all that the Swiss banker would have started any meeting like a negotiation.

"Unless the assassin knew nothing about the meeting," Tiberius offered slowly, raising his hands immediately to others before they could question the statement. "Just think about it. The only way that the method of the hit makes sense is that timing was not an issue. We know Zeidt was a man of habit and he liked his creature comforts. I'd be willing to bet he regularly went to that café, offering the perfect place for an attempt on his life. The killer didn't expect him to be meeting anyone and the subject of our meeting had no bearing on Zeidt's death."

"That makes sense to me," Morgan concurred.

"To me as well," Dufresne agreed tentatively. "But I don't think we can just shrug and say poor Herr Zeidt was killed for some other reason. We need to know why he was killed, in case it has something to do with the Manor."

"Agreed. Sadly our best lead on that was just removed from underneath a BMW," Tiberius continued, unhappily drinking from his own mug of beer. "I think our hitman was struck on purpose to sever the connection between the victim and the client."

"It's a pretty suspicious coincidence, but I'm not completely sold," Morgan countered, playing the devil's advocate. "Who's to say our hitman even gets on the scooter if we're not chasing him. He probably had a couple escape routes out of the city once the deed was done."

"I suppose," Tiberius conceded bitterly, his frustration growing. "Shit! We just don't have enough information."

"So what do you want to do?"

"I think we need to go back to the Manor and report to Lord Lodge," Tiberius announced without hesitation. "This was only supposed to be a short excursion, so chasing leads around Luxembourg and who knows where else will only delay our return and cause him undue concern. When we get back I'll report to Lord Lodge while you gentleman prepare for a much longer return trip. I have a feeling we're going to need much more than some radios, pistols and fake id's."

"What about the mole?"

"What mole?" Tiberius replied with feigned confusion. "All we have is the unconfirmed testimony of a desperate traitor looking to save himself. He might have been killed because of that information, but he might have also stolen money from a gangster. Until we know more, you keep that information to yourselves. I'll tell those who need to know."

"But what if it's true," Dufresne persisted.

"Then the mole could be anyone at the Manor, and those who know the truth could be the next target."

Chapter 5

1995. The hum of the jet's engines and the view through the tiny window twenty thousand feet above the earth was only adding to Jane's already nervous state. Her first official operation for the Black Tower Hunt Club through the portals had been meant to ease her into the jolting reality of travelling through time and space. However this had not taken into account the fact that Jane had grown up on the Island and had never really seen anything more modern than a grandfather clock. But it was more than the continual bombardment of impossibly advanced technology that was wrenching Jane's nerves into knots. Looking at the briefcase that sat on the seat beside her, she knew that the file within it was the real cause for her current state.

A few weeks after Dr. Cleaver had fled Ravenwood Manor, Lord Lodge had called her into his office. Hoping she'd be elevated from her position as a maid, she nevertheless entered with realistic expectations. But to the shock of both herself and some of those assembled, he announced that she would be replacing the deceased

Percival Drummond as Secretary of the Hunt. This move sent a minor shockwave through the Manor and was felt by both members and staff alike.

So Jane took on the task with an almost addictive zeal, working and studying impossibly long hours everyday. She knew that one of the reasons she'd been appointed to the position was due to a sense of appreciation Lodge felt towards her for helping him escape the clutches of Dr. Cleaver. But she was desperate to prove that that was not the only reason for his decision. She spent the majority of her time learning how the Secretary's office worked from Drummond's assistant and small staff; where files were, how they were tracked, and other administrative tasks. She also met with Tiberius daily, since after taking over for Dr. Cleaver she reported to him as Master of the Hunt.

Within weeks the general consensus around the Manor was that Jane was a significant improvement over the pompous and conniving Percy Drummond. But she still had to prove that she could operate in the real world beyond the portals. Her two main responsibilities as the Secretary of the Hunt were setting up the hunts and recruiting potential staff and members. This required regular passage beyond the portals and she was the first Hunt Secretary to be from the Island, which seemed to be perpetually stuck in the Victorian era.

Wanting to tackle the problem head on, Jane spoke to Tiberius before he set out to investigate a suspicious invitation through the 1988 Luxembourg portal. With increased confidence from her new position, she reasoned that with the departure of Dr. Cleaver, Malicio, and four other members of the Black Pack, new recruits were needed to fill the vacated positions. But Tiberius was unconvinced that she could handle that many recruitments alone and asked her to hold off until both he and Lodge had more time to oversee the process. Undeterred by his doubts, she pleaded her case for the opportunity to recruit one staff with a free reign as a test of her abilities. If she found it overwhelming or she made a poor choice she'd hold off further recruiting efforts until she could be supervised.

Jane was still surprised that he'd agreed to the proposal as she shot another glance at the briefcase beside her. She knew that her future was intrinsically linked to the file within and the person she was preparing to meet. She'd spent days poring over files for potential recruits, looking for the right combination of intelligence, skills, and desperation.

She'd spent the majority of her life living within the intrigue and danger of the Manor, among the constantly feuding members of the Black Tower Hunt Club and the staff who served them. So she knew that in order to survive and thrive in her new position, she'd need allies. By siding with Lord Lodge against Dr. Cleaver, she'd gained his support and that of his powerful right hand, Tiberius. But Jane knew better than most that potential danger could come from below as much as above. She needed an assistant of her own that she could rely on to protect her, both professionally and physically. None of the existing staff at the Manor could be trusted to fulfill that role, so she'd convinced Tiberius to allow her to recruit someone new. The fact that he would be assigned specifically to her rather than the Black Pack and the Manor as a whole had been left out of the discussion. She was sure Tiberius would understand, after all he had two such men himself in Morgan and Dufresne.

Her thoughts were disturbed as the captain announced over the intercom that they were starting their descent into Aviano Air Force Base and would be landing in twenty minutes. A feeling of excitement and terror shot through Jane as the plane pointed noticeably downward. She felt butterflies in her stomach and gripped the arms of her chair with white knuckled force.

"Not a good flyer?" asked a blue uniformed man sitting across the aisle from her. She couldn't tell if he was being sincere or mocking her. Due to her intense studying she could tell from his uniform that he was a Major with the US Air Force and had the gold wings of a pilot on his breast.

"No I'm not Major," she replied tersely, careful to omit that this was her first time on a plane. Emerging from the portal, she had donned a new persona in order to complete her mission and any slip up could be dangerous.

"Call me John and don't worry about the landing," he smiled easily, glad to finally be talking to the black haired beauty across the aisle. "I went to the Academy with the pilot and he's pretty good. Not good enough to fly an F-15 like me, but good enough to land this boat."

Jane merely smiled in response, initially confused by his terminology. She was glad for the reassurance, but she also could also pick out an approaching proposition with skill. She had no wish to make friends on this mission, certainly not with the likes of the Major with his bravado and bad teeth.

Despite the calm demeanour of the Major, she found the next twenty minutes the most thrilling and terrifying of her life, much worse than the takeoff a few hours prior. When the wheels of the plane bumped to the ground heavily, she briefly believed that she was going to die a horrific death in this steel tube. A wave of despair flooded over her as she thought of dying far from home. The image of Patrick flew to her mind instantly and the lost possibilities of the future.

He'd left to hunt down one of the escaped Members of the Hunt, some strange Russian, immediately after she'd been appointed Secretary of the Hunt. Since then they'd not seen each other and she'd been too busy with her work to truly think about him. Although she had strong feelings for the newest Member of the Hunt, Jane didn't know if she could handle a new job and a new man in her life.

"Mrs. Pierce," prompted an Air Force steward standing in the aisle beside her as the plane taxied along the runway. "You gave instructions to be let off first?"

"That's right," Jane nodded briskly, hiding the smile she felt inside. The forgers at the Manor had a strange sense of humour and had no doubt giggled slightly as they had made her fake documents.

Her cover was that of a high ranking CIA operative on special assignment with a joint military intelligence task force. Jane had studied for months in order to prepare; reading documents, reports, and even novels on intelligence agencies and their activities. But despite all the work, she knew that she wouldn't be able to keep up the façade for an extended amount of time. Because of this, Jane hoped that her documents, her attitude, and her looks would provide enough cover to get the job done quickly.

So far the combination of those three things had worked well. She had managed to get from the portal in Copenhagen to Mannheim Air Force Base in Germany without any issues. A flash of her id and the undone top two buttons on her silk blouse had then ensured that the sergeant at the air field had squeezed her onto a departing military transport flight to Aviano Air Force Base in Northern Italy.

As the steward led her to the front of the plane, she didn't bother to hide the smile on her face as she walked up the aisle. She knew that the majority of the plane was filled with men in military uniforms, staring at her alluring form as she departed. She hoped that the rest of the men she encountered were as easily distracted.

With Pierce gone from the Manor through one of the portals, his valet Melrose had seemingly adopted Jane as his secondary duty. When he learned that she'd be travelling through one of the portals herself, Melrose had jumped into action in order to help her prepare. With an impressive eye for her size and colouring, he'd put together a stylish collection of clothing that complemented her perfectly. Taking her cover into account, he'd dressed her in outfits that were both acceptable for a female businesswoman of the time, but also displayed her physical attributes.

The early morning sun burst through the opened doorway after the plane had stopped its progress. Jane immediately felt the safety of stillness as she followed the steward down the stairs to a waiting car on the tarmac. Glad to be out of the death contraption, she loosened her grip on the briefcase in her hand as the steward passed her valise to the driver.

"Mrs. Pierce?" inquired a young man in sunglasses and a light gray suit, stepping forward from the car as the driver took her bag to the back.

"Yes?"

"I'm Spencer Sands, the Agency liaison here at Aviano," he offered genially, putting his hand out with a smile.

"Jane," she replied with a smile of her own, shaking his hand quickly.

"I received your message from the Embassy in Copenhagen and set up a meeting with the base commander," he reported with slight hesitancy as the driver opened the door for them.

"Is there a problem?" Jane asked as she followed him into the back seat, slightly concerned by Sands' change in tone.

"Well, the Colonel's old school military," Sands began almost apologetically as the car fell in behind a parade of airport vehicles heading towards the various hangars and buildings. "He's not going to take very kindly to any outside interference, especially from us."

"The Colonel doesn't have much say in the matter," Jane countered confidently as she watched in awe as two sets of fighter planes took off in tandem formation, their jets engines shooting blue flames as they rose with impossible speed.

"If you say so," Sands shrugged without the same confidence. "But the subject is military and we don't have much clout when it comes to their personnel."

"In this case we do," she pronounced, eyeing the driver suspiciously.

"Don't worry, he's one of ours," Sands answered Jane's questioning glance as he nodded to the driver in front of him. "You can speak freely."

"I'd rather keep things between us at the moment, no offense intended," She replied evenly, taking an envelope out of her briefcase. "Read this."

Sands took the letter and opened it carefully reading it over twice before whistling quietly and handing it back. With nothing left to say he put his sunglasses back on and stared at the alpine view out of the window.

*

"The Colonel is currently on the phone and will be with you shortly," explained an attractive female corporal from behind her desk when Jane and Sands walked in. Without waiting for a response she went back to her typing, an impressive staccato of tapping keys filling the anteroom outside the base commander's office.

They both turned and sat on a pair of chairs beside the door, the material a hideous light blue that had seen better days. Despite the space, the office seemed cramped with just the three of them in it. The walls were covered with mementos, plaques and frames, all belonging to the current inhabitant of the office beyond. Jane knew this type well from her time at the Manor. Some of the members loved to put up displays of their prowess on the walls and she was sure they'd see even more on the Colonels' walls beyond.

"The Colonel does this to everyone he meets," Sands whispered as he leafed through a magazine that had been left on his chair. "He tries to show how important he is by appearing busy and making them wait."

"Don't worry, I know the type."

After five minutes of patient waiting, both stood up as the corporal received a quick message on the phone. Moving to the door, she ushered them through and announced their names to the Colonel.

As Jane predicted, the Colonel's office was a museum to the great man he believed he was. The walls were so full that Jane couldn't tell what the actual paint colour was. Predictably the Colonel didn't stand up when they entered and began his offensive before they could even sit down.

"I told you before Sands, that I won't allow interference by the god-damned CIA on my base on military matters!"

Undoubtedly reminded of previous conversations with the Colonel, Sands remained standing in front of the man's desk, ready to make a quick retreat. Jane however intended to get what she wanted and knew she'd have to show her strength, so she sat down calmly and motioned Sands to do the same.

"Listen lady, I don't know who you are but I wouldn't get too comfortable," the Colonel continued, his grey mustache bouncing as he spoke. "You're not going to get what you want."

"But you haven't even heard what I want Colonel," Jane replied pleasantly, crossing her legs slowly and leaning back into the chair. Her heart was pounding and she felt like she'd break into a sweat at any moment. This was the first big test she'd had since emerging in Copenhagen. Fooling the staff at the embassy and Sands had been easy as soon as she flashed her ID and smile. But neither of those things was going to work on the Colonel. He was an angry little man who coveted power and used it whenever he could.

Her reply and demeanour caught him off guard, unused to it in people that entered his office. Looking at the cool confident woman across the desk, he was immediately intrigued and decided he'd hear her piece before throwing her and the other fool out his door. The Colonel had no time to play spy games with amateurs, not with a war on. Fighter planes from *his* base were currently conducting bombing missions in the Former Yugoslavia. He was a vital cog to the NATO mission there.

"Fine, tell me what it is that you want so that I can say no and return to more important matters."

"I'll start off with an easy request," Jane smiled as she reached down to get the briefcase from the floor, intentionally offering a brief view of her cleavage. "I'd like you to get your Provost Marshall to come in."

Ready to deny her first request in order to set the rules for their encounter, the Colonel was once again caught off guard. The Provost Marshall was in charge of the Military Police on the base and responsible for security. Unsure where this was leading, he slowly lifted his phone and asked his secretary to send Major Sullivan to his office. All three sat quietly in the brief time it took Major Sullivan to knock and enter the office.

"You wanted to see me sir?" asked the Major as he walked up to the Colonel's desk, shooting a quick inquiring glance at the pair already sitting there.

"She did," was all the Colonel could utter as he leaned back in his large leather chair.

"Ma'am?" the Major asked looking down at Jane in confusion.

"Major please a take a seat and I'll get down to business," Jane ordered as she removed a file from her briefcase. When he did so, she continued in a quick business like tone. "Like Mr. Sands here, I am with the Agency and for the purposes of this meeting my name is Jane Pierce. I'm currently part of a joint CIA - DIA task force concerning aspects of the fighting in the former provinces of Yugoslavia."

"I haven't heard of this task force," countered the Colonel sceptically. "What's its mandate?"

"Need to know Colonel," she stated firmly, before flashing a smile as she continued. "To be fair I only really need to speak to the Major here, but decided to include you out of courtesy to the chain of command."

"Now see here this is my base and..."

"Please Colonel," Jane cut him off gently with an upraised hand. "Before you say something you'll regret I'd like you to read this letter."

"No piece of paper is going to tell me what to do on my own base!" He shouted as he leaned forward, his hands on his desk. Jane didn't blink, keeping the letter outstretched in her hand towards him. Seeing she wouldn't back down, the Colonel reached across the desk and snatched it from her hands. His mouth began moving silently as his eyes went left to right across the page.

"Out loud if you please," Jane interrupted him politely as he read. "For the Major's sake and so that we all understand each others positions."

"Fine," murmured the Colonel, the letterhead on the page making him re-evaluate the importance of his mysterious visitor. *"The holder of this letter, Officer Pierce, is operating under the auspices of this office. All officers, regardless of rank, shall provide her with any and all assistance required for any undertakings under CIA-DIA Task Force Broadsword. Signed-* holy shit."

"What is it sir?" Major Sullivan asked after the Colonel's whispered curse.

"It's signed by the Secretary of Defense," the Colonel finally answered after composing himself. With a wary stare he handed the letter back to Jane and leaned back in his chair. "So how can I be of assistance?"

"You've done enough already Colonel," Jane replied frostily as she put the letter back in her briefcase and stood up. "Major Sullivan and I will leave you to your important work."

Before he could reply, Jane stood up and walked out of the office. Her adrenaline was pumping and her fingers were tingling. She knew the forger at the Manor was good, but she'd expected the Colonel to question the letter or call someone before he offered her any assistance. When she stopped to compose herself in the anteroom Sands and Sullivan almost bumped into her.

"Thank you for your help Spencer," Jane acknowledge after a few calming breaths. "I'll be in touch if I need anything else."

They shook hands quickly, with Sands trying hard not to look disappointed in being dismissed from assisting with what appeared to be a high level operation. He followed them into the corridor and then left to return to the parking lot out front.

"Where to now Ma'am?" Major Sullivan inquired with a slight gleam in his eye.

Jane had taken a quick appraisal of the Major when he'd entered the Colonel's office. Unlike the glory hound prima donna that occupied the office, she had pegged him as a worker. More interested in the job he currently worked in and doing it right than aspirations for the next rank. She felt this first impression was an accurate depiction as they stood together in the corridor. He had a tough but honest face, with thinning hair and an extra couple pounds at his waist. She didn't know it, but others would have said he looked like a cop.

"How about a drink?" she asked after checking her watch. It was approaching noon and she needed something after the stressful flight and the anticlimactic meeting.

"Sure," he chuckled after checking his own watch. "The Officer's Club should be open by now. It's just down the street, so we can just walk over. If that's ok with you ma'am."

"It's Jane, and that sounds fine."

"Sully," he replied as they made their way out into the sun drenched alpine air base. They walked down the sidewalk without speaking, the sounds of jets taking off in the distance breaking the silence. Within minutes they reached the Officer's Club, a stylish and welcoming building compared to the drab military buildings of the base.

There was only a smattering of uniformed clients within the dark and smoky bar when they entered, most of them high ranking enough to not worry about their bosses finding them there.

"What can I get for you Sherriff?" called the bartender jokingly when he saw Sullivan walk in. He then winked when Jane sat down with him at table near one of the windows.

"What's your pleasure?" Sully asked Jane as they sat, trying to ignore the bastard behind the bar.

"Whiskey."

"Sounds good to me. Two whiskeys," he called over to the bartender. Within seconds the drinks where poured and he brought them over to the table.

"Here you go," he said depositing them on the table. "Do you or your lady friend need anything else?"

"This is a business meeting," Sully replied with an easy smile. "But that doesn't mean my wife should find out."

The bartender laughed and retreated back to the bar.

"Sorry about that, but people in this place get all riled up when attractive women walk in."

"I'm used to it, trust me," Jane waved the issue aside. The more time she spent on military bases, the more similarities she discovered with the Manor.

"So now that we're away from prying eyes and ears, what's this all about?"

"Staff Sergeant Logan," she replied simply as they both took a sip of their drinks.

"What!?" The Major exclaimed, almost spitting his whiskey out. "You can't be serious."

"I am," she stated simply, returning his questioning gaze with a steely one of her own.

Sully shot back the rest of his drink and leaned back with a smile. "Fair enough. I think I'd like to see this. You realize that he's just been released from the infirmary and the interrogation has probably just started."

"That's why I'm here now. I need to speak to him before the interrogators and lawyers get their claws too deep into him."

"It's not going to be easy," Sully observed thoughtfully after a moment. "A whole crew flew in from Washington a week ago after this whole fiasco exploded. They've practically taken over my entire building. I'm allowed in and out, but that's just about it."

"Well that's all I need, a foot in the door."

"Good because that's all I can promise," Sully laughed as they stood up and left the bar. A cloudless sky greeted them as they emerged, the sun blinding both as they groped for sunglasses. Jane had never had a pair until Melrose had slipped them into her jacket pocket. They'd felt strange at first, but now she wondered how she'd ever lived without them. Not only did they protect the eyes from the sun, they could hide the intentions of the wearer.

As they walked towards the stockade, Jane was struck by the uniformity of the base. She was used to the jumbled buildings of Rooks Bay and the organized chaos of the Manor. There was something unnatural about the duplicate buildings evenly spaced on the immaculate lawns. Even the people they passed seemed to walk in unison, sometimes in large groups.

"The stockade is just up ahead," Major Sullivan pointed out as they turned a corner. A collection of black

SUV's were parked out front along with some uniformed guards armed with rifles.

"Seems like an unnecessary amount of security for one man," Jane observed as they approached the block-like building. "Especially one of your own."

"To be honest I just posted the guards to impress the visitors," Sully offered with a shrug. "It's what they expect. Have your ID ready."

"Afternoon sir," called one of the guards mechanically when he spotted the Major approach. It took all of his training to keep his eyes on the officer as he saluted, rather than the bust line of his hot companion. "ID miss?"

Jane handed it over to the guard, receiving a flash of surprise before it was hidden beneath his standard stone faced expression. He quickly handed her ID back and motioned for the other guard to open the door for them, once again saluting as they entered.

"You're surely gaining a large group of admirers," smiled Sully as they passed the front desk manned by one of the junior officers.

"Must be my personality," Jane allowed with a smile of her own. But before she could follow the Major past the desk, the young Lieutenant waved her down. "Yes?"

"Sorry ma'am, but all visitors are required to sign in," he said with a wary glance at his boss.

"Lieutenant," she began pleasantly as she removed her ID and showed it to him. "How can I sign in if I was never here?"

Having never encountered anyone from the CIA, he was confused on how to proceed. When no help came from Major Sullivan, he finally nodded slowly and closed the log book in front of him.

"My God you're good," Sully commented as they continued down the hallway. "But you'll need more than that with this next group."

"Major, I can do this all day long," Jane declared as they stopped at a security door. She was feeling very confident as she passed each consecutive hurdle. But there was still a small icy ball of anxiety that she could feel within her. However rather than try and ignore it, she embraced the feeling, knowing it would keep her grounded. Despite the ease she'd dealt with all of the potential problems so far, she couldn't afford to get caught off guard due to arrogance.

The hallway beyond the security door was completely white, with naked fluorescent lights and shining linoleum floor making Jane want to put her sunglasses back on. Another set of armed guards were positioned by a door further down, but Major Sullivan opened a closer door before they reached them.

The room they stepped into seemed completely black in contrast to the hall, but after a few seconds of blinking Jane was able to focus properly. The room was packed full of people, monitors, sound equipment and blinking displays. Those inside looked up at them briefly before turning their attention back to a large window that took up an entire wall.

Jane followed their glance through the window and shuddered briefly at the scene before her. A dark skinned man in a blue jump suit was handcuffed to a metal table in the middle of a spotlessly white room. Two expressionless armed guards stood in opposite corners, while two other men circled and yelled at the manacled man. A fifth man in a green army uniform sat across from the prisoner, leafing through a thick file folder.

"Your orders were to rescue and evade!" yelled a stern faced man in a black suit. "Are you too good to obey orders?!"

"Or are you some kind of glory hound?!" growled the second standing man, his striped tie loosened and his shirtsleeves rolled up. "Guys like you get people killed!"

The prisoner just stared at the window without flinching, ignoring the buzzards overhead.

"This isn't the first time this has happened to you is it?" observed the Army officer as he pulled a document from the file, finally eliciting a reaction form the prisoner. "Remember Desert Storm?"

"I was cleared of that," he replied calmly.

"Not by me," retorted the officer with a sneer. "You got lucky, that was during a real war and was ignored. You shot up a van full of Iraqis, killing most of them."

"They were Republican Guard."

"So you say, but lucky for you the van exploded and destroyed the evidence."

"You get your kicks shooting up civilians?" challenged black suit from behind the prisoner.

"Fuck you," he mumbled in response, getting a backhanded slap from shirtsleeves for his trouble.

"This asshole has fucked us all," observed a well coifed suited man in the dark room as the officer continued his questions. "The Russians and Serbians want his heart on a plate."

Heads nodded in reply as they continued to watch the proceedings in the room beyond. Jane looked at the collection of people in the room and was immediately able to sort them into two categories; there were the workers at the different machines, and there were the suits watching with perverse enjoyment.

"Who is everybody?" Jane whispered to Sully cautiously.

"The two goons in the room are Investigators from Army CID and the Lieutenant Colonel is a lawyer from the Judge Advocate General's Corps," Sully answered quietly, before nodding at the men within the dark room. "Those two are from the Public Affairs office and the other two are from the State Department."

"Who's in charge?"

"Officially? Well that's the Colonel, he's going to be prosecuting Sergeant Logan if it comes to that. But the jerk from State is really pulling the strings."

"Listen Sergeant, you fired on an unmarked civilian car," continued the Colonel in the interrogation room. "You killed three of the four men, without provocation."

"One of them was a Russian diplomat, dickhead!" yelled the man in the dark suit.

"That's not how it happened sir," Logan countered shaking his head slightly.

"Not according to the surviving witness," concluded the Colonel closing the file. "You had a bright future ahead of you; chosen for Officer Candidate School with a choice of degree. I've seen your test scores, you're a bright guy and probably could have gone far. But you threw it all away because of an itchy trigger finger. I've got a simple statement here for you to read and sign. If you do that I might be able to help you and offer a reduced sentence. If not…"

"I've heard enough," Jane whispered to the Major. "Please invite the Colonel, with all due respect, to stop the interrogation and come in here. I need to speak to Sergeant Logan before he signs anything."

Major Sullivan nodded and hid the smile that had crept over his face. He silently left the room and walked down the hall to the guarded door. Nodding to his two men at the door he silently knocked on the door before entering, not waiting for a response.

"What the hell is this all about?" asked the suited man from State within the observation room. "I thought we told that old policeman to stay out of this."

They all watched with collective curiosity as the Major opened the door and walked directly to the seated officer. He leaned down and whispered a few brief words before straightening up. The Colonel shot a dark look over his shoulder at the two way mirror, obviously displeased by the interruption. After a few moments he stood up and walked as calmly as he could out of the door.

"Here we go," Jane whispered to herself, preparing for her biggest challenge on this mission so far. This was uncharted territory and she just hoped she'd studied enough and could keep her nerve for the onslaught that was moments away.

Chapter 6

"No one's speaking to the prisoner until I'm done my interrogation!" bellowed the Lieutenant Colonel as he slammed open the door to the observation room. Looking at those assembled in the room, his eyes immediately feel upon the only new face. "Is this your doing?"

"Yes," Jane replied coolly, having taken a few calming breaths in advance.

"Who the hell do you think you are?" he continued his barrage, towering over the significantly smaller woman. His square face, crew cut, and large frame were probably intimidating to most people he encountered. But Jane was used to such men, most of them more dangerous than the lawyer playing soldier in front of her.

"This is who the hell I am," Jane countered firmly as she held up her ID to the Colonel's face.

"I don't take orders from the CIA," he said with more control.

"Why the hell is the Agency involved with this?" questioned the polished suit from the Sate Department.

"I could ask you the same thing," Jane retorted quickly, having already decided she disliked the man.

"I'm here trying to prevent an international incident," he answered, puffing up slightly as he spoke. "Because Rambo in there went ballistic. Someone has to be held accountable."

"Why don't you hold the wanted war criminal that Sgt. Logan killed responsible?"

"He killed a Russian diplomat!" chimed in one of the lackeys from behind, covering for his temporarily silenced boss.

"Maybe you should be asking why a Russian diplomat was driving with a war criminal in the first place, rather than putting the screws to an honest soldier," Jane offered icily to those assembled. "You're a soldier Colonel. You really think Sgt. Logan should be treated like this."

"I'm also a lawyer and have to pursue my duties with impartiality and without prejudice. I've been ordered to prosecute Sgt. Logan and that's what I'm going to do."

"Those orders have just been put on hold," Jane stated firmly as she reached into her briefcase.

"On who's authority?" challenged the man from State, having regained his voice.

Jane ignored him and produced her forged letter, handing it to the Colonel. Like before she asked him to read it aloud.

"What the hell is Task Force Broadsword?" asked the bureaucrat dubiously.

"Like I told the Base Commander, it's need to know," Jane smiled sweetly taking the letter back. "And you don't need to know."

"But…"

"But nothing," She cut him off quickly before turning to the two uniformed men by the door. "Colonel, I'm going to go in and talk to Sgt. Logan in private. You and your investigators can wait in here if you like, I shouldn't be too long. Major?"

"Yes ma'am?" Major Sullivan answered cheerfully, amused at the scene he had just watched and ready for act two.

"I want all of the recording equipment and microphones turned off," she ordered looking at the array of technology within the room. Her eyes briefly rested on the men from Public Affairs and State huddled in the corner together. "No one in this room is cleared for the conversation I'm about to have. So if they try and listen in, escort them out of the building immediately. Preferably with extreme force, but they'll probably go along gently. I know their type."

"Yes ma'am!" Sully accepted enthusiastically, quickly overseeing the shut down of the equipment. Everyone inside the room would still be able to see her and Logan, but she wasn't worried about that. Once everything was shut down she left the room and walked over to the next door where the Colonel, the CID men, and the guards were all congregating. She ignored the angry glares of the CID men and asked the guards for the keys for the prisoner's handcuffs.

"That goes against protocols ma'am," answered the head guard as he pulled out the keys and handed them over.

"Sergeant, protocols are for suckers," Jane replied coolly, giving him a wink as she accepted the keys. "I'll bang on the door when I want back out."

One of the guards opened the door for her and she walked into the interrogation room with feigned confidence. Despite the fact that the deception had worked well to this point, Jane knew she was still in danger. While she sat secluded in the interrogation room with Logan, any one of the men in the other room could be on the phone with their superiors. There was a distinct possibility that she might be led out in the same chains that were now on the prisoner before her.

Sergeant Logan looked up at her as she walked into the interrogation room. The room seemed even whiter and brighter than the hallway, with an almost overpowering scent of industrial cleaner. The metal table in the middle of the room was bolted to the floor, but the flimsy plastic chairs were not. She pulled back the chair previously occupied by the Colonel and sat in it with poise, gracefully crossing her legs.

"Here, take those bracelets off," Jane offered sarcastically as she threw the keys across the table. "Steel really isn't your colour."

"Are you supposed to by the good cop ma'am?" Logan enquired after a moment's hesitation before picking up the keys and putting them to work.

"I'm not good and I'm definitely not a cop," Jane replied smirking, pulling out a file from her briefcase. She didn't really need the file on Staff Sergeant Logan, having memorised its contents before she left the Manor. But she thought it might confuse those inside the observation room, while putting Sgt. Logan at ease at the same time.

Staff Sergeant Logan had been born into a mixed race family in Florida almost twenty seven years prior, his mother was a black nurse and his white father worked at a thoroughbred horse farm. He'd been a star athlete in high school, playing in every sport that he could. But despite a clever mind, young Logan found grades less appealing than athletic accolades. Unwilling to offer a scholarship to a small town high school star with bad grades, no colleges came calling. In need of a job that offered the same camaraderie and physicality as sports, he decided to join the army.

Basic training came as a shock to the young man used to sleeping in and showing up late for class. But he quickly adapted to his environment and thrived with the continuous challenges. He gravitated towards the infantry and was quickly selected for Ranger School, graduating at the top of the class. Promoted to sergeant within a few years, Logan continuously found himself at the sharp end of the US military machine; fighting in Iraq in 1991, then Somalia in 1993, and finally in Bosnia in 1995. It was because of recent events in Bosnia that Logan now found himself as a pawn within a greater political game.

When the NATO led bombing campaign began in mid 1995 against Serbian targets in Bosnia, Logan found himself assigned to a special group assigned to recover downed airmen. Three weeks prior he'd parachuted in with his team to find an F-16 pilot who'd ejected from his plane after a mechanical failure. The area was completely controlled by Serbian forces and Logan found himself separated from his team. Undeterred he started towards the last known location of the pilot, who was hiding in a dense forest kilometers away. However before he could reach the area, Logan came upon a suspicious meeting on an empty country road. He quickly recognized one of the men as a wanted war criminal, his picture having been passed around during intelligence briefings. Having seen first hand the devastating ethnic cleansing in the area, Logan could not keep his head down and carry on with his original mission. When the meeting broke up Logan approached the car with his rifle up, hoping to apprehend the wanted man. Panicking, the driver started firing his weapon blindly out the window, forcing Logan to return fire for protection. Knowing he wouldn't be able to catch the bastard, Logan put a bullet in the war criminal's head before retreating into the woods.

Receiving a small wound on his shoulder, Logan was able to make it to the rendezvous point where the rest of his team was awaiting pick-up. They were airlifted by helicopter and transferred to a navy aircraft carrier, but due to his wound he was separated from his team and flown back to Aviano for treatment. The doctors discovered his wound had become infected and the sergeant soon fell into a fever. During his time in the hospital, news of a rogue assassination attempt by the US military erupted. The Serbians denied the allegations against the wanted war criminal, claiming he was a prominent military leader. Plus unbeknownst to Logan, a Russian intelligence operative from the SVR covered as a diplomat had been shot in the car.

Embarrassed by being caught off guard the US government went into full defensive mode, ready to throw Staff Sergeant Logan to the wolves in order to keep the international community content. So a team had been sent from Washington to Aviano to investigate the incident and charge Logan in a manner that would generally appease the other parties.

Jane hoped that she could convince Sgt. Logan to join her before it went that far. It had only taken seconds looking over his file for her to realize he was perfect for the new direction Lord Lodge and Tiberius wanted for the Manor. He was an intelligent, honourable man, who thought for himself.

"So if you're not a cop, who are you?" Logan asked, gingerly stretching his arms over his head after hours in restraints. "You're a spook, aren't you?"

"Had much experience with spooks?" Jane answered the question with a question.

"I met a few during Desert Storm," he replied with a shrug. "Plus some more after the shoot out in Mogadishu." Although he tried to look at ease, his eyes betrayed his nonchalant attitude. He had clever dark eyes that seemed to be constantly evaluating.

"Let's just say I'm your fairy godmother," Jane answered cryptically, receiving a broad smile in return. It was a smile that Jane was sure appealed to many young women, much like the rest of the Sergeant. His light brown skin and smooth features made it possible for him to appear Persian, Arabic, or even South American. She could also tell he was also in perfect physical shape, despite recovering from his brief illness and wearing an extra large jumpsuit. "Looks like you're in a pretty tough spot Sarge."

"Yes ma'am," he replied, the smile evaporating as quickly as it appeared. He remained silent, unwilling to continue until he knew more about the reason for his visitor's arrival.

"The Colonel says that you shot up a car with a Serbian General and Russian diplomat inside. He's been ordered to throw the book at you," Jane summarized dispassionately. "Did you do it?"

"It wasn't like that..."

"Sergeant, I don't have time for evasiveness," she cut in mid sentence. "If you want to equivocate you can do it with the lawyer. The camera's are off and no one's recording our conversation. Want to know why?"

Logan raised his eyebrows in silent response. He'd noticed the reds lights go off the cameras when the guards had left. Since then his curiosity had not been satisfied.

"It's because I'm not here," Jane offered conspiratorially. "Listen, I don't care who you shot, where you shot them, or how many times. But what I do care about is if you can answer my questions honestly. So let's try this again, did you shoot the Serbian and the rest of the guys in that car?"

"Yes, ma'am," Logan answered simply in his best boot camp style.

"Why?"

He sat silent for a moment, slightly surprised by the question. Up until this point nobody had asked him why he'd done what he did. They were so eager to place the blame on him that they didn't care about his motivation or the particulars of the encounter. But looking at the serious woman across the table from him, his gut told him he should follow her request and answer her directly.

"The first pilot they sent us to retrieve was captured just before we got on the ground," Logan began slowly, deciding to put words to the emotions he'd felt. "The place was crawling with the enemy, so we spent two weeks evading capture trying to get to an extraction point. During that time we passed a mass grave and watched helplessly as half a village was slaughtered. Our orders then were to avoid contact at all costs and to not engage the enemy unless our lives were at risk."

"Go on," urged Jane as Logan trailed off, his eyes focused on some distant point before clearing.

"I couldn't look in the mirror for days afterwards," he continued bitterly. "I mean what the fuck are we doing here? Pussy footing around these bastards while they're killing entire villages! So yeah, I shot that general directly in the forehead when I realized I couldn't take him alive and I'd do it again."

"You ride horses?" Jane asked casually despite the agitation of the prisoner across the table.

"What?"

"Do you know how to ride a horse?" she repeated slowly, deliberately provoking him.

"Uh yeah," the Sergeant replied, still slightly confused. "My dad worked for a thoroughbred owner. He wasn't one of the main trainers, but he was good with horses and he taught me to ride when I was young. Why?"

"I ask the questions," Jane continued, working through the checklist in her head. "And both your parents are now deceased?"

"Yes, cancer for both. My dad six years ago and my mom the year before."

"Brother's, sisters…?" Jane rhymed off quickly, receiving a shake of the head in reply.

"No living relatives, with no one to miss me," he answered perceptively.

"Ahh, you catch on pretty quick," Jane smiled, satisfied that he'd connected the dots. She already knew there was no one who would miss him if he disappeared. It was one of the requirements for prospective recruits to the Manor. They couldn't have their secrecy uncovered by a relentless wife or sibling.

"What do you want from me?" Logan asked pointedly, tired of the games.

"I'm looking to recruit someone with your skill set, but more importantly someone with a conscience and a sense of loyalty and honour. I don't need a psychopathic killing machine, but I also don't want a priest. Are you interested?"

Logan hesitated, unsure how he felt. All he really wanted to do was to be let out, rejoin his team, and stay in the Army.

"Listen Sarge, the Army's going to hang you out to dry," Jane pointed out honestly, knowing the dilemma Logan was facing. "They're going to charge you with everything they can, even if you sign the statement the Colonel waved in your face. You'll spend years in Leavenworth and will be basically unemployable when released. Sure you might get a job as a janitor or flipping burgers somewhere, but that's about the best your future holds."

"You don't know that," Logan rebuffed weakly, the full impact of his situation dawning on him.

"If you're dense enough to believe that, then I don't even want to recruit you," Jane countered sharply, putting the file back into her briefcase.

"Wait! What do I have to do?" he called out desperately.

"If I recruit you, you will belong to me," Jane began, leaning back into her chair. "You will cease to exist, no more friends and no more army. You'll receive a decent wage and see some pretty incredible things. But make no mistake, any foul ups and you will disappear for real. Are you still interested?"

"Let's do it," Logan shrugged in response after a moments thought. "Doesn't look like I've got much of a choice."

"I knew you'd see it my way in the end," Jane smiled back, failing to hide the excitement she was feeling from her first recruitment. "Do you have any regular clothes other than that awful jumpsuit?"

"No ma'am," he answered slowly, confusion setting in once again. "Why?"

"Well we can't have you walking around the base looking like an escapee," Jane answered, looking over the soldier in front of her. "Leave it to me."

Without adding anything Jane stood up and walked over to the door, banging on it twice. Within seconds the door was opened by one of the guards. She shot him a brief smile that melted the stone faced soldier before walking to the observation room door. There were only a few hurdles left for her mission, but they seemed to be getting taller. Getting in to see the prisoner had been fairly straight forward, however she knew getting him out might be tougher.

"Gentlemen," Jane announced upon entering the observation room, silencing the whispered conversations within. "I think I can find a way to make everyone happy. Well I'll be happy at least and the rest of you might only end up slightly content."

The faces looking at her ranged from suspicious, to doubtful, to downright upset. Jane offered her most angelic smile as she prepared her final gambit.

"Sgt. Logan will be leaving here with me today," she began despite the atmosphere of the room. "He has vital information required by Task Force Broadsword."

The room erupted in a cacophony of voices, challenging the surprise announcement.

"What about his trial?!"

"There are procedures to be followed!"

"What about the Russians?!"

"What will we tell the press?!"

Jane patiently waited before raising her hand to signal silence. Despite the bravado and tension of the men in the room, they all quieted down for her. Without removing the smile on her face, Jane continued.

"Let me explain how things will go from here and hopefully you will all see how beneficial this will be to everyone. In a few minutes I will leave here with Major

Sullivan, who will escort me to the base hospital. We will meet with the head doctor and the coroner."

"Colonel Davenport and Dr. Charles," offered Major Sullivan helpfully, signalling to everyone in the room who's side he was on.

"Yes thank you," Jane acknowledged, her smile broadening briefly. "I will present those men with the same letter you all saw. They will then file a report and sign a death certificate stating that Staff Sergeant Logan tragically died from the infection of the wounds he received in Bosnia."

"But what about the charges against him?" the Colonel asked too quickly, realizing the reality almost immediately.

"If you want to charge a corpse and take it to trial, then by all means have fun," Jane laughed in response. "Gentlemen, in fifteen minutes Sgt. Logan will be officially dead. The Russians, Serbians, and Washington will then lose interest and we can all go about some real business."

"What if we don't go along with your lies and reveal the truth," questioned the jerk from State. "That fancy letter in your pocket only applies to people under the Department of Defense, not the State Department."

"Colonel do you want to handle this one or should I?"

"Sir, I think I can safely assume that Task Force Broadsword is at the highest National Security level, well above Top Secret," The Colonel answered the bureaucrat, grateful for an opportunity to redeem himself from his previous misstep. "As such, revealing any related information to anyone not cleared could result in prosecution."

At this pronouncement, everyone slowly came to realize that Jane's solution would actually save them all a lot of work. The soldiers were only too eager to follow what they believed was a legitimate order. Even the bureaucrats realized they'd just received a paid vacation to Italy and slowly left the room in significantly better spirits than when they'd entered.

"Major, have a copy of the doctor's report and the death certificate sent to me when it's done," The Lieutenant Colonel ordered as he gathered his briefcase and hat from a side table. "I'll be at the Officer's Club and will be out of your hair as soon as I get both."

"Yes sir."

"Officer Pierce, this has been quite the experience," the Colonel smiled as he shook Jane's hand, clearly amused by what had just happened. "I don't suppose I can tell anybody about this?"

"What do you think?" Jane replied with a cocked eyebrow. "None of this ever happened. By the time you got to the base, Sgt. Logan was already dead."

Shaking his head, the Colonel left the room. The Army CID investigators were in the hall and would have to be briefed on the new story.

"Before we go to the hospital, could you give me any tapes that show Sgt. Logan in the building," Jane ordered politely, closing the last loophole at the stockade. At Sullivan's order the techs ejected the video cassettes and handed them over to Jane. She quickly put them in her briefcase and followed the Major out to the lobby.

"What do you want me to do with Sgt. Logan?" Sully asked as they reached the front desk, still manned by the young Lieutenant.

"Who's on duty that you can trust?" Jane asked looking from the Major to the Lieutenant.

"Corporal Dodd," the Lieutenant answered quickly, hoping to impress his boss by knowing his people. Major Sullivan thought for a moment and then nodded in concurrence.

"Good. Have Cpl Dodd give Sgt. Logan some camo fatigues," Jane began as she reached into her purse. "Don't worry they don't have to fit, but he can't be seen outside of the building in his prison jumpsuit. Once he's presentable, Cpl Dodd will then take Logan to the PX or whatever store is on the base to buy some clothes."

"Who's going to pay for a new wardrobe?" the Major asked dubiously, not wanting to have to explain the expense to the bean counters.

"Don't worry, this should take care of it," she replied, pulling some crisp hundred dollar bills from her purse. The Lieutenant's eyes widened as he stared at the roll of cash Jane held, sighing slightly as she put three bills in his hand. "Have him taken to the NCO's club when they're done. I'll meet him there once we're finished at the hospital. Got it?"

"Yes ma'am!" exclaimed the young officer, eager to please a seemingly important guest. He quickly had one of the dispatcher's call Cpl Dodd and ordered him back to the stockade from patrol.

"The hospital's on the other side of the base, so I'll drive us over," Sullivan offered as they left the building, the armed guards at the doors no longer at their post. They walked over to the motor pool, where Sully directed Jane to one of the Humvees. A red light was on the top and *Military Police* was written across the hood and doors. Jane hesitated slightly before trying to get into the green painted monster, having never seen a vehicle like it. The Major noticed her reticence and couldn't help but comment. "First time in a Humvee?"

Jane nodded slowly after climbing into the passenger seat. The seat was stiff and the interior was a collection of plain metal parts with a gun rack mounted on the console between her and the driver. But she calmed herself down once he started driving, realizing that it was basically a car.

The roads were largely empty as they drove to the hospital, Major Sullivan explaining that it was lunch time and most of the people on the base would be crowded into the mess halls. The hospital itself was an undistinguished building with more windows than most of the others on the base. Sully pulled the Humvee into a reserved space for emergency vehicles and jumped out with ease. Jane however, had a much harder time descending. Between her heels, her suit, and her collection of bags, she basically fell to the pavement.

Jane recovered her composure quickly as Sully rushed over to help her. She waved away his apologies for not helping her out, regaining the role of the strong professional woman. They entered the hospital without another word, quickly finding Colonel Davenport in his office. The forged letter was presented to him and he diligently completed the medical report on Sgt. Logan with only a minor protest. The coroner, Dr. Charles, was even easier to deal with. An older man at the end of his career, the letter was more than enough to get the faked death certificate. Jane was pretty sure that she could have convinced the dirty old man with nothing more than her cleavage.

The doctor's assistant made photocopies of the documents and passed them over to Major Sullivan, who in turn gave Jane a copy of each. Satisfied that Sgt. Logan was finally administratively dead, Jane followed Sully out of the hospital in a thrilled daze. She'd successfully completed her first recruitment for the Manor! But more importantly, she'd done it alone and on her terms.

"That was quite the performance today," observed Sully as he drove Jane to the NCO's Club to pick up Logan. He had watched the satisfied look of success on Jane's face as they'd entered the Humvee and drove away. He was incredibly impressed with the iron willed woman sitting beside him. She'd argued, cajoled, and forced her requirements past multiple equally strong willed senior military and government officials. Himself included. But the fact that she'd done it with everyone seemingly content with the outcome was the most impressive part.

"Thanks Sully," she accepted graciously, still beaming in the moment. This time when he parked the Hummvee, Major Sullivan quickly got out first in order to help Jane out of the combat vehicle. She thanked him again and confidently walked through the front doors of the NCO's Club.

She ignored the duty Sergeant at the door and kept walking in to the dining room. Her clicking heels on the hardwood floor drew a number of glances from the men eating a late lunch. These glances turned to stares once they saw her full form. But Jane didn't even register the attention she was drawing, too focused on Sgt. Logan's table in a dark corner.

He was sitting with Cpl. Dodd and eagerly finishing off a plate of spaghetti with a glass of red wine. Jane dismissed Dodd after he helped her into a seat with gentlemanly pride. He was immediately replaced by a waiter who eagerly took Jane's order. Too nervous to eat all morning, she realized she was famished and thought she'd better eat before she passed out. She ordered the same thing as Logan, receiving her own glass of wine with speedy efficiency.

"So what now?" Logan asked after wiping his face and taking a sip of wine.

"A slight celebration," Jane smiled back at him as she took a sip of her own wine. With some regret she put the delicious vintage down and reached into her briefcase, throwing the photocopied documents on the table theatrically. "Congratulations Staff Sergeant Logan, you're dead!"

Chapter 7

The intangible malevolent atmosphere of the Manor had seemingly disappeared with Dr. Cleaver and his cronies, only to be replaced by a feeling of confusion and unease. The Manor had stood for centuries, changing only slightly in all that time. So the unexplained disappearance of so many Hunt members and their staff had not gone unnoticed and made many feel as though it signalled an uncertain future.

The North Tower, once a curiously forbidden part of the Manor to the staff, was now avoided at all costs. The only entrance to the dark monolith was now under constant guard by two well armed guards.

Pierce hesitantly nodded to both men as he led half of his Pack out of the North Tower and into the main part of Ravenwood Manor. MacDuff trailed behind him with a still drugged Leon while Kat brought up the rear. He looked expectantly towards the office door of the Hunt Secretary, slightly disappointed by the person who emerged.

"Ty!" shouted Kat from behind, charging past MacDuff and making him drop Leon to the ground. With youthful exuberance that belied her age, Kat ran and jumped onto Tiberius' muscular frame. They exchanged a passionate kiss before he lowered her back down, both sporting a satisfied smile.

"Well done Patrick!" Tiberius exclaimed once he recovered from his brief reunion, staring at Leon's drugged form. He stepped over the body and shook hands with Pierce first and then his old comrade MacDuff. "I wasn't even sure it would be possible to track any of them down. You, take this filth down to interrogation room five."

One of the guards immediately responded to Tiberius' order, lifting Leon's prone body onto his shoulders and shuffling away.

"What's with the guards?" Pierce inquired as he looked back at the remaining sentinel.

"I've got some new developments," Tiberius answered equivocally, refusing to elaborate.

"Like what?" Pierce prodded for more info, but to no effect. He then shrugged and turned towards the Secretary of the Hunt's office. "Well if there's nothing else you can't tell me, I'll just head in there…"

"She's not there. She went to recruit a new Hound for the Black Pack," he stated calmly. Seeing the look of concern that spread across Pierce's face, he tried to set the man's mind at ease. "Don't worry she can take care of herself."

"Yeah, I know," Pierce eventually agreed, knowing it was true. Jane had been instrumental in hunting down Colonel Bufford over six months ago. She'd also saved his life during the final showdown, but that didn't make him feel any easier. He needed to know more, "Where and when?"

"Italy, 1995," Tiberius sighed in response, knowing the argument that was coming.

"What?!" Pierce exclaimed in shock. "She was born on the Island and has never been through a portal except once. That was to 1830's France, where there weren't any phones, cars, or planes. How do you expect her to fit in there?"

"It was her idea," Tiberius countered coolly. "She picked the file and the target. Don't worry; she went through the portal many times before heading out on the actual mission. She studied incredibly hard and got acclimatised to the era. I wouldn't have let her go otherwise."

"Fine, but if anything happens to her..." Pierce let the warning hang in the air, inwardly surprised by his outburst. Events at the Manor had pulled them apart just as they had found each other. It wasn't until that moment that Pierce realised the impact she'd had on him and that he now worried for her safety as much as his own.

"Trust me," said Tiberius, wrapping his arm around Pierce's shoulder and leading him away from the office. "Get yourself cleaned up, fed and rested. I'll meet with you and your men tomorrow and you can debrief me on your mission so far."

"Sounds like a plan," Pierce grudgingly accepted. MacDuff silently followed him down a series of halls and corridors until they reached the Main Hall. His mood lightened as they stopped in the middle of the enormous circular mosaic floor and stared up at the domed ceiling five stories above. He remembered his first time entering the imposing space and it felt like a lifetime had passed. He'd been confused and intimidated by the Manor, but now it was home and he was glad to be back.

"Good night my Lord," MacDuff offered as he quietly departed.

"'Night," Pierce mumbled in reply before he walked to one of the grand staircases that led to his rooms located in one of the Manor's towers. The familiar walk through the building made him anxious for the relaxing atmosphere of his own space. He yearned to return to his comfortable leather loungers in front of a crackling fire, with glass of scotch in hand. He finally reached a large door with a brass plaque scrolled with *Commandant Pierce* on it. He stared angrily at the name, feeling it mock him as he opened the door and walked past it.

He had been recruited prematurely by the Black Tower Hunt Club the previous year, based on the experience and skills of his future self. Commandant Pierce was a cold blooded bureaucrat in charge of a misguided and horrific prison system. When he discovered this, Pierce had hoped that by arriving at the Manor that fate was no longer possible. However the longer he stayed, the more he worried that his fate was sealed.

"Welcome back my Lord," greeted his valet as Pierce entered. Melrose was the epitome of the professional servant, always appearing when required. "How did the hunt go?"

"Stop with that *my Lord* stuff when we're in here," Pierce ordered as he handed his bag and swordstick over.

"Yes sir."

"We caught Leonardo, or Leon as he was going by," Pierce answered, ignoring Melrose's inability at informality.

"Hopefully that's all you caught," sniffed Melrose as he took in Pierce's dishevelled attire.

Confused at first, Pierce shot a quick glance in the mirror and realized he was still dressed like a downtrodden war vet from the seventies. He almost didn't recognize himself with the long hair and scraggily beard. His Hawaiian shirt and ripped combat pants only added to his rough look.

"Ok, I guess a bath wouldn't be out of the question," Pierce allowed with a smile.

"Very good sir," Melrose accepted, barely cracking a smile.

After thirty glorious minutes in his large claw footed tub, he emerged refreshed and clean. Melrose insisted on cutting his hair back to a respectable length and giving him a shave, despite Pierce saying it would ruin his roguish appearance. Once more recognizable, Pierce entered his lounge in a pair of pressed pants and smoking jacket. The clothing was rich and expensive, but lacked the comfort of his old jogging pants. However his valet had yet again ruled the day, refusing to allow a lord of the Manor to wear such simple clothing.

"Melrose, could you come in here for a second," Pierce called out when he noticed a black bottle of scotch and a single glass on a table beside his brown leather lounge chair.

"Is there a problem?" Melrose inquired as he entered the lounge from the bathroom, folding a small white towel.

"Big problem," he replied seriously, pointing at the single glass. "I've been gone for months and the day I get back you want me to drink alone? No chance, grab another glass and have a drink with me."

Melrose flashed a quick smile, relieved at not having done anything wrong. He grabbed a glass at the bar and then sat down gently in a chair across from his master. He frowned slightly as Pierce leaned over and poured him a drink, uncomfortable with being served.

"So what's the gossip? What's happened since I've been gone?" Pierce asked as he leaned back and poured himself a drink. They toasted each other and took a sip simultaneously.

"The fallout from Lord... I mean Dr. Cleaver's departure has actually been fairly minimal," Melrose began after savouring the scotch. "As you know only eight of the Hunt members left that fateful night..."

"Cleaver, Zeidt, Debochev, De La Gena, Laflamme, and three others I didn't really know," Pierce cut in, counting them off on his fingers.

"Correct; Lord Van der Hees of the Orange Pack, Fraulein Muller of the Violet Pack, and Lord Donnelly of the Green Pack," Melrose finished, filling in the blanks. "This left twelve, after the death of Colonel Bufford. More than enough to keep the Manor staff occupied. Those that remained have acted normally, carrying on as they did before in seemingly contented ignorance."

"What about the staff?"

"Well that's just the thing," Melrose answered, setting his glass down and leaning forward. "The staff have not been formally told anything. Rumours and conjectures are flying around below stairs, from the ridiculous to the volatile."

"Why hasn't Lord Lodge made an announcement? Surely his voice would put everyone at ease, no matter how dire the situation."

"Lord Lodge has shut himself in his rooms," Melrose replied sadly. "This time for real. I've only been able to see him a few times since you've left. He sits in his office all day long, poring over books and papers that are brought in on a trolley each morning."

Pierce could feel the concern in Melrose's voice, his valet having once worked for Lord Lodge directly. The Master of the Manor was undoubtedly the greatest intellect he had ever met. But Pierce knew that such men often walked a fine line between genius and insanity. This made him share Melrose's concern and he decided he'd check in on Lodge after his meeting with Tiberius the next day.

"I'll talk to Tiberius about it and try and get in to see Lord Lodge tomorrow," Pierce advised his valet, hoping it would ease his mind. "What else is going on? How's the reaction to the promotions been?"

"Generally good, although there's always jealousy and intrigue in this place, so it's hard to tell," Melrose allowed, leaning back into his chair. "I think some of the members were shocked by Tiberius being named Master of the Hunt, going from a servant to their superior. However no one can really argue he doesn't deserve the position and the grumblings didn't last very long. The staff however are overjoyed with the change. Cleaver might have been respected by most, but he was feared by everyone. Tiberius's move upwards has been celebrated by everyone below stairs, many seeing it as a positive precedent."

"I hope too many of the servants aren't expecting to become members of the Hunt anytime soon," Pierce observed doubtfully. "Don't get me wrong, I'm not a supporter of this upstairs/downstairs division. I'm a Canadian after all and no limit should be placed on what a person can achieve. I just don't want anyone to get hurt and disappointed when the next member of the Hunt isn't recruited from within."

"I wouldn't worry about that," Melrose allowed. "The staff know all too well how slowly change happens here. Although the additional promotion of Miss Piper has created a stir."

"Miss Piper?" Pierce asked absently.

"Miss *Jane* Piper," Melrose elaborated followed by an audible sigh. "The woman you're infatuated with."

"Infatuated is a strong word," Pierce argued, hoping he wasn't blushing. Ever since meeting her, Jane was the only name he'd heard her referred by. He'd probably been the second most excited person, after herself, when Jane had been named Drummond's successor. He knew she was clever, intelligent, capable, and deserved to be more than just a maid. But they hadn't seen each other since the night she'd received the good news.

"None of the jealousy one would expect from the other servants has surfaced since she was promoted," Melrose continued, inwardly proud at the professionalism of his colleagues. "In truth I don't think many of the servants aspire to anything beyond their current position, so everyone seems to be happy for her."

"Well that may not last too long," Pierce observed prophetically. "She just showed to the others what is possible. Sure the situation she found herself in was very unique and I doubt many of the staff would want to go through everything she did in order to move up. But nonetheless the seeds of ambition and possibility may have been planted."

"From the stories I heard the night you returned from the portal, I can't think of many people who would want a promotion that badly."

"Well you never know," Pierce shrugged before looking at Melrose with renewed interest. "What about you? You've been working at the Manor for what, fifty some years?"

"Something like that, though to be honest I've lost track."

"Have you ever dreamt about doing something different?" Pierce inquired

"I'm quite content with my life and occupation," Melrose replied after a moments thought. "To be honest I've never thought about a change."

"Fair enough," Pierce allowed, not wanting to push Melrose too far in case he inadvertently offended him. The last thing he wanted to do was imply that Melrose was wasting his life serving others, since he knew his valet was proud of his position.

They both finished off their drinks and Pierce retired to his bedroom, where he practically collapsed into the bed. After six months of sleeping in flea infested motels and car seats, his luxurious four poster bed put him to sleep instantly.

*

"Have these instructions delivered to Lord Pierce and the Brown Pack," Tiberius instructed the porter at his door, handing over two small notes. The porter accepted them in his spotless white gloves and left after delivering a small bow. Tiberius closed the door with a smile, still unused to being the Lord of the Hunt. He walked back over to his large desk, picking up a third note.

His private rooms were almost identical to the ones Pierce occupied, situated in the tower opposite that of the Lord of the Brown Pack. Although his official office was beside Lord Lodge's on the second floor off the Main Hall, Tiberius preferred doing most of his work from the privacy of his personal rooms. Unlike the other members of the Hunt, there was no brass plaque with his name on it attached to the door. Its absence didn't mean that no one knew where he was, it simply warned people he wasn't to be bothered here unless summoned.

"I've got your invitation to the debriefing tomorrow," Tiberius announced after walking across the hall into his bedroom. The faint glow from a half dozen candelabra's stopped him instantly after he closed the door behind him. He hadn't used them in years, preferring the ease and safety of electricity.

"That's nice," replied a feminine voice from the bathroom.

"I thought you'd be pleased to be included," he replied, easing out of his leather jacket and placing it on a nearby chair.

"I am, but I've got better things on my mind right now."

"Like what?" Tiberius asked walking towards the bathroom door, unwilling to converse through the walls.

"Like you," Kat replied, seductively stepping past the door before Tiberius could reach it.

His eyes widened by the sight before him, prompting Tiberius to flick the note he held over his shoulder theatrically. Kat stood smiling at him in a stunning black and red lingerie ensemble. The sheer stockings matched her perfectly fitted bra, leaving nothing to the imagination. She cat walked over to him, her crimson high heels clicking across the hardwood floor.

"Where did you get this?" he asked in awe as she shoved him onto the bed.

"A nice little shop in Los Angeles," she replied taking a step back from the bed, giving Tiberius a full view of her purchase. "I saw this in a magazine and wanted to surprise you. So I asked Liam if he could help me find a store."

"I'm sure he could."

"He knew one right away and even told me what my measurements were," Kat teased, running her hand through her vibrant auburn hair.

"I'm sure he did."

"Do you like it?" she asked slinking back towards him, smiling at his brief flashes of jealousy.

"It's the greatest thing I've seen in a long time," he answered truthfully staring into her eyes. Tiberius had not lived his many years at the Manor like the monkish Templar he'd once been. But he'd also refrained from the life of debauchery the portals of the North Tower could make possible. He'd had many women in the past, enjoyed the company of a few, but loved none of them.

"That's just what Liam said when I showed it to him at the store," Kat lied innocently as she leaned over and began unbuttoning his shirt.

"What?!" Tiberius exclaimed, feeling as though his blood were on fire. Even though he knew it wasn't true, the thought of anyone else seeing her like this made him furious. Without realizing it, he'd gripped Kat's wrists with a surge of force. But rather than grimace in pain, the young beauty's eyes and mouth opened wide with pleasure.

Before he knew it, Tiberius was pushed back onto the bed and a pair of soft hands ripped the rest of his shirt open, shooting buttons in all directions. She immediately started kissing his scar riddled muscular chest. More aroused than he'd ever been in his life he reached down and pulled Kat towards him, locking lips with her at once.

Six months of pent up desire exploded on to the bed as they let their hands and fingers explore each other's bodies. Kat removed the rest of his clothes with the same destructive forces she'd used on his shirt. Her urgent fingers tingled as she felt the hard muscles of his powerful frame. The random scars she discovered only made her want the ancient warrior even more.

Tiberius ran his fingers along her soft and toned body, fulfilling a desire he'd felt from their first meeting. He slowly began undoing her garter with a simple one handed flick he'd learned in Paris before the Revolution. More lessons from his past came rushing back as he confidently undressed her, eliciting pleasurable moans in reply.

Their naked bodies came together in a flurry of skin and limbs, using every inch of the giant four poster bed. The intensity of their love making did nothing to shorten the experience. Their mutual energy only fuelled the yearning each felt for the other, culminating in a storm of oaths and screams.

They crumbled into each other's arms at the end, panting in synchronised satisfaction. Both lay staring at the intricately carved ceiling, unable to stop smiling from their exertions. Eventually Tiberius noticed a bottle of wine and some glasses on the bedside table. Without disturbing the angel entwined with him, he stretched his arm and grabbed the bottle. Luckily the cork was already out, so he just took a gulp straight from the bottle. He passed it over absently, where Kat took it and had a drink herself.

The bottle was passed back and forth a few times before Kat ended up spilling some on herself. The dark red liquid trickled down her neck, so Tiberius leaned over and sucked it off. Smiling at the sensation, Kat poured some more of the wine along her neck line and then on to her breasts and stomach. Without hesitating, Tiberius moved his head along her body, eagerly cleaning her off. Before he could finish, he felt the warm wine hit his shoulder and trickle down his back and chest. This was quickly followed by the feeling of Kat's soft lips on his own body.

This sensual caressing reignited their desire and both were soon engulfed in another passionate exchange. However this time they were more deliberate with their attention to each other. Their bodies moved together in rhythmic unison, reaching sexual peaks and valleys more slowly than before. Like an experienced dance team, they instinctively knew what the other needed and answered it effortlessly.

"You were right," Kat exhaled breathlessly as she flopped back down onto the bed. "You always have control of your weapon."

Tiberius looked over at her in confusion before her impish grin made him recall a clever line he'd uttered outside the Raven's Vale six months ago. He'd meant it as a double entendre when he'd said it, but he hadn't been sure she had understood. The small village of Rivermead wasn't very worldly, but apparently she'd had some experiences before their first meeting.

"You were fantastic," he praised, happy to see her grin broaden into a full smile before she laid her head on his chest. "So how was your first trip through the portals?"

"Until now I would have said it was the most incredible experience of my life," she replied with renewed animation. "I was so excited when you came and told me Lord Pierce needed some help. I thought we'd be riding through the countryside again, chasing down thugs like before. So I was a little disappointed when I followed him to the North Tower. I didn't really know what was inside and Jane's explanations didn't make any sense. But nothing could have prepared me for walking through the portal. It was magic! All those people, and the cars, and the buildings, and the sun. My god the sun was bright and warm everyday."

"It wasn't too overwhelming?" Tiberius asked, still slightly apprehensive for having suggested to Pierce he use her on the hunt. Despite her adventurous spirit, she was an Island girl like Jane.

"No, it was exhilarating," Kat exclaimed rolling over on to her stomach beside him. She propped herself on to her elbows as she continued her speech on all the great things she saw. "But the best part was when that bastard came over to me and offered me a cigarette. From that point I knew we had him. He fell into the trap perfectly."

"With you as the bait," Tiberius muttered.

"Can you think off anything more enticing?" she replied, tossing her thick hair to the side while batting her eyes. "Don't worry, you're not the only one that travels with a posse. I was safe the whole time."

"I take it then that you'll go back with them if he asks?"

"In a heartbeat," she agreed quickly before hesitating slightly. "Wait, you mean there's a chance he won't ask me?"

"Well you're not actually a member of the Brown Pack," Tiberius explained carefully. "It's up to Lord Pierce how he conducts the hunt."

"Oh."

"Don't worry, I'm sure he'll take you again," he replied confidently as he ran his fingers through her hair. "You're fearless, smart, and the most appealing bait I've ever seen. If Pierce has an once of sense he'll invite you back."

"What do you think of him, Lord Pierce," Kat asked absently, enjoying the sensation of his playing with her hair.

"He's a bit of an enigma," Tiberius answered thoughtfully as he reached over and grabbed the discarded bottle of wine. "When I first met him, he'd just finished beating up Morgan and Dufresne with nothing more than a book. He did the same thing a few weeks later when he handily beat Sean in a duel. Time and time again he appears like a harmless nobody, only to strike with effective force. I almost thought it was some kind of cunning act, but the man's completely honest and straightforward."

"That's what I thought as well," Kat agreed, remembering their first meeting. "I couldn't understand how Jane was attracted to him. He wasn't a dark and dashing figure with a slight scar above his eye."

Tiberius smiled at the compliment as she gently touched the small line above his brow. He passed her the wine bottle and watched her take a small sip, hoping that it would trickle down her front again.

"But after spending months with him in California, I can see where the attraction comes from," she continued, handing the bottle back. "He has an inner strength that's hard to measure and he's very smart. You know he almost reminds me of Lord Lodge."

"Well if he's as smart as we both think, he'll demand that you join him again," Tiberius allowed, emptying the bottle with a final gulp. The thought of her getting hurt beyond the portal worried him. But he also knew that her desire to go was one of the qualities that attracted him to her.

"Are you sure you can't make a slight suggestion in case he's not as convinced," Kat pleaded seductively.

"I'm not about to interfere with Lord Pierce's mission, not matter how much I love you." The words slid easily out of his mouth before he realized it, eliciting a pleased smile from Kat. He smiled back in return, having never spoken those words before and not really sure what to do. Luckily Kat had no such hesitation as she jumped across the bed, grabbing him a third time.

Chapter 8

"We smile and shed tears of delight as she ascends towards the light," intoned a surprisingly soft voice to the white robed congregation holding hands in a circle. They were all humming at various levels, slightly swaying back and forth. "Our sister gets to climb the glorious path to enlightenment. We should all be so lucky!"

The leader joined in the humming as he slowly walked behind the circle, lighting torches sticking out of the ground. When he completed his first circuit of the circle he started another, this time watching those assembled and looking for any doubters. But he found none; they were all deep in meditation and ignorant of their surroundings.

"But our sister must be free of all physical bonds to make her journey," he continued his address, stepping onto a large rock. "Who will help her?!"

"I will!" "I will!" "Me too!" rang out a chorus of voices as they eagerly grabbed the torches behind them and lifted them up. They all closed in on a wooden platform built in the center of the circle, holding the blazing torches above their head.

"Brothers and sisters, set her free!" exclaimed the leader, the firelight gleaming in his crazed eyes. The crowd obeyed at once and tossed the torches onto the platform, backing away quickly as it erupted into flames. Within seconds the shape of a body disappeared in the raging fire.

"May the light shine upon each of us," he proclaimed, stepping down from the rock. The crowd returned to their circle, resuming their hand holding and chants. The leader sat upon the rock and stared into the fire, a smile creeping upon his face. He had travelled all over the world and had never found such a fertile land, full of desperate people searching for anything to believe in.

He gave them something to believe in, himself. Despite his flat greasy hair and scraggily beard, people never shied away from him. Just the opposite, when they looked into his mesmerizing dark eyes and listened to his soft voice, they flocked to him. None of them really cared about the nonsense he spouted, they just needed to hear the sincerity of the delivery.

"Pardon my Lord," whispered a voice behind him, forcing him to turn from the joyous scene by the fire.

"What is it Yves?" he asked with minor irritation.

"I thought you might like to know that we've heard from one of our agents," he began quickly but quietly. "Leonardo has discovered another *recruit* and will be picking her up."

"That is good news my friend," smiled the leader rubbing his hands together.

"Shame about young Evelyn," Yves observed with little feeling as he looked at the raging funeral pyre beyond. "She was such a nice little whore, so accommodating. Sadly she just insisted on leaving."

"You removed the teeth this time?"

"Yes sir," Yves nodded with a smile. "Most of them after she died."

"Good. I don't want to have to leave this place like the last one," the leader reprimanded softly. "I really like it here."

He breathed in deeply, ignoring the smoke and instead enjoying the fresh floral scented air as he looked over the clearing they all occupied. The ground was soft and spongy, with layers of dirt, pines needles, and ferns spread out over the forest floor. Towering pine and cedars rose towards the sky, their tops seemingly pointing at the bright stars above. Heavy rain from the night before nullified the possibility of the fire setting any of them ablaze.

There were no other inhabitants for miles, creating an idealistically isolated commune for this small but faithful sect. The land was owned by a shell corporation and its steep hills descended towards a large bay. The shoreline was periodically used by campers as they paddled along the water, but they never bothered with the white robbed inhabitants. They could do whatever they wished here, far from the prying eyes of society.

"They'll be here until the sun comes up," observed the leader as he looked over his dogmatic flock. "We might as well go have some fun."

Yves followed in step behind him as the walked along a well worn path through the dark forest. After a short distance they could see the twinkling lights of the compound shining through the branches. Another clearing soon opened up as they made their way past a set of buildings. It was an old summer camp that they'd bought and taken over. A collection of small cabins stood by the edge of the forest, pointing towards a large hall made of logs. Once the main meeting and dining hall, it now belonged to the leader and his entourage.

A brown robbed sentinel stood at the door and held it open for the leader and Yves as they climbed the large front staircase.

"My Lord," nodded the acolyte as he bowed his head in deference.

Immediately inside were a collection of benches all pointed towards a small platform. A high backed wooden arm chair sat alone on the platform, the leader's pulpit. They walked past this seemingly innocent room into the bowels of the building beyond.

A shiny brass key chained to the leaders waist opened a heavy wooden door and led to a scene straight out of a sheik's harem or a Parisian bordello. Through a fog of smoke, half naked women were strewn across a pillow filled room. Soft carpets overlapped each other along the floor, with two large hookahs sitting predominantly in the middle.

Seeing the entrance of the two men, a short but lean man stood from his place beside one of the hookahs. Clapping twice, he resurrected the lounging women from their drug induced lethargy. They walked over and began slowly removing the men's robes, pressing their bodies against them flirtatiously. They led the leader to a comfortable chaise in the corner as Yves took the other man aside.

"I just heard that Leonardo has got another one for us," Yves smiled as two of the girls called to him. "Apparently she's a real spitfire, but he'll break her."

"I don't know," replied his companion contemplatively. "I think I might like one with a bit more spirit."

"Perhaps," Yves acknowledged as they sat down by the hookah. "But Lord Debochev likes his women subservient and adoring. Who are we to argue?"

*

"Is this where we get the free hair cuts?" Liam asked as he poked his head past the door, holding up the note Tiberius had sent.

"Shut up and get in here," Tiberius growled, motioning Liam and Sean towards a pair of wooden chairs by the wall. "You're late."

"Apologies, but we just got back," Sean offered as he followed Liam into the office.

"Leon's car is in place at his warehouse?" Pierce asked his two men as they sat down, receiving a simple nod in reply. "Good."

"So how the hell did you track him down?" Tiberius posed to the assembled crowd. Pierce and MacDuff sat in the comfortable chairs across from the desk, with Morgan, Dufresne, Kat, Liam, and Sean occupying smaller chairs along the walls. The space was tight, but Tiberius wasn't willing to meet anywhere else in the Manor.

"It wasn't easy," Pierce began with a sigh. "We spent months sifting through the list of aliases that you gave us. It took forever since we didn't even know which Packs had gone through the portal, so we had to check all of them."

"We went through directories, phone books, and even broke into a DMV office to check their files," continued MacDuff. "We even checked newspapers to watch for miraculous gambling winnings to see if any of them were stupid enough to bet on a game or race they knew the result for."

"But we came up blank," Pierce finished shaking his head. "Honestly I was ready to call it a day."

"Luckily Liam's a smart mouth and never refrains from showing it," Sean jumped in.

"It worked didn't it?" Liam argued with a shrug. "All I said was that some of the guys we're looking for are really dumb and I wouldn't be surprised if they used their real name."

"It couldn't have been that easy," Tiberius laughed leaning back into his chair, thoroughly enjoying the tale.

"Not quite," Pierce allowed a quick smiled in recollection. "Our first try using their real names also produced nothing. But then we tried a slight variation; using their Pack's names. So we discovered that Leonardo Scapitti was living in Los Angeles as Leon White."

"Once we had his name and address it was simple," MacDuff said. "We tracked him down and observed him for a few weeks, discovering his work at the youth shelter."

"That's when you asked to use Kat as a way to capture him," Tiberius concluded, knowing that part of the story.

"Yeah, we knew he was up to something," Pierce continued, his face growing darker. "He seemed like he was hunting, so we threw some bait out to see if we got a bite."

Tiberius smiled at the choice of words, his grin broadening as the group retold the full story of Leon's apprehension and subsequent interrogation. It would seem like a holiday compared to the interrogation Tiberius had planned for the bastard. He'd heard rumours of Leonardo's penchant for sadism, but nothing concrete. The fact that he'd belonged to the White Pack meant that he'd been beyond Tiberius' control. But that was no longer the case.

"I doubt we'll get much more out of him concerning Debochev's whereabouts," MacDuff offered sagely. "His answers on the boat seemed truthful and that Russian bastard is canny enough to keep this imbecile in the dark."

"Indeed," Tiberius agreed with a nod. "From what you've said it sounds like Grigori went to great lengths to keep Leon at a distance. The use of messengers and agents seems an unnecessary step otherwise. But don't worry, there's other information I want from that hoodlum from Chicago."

"Like what?" Sean asked.

"I imagine you're hoping that Leon knows which portals the other Packs used. They might have decided as a large group," Pierce offered as he watched Tiberius hesitate in answering. "He might even know something of Cleaver's plan."

"Those are some of things we'll be asking him, but there's more," Tiberius sighed wearily. He'd been debating on how much to tell Lord Pierce since returning to the Manor. The arguments had been pounding within his head until he finally made a decision to trust him. "There might be a mole in the Manor."

"So get a cat," offered Liam lamely, receiving a glowering look from almost everyone in the room. "Sorry."

Tiberius hated himself for it, but he'd made sure to watch all of those present when he made his pronouncement. He knew that everyone in the room was on his side, but he had to be sure. The fact that nobody reacted with shock didn't surprise him. Even Pierce, with his limited exposure to the Manor, had come to know the place well enough to know that allegiances continually shifted.

"Tiberius, that's not exactly earth shattering," MacDuff finally admitted after taking a note to hit Liam later. "I'd be willing to bet that Cleaver has his claws into a number of maids, groundskeepers, or any other servants. Hell; you do, I do, we all do."

"Yes I know," Tiberius waved the argument aside. "But this appears to be much more than that. You're not the only one who succeeded in finding an escapee."

The Brown pack sat and listened in rapt attention to Tiberius' activities in Luxembourg, from the discovery of the note, to the meeting with Zeidt, and culminating in the assassin's death.

"So what do you plan on doing?" Pierce asked after hearing the news.

"I'm taking my men back to Luxembourg to follow the trail while it's still warm," Tiberius announced, generating smiles from both his men. "But under no circumstance does the mention of a mole leave this room. If there is one, it will only warn them off and create a target to anyone with the knowledge."

"And if there isn't one, it will only create panic and breed suspicion," Pierce concluded.

"The only people who know are in this room. Let's keep it that way," Tiberius warned, the unspoken hint of a threat hanging over the room. "Now back to your mission. What's your next step?"

"Leon phoned his contact from the café, which initiated the chain," Pierce began confidently. "The boys placed his car at the warehouse, where one of the links will drop a matchbook with instructions into his car. We'll tail whoever drops off the matchbook and keep the appointment at whichever diner we're directed to."

"Follow the links of the chain until you reach the end," Tiberius nodded in agreement.

"If it's alright with you, I'd like to keep Kat on the team," Pierce added cautiously. Tiberius' and Kat's relationship was the worst kept secret in the Manor and he didn't want to be the reason for keeping them apart. He thought of Jane and wanted nothing better than to be close to her again.

"Of course it's fine with me," Tiberius said, trying to ignore Kat's excited face in the back of the room.

"Good. If they're really abducting girls we'll need her help again," Pierce relaxed, happy that he hadn't ruffled any feathers. "So, who is this Debochev guy? We went through the portal with not much more than that list of names. We got lucky with Leon, but I'd like to be better prepared for the rest of them."

Glad that Pierce had realized the need for more information, Tiberius opened a desk drawer and took out a large manila folder, dropping it onto the center of his desk. He opened it up carefully, but leaned back in his chair rather than start reading from it. He had memorised the files of all those who had fled the Manor.

"Grigori Debochev," he began slowly as he pointed to the wall on his right. A collection of photos were hanging on the wall, everyone that had fled the Manor. A bright red X was painted across the faces of Zeidt and Leon.

"America's Most Wanted, eat your heart out," Liam whispered to no one in particular.

"The Lord of the White Pack; he's cunning, ruthless, and intelligent," Tiberius rhymed off. "Though he's not as physically dangerous as Colonel Bufford, he's infinitely more treacherous as an adversary. He was born in Tsarist Russia, in a desolate farming community. In a time of intense classism, he rose to the very peak with little more than his brains and charisma. He left a trail of bodies and broken dreams from the vast Russian steppes to the canal lined streets of St-Petersburg. Labelling himself as a holy man and spiritual healer, he connived his way into people's hearts and wallets."

"Sounds like he was just a hustler," Pierce observed unimpressed.

"Oh he's a hustler, there's no doubt about that," Tiberius continued. "But he's a dangerous one. He had a gift at differentiating hypochondriacs from the truly sick. He was able to fool the former into believing they were healed with nothing more than soft words and a mesmerizing stare. The latter were given useless concoctions for a ridiculous fee. Those that were *healed* praised him and those that remained ill eventually died penniless. Within a few years his fame as a healer and intensely spiritual man spread, along with a large number of faithful followers.

"Eventually he gained the attention of the Tsarina, a desperate woman tired of the court doctors. Grigori proved successful from the beginning, using a combination of common sense and hypnosis in his treatments. These successes led to him becoming a permanent fixture at court. From there he accepted bribes for favours, used his influence to silence detractors, and generally enjoyed himself. He preached that sin and repentance were required for salvation."

"So he sinned a ton and repented a little?" Pierce inquired with a raised eyebrow.

"Indeed. He enjoyed group sinning with his largely female following, though he apparently was not opposed to sinning in smaller numbers."

"I could join that church," Liam observed.

"He must have been incredibly charming to get that many women to sin with him," Kat offered sceptically as she looked at his photograph on the wall. "He looks like a bum."

"Power can be a strong appeal, and he wielded an impressive amount of it," Tiberius explained. "But power also brings rivals and enemies. For years Grigori stayed one step ahead of bureaucrats, the church, but most importantly the secret police. They hated him and constantly tried to have him arrested from evidence they discovered or fabricated. But he remained in place despite all their efforts. You can see how he uses some of those tricks today; messengers, go betweens, and lackeys all do the dirty work."

"All things must come to an end," MacDuff offered sagely. "How did Lord Debochev get recruited here?"

"After avoiding two different assassination attempts, Drummond was sent to recruit him. He was intrigued with the offer but had been invited to a party he wished to attend. Not wishing to throw the opportunity away, he sent a double to the party until he could finish his business with Drummond. However the two talked into the night and before Grigori knew it the sun was up and one of his spies was banging at the door."

"The assassins didn't miss the third time?" Morgan spoke up for the first time.

"The double was found poisoned, shot, beaten, and drowned."

"Very sloppy," Morgan shook his head with professional disdain.

"Drummond and Debochev were on the next train out of St-Petersburg," Tiberius concluded. "He wasn't about to sit around for a fourth time and the death was a fortuitous way for him to disappear."

"I don't know if he'll be that much tougher of an adversary than Bufford," Pierce said doubtfully. "He doesn't sound like a big threat as long as we don't fall under his mystical allure."

"You forget you're not only hunting Debochev ," Tiberius cautioned quickly. "He still has two of his men with him, plus other followers he has undoubtedly recruited. What makes him so dangerous is his ability to make others fall under his spell. Look at what we know already from Leon. There are at least three new people working for him, one way or another."

"Three?" Kat asked, counting on her fingers.

"The owner of the café, the man Leon called from the café, and whoever drops off the matchbook and swaps the cars at the diner," Pierce answered, quick to realize the situation. "There's probably more people than that."

"Exactly, we must also take into account the hunting grounds," MacDuff added, unwilling to take the Russian too easily. "In Marseille we had more anonymity, plus a few pieces of gold could get you a lot more. In 1971 there are databases, licences, and well trained police. Not just thugs with clubs. Infinitely more things can go wrong there. We'll need to be fully prepared to be successful this time."

"I agree with MacDuff, you'll need to tread carefully. Good luck" Tiberius finished, signalling an end to the briefing. Everyone stood up and filed out of the office, with only Pierce remaining in his seat. "Is there something else Lord Pierce?"

"Cut it out," Pierce laughed at his formal tone, receiving a genial smile in return.

"What's on your mind?"

"I'd like to see Lord Lodge," Pierce began, trying to keep his tone friendly. "I haven't spoken to him since that night I came back from Marseille."

"I'm afraid it's not a good time," Tiberius wavered, closing the file on his desk. "He's very busy with Manor business. What with everything that's happened…"

"Cut the bullshit," Pierce interrupted swiftly. "I'm not the naïve newbie anymore. Melrose filled me in last night."

"What can I say," Tiberius sighed as he stopped fiddling with things on his desk. "I've never seen him like this. Cleaver's actions took him completely by surprise and now he's obsessed with finding him."

"Obsessed how?"

"I don't really know how to explain it," Tiberius offered with a shrug. "Since I know you won't be satisfied otherwise I'll bring you in to see him and you can decide for yourself. It's almost the time when I look in on him."

Tiberius stood up and walked over to a large map of the Island that took up half of the wall. He looked at Pierce conspiratorially, winking as he pushed a small wooden button hidden within the design of the frame. Pierce heard a quiet click, and then the movement of gears. The map suddenly moved backwards and then shifted to the right behind the rest of the wall, exposing a poorly lit corridor beyond.

"A secret passageway?" Pierce intoned with youthful enthusiasm. He was surprised that he hadn't been in one since arriving at the Manor. The building was an enormous labyrinthine structure, with countless rooms, halls, and corridors. Numerous architectural styles had also been employed in the various stages of construction, so it just seemed like it should be filled with secret passages.

"Careful when you step in," Tiberius instructed as he motioned Pierce to follow him in. "Few people know about this little secret and I don't want scuff marks on the wall giving it away."

Pierce nodded and made a deliberately large step over the two foot section of wall that remained. He followed Tiberius closely, avoiding the bare lightbulbs that hung from the ceiling. They passed a couple of doors as they walked, but Tiberius remained quiet as to where they led. Eventually they came to the end of the corridor, where a large doorway stood. Two thin horizontal openings let beams of light into the dark space and Pierce walked over to look through.

Squinting through the highest opening, Pierce could only see the tops of some shelved books. But he had a hard time focusing any further. Another quiet click from behind him made Pierce take a step back as the door swung open, revealing a large white room beyond.

Chapter 9

Pierce was pretty sure they were standing in Lord Lodge's office, but the room bared little resemblance to how he remembered it. That last time he'd been here, he'd discovered the true history of Ravenwood Manor after returning from his mission in Marseille. Lord Lodge had just settled in and the large white space had looked deserted. The few pieces of furniture had been shoved into a corner and covered with sheets to protect them from dust and the table tops were all devoid of any papers or writing instruments.

But the scene before Pierce was completely different. Piles of books, documents, and boxes were haphazardly scattered along the floor and balancing on any flat surface available. Tiny paths free of the piles snaked randomly along the floor in no specific direction. An almost overpowering smell of pipe smoke attacked Pierce's nostrils and made his eyes water slightly. He was glad for the high ceiling of the room, since it kept the lingering cloud of smoke well above their heads.

"Where is…?" Pierce began to ask, looking around for Lord Lodge before Tiberius shushed him.

"Heidelberg!" Lord Lodge exclaimed, standing up from behind a pile of boxes in the middle of the room. "How could I have missed that?!"

Pierce was shocked by the man before him, not at all how he remembered the Master of the Manor. Lodge paced slowly amongst the organized chaos, tapping a collection of newspapers against his leg as he went.

"Sir, Lord Pierce is here and..." Tiberius announced despite Lodge not registering their sudden appearance from behind the bookcase.

"Seven different post offices have been robbed in less than six months," Lodge cut him off as he waved the newspapers at them. "What do you make of that? Something to keep our eye on."

"Sir, what exactly is..." Pierce started, taking a step forward.

"Don't move!" Lodge exclaimed excitedly. "You almost knocked over the stack concerning ferry movements on the Baltic!"

Pierce looked down at his feet and noticed a few books and some pamphlets lying on some faded newspapers. When he looked back up, Lodge was weaving through the piles to approach them, obviously unwilling to allow them to walk through his work. The top button of his shirt was undone and the ends of an unravelled black bowtie peeked through the collar. Three different pipes poked out of the pockets of his wrinkled beige smoking jacket. Pierce suddenly understood Tiberius' inability to describe the man before them. Apart from the piercing gaze of his eyes, Lord Lodge looked like a different man.

"So who did you catch? Was it one of Debochev's men?" Lodge asked absently as he reached them. His eyes moved from one of the newspapers in his hand to the piles on the floor as he decided where to place it.

"Yes it was, Leonardo," Pierce answered with obvious surprise. Seeing Lodge like this, he'd forgotten that the man possessed a rare intellect. "But how did you know?"

"Moths," was all that he said before letting out a breath of success and placing the newspaper on the correct pile. "Keep him in one of the interrogation rooms and go over the following questions."

Lodge quickly walked back over to the pair, rummaging in his pockets as he went. He finally pulled out a small folded piece of paper that Tiberius accepted calmly. He unfolded and peered over the list quickly before putting it in his own jacket pocket.

"Good, well unless either of you possess a running knowledge of Romanian chess champions during the cold war…" he trailed off as he retreated to the middle of the room, stopping momentarily to light a pipe.

Pierce didn't know how to react to their quick meeting, so he simply followed Tiberius back through the passage, returning to the office they had started from. The scene he just witnessed was so unexpected that he just sat down in silence once the secret door shut behind them.

"What the hell was that?" he finally blurted out, seeing Tiberius flinch as he said it. "I think that goes beyond obsessed, he's manic."

"His brain doesn't work like ours," Tiberius defended quickly. "He's a genius who's able to solve problems at multiple levels."

"I know that," Pierce countered as he leaned onto Tiberius' desk. "Listen you don't have to convince me that he's in a class by himself. But that in there is something different."

"You just caught him on a bad day," Tiberius argued, not entirely convinced.

"Did you just see what I did?" Pierce shot back. The episode had left him feeling both anger and concern. He'd taken a genuine liking to Victor Lodge and had enjoyed the few discussions he'd had with the man and didn't want him to have a nervous breakdown. But on the other hand they still had other Hunt members to track down and could use his abilities. "That pile of junk didn't just show up yesterday. Maybe you don't see it because you've been here the whole time. But that room scared me and I'm not sure he can see the forest from the trees anymore. I mean, Baltic ferry movements?!"

"What would you have me do!" Tiberius retorted angrily, throwing the pen he'd been twirling into the corner. "Lock him up?! Because that is the only way to keep him from working. He won't stop until he finds Cleaver. Nothing else matters; not you, me, or catching any of the rest of them."

They both sat staring at each other in silence for a few minutes, neither willing to back down. Pierce finally broke the ice by getting up and retrieving the pen from the corner and placing it on Tiberius' desk.

"Thanks."

"Sure," Pierce accepted solemnly before a smile broke out on his face. "Locking him up wouldn't work. He'd just break out and continue working before you could clean up his office."

Tiberius immediately laughed in reply, accepting the truth of the statement. Lord Lodge was as persistent as he was perceptive.

"So what do we do about it?" Tiberius asked, quickly turning the conversation back to serious matters.

"I'm not sure there's anything we can do about Lord Lodge right now," Pierce allowed with dismay. "But you will have to address the staff on what occurred that fateful night. Without a clear statement the rumours have been flying around. So far it's been mostly idle gossip, but I think it will become more destructive as time goes by."

"You're probably right," Tiberius nodded. "We've just been so busy around here since then."

"Hey I'm not blaming anyone," Pierce replied holding his hands up defensively. "What about the Hunt. They'll have to be spoken to as well. From what Melrose told me, they're pretty much content in their usual idleness, but that won't last for long."

"I suppose I should be the one to speak with them as well," Tiberius decided, weighing the situation in his mind. "If they were to see Lord Lodge in his current condition, we might find more of them switching sides."

"That's a possibility. What do you plan on telling them?"

"I think I'm going to read them the riot act," Tiberius answered firmly. "I'll figure out the right words, but the message will be clear. The North Tower is closed for business and anyone acting against the Hunt or the Manor will be dealt with very harshly."

*

Although the train wasn't nearly as frightening as the plane ride, Jane still felt uncomfortable looking out the window as the Italian Alps flew past. The idea of travelling at such a high speed, though exhilarating, filled her with trepidation. But she had to admit the soft first class seats were significantly more comfortable than any carriage the Manor could offer.

"Would you like the newspaper?" asked a gentle Spanish voice across from her. After years of being berated by Senor De la Gena, Jane knew enough Spanish to understand and accept the offer. She leaned over and took the newspaper from Logan, who was also gifted at languages.

They had finished their meal at the NCO's club at Aviano quickly and got a ride to Venice from an obliging Spencer Sands. Eager to distance herself from the American Military, Jane decided that returning to the Copenhagen portal by a different route would be best. So they had boarded the last train to Vienna with minutes to spare, grabbing the last two first class tickets separately.

Logan was travelling with a fake Spanish passport Jane had brought from the Manor. Knowing his history back to front, she had also devised a cover for him at the same time. With the lessons he'd learned by the side of his father, she decided he could probably pass himself off as a horse trainer. With this in mind she'd had the forgers prepare a full package that would pass all but the most intense scrutiny.

Since she didn't want to arouse too much suspicion, they were travelling separately. So she had hid her American passport and CIA ID in the false bottom of her briefcase and was travelling as a beer wholesaler with a British passport.

Intrigued by all of the information in the paper, Jane's eyes were glued to it as she tried to absorb as much as possible. But a lot of it was barely comprehensible to her, to the point she felt like she was reading something in a different language. She could pronounce all the words, but she had no idea what they meant. One article decried the re-emergence of right wing conservatives in Austrian politics. What the hell did wings have to do with politics and what did their direction have to do with anything? The longer she read the more discouraged she became with her future as the Secretary of the Hunt. There was simply too much to learn in order to operate effectively outside of the Manor.

She remembered her confusion trying to get a drink out of a vending machine at the train station. After five minutes of staring at it, she'd finally taken a step back and waited for someone else to try. After seeing a kid put coins into the machine and push a button, she'd walked up and repeated the process. She found the bubbly sweet drink delicious, but it had not helped her feel much better.

Finished with the infuriatingly confusing paper she set it down across her knees and looked out the window. She realized how intensely she'd been reading by the darkness that now covered the land outside. Turning her head from the emptiness outside, she was somewhat startled to see that the first class cabin was empty except for her and Logan.

"You really zone out when you're reading," Logan observed with a yawn as he stretched in his seat. "The other two went to the dining car for some supper half an hour ago."

They were sharing the compartment with a pair of older Italian gentlemen that sat across from each by the door. They spoke little to each other, both reviewing documents from their respective briefcases.

"Are you hungry?" Jane offered, sensing the hidden suggestion.

"I could eat," Logan replied casually, hoping she didn't hear his growling stomach. Though it was only a short time since his meal at the NCO's club, Logan couldn't remember eating before that with all of his time in the hospital.

"You head out first and I'll meet up with you in a few minutes," Jane ordered. Despite having recruited Logan with no issues and seemingly being in the clear, Jane had a nagging sense that they had to remain careful. She was determined to stay vigilant until she returned through the portal to the Manor.

Logan accepted her plan without question and left the compartment without another word. He was only gone for a few minutes before the door once again opened up and the two Italian gentlemen entered and returned to their seats. Fully fed and with a few glasses of wine from the dining car, they ignored their briefcases and continued a discussion on soccer and the merits of AS Roma. As the conversation became more animated, Jane stood up and politely passed by them to the door. As she left they quieted down slightly and from the corner of her eye saw them appreciating her assets. She almost laughed to herself; dirty old men were the same everywhere.

The dining car was the next one behind first class and Jane made her way along the passage without passing anyone. The feeling of walking on a moving train also felt strange to her, so she was glad that she didn't have to walk too far.

Most of the tables were occupied with diners finishing their meals when she entered and Logan was the only one waiting to be served. Grateful this was the case; Jane walked slowly over to his table and asked if she could join him. Logan motioned towards the seat across from him with a nod, barely able to keep a straight face.

"I can't believe you agency types actually act like this," he observed shaking his head in amusement. "I thought it was only in the movies."

"Better to be safe than sorry," Jane replied absently as she picked up her menu. She raised it up to her face but ignored the contents, merely using it to casually scrutinize the other patrons. When she didn't register any familiar or threatening faces she lowered her eyes and perused the drinks list.

The waiter soon returned delivering Logan's beer and turning an inquiring glance at Jane. She ordered a whiskey and the lamb, to which he complimented her on her choice before quickly departing to another table.

"How's the wound?" Jane asked as she watched Logan gingerly rotate his shoulder. She'd almost forgotten he'd just gotten out of the hospital that morning.

"Fine, just a little stiff," Logan brushed it off, unwilling to admit to anything more than that. The macho identity of the army was too ingrained in him to complain about a wound that was no longer life threatening.

"Good, because you're now on the clock," Jane said seriously, knowing he wasn't being truthful but unwilling to call him out on it. She then changed her demeanour in an instant and was almost gushing. "So how long have you worked with horses? I simply adore the creatures."

The waiter had returned with her whiskey and both of their dinners, gently placing them on the table in front of them. When they declined anything further the waiter smiled and turned away, slightly jealous of the Spanish gentlemen. Another romance born on the tracks appeared to be blossoming.

"How do you turn it on and off so fast?" Logan asked dumbfounded as he watched Jane cut into her lamb kebab. One moment she was busting his balls and the next she was gushing like a schollgirl.

"Years of practice," she replied obliquely. Unimpressed with the mysterious woman routine, Logan continued staring at her without touching his meal. Noticing this, Jane decided to elaborate a bit more. "I'm not strong enough to fight and I'm not fast enough to outrun anyone. So I learned a long time ago that my best defence was to avoid a confrontation from the beginning. For me that means changing my appearance for those I encounter."

"So is this the real you now or are you playing a role?"

Jane merely smiled in reply, unwilling to delve any further into her chameleon-like tendencies with him. However this seemed to satisfy the ex-soldier as he finally dug into his schnitzel and chewed happily. They ate their meal in silence, concentrating on not dropping anything as the train continued rolling along.

"What did you mean I'm on the clock?" Logan asked after their meal was cleared and they waited for their coffee. There was only one other occupied table in the car, so he felt they could speak freely.

"It means that if the bus boy clearing the table behind me suddenly lunges this way with a steak knife you'll stop him," she replied coolly, studying him closely. "As I said in the interrogation room, you belong to me. So when I'm on the job, you're on the job. If that means protecting me or carrying the luggage, that's what you'll do."

"That's what I thought." They both became silent as the waiter delivered their coffees and asked about dessert.

"So where are we heading after Vienna?" inquired Logan after the waiter left them. But all he got out of Jane was another of her elusive smiles. "Come on, you trust me enough to protect you but not enough to know what we're doing?"

"Precisely," Jane agreed after taking a sip of her coffee. "Trust is a funny thing. At this moment I trust that you will do what is beneficial to you. You're clever enough to know that following along with what I say is best for you right now. After all, I just got you out of prison and had you administratively assassinated. But I'm not prepared to trust that you'll do what's beneficial to me."

"What do you mean?"

"Right now you're like a dog on a leash, a very dangerous dog," she began, ignoring his continued puzzlement. "You're going to follow the directions of the person holding the leash, which is me. If a mugger were to come at me, you'd attack him because that's what you've been trained to do. But what happens if the leash comes off? Will you attack the mugger, run away, or attack me?"

"You've seen my file, what do you think I'd do," Logan replied, slightly hurt that she could think he wouldn't do the right thing.

"You mean the file where you've been reprimanded multiple times for the reckless use of force and potentially killing innocent civilians?" Jane answered sharply.

"It doesn't give the whole story," he countered, angrily shoving his empty coffee cup aside.

"Exactly my point," Jane concurred quickly. "All I know about you is from the file and the few hours we've spent together. So I'll continue to hold the proverbial leash until I can trust you to place my well being alongside your own."

"Fine," Logan offered stonily, crossing his arms.

"Logan," Jane began in a gentler tone, realizing she had stung him with her lack of trust. "If I didn't think you were right for this job I would have let those hyenas tear into you back at Aviano."

"I guess I still haven't thanked you for all you've done so far," he admitted, softening his attitude. "Thanks."

"Your welcome," Jane smiled brightly, unprepared for his quick turn around. The blare of the trains whistle made her look up at the clock above the door at the far side of the dining car. "We're almost there. We should return to our compartment and collect our things."

They walked the short distance to their first class compartment with stiff legs, realizing that they'd been sitting for a prolonged period of time. Their travelling companions were dozing in their seats, forcing Jane and Logan to step over their legs in order to avoid waking them. By ten o'clock the bright lights of a major city were flashing past the darkened windows and the porter walked by announcing their imminent arrival in Vienna.

They descended the train separately when it came to a halt and split up as Jane had directed. The late hour meant that the Westbahnhof wasn't very busy, so they had to be even more obvious about their dissociation. Jane walked directly to the taxi stand with a porter following dutifully behind with her luggage. Meanwhile Logan meandered through the station, stopping at the washroom and the café. He only had a backpack, so he decided to walk the short distance to their hotel once he was done.

After they had obtained their train tickets in Venice, Jane had phoned the hotel to make reservations. She had called twice, first for herself and the second time as Logan's secretary. She had a list of rooms that were adjoined and had been able to book two adjoining rooms without arousing any suspicion.

Logan almost walked past the boutique hotel Jane had reserved for them, making him realize how tired he truly was. He hadn't slept well in the hospital as he battled the fever resulting from his infected wound. Mixed with the stress of the interrogation, he was a walking zombie. So it wasn't surprising that when he doubled back to the front door, he didn't notice the man in the dark coat that had been trailing him from the train station.

*

The name on the credit card he'd used for the train ticket in Venice said he was Marco Arpicci, however that was not the case. His real name was Marek Arpek and he was not the freelance photojournalist his business cards or cameras suggested. He was in fact a freelance clandestine operative, trained in surveillance and assassination. He'd actually been born in Albania and been a part of the Sigurimi, the Albanian secret police. His talent for the work led to his being sent to Moscow to be further trained by the KGB.

Like many of his comrades, he found himself abandoned and out of work when the Iron Curtain fell and communism was replaced throughout Eastern Europe. However this was only temporary, as people like him were nothing if not resourceful. Organized crime and large corporations soon sprang up all over the former Communist States and they needed the same expertise Marek and men like him had. But best of all was that they paid much better.

After a few jobs, Marek set himself up in Italy under his new cover name and worked toward an early retirement. Most of the work was legitimate surveillance operations, peppered with the odd physical intimidation job to keep himself in the game.

So when he received a call from a long forgotten contact from his Moscow days, Marco's ears perked up. The KGB might have been disbanded but its replacement, the SVR, was basically the same organization. Those with enough talent, connections, or both, had stayed on and kept their old rolodex of contacts.

Apparently some cowboy of an American soldier had shot an SVR man under diplomatic cover in Bosnia. This went against the unwritten non-violence code of conduct for clandestine operations. The killing of foreign agents was avoided at all costs and the Russians felt that they had to respond in order to flex their muscle. Freelancers would be sent throughout Europe to watch for this Sgt. Logan if he appeared and terminate him if possible. Marco was assigned the Venice train station, as it was a main thoroughfare close to Aviano Air Force Base.

After three days of watching, Marco became tired of the job but was unwilling to abandon it in fear of any repercussions. So when he heard his name called over the station PA system, he hoped a message was waiting for him with instructions to shut down. The girl at the assistance counter passed him a telephone number and he eagerly went to the nearest pay phone and hoped he could return to his little villa.

The voice on the phone was coldly mechanical and succinct. Logan had died in the hospital of his wounds and that the mission was cancelled. He would be compensated for his time and would not be contacted again.

But Marco's smile was immediately wiped off his face as he turned to the main entrance. Walking in to the train station behind an extremely attractive black haired woman, was the spitting image of the photo Marco had memorised. He couldn't believe his misfortune and cursed the timing of the phone call. A few minutes earlier he could have left the train station and been on his way out of Venice, happily ignorant that his target was still alive. He toyed with the idea of ignoring the fact that he'd seen Logan, despite knowing it wasn't an option. Part of him truly enjoyed the deadly game of his profession. But more importantly he feared the repercussions that he would face if the SVR discovered he'd let Logan go. There would be nowhere to hide and no one to turn to for help.

So he casually made his way to the ticket counter and joined the queue two lines over from Logan. Luckily his line moved quick enough that he remained close enough to the American when he purchased his ticket. Marco had little time to question what he was doing heading to Vienna, before it was his turn at the ticket window. Wanting to stay close to his target, Marco also asked for a first class ticket to Vienna. However he had to settle for second-class when he was told first was fully booked.

Marco had to remain patient and resist the urge to leave his seat and check his target as the train made its alpine journey through Italy to Austria. Although he knew the rules were pretty lax on these trains, he still didn't want to get caught snooping around the first class cars. So he'd simply sat and tried to stay calm as the train barrelled through the darkness, desperately hoping that Logan was really going to Vienna.

When the train finally approached the Westbahnhof, Marco got up from his seat and moved to the end of the car. This allowed him to get out first after the conductor opened the door and lowered the steps to the platform. The station was mostly empty as he walked towards a row of phone booths by the front door. He cautiously watched a pair of policemen walk past him as he picked up the receiver and pretended to dial a number. He was carrying a small .22 caliber pistol in a shoulder holster and hoped the small bulge under his arm was imperceptible from across the lobby. Finally after an increasingly frustrating wait, Logan appeared from the station café.

He followed him with ease along the quiet streets of Vienna as they walked north, however there were just enough people out that he couldn't make an attempt. After turning onto a quiet side street he thought he'd been spotted for a split second. Logan had suddenly turned around and was looking back in his direction. It was almost the kind of trick a trained agent would employ for counter-detection. However Marco breathed a sigh of relief when Logan quickly moved to his right and walked up the few steps of a non-descript hotel.

Risking an even greater chance at detection, Marco followed Logan into the hotel and loitered around the lobby as the other man checked in. There was a small hotel bar just off the lobby and Marco spent an enormous amount of time looking over their small menu. But his well trained glances at the front counter made it possible for him to clearly see the attendant hand Logan the key to room number 12.

Satisfied he walked into the bar and ordered vodka on the rocks. The drink would have a calming effect on what he had to do next. He would wait for fifteen minutes and if Logan didn't reappear in the lobby, Marco would go up to his room and complete his assignment.

Chapter 10

After hearing the soft knock on the connecting door, Jane sauntered over in her sock feet to open it up. After spending countless tense hours in uncomfortable business clothes and deadly high heels, she was glad to finally feel something close to relaxation. Logan was standing a few steps from the door when she opened it, looking slightly abashed.

"I hope I'm not intruding," he offered politely. "I just thought I'd let you know I got here with no problems."

"Good, well you should get some sleep," Jane replied absently, before she noticed him hesitate at the door. "Was there something else?"

"Just a quick question," Logan started, remaining on his side of the room. "Who the hell are you really? You're not with the CIA and since I *belong to you*, I'd like to have a better idea of what I'm getting myself into."

"What do you…?"

"Don't," Logan cut her off before she could continue, taking a single step across the threshold. "Like I said, I've met some agency types in the past. But you're not like any of the ones I've met. There's something not quite right that I can't put my finger on."

"Listen…"

Jane didn't really know how she was going to reply to Logan's accurate accusations, but she didn't have the chance as the door to his room suddenly slammed open. A rush of footsteps raced into his room and before she knew it, Logan had thrown her to the floor behind the bed.

She watched anxiously as Logan stepped to the side of the connecting door in time to surprise a rough looking man in a dark coat. He pointed a small pistol with a silencer at the middle of her room as he raced in. Logan swatted the pistol to the ground with a violent chop before using his other hand to slam the intruders head into the wall.

Doubled over, the intruder had just enough awareness to throw a punch into Logan's mid section. Under normal circumstances, the ex-Ranger would have easily taken down the smaller Albanian with little trouble. However in his tired and weakened state, the altercation was slightly more even. They grappled roughly, knocking over a lamp and breaking a chair with neither gaining the upper hand.

Jane was able to grab the dropped pistol as the two men fought, but didn't trust her aim to take a shot. But this proved of little consequence as Logan was finally able to get behind Marco and put him into a solid choke hold.

"Who sent you?!" Jane demanded as she approached pointing the pistol at Marco.

"The Russians," wheezed Marco from the increasing pressure being applied by Logan's large arms.

"Are you alone?"

He nodded quickly and then tapped Logan's bicep as his faced turned even redder. Jane motioned for him to loosen his grasp, since the intruder looked like he had something further to say.

"But Russians heard that he was dead and called it off," Marco reported between breaths. "I just happened to see you on my way out of the train station."

"Bad luck for you then comrade," Logan whispered, making Marco's eyes widen in shock before he violently twisted his neck. An audible snap seemed to echo in the room.

"What the hell…" Jane was once again cut off as she stared at Logan in disbelief. She was feeling a mixture of anger and shock after watching him kill the man so suddenly. But a knock at the door quieted her at once.

"Fraulein?" intoned a male voice, clearly someone from the staff. "Is everything alright?"

Jane looked around the room, knowing everything wasn't alright, but realizing she'd have to answer the door. Some of the furniture was knocked over and there was a dead body on the floor. Logan's face was red from the exertion of the fight. Thinking quickly she motioned Logan to shove the body beside the bed. At the same time she ripped the sheets off the bed.

As the bell boy knocked a second time, Jane rushed over to the door, ripping her shirt open as she went. A button flew into the washroom, bouncing on the marble floor.

"Yes?" she asked as she opened the door a crack.

"Is everything alright?" the bell boy asked in English, having seen the British passport of the woman from room ten. "Some other guests heard a commotion."

"Oh," Jane raised her hand to her mouth in embarrassment, letting the door slowly creep open. "I'm terribly sorry."

Now it was the bell boys turn to feel embarrassed. It took an enormous effort to keep his eyes away from Jane's lace covered curves under her ripped shirt. He then peered over her shoulder at the physically impressive man in the room beyond. He was replacing a toppled chair and looked as though he'd just got out of a gym. Coming to the conclusion the inhabitants of the room wanted him to reach, the bell boy apologised for the interruption and quickly left.

Jane closed the door behind him and did her shirt back up with the remaining buttons as she turned back towards the room. She thought she saw a brief look of disappointment on Logan's face as she became fully dressed again, but she ignored it completely. There was no denying that he was fit and handsome, but Jane wasn't attracted to him enough to muddy the waters between them. Although his straightforward openness made him the perfect employee, it wasn't what she looked for in a lover.

Eyeing the broken chair, she decided to sit down on the bed instead. She needed to think things through now that their cover was potentially blown and there was a dead body in her room.

"We need to get rid of this body and get out of here," Jane stated simply after quickly regaining her composure. "Any ideas?"

"I saw a laundry chute on the way from the elevators," Logan offered after a thoughtful pause. "But that might be a little too theatrical."

"Plus it's too busy there," Jane agreed at once. The last thing they need was for an elevator full of people to turn up as they shoved a body down a chute. "What about the stairs?"

"Perfect," Logan nodded. "I should have thought of that first. I must be really tired. Plus with the broken neck it might even look like an accident."

"Exactly," Jane walked over to the door and looked at the emergency map for the floor. There was a stair well around the corner from Logan's room with only one room in between.

Together they grabbed Marco's body and then lifted him up between them. A body seems to gain a significant amount of weight when it dies and becomes ungainly to move. So Jane was forced to help Logan drag the body into his room and then quietly out into the hall. It was mercifully empty and they quickly stumbled their way to the stairwell. Despite the weight and their increasing exhaustion, they decided to take him down a few flights before dumping him down unceremoniously.

"What now?" Logan asked back in his room, barely able to stay awake.

"I think we risk staying the night, if we leave now it will be a little suspicious. It's close to midnight and I'm too tired to go anywhere else right now," Jane yawned, mimicking Logan across from her.

"Are you sure you'll be able to sleep with everything that just happened?" Logan asked as he got up to leave.

"I'll be fine, just leave the door open in case something comes up." Jane had seen dead bodies before and had witnessed men killed in front of her eyes. She wasn't numb to it, but she was too exhausted for the full weight of events to register completely.

Both slept soundly until morning, eventually waking up after seven to the ringing of Logan's alarm. Jane instructed Logan to go to the rental car booth at the train station after he was done showering. She would meet him at the café around the corner when he was done and they would drive to their next destination.

She jumped into her own shower and let the warm water flow over her. Her previous life as a maid at the Manor had forced her to become a morning person, so she didn't need the shower to wake her up. However she did stay in it longer than normal, feeling her muscles relax from the massaging patter of the warm droplets.

When she eventually emerged from the bathroom she dried her hair and pulled out some clothes from her valise. She decided to wear something more comfortable than she had yesterday with the prospect of a full day in a car ahead. She pulled on a tight pair of designer jeans and put on a cashmere sweater, completing the outfit with leather boots and her jacket from the previous day. She smiled as the shoved her ripped shirt from the night before into her bag, congratulating herself on thinking quickly. With a satisfied appraisal of her reflection in the full length mirror, she left the room and took the elevator to the lobby.

Checking out was simple and she was at the café around the corner in time to see Logan pull up in a black BMW sedan. He got out and opened the trunk, taking her bag and placing it inside.

"We'll have some breakfast before we head out," Jane suggested as she led the way into the small café.

"Which is where exactly?" Logan asked hoping for an answer but not really expecting one.

They ate a collection of pastries with their coffee, silently enjoying the bright fall morning. Vienna sprung to life before their eyes and the sidewalks were soon full of pedestrians busily walking past. Jane could have sat there all morning, but she also had a pulling desire to return to the Manor.

"So where are we going?" Logan asked a second time as they buckled themselves into the BMW. "I'll at least need a hint if I'm going to drive."

"Head towards Munich," Jane replied vaguely.

"You still don't trust me? Even after that assassin could have killed you last night?"

"A little bit more. But Logan, you were the target," Jane smiled as she donned a pair of sunglasses.

*

"Starsky and Hutch called, they want their clothes back," Pierce observed sarcastically as he watched Sean and Liam walk out of their respective change rooms.

"What? I think we look cool," Liam countered looking in the nearest mirror. "They were cops in the 70's right?"

"Yeah but when I said we're going to be masquerading as policemen, I didn't mean you should dress like fake television cops." Pierce shook his head in amusement as Sean and Liam both shrugged. They were dressed exactly like the television duo, right down to the ridiculous turtle neck and the knitted sweater. Luckily the show wouldn't air for another couple years when they went back through the portal.

"Well at least we'll blend in," Sean offered as he looked over Pierce's plain gray suit, white shirt, and black tie. "You look like a square in that suit."

"I'm supposed to look like this, I'm in the FBI," Pierce replied looking down at his clothes. "Since when do you use the word square?"

"I heard some girl yell it at MacDuff when we were spying on Leon."

MacDuff then walked out of his change room and everyone stopped talking. He was wearing a three piece plaid suit made of something close to the Black Watch tartan. Although appearing like a normal black suit from a distance, up close it was unmistakably tacky.

"Aye, this is a fine suit," he intoned happily as he adjusted it slightly on his large frame.

Pierce gave up and just stared up at the ceiling. They were in an area of the Manor that many called the Costume Department. Aisles of racks covered the large room, filled with clothing from every era that the portals of the North Tower had access to. It was a staggering amount of clothing and accessories that offered a tangible example of the power of those portals.

Groups of change rooms lined the outer walls of the Costume Department, making it possible for multiple packs to be outfitted at the same time if the need arose. But Pierce and the Brown Pack were the only ones present at that time, apart from the staff that ran the place. The head of the Costume Department was an older German named Isaac who had been recruited to the Manor just before the Nazi's took power. Being a Jew in the theatre business as a costume designer, he'd leapt at the opportunity to continue in his field and escape the fascists.

"Now that we have your sizes we'll put a few more outfits together and send them up to your room," he replied, quickly moving into the forest of clothes with two assistants in tow. Safety beyond the portal doors required the ability to blend in and the Costume Department worked tirelessly to ensure the clothing the members took with them were authentic to the period. Pierce called out thanks to the staff and then instructed his men to change back into their normal clothes.

When they all emerged, they looked like some sort of Scottish gang. After returning from their mission in Marseille, they were a close knit group and dressed like it. As staff of the Hunt, MacDuff and the others had to wear the tunics of their Pack. In their case short brown leather ones, the high collars emblazoned with the Pack emblem of a majestic stag. But unlike the dark trousers that many of the other Hounds wore, Pierce's men wore kilts with sporrans.

They had given Pierce a kilt made of the Maple Leaf tartan when he'd first arrived at the Manor. It had been a kind act to welcome a new member who was bewildered by his new surroundings. Pierce had immediately felt gratitude for the nod towards his Scottish and Canadian heritage, doubly pleased when they also wore the same thing. But unlike his men, Pierce was not forced to wear the brown tunic. Instead he wore a brown tweed jacket, with the insignia of his position as Lord of the Brown Pack on the left lapel. The outfit was topped off by his ever present ebony swordstick.

"The forger should be done with our new ID's," MacDuff pointed out as they left the Costume Department. It was located on the third floor close to the Hall of Hounds, as Isaac argued that he needed the light to properly see fabric and worried about the dampness a basement room would offer. The forger meanwhile preferred the basement and kept his offices near the Secretary of the Hunt's staff. This meant a long meandering walk through the halls and corridors of the Manor.

The four men walked purposefully through the Manor, their Highland clothing and genial chatter a strange sight to those they encountered. The apprehensive atmosphere of the building was still being felt by the inhabitants, the staff most of all. This was further reinforced for Pierce as they walked past the massive doors to the Hall of Hounds. The sound of wood breaking and loud yells seeped out into the corridor as they passed by.

Pierce stayed out in the corridor as his men investigated, since members of the Hunt were encouraged to stay out of the sanctum of their staff. The noise dropped off immediately as they entered, but picked up again seconds later as MacDuff and the others rejoined Pierce.

"Just a little bit of the rough stuff," MacDuff explained when Pierce raised an enquiring eyebrow. "Boys will be boys."

"Don't forget the girls as well," Liam interjected solemnly. "Violet was in the mix there too. I think she was the one who broke the chair."

"I think it's more than just that," Pierce disagreed as they descended an empty staircase. "You and I both know that there's a building pressure within these walls. I'm hoping that Tiberius can release some of it when he speaks with everyone."

"You believe there could be trouble?" Sean asked from behind.

"Don't you?" Pierce replied seriously. "Lord Lodge has blocked off access to the North Tower in an attempt to keep order. The only problem is that that's not the only door in this place. The front door is wide open."

"With an island full of innocent people potentially in danger," Sean understood Pierce's worry.

"Exactly," Pierce concurred as they finally reached the office of the Manor's resident forger.

"Ahh Monsieur Pierce, your timing is perfect," welcomed the small balding gentleman from behind a wooden counter. A number of desks were lined up behind him, many with his assistants bent over and peering at documents through magnifying glasses. The whole room had the atmosphere of a library, with the smell of paper and leather mingling with the hushed voices of the workers. "This way if you please."

They all followed him into an adjoining office that was more of a conference room, with a single large desk in the middle with a number of chairs surrounding it. It was used to meet with the various Hunt members without disturbing the work in the main room beyond.

"What have you got for us Pierre?" MacDuff asked excitedly, always an admirer of the forger's work and sense of humour.

"I have the usual collection of items one would expect; driver's license, library card, blood donor card," Pierre rhymed these off as he passed out a leather wallet for each man. "But I'm sure you're really here for your badges."

When everyone nodded expectantly, Pierre lifted four more leather bundles that looked like wallets from a box beside him. A clever smile briefly appeared as he opened each one before distributing them around the table.

"For the two hooligans, you're covered as Deputy US Marshals," he announced handing the ID's to Liam and then Sean. "Deputy Mick, Deputy Donald."

"That's racist," Liam observed as he fingered the silver star. "Wait I get it, that's funny."

"For the imposing Scotsman and Lord Pierce, you're in the FBI," Pierre continued, passing the last two ID's over. "Agent Bruce and Agent Gunn."

Pierce accepted his ID and opened the worn black leather holder. It was soft and wrinkled, distressed to appear much older than it was. Inside was a plastic ID card with his picture on it and his information. To avoid too much confusion, everyone kept their real first names. Below the card was the gold badge of the FBI, and Pierce smiled at it. This was like a skeleton key for the real world, able to open most doors they might come across.

"Anything else in that magical box of yours," MacDuff smiled after looking at his own ID and placing it in his tunic pocket.

"Mais oui," Pierre said as he dug back into his box, pulling out a file folder. "I have blank arrest and search warrants that you can use at your discretion with the correctly forged signatures of various judges. All you need is a typewriter to add the names in once you're over there. I've kept a few here in order to put in the aliases the White Pack are using. Lord Tiberius said that he would get them for me to make the documents look more realistic."

They collected their new presents from Pierre and left after thanking him for his excellent work. Pierre and the forgers were indispensible to missions beyond the portals. The documents they provided made it possible for the Hunt to avoid problems with the law that money couldn't get them out of.

"I wonder how Tiberius is going to get those names," Sean wondered absently as they reached the large stag carved door to their lair.

"If Leonardo has any sense he'll have them typed up and ready for him," Liam laughed lightly, but then shivered. "I'm sure glad I'm not in his shoes."

"Tiberius won't do anything drastic," Pierce reasoned calmly before a shadow of doubt crossed his mind. "Will he?"

"What would you do to the guy that betrayed your mentor, abducted innocent girls, and then drugged someone you really cared about?" Liam asked rhetorically. "What would you do if it had been Jane instead of Kat in that trunk?"

"MacDuff, get me down to the cells now!" Pierce exclaimed, realizing that if the positions were reversed Leonardo might already be dead.

Chapter 11

Tiberius let the door swing open slowly, the creaking of the hinges making an eerie sound. But instead of walking in right away, he just stood at the threshold, staring into the dark stone cell with steely eyes. The room smelt of straw mingled with body odour, making him even more disgusted with the curled up form lying in the corner. A single pot light in the ceiling provided a small amount of light, just enough to let the prisoner realize the terrible situation he was in.

After a brief moment the prisoner on the floor slowly propped himself up and leaned his back against the wall, squinting at the doorway until he could properly focus on the man standing there. He started to breath quickly when he realized who had opened the door.

"Ti…Tiberius, listen," he started, stuttering slightly from the cold, but mainly from anxiety over his future. But a stern stare from Tiberius made him stop before he could say another word.

Tiberius slowly walked into the room, soon followed by his men. Duschene brought in a folded wooden chair, opening it up and placing it against the wall behind Tiberius. Morgan followed them in with a wooden box that offered a metallic jangle as he walked, setting it down beside the chair. Both then left the room, closing the door loudly behind them.

"I already told Lord Pierce what I know," Leon finally uttered after finding his remaining courage. "No amount of torture is going to get anything else out of me."

"Really?" Tiberius asked, almost laughing at the brute before him. "I suppose some might classify you as a hard case. You would have to be, growing up on the mean streets of Chicago in the midst of gangland fighting. You beat some guys and they beat you. You killed some guys and dodged the bullets aimed at you."

As he rhymed off the tawdry exploits of a small time hoodlum, Leon's chest started to swell with pride. He needed to build him up on order to tear him down. Despite his time at the Manor, Leon was still just a small time thug. He was another reminder of the poor judge of character Drummond employed for recruiting staff.

"Perhaps you're being truthful about your first interrogation. Perhaps you really did tell them everything you know. After all, I heard that Lord Pierce was able to trick you into talking by making you think he'd feed you to sharks," Tiberius continued, seeing a flicker of doubt cross Leon's face. "Don't worry, I'm not actually going to feed you to sharks. But what I really loved about the story was how he set it up by talking about Jaws. You might not know it, but I'm a bit of a movie buff so I could appreciate the genius of it. Do you enjoy movies Leonardo?"

"What? Ya, I guess," Leon mumbled in confusion.

"Good. Have you ever seen Pulp Fiction?" Tiberius asked coolly. "It seems like a movie you'd like; there are hit men, drugs, and killing in it. Well there's a line in it that I think really applies to our situation."

"What's that?" Leon challenged, no longer really worried. He'd expected his interrogators to come in and start beating him before asking any questions. After all, that's what he would have done. But all these questions seemed pointless and made him feel like Tiberius was merely killing time before releasing him.

"*I'm going to go medieval on his ass,*" Tiberius said icily, his stare turning even colder. "I lived through the medieval era and prohibition Chicago was a walk in the park by comparison. You think living with roving gangsters with itchy trigger fingers is impressive? You believe you're tough because you roughed up newsagents and barbershops for your cut? I lived through the Black Death, the Crusades, and roving *armies* bent on killing, raping, and pillaging. It was called the Dark Ages for a reason and I'm going to teach you why."

Leon's confidence in walking out of the room any time soon evaporated immediately and the sour taste of fear started to creep up his throat. It was the same feeling he'd felt on the boat as Liam threw fish parts into the sea behind him. He'd truly believed that there were sharks and was deathly afraid of the pain they'd inflict. However learning about the absence of the sharks did nothing to ease his mind about his current interrogation. He didn't doubt Tiberius' resolve and was truly frightened by what he might do.

Tiberius watched with delight as the prisoner's false bravado started to crumble. But he knew that he'd have to push further for results. When Leon's eyes lowered to the floor, Tiberius kicked the wooden box beside him, receiving his full attention again.

"You see I'm *actually* going to medieval on your ass," Tiberius stated calmly as he started removing some of the contents of the box. There were a few rusty jagged blades, a couple lengths of chain, and some indecipherable but terrifying devices. "I'm not proud of the skills I learned before being recruited to the Manor and would ordinarily never employ them. But in your case, you fucking sadist, I'm willing to make an exception. After all, how many girls did you torment before delivering them to Debochev?"

"Now wait…"

"I thought with your record you would have experience with an interrogation," Tiberius shook his head sadly. "You're supposed to answer the questions that I ask. Although to be perfectly honest it won't make things any easier. You see, I'm going to take you apart piece by piece no matter what you tell me."

Grabbing a length of steel chain, he slowly wrapped it around his knuckles, creating a lethal fist. Although Tiberius remained sitting on the chair, Leon had scrambled into the corner, weeping silently.

"How many girls?!" Tiberius growled, his anger at the prisoner only increasing by his pitiful display.

"I don't rem…" Before he could finish the sentence Tiberius swiftly rushed off his chair and planted a steel jab into Leon's gut, dropping him to the ground.

"You don't remember?" Tiberius challenged after taking a step backwards. "Sociopaths always remember all of their victims. It's what gets you high. So you must be ashamed by the total number. I'll just have to take a guess and punish you accordingly."

With all his power he threw a second punch down on Leon's prone frame, still coughing on the floor. He knew he had to calm down, but all Tiberius could think about was what would have happened if the sick fuck had gotten his hands on Kat. It took an enormous effort, but he finally took a step back and took a calming breath.

"The trick to cutting a body properly is to tenderize it," Tiberius lectured as he removed the chain from his right hand and shifted to his left. "Otherwise you spend too much time cutting through the tough muscle and tendons. Unless you've got a really sharp knife, but I don't think any of the ones I brought classify as sharp."

Leon had risen to his hands and knees and looked over at the collection of rusty blades with teary eyes. He'd always taken pleasure in torturing others, feeling a rush as he watched them feel pain. Never once had he ever wondered what it must be like on the receiving end. But now he understood why his victims had behaved the way they did. He was so scared he could barely control his body and his weeping pleas echoed in the empty room. The idea of the rusty blades ripping through his skin terrified him so much he didn't even notice the warm liquid trickling down his legs.

"Since you're being such a sissy about this, I'll do you a favour," Tiberius sneered. "I'll just go ahead and get the beatings out of the way without stopping for questions. This way we can move to the next stage quicker. It's just too hard to get answers out of someone who's too winded from punches to speak. Trust me; it will be much easier this way."

He lifted Leon's head with his right hand and wound up to deliver a blow with his left, but hesitated when Leon let out a long terrified wail.

"I'll tell you everything!" he sobbed loudly, his whole body shaking.

"Yes, I think you will," Tiberius uttered with distaste before delivering a knee to the head. Leon dropped backwards in a heap, knocked unconscious. Tiberius removed the chain from his hand and dropped it back in the box. He'd hoped that Leon would have offered more of a resistance in order to give him an outlet for his frustration. However he was actually glad that it hadn't come to that. He was experienced enough to know that the anger he felt would quickly disappear and he would have been left with a big hole filled with guilt and shame if it had gone any further.

Without another glance he turned and opened the cell door, ordering his men outside to take the prisoner to a real interrogation room. He passed them at the door and was surprised when he saw two men in kilts running towards him down the prison corridor.

"What did you do?!" Pierce yelled as he drew close enough to see Tiberius' calm face.

"What had to be done," Tiberius replied, not really understanding Pierce's question or his presence there.

"God damn it!" Pierce cursed, stopping in place before he reached the cell door. "If you killed him I'm out of here! I'm fucking done! I didn't agree to stay so that one killer could be replaced with another. We're supposed to be the good guys!"

"Sir," MacDuff offered calmly.

"No Duffy! Not this time," Pierce ignored his friends attempt to calm him. "You said we were going to change this place and I believed you. You and Lord Lodge both said that to me in his office. So if you just killed a man for some twisted sense of revenge or justice, then you lied and I'll burn this fucking place to the ground."

Before Tiberius could respond, Morgan and Dufresen pushed passed him with Leon draped between them still very much alive. He even started mumbling again as they passed Pierce and headed down the corridor towards the stairs.

"You were saying?" Tiberius asked gruffly.

"I, uh…Sorry," Pierce apologised stubbornly. "But I meant what I said."

"I know and I don't blame your reaction. There was a moment in there when I was worried I would lose control and do something I would regret. But the moment passed quickly, since I also meant what I said. We will change this place."

Pierce nodded in acceptance, though he knew it would be a lengthy and difficult process. He fell in step beside Tiberius as they walked up to the floor above where the interrogation rooms were kept. Instead of joining Leon immediately, both men went to the observation room next door and watched him through the two way mirror.

"I already got a lot of good info on Debochev from him on the boat," Pierce offered as he watched Leon become less disoriented in the other room. "What else are you trying to find out?"

"Cleaver," Tiberius stated simply.

"You think he knows anything about Cleaver's disappearance?"

"I won't know unless I ask," Tiberius replied. "I need to get some real leads on Cleaver before Lord Lodge becomes unreachable. Anything to get him out of that damned office and all his piles of notes."

"I doubt he really knows anything," Pierce offered realistically. "But you never know. There could be a nugget of information in the back of his head that he's not even aware of."

"If it's there, I'll find it."

"Well, before you go digging too deeply in search of this possible lead, could you ask him about the aliases his compatriots are using? I could use it before we go back."

"Good thinking," Tiberius smiled as he opened the door and walked towards the interrogation room. "It's always better to start off with easy questions."

*

Only the sound of their engine and those of passing cars broke the silence on their morning drive to Munich. Their route took them along the majestic Alps, and Jane found herself mesmerized by the towering snow topped peaks. The only time she was able to pull her gaze from the mountains was when other cars flew past them with remarkable speed.

So far most of her travelling had taken place within the confines of planes and trains, where the outside world was not as easily observed. So she found their journey on the Autobahn to be just as exhilarating and terrifying as anything she had experienced so far. Cars mere feet from them zoomed past in the blink of an eye, disappearing down the road in seconds. A few times she found herself gripping the door handle as they became the speeders and passed slower cars.

But apart from the exploits of the other motorists, Jane was also in awe of the sheer size of the land. She'd looked over a map as they set out from Vienna and the few inches to Munich seemed fairly close. But after an hour of driving she'd looked back down at the scale and blinked in amazement. Unfolding the map to see the entire area it covered, she suddenly felt small and insignificant. Cities and towns seemed to be everywhere, with roads crisscrossing over the entire area. All the books and maps she'd studied before arriving did not do justice to the real thing.

Arriving in Munich did little to erase this feeling as she observed the enormous number of people, cars and buildings. Feeling overwhelmed by it all, Jane told Logan to drive through and that they'd stop once they were outside the city.

They found a service station a few kilometres outside the suburbs of Munich that was moderately busy with fellow travellers. While Logan put gas in the car Jane went in to use the washroom. As she washed her hands she looked in the mirror and saw a strong woman looking back at her. It made Jane remember everything she'd accomplished and how far she'd come. Rather than be intimidated by the world beyond the portals, she decided to embrace it as a sign of her progress and future. If she wanted to continue to move up at the Manor, she'd be here all the time. With renewed confidence and poise, she strolled out of the washroom and into the service center lobby.

Logan finished paying for the gas at the counter and turned in time to see her emerge from the washroom. He held a tray of sandwiches and coffee and motioned for her to find a seat beyond the racks of candy and newspapers. There were only a few tables unoccupied, so they had to settle on one beside another young couple.

"First time seeing the Alps then?" Logan asked sociably after sipping from the paper coffee cup.

"From below yes," Jane answered. "I've seen them from planes, but it's not really the same thing. It was my first time on the Autobahn as well."

"Me too. If I had known what it was like I would have rented a faster car."

"I think we were going fast enough," Jane replied, receiving a shrug in response.

"So what's our next checkpoint boss?" Logan inquired after finishing his sandwich in a few large bites and crumpling up the paper wrapper.

"Boss, I like that," Jane smiled, pushing the rest of her unappealing sandwich to the side. The Manor might have been missing the advanced technology that now surrounded her, but the food there was significantly better. "We're going to Berlin."

"Well we better get back on the road then," Logan whistled. He picked up the tray, dumping the contents in a garbage bin before opening the door for her. They were quickly back on the road, the rolling Bavarian countryside speeding past as Logan confidently shifted gears. The traffic cleared considerably the farther they drove, allowing Logan to relax slightly behind the wheel.

"I think it's time we revisit our conversation from before," he said calmly, keeping his eyes straight ahead. "The one that got interrupted by the assassin."

Jane had known it was coming, but had hoped that he would have let it go for a little bit longer. Ideally he would have forgotten about it until they got to Copenhagen. But with a slight sigh she realized she wouldn't be able to avoid the conversation he wanted to have.

"Why don't you think I'm with the CIA?" she asked defensively, wondering what had tipped him off and if she could explain it away. "Everyone at the base clearly understood that I was."

William Scott

"I'm not really sure," he allowed, shooting her a sceptical glance. "But there's something's not right about you."

"Like what?" Jane yawned, hoping to show she wasn't concerned with the questions.

"For starters you didn't know how to use the drink machine and stared at the displays at the train station like they were magic," he listed in amusement. "And then there's your problem with speed."

"What problem with speed?" she asked moments before cringing as Logan swerved to pass a slow Volkswagen, shooting past it at high speed.

"Seriously?" Logan smiled at her as he slowed down. "You're going to pretend that your hands weren't gripping your arm rest on the train yesterday or the door of the car this morning?'

"So I don't enjoy speed," Jane retorted with slight embarrassment. "I don't recall it being prerequisite when I was in training at Quantico."

"Fine," Logan allowed before resuming his interrogation. "Like I said before, I met a couple Agency types before. Maybe you know them; Wayne Gretzky from section 99, or Joe Montana the Chief of section 49?"

"I've never heard of either of those guys," Jane answered easily, already prepared for questions such as these. She knew that if she acted like she knew them, and they were fake names, then it would give her away. "But the CIA is a big place and very compartmentalized. Those probably weren't even their real names."

"No kidding," Logan laughed. "What about the boss then, you must know him? Bruce Springsteen?"

"Sure I know him, but it's not like I pass him in the halls or eat lunch with him," Jane countered with increasing confidence. If this was all Logan had to go on,

169

she might be able to fool him after all. "I mean, you didn't just go waltzing into your General's office did you?"

"No, but then again my boss isn't a rock star," Logan replied coldly. "Who the hell are you really?"

"I already said, I'm agent…"

"Stop!" Logan yelled, banging his hand on the steering wheel. "Stop lying to me. I know you're not with the CIA and I've got a pretty good feeling you're not even American. Just tell me the truth. Like you said, you own me now, so it's not like I'm going to run away or do something stupid. But I need to know what you got me into."

Jane reacted like she'd been slapped, unprepared for Logan's outburst. She thought she'd answered the questions alright, but clearly there was more to them that she didn't understand. Realizing she had to tell him something, she decided she'd provide him with a secondary story she'd developed in case her CIA cover became questioned. She couldn't risk telling him the whole truth and he probably wouldn't believe it anyway.

"Fine, you're right I'm not with the CIA," Jane began slowly, regaining her composure quickly. "I work for a private firm called Black Tower, a sort of independent security agency. We do the things that governments can't or won't do."

"So what does that have to do with me?"

"We're always looking out for recruits from the western world's elite military units; Navy SEAL's, Delta Force, British SAS, Canadian JTF 2, and so on. We don't exactly pick up the rejects, but we do believe in offering second chances," Jane explained from memory, inwardly happy when Logan nodded to continue. "You showed up on the company radar after the incident in Iraq and we started a file on you. After some research we thought you'd be the perfect candidate if the opportunity arose."

"So after this thing in Bosnia…"

"We jumped at the chance to recruit you before you were demonized and out of our reach in a military prison," Jane finished, confident he was buying the story.

"Wait a second, one of the MP's guarding me said that you had a letter signed by the Secretary of Defence. He said that you used it to get me out," Logan began with a questioning look.

"That's right."

"How did you even get that?" Logan asked incredulously.

"Well I had a clerk print it up, but since the Secretary's such a busy man I had to sign it for him," Jane smiled, since it was the closest thing to the truth she'd said so far.

"And that worked?!"

She replied with a raised eyebrow, as it clearly had worked. Logan continued driving silently for a moment before letting out a slow whistle.

"You've got a pair of brass ones lady," he offered clearly impressed. Jane didn't understand the reference but took it as a compliment. "So with nothing more than a forgery, you walked into the lion's den and bluffed everyone into letting me leave with you."

"Don't forget I got them to kill you as well," Jane added, enjoying having her exploits recounted back to her in awe.

"Why go to all the trouble for me?" Logan asked curiously. "There's a ton of guys like me in the Rangers alone."

"Like I said, we believe in second chances and you seemed to need one more than anyone else," Jane offered.

"Plus you didn't have any, um ties, to sever. The job isn't exactly 9-5."

"So you needed someone with nothing to lose and no one to miss," Logan stated without any bitterness.

"Something like that."

Logan smiled with seeming acceptance and continued driving without asking any further questions. Jane was glad that it had gone so well, but a part of her felt as though he wasn't completely fooled. She thought she'd seen a hint of scepticism in his eyes, but didn't know if she was just imagining it.

They reached Berlin after nightfall, having stopped a few times on the way for food, gas, and to stretch their legs. The weather had been good and the driving easy, but they were both tired when they pulled up to the main train station in Berlin, the Lehrter Statdbahnhof. A porter directed them to the car rental agency kiosks and the BMW was quickly returned when Jane flashed the haughty clerk a flirty smile.

Logan grabbed Jane's bag and followed her in to the station, struggling to keep up with her as she darted through the crowd towards the ticket counter. Once she got in line he wandered over to the newsstand and looked for an English paper to see if there was anything interesting going on. Air strikes into Bosnia were still dominating the headlines and a part of him was happy to be done with the conflict. However he couldn't be sure that that would be the case, since this Black Tower company seemed like the type of group that would send him back in to a warzone.

"Two sleeping cabins on the overnight train to Copenhagen," Jane announced contently as she approached from the ticket counter, handing Logan his ticket. "Boarding has already started so we should head over to the platform."

"Adjoining cabins?" Logan asked after looking between his and Jane's tickets.

"Yes, but this time if an assassin breaks in, kill him in your own room."

Chapter 12

Despite the constant motion of the train, Jane found it easy to sleep and awoke refreshed to find a foggy Danish morning out of her window. She could barely see anything beyond the repetitive green fields that followed along the tracks. The lightness of the gray mist told her that the sun was up and a quick check of her watch told her that the breakfast service had started.

She dressed in her clothes from the previous day, unwilling to wrestle with her luggage in the confines of the small cabin. After pulling on her leather boots she exited her cabin, just missing an elderly woman slowly waddling along the corridor.

The dining car was two up from her own and she arrived in time to see a waiter remove the remnants of Logan's breakfast. As before she walked up and asked him if anyone was sitting there. He just shook his head and offered her a seat, used to the routine.

"How'd you sleep?" Logan asked after Jane gave her order to the waiter.

"Fine," she replied easily.

"Well this train is much slower than the last one."

Jane accepted the little joke at her expense with a stiff smile before ignoring him and turning her attentions to the delicious coffee deposited in front of her. She was actually glad that Logan felt comfortable enough to tease her. There would have to be a certain easiness in their relationship if he were to be useful to her.

As she chewed on her toast, Jane watched Logan happily sip his refilled cup of coffee and felt a twinge of guilt. Although he'd accepted the story of Black Tower, she didn't feel comfortable taking him through the portal without explaining the whole truth. She knew there was a danger in this, but she felt it was the right thing to do. In spite of all her preparation, she'd felt disoriented when she first emerged from the portal in Copenhagen. After a few hours she'd quickly returned to the Manor, overwhelmed by the magnitude of what she'd experienced. But Logan didn't have this option. With the increased security, he'd be stuck in the Manor after using the portal. Returning back wouldn't be an option and the more trouble he caused because of it would look bad on her. Tiberius might not believe she could complete a recruitment by herself and stop her from trying again.

She couldn't allow that to happen. Her future and safety at the Manor rested on her ability to operate and recruit staff beyond the portals. She needed the freedom to recruit the people she wanted, building a strong loyalty among the tough and dangerous Hounds of the Black Tower Hunt Club.

"What's on your mind?" Logan asked with friendly curiosity.

"Hmm, oh nothing really," Jane replied quickly. "Just some work issues I'm trying to sort out."

When she didn't elaborate Logan merely shrugged, got up, and returned to his room without another word. Jane finished her meal alone and then returned to her room as well. They would be arriving shortly and she decided she'd wait until they got to the portal before telling Logan the truth.

Their train arrived at the Copenhagen Central Station in the mid morning and disgorged its occupants onto a bustling platform of rushed commuters. Unlike their previous attempts at concealing their relationship, the station was too busy for Jane or Logan to keep up the pretext. So together they weaved their way through the station lobby to the front door, joining the queue at the taxi stand outside.

The autumn sun had finally burned through the morning fog, revealing another beautiful day. Despite the number of people in line, it moved fairly quickly and the pair were soon at the front. They didn't have to wait too long before a beat up taxi pulled up and they were comfortably sitting in the back seat. Jane only had to repeat herself twice before the driver understood where to go and sped off.

Since Copenhagen was the first place she'd visited after leaving the Island, Jane felt a sense of homecoming as the taxi drove over bridges and past the canals of the older section of the city. After a few days of always being in a new place and seeing new things, she enjoyed being able to recognize familiar landmarks. They passed one of her favourites, the beautifully multicoloured old houses of Nyhavn, and Jane smiled remembering the first time she had been there. All of the houses were a different vibrant colour, easily putting the trees of the nearby parks to shame. The buildings and harbour were reminiscent of her hometown of Rooks Bay and she wondered if she could convince some of the owners to paint their houses in similar colours.

After a series of turns on small side streets, the taxi stopped in front of an old stone four story building. Once the opulent town home a wealthy ship owner, it had been converted into offices after the war and housed a collection of small businesses.

Logan fumbled in his jacket pocket for the right currency to pay the driver after he pulled Jane's luggage from the trunk. However before he could find the right amount, Jane pulled out a few bills and gave them to the driver, receiving a toothy smile in return.

A set of elegant double doors faced them a few steps up from the sidewalk. Logan grabbed Jane's bag and followed her up and into the building, impressed by the interior décor. When the building changed hands in the 1950's, the new owner had been adamant about keeping the original entrance and staircase intact. Therefore Logan and Jane seemingly walked back in time as they entered.

The lobby of the building was awash with white marble floors and columns. A golden chandelier hung from the ceiling, perfectly matching the golden framed paintings that adorned the walls. The only wooden object in the room was a small but expensive hand crafted desk by the staircase. A middle aged security guard in a perfectly tailored blue blazer nodded to them from the desk, recognizing Jane immediately.

Jane smiled back at the guard and led Logan to the grand marble staircase that ran up the left hand side of the building. The dazzling white of the steps was somewhat muted by the golden carpet and railings that ascended with them. At the top of the staircase they stepped onto a large balcony with three doors leading off it. Each door was the same carved oak, with a small brass plaque proclaiming the occupant. This same scene was repeated as they walked up the next two floors. But when they reached the top, there were only two doors there. Jane walked to the second door with the plaque *Chronos Investments* on it and opened it with a small brass key from her pocket.

The small foyer inside the door matched the hall and lobby below, with a white marble floor and gold carpet. There was a pair of clothes trees in two corners with a few reception room type chairs lining the walls. Otherwise the foyer was empty except for a single door on the left that read *Private*. Logan followed Jane to this door where she unlocked it with a second key.

The room within was just as breathtaking as the rest of the building. Highly polished hardwood flooring ran along the length of a huge room that took up almost half of the top floor. White moulded wainscoting covered the bottom third of the walls, with a luxurious blood red fabric covering the rest. Paintings were interspersed between large windows that provided an impressive view of the city beyond.

Logan followed Jane as she passed a massive wooden conference table that he thought could heat the imposing fireplace at the end of the room for years. When they reached the fireplace, Jane sat down behind a desk beside it. She motioned for Logan to sit down on one of the leather chairs across from her.

"So is this where you work?" Logan asked, obviously impressed with the room.

"Sometimes," Jane answered somewhat truthfully. "This office provides a certain amount of discretion and anonymity. Would you care for a drink?"

"It's not even noon yet," Logan remarked incredulously as Jane pointed towards a small drinks table beside her. "But what the hell, it's five o'clock somewhere right? What's your poison?"

"Whiskey," Jane said at once, pointing him towards the right bottle. She was nervous about what she had to do next and hoped that a fortifying drink would help settle her growing jitters. She smiled in thanks as he set their drinks down on the table between them.

"So is this our final destination?"

"Not exactly," Jane replied motioning for him to join her in taking a drink. "I need to tell you exactly what awaits you beyond this room. I am going to be completely honest with you, but some of it might not make sense at first. So you need to wait until I'm done before asking any questions."

"Sounds ominous," Logan smiled, clearly entertained.

"It should," Jane countered seriously, immediately making him wary. "The minute you walked out of that interrogation room at Aviano, you made a binding agreement. I couldn't go into the full details of the agreement at that time and have held off until now, for fear you might do something stupid like run. If that had happened you would have become a real dead man, not just administratively."

"So that means if I don't like what you say and run out of here…"

"You'll be a marked man and will probably be dead within a month," Jane concluded. "What you're about to hear is one of the most closely guarded secrets in the world and it's the reason you can never leave."

"Well seeing as I don't have much of a choice," Logan shrugged after a moments pause. He didn't know what could be so important, but he recognized the reality of his situation. He had no where to turn for help even if he wanted to run. The Army would probably ignore him completely if he turned back up, unwilling to deal with him and the obvious cover up that had occurred. Plus looking around the lavish office, the future didn't seem that bad.

"Black Tower is more than just a corporation, it is an ancient order called the Black Tower Hunt Club. It operates out of Ravenwood Manor on an island that's not on any known maps and exists outside any timelines. It is run by the Master of the Manor, Lord Victor Lodge and the Master of the Hunt, Lord Tiberius. There are roughly twenty members of the Hunt that reside at the Manor and partake in the hunts."

"Like some kind of fancy English thing with guys riding around in red jackets?"

"No. Nothing like that in fact," Jane continued solemnly. "The members are recruited throughout history and they hunt people."

"Come again," Logan interrupted despite Jane's instructions. "Did you just say what I think you just said?"

"Yes, but…"

"Are you off you're fucking meds? That doesn't make sense. It's impossible."

"It's the truth," Jane stated simply before continuing. "Apart from not being on any maps, the Island is also not affected by time the same way as here. Islanders are known to live until the age of 150. Staff members at the Manor live almost double that and there is no known Hunt member that has died from old age. Guess how old I am."

"I don't know, twenty five-ish?"

"I'm forty five."

"Bullshit."

"I was born on the Island in the town of Rooks Bay and have lived through forty five winters," Jane said, staring at Logan honestly. "I am telling you the truth and the faster you accept that the better."

Logan sat stunned for a while, his brain unwilling to accept Jane's statement. But his gut told him that she was telling him the truth. He'd been correct in thinking she wasn't an American after she'd failed his little test. There were many things about her that had seemed a little strange to him before, that now made more sense. He shot the rest of his drink and nodded for her to continue.

"The Manor had been used as a prison for some of histories worst criminals; murderers, zealots, sociopaths, and the like. Until a year ago the former Master of the Hunt, Dr. Cleaver, had organized excursions where they hunted people. The targets were mostly other criminals that no one would miss."

"So what happened a year ago?"

"Lord Pierce arrived," Jane proclaimed proudly. "He arrived and uncovered a plot to kill Lord Lodge and then stopped another member from tampering with history. But he wasn't quick enough to catch Dr. Cleaver, who disappeared. Which brings us to you."

"Me? How?"

"The Manor is currently in disarray, with a number of dangerous people missing. So I've started recruiting replacements, people just as dangerous." Jane offered Logan a brief smile before continuing. "Each Hunt member has a staff of three, called hounds, and they act as their private soldiers. Together all four are called a Pack and are identified by a colour, with their own distinct symbol and uniform. To offset the power of the individual packs the Manor has its own Pack, the Black Pack. They answer to the Master of the Hunt and the Hunt Secretary. The problem is that Dr. Cleaver did not leave the Manor alone. He took seven other packs with him, along with a number of hounds from the Black Pack. So I've started refilling the stables so to speak, making you the newest Hound of the Black Pack."

Logan had seen this coming as Jane explained the hierarchy of the Manor, so he didn't physically react with a shocked face. But underneath his calm demeanour, his brain was spinning while he tried to turn her words into sense. "This is really happening, isn't it?"

"I'm afraid it is."

"I'm going to need another drink."

Jane stood up and grabbed the bottle, pouring one for both of them. Logan drained his second glass in one straight shot, slamming the glass down harder than he intended. When he let go of it he slapped himself in the face, making a loud snapping sound that surprised Jane.

"Sorry about that," he offered quietly. "I just had to make sure."

"I assure you this is no dream," Jane observed seriously. "But it could turn into a nightmare. There are over twenty well armed and well trained deviants running through time, doing who knows what. They need to be hunted down and stopped."

"Which is where I come in."

"Not immediately, but yes," Jane replied. "I need new people that I can trust, without the taint of the last administration. Lord Tiberius and I plan on filling the Black Pack with dangerous but honourable people. I want you to be the first."

"What do I have to do?"

"Whatever I say," she answered simply. "Unless you haven't guessed, I am the Secretary of the Hunt. I wasn't joking before when I said that you belong to me. I need a bodyguard with a brain, but more importantly someone I can trust. Despite what I said on the train I trust you. Do you trust me?"

"Well, you got me out of that messy situation in Aviano," Logan began slowly. "I'm not really sure I trust you, but I know damned well that I owe you."

Jane accepted his statement for what it was, inwardly happy that things were progressing as she'd hoped. With luck Tiberius would be impressed enough with Logan to allow her to continue recruiting alone.

"So how does this time travel thing work?" Logan asked with a wry smile across his face. "I didn't see a DeLorean parked out front."

"A De-what?"

"Never mind," Logan waved her off, remembering she didn't even know who the Boss was. "How do we get to this mysterious Manor that's on an island no one can find?"

"Through that door," Jane answered simply, pointing towards a door behind her. Logan hadn't taken any notice of it when he sat down, but it seemed like a normal door to a closet or washroom.

"That doesn't seem very impressive," he replied dejectedly, thinking it would be much more fun to go 88 mph in order to travel through time rather than walking through a lame door.

"We'll see."

*

"My master won't appreciate you going through his things like this."

"I don't give a shit about what you master appreciates," Pierce retorted as he stalked towards Debochev's valet.

"That's not entirely true sir," Melrose offered from beside his fellow servant, a firm grip around the other's arms.

"No you're right, I do care about a few things concerning Lord Debochev," Pierce allowed, staring the valet in the eye. "Like where he is, how I'm going to hunt him down, and what I'll do when I find him."

An innocuous comment from Melrose that morning had made Pierce realize that he was ignoring a potential source of information. This made him angry with himself for succumbing to the ignorance of the privileged by forgetting about the knowledge servants gain of their masters. So after his confrontation with Tiberius, he and his men marched into Debochev's quarters on the East side of the Manor. His valet had not offered any resistance, but had eyed Melrose with distaste when he'd followed Pierce in.

"Have a seat and we'll have a little chat while my men ransack the place," Pierce ordered, kicking a chair towards the valet. Pierce sat down on a comfortable leather chair across from him and motioned for him to follow. When the valet hesitated, Melrose gave him a shove from behind onto the chair. Despite the show the staff of the Manor put on, they were not one big happy family. Their loyalties were just as divided as those they served and there were long standing grudges aplenty.

Though Cleaver and his followers had fled the Manor, their servants had remained and quickly found life at the Manor very difficult. They were ostracized by the staff of the loyal members and at risk of losing their positions. Although some had not known about plans to leave the Manor, many probably did.

"Where did your master go?" Pierce began with an easy question.

"I don't know."

"What was he planning on doing when he got there?"

"I don't know."

"What did he take with him?"

"I don't know."

"Well I tried my best to save you," Pierce lamented insincerely. "MacDuff! Take him to the cell Leonardo just vacated."

"You... you have Leonardo?" the valet stammered in confusion. As one of Debochev's hounds, he knew him well.

"Had Leonard," Pierce corrected while he tapped his fingers on the handle of his swordstick. "We found him, captured him, and then interrogated him. Sadly we put our questions a little too... what's the word I'm looking for?"

"Violently?" Liam offered from the other side of the room as he cut through a sofa pillow with his knife.

"No, it wasn't very violent," Pierce thought, ignoring the increasing look of horror on the valet's face. "I guess forcefully would describe it better. What's your name?"

"Hector," he answered slowly.

"Well Hector, there seems to be a slight problem," Pierce began amiably. "I just asked you three simple questions and you answered very succinctly. Apparently you don't know anything."

"Yes."

"But that's not what Leonardo told us," Pierce continued, his voice still calm and friendly. "He told us that you were in the room for enough conversations to know at least something."

"He was lying."

"That's exactly what I would say in your position," Pierce agreed. "The problem is that he was a little more persuasive in his answers than you. Now do I look like an idiot to you?"

"What?" Hector asked with a mixture of wariness and renewed confusion.

"The answer to that is supposed to be no, not what, Hector," Pierce countered, enjoying the interrogation. "But for some reason you're treating me like an idiot. Even if Leonardo was lying, I can't believe you know nothing about Debochev's plans.

"Well I don't."

"Fair enough, if that's the story you want to stick with," Pierce shrugged and then nodded towards Melrose. Despite his gentle appearance and crisp uniform, Pierce's valet was very strong. So it took almost no effort for him to grab Hectors arms and hold them behind the back of the chair. "I'm ready to believe your story Hector, if you can convince me the same way Leonard did."

"Wait! What?" Hector exclaimed, struggling in Melrose's strong grasp.

Without a further explanation Pierce pushed the small button on the handle of his swordstick, pulling out the long thin steel blade. Leaning forward from his chair he slowly and expertly cut off Hector's jacket buttons with casual flicks.

"My master is a great and holy man!" Hector wailed, staring on the glinting blade at his chest.

"Your master is a fraud who uses others for his own gain," Pierce spat, pulling the sword back from Hector's body. "He's a parasite who ruins lives and I'm going to bring him back here whether you say anything or not. But the question is, how are you going to serve him when you don't have any fingers left? Liam, how many did it take before Leonardo started talking?"

"Three I think," Liam smiled after smashing a picture frame with his knee. "Wait, do thumbs count as fingers?"

"Sure," Pierce accepted, his gaze never leaving Hector. "Well let's see who can last longer. Hector, be so kind as to raise your right hand. Don't worry this blade is razor sharp, so you won't feel a thing. At first."

"Stop!" Hector yelled as his fists clenched onto his striped trousers. Pierce lowered his sword and raised an inquiring eyebrow. "I swore an oath to Lord Debochev that I can't ignore. I won't tell you anything that could hurt him. However…"

"Yes," Pierce smiled, expecting a small proviso on Hector's honour to his departed master.

"If you were to somehow check under a square of the parquet floor of his study, two down and three across from the corner window, you might find some answers you're looking for."

"Liam, watch him," Pierce ordered as he followed MacDuff into Debochev's study. It was similar to his own, but with more personal items adorning the walls and the faint scent of incense floating in the air. They moved to the window and counted off the squares on the floor, finally pointing at the one Hector directed them to. MacDuff pulled out a small blade and bent down to the floor. He wedged it into a small space along the square's edge and pried it open enough to fit his fingers in. Checking that there were no booby traps, MacDuff then lifted the square up and placed it beside the newly discovered hiding place.

"What have we got here," MacDuff whispered as he leaned over and examined the space more closely. "A few books and a file folder."

"*New Age Medicine, The Power of Positive Inference, Cults in America*," Pierce listed off the titles as MacDuff handed them to him. "I think I know where this is heading. What's in that folder?"

"Just a list of names and some newspaper clippings."

"Looks like a target list to me," Pierce frowned as he leafed through the pages. Most of the names corresponded to the newspaper clippings. Pierce immediately noticed the number of articles about recent lottery winners, and socialites from the society pages. With no royalty to get close to in 1970's America, Debochev was going to weasel his way to the next best thing. "This should get us something if our current lead ends up turning a blank."

"So what should we do about Hector?" MacDuff asked with little concern.

"Let the little cockroach sweat it out in one of the nicer holding cells. Then we'll get him released to kitchen duty or something equally demeaning."

"Aye, that's good," MacDuff laughed.

"While you take care of that I'll talk with Tiberius and get these rooms sealed off. There might be some other tidbits hidden away."

They emptied out of Debochev's quarter's, locking the door as they left. MacDuff, Sean and Liam escorted Hector towards the dungeons below, while Pierce and Melrose walked towards Tiberius' office. Melrose led most of the way, since they were in a part of the Manor that Pierce wasn't very familiar with. Eventually they turned onto the gallery that led to Tiberius' office and Pierce was finally able to recognize his surroundings.

Not wishing to interrupt any meeting within the room, Pierce decided he had better knock first, rather than just barge in. But as he raised his hand to knock the door swung open and he was utterly surprised by the person that almost barrelled into him.

"Jane!" he exclaimed in delighted shock.

"Patr- I mean Lord Pierce," she replied with equal surprise before regaining a calm demeanour.

"It's fantastic to see you," Pierce gushed, embracing her with both arms.

"And you," Jane replied less effusively, giving him a small peck on the cheek.

"I heard you were in Italy," Pierce continued after taking a step back, slightly baffled by her casual attitude. "How did it go? I want to hear all about it."

"Yes I did, but I can't really talk about it," she answered quickly, looking around the gallery. "I'm afraid Lord Tiberius has called a meeting in the Hunt Room this afternoon and I must prepare for it. I'm absolutely rushed off my feet. We'll talk later."

"Sure," Pierce replied to Jane's departing form as she left before he could say anything else. The last time they'd seen each other, she'd been all over him. Sure they had just lived through an incredibly dangerous adventure and they were both drinking, but Pierce had been sure there was something there. He still felt that way towards her, but based on her almost cold reception he wasn't sure the feeling was mutual. "What the hell was that?"

"Sir?" Melrose asked absently from behind him.

"Stop it. What the hell just happened?"

"I think a beautiful woman just brushed you off sir."

"Thanks for that," Pierce scowled at him. "I need a drink."

Chapter 13

A bright afternoon sun flowed through the stained glass skylight that ran along the length of the Hunt Room, filling the majestic space with a multitude of dull colours. Reminiscent of the House of Commons, the Hunt Room was filled with carved wooden furniture facing each other from two sides of the room. A blood red carpet separated the two banks of seating with only a simple table in the middle and a platform with two imposing chairs at the end.

The remaining members of the Hunt had been called to the meeting and the number of empty chairs easily told those assembled as to the subject. The front row consisted of twenty seats, one for each member and adorned with their pack's symbol. Their respective hounds sat on tiered seating behind them. It was a cold and solemn room, the very heart of Ravenwood Manor.

Looking around the room Pierce was struck by the difference from the last time he had been there. It had been a stormy night and every seat was filled. They had received their target for the hunt, an arms dealer in 1930's Spain, and he'd felt the chill of the place. The bloodlust of almost eighty people had been palpable and he shuddered in recollection.

But today the room was subdued, for which Pierce was very glad. He'd returned to his room after running in to Jane and had polished off half a bottle of scotch before MacDuff had fetched him for the meeting. He'd drank it so fast that the walk over had been fairly easy. But now he was starting to feel the full effects; partly drunk and partly hung over.

"Liam said that he could take you down to the village," MacDuff whispered to him from the seat behind. "He knows a couple girls that would jump at the chance to spend some time with a Lord of the Manor."

"I'm in no mood Duffy," Pierce growled, his heading pounding. "You tell that annoying leprechaun that if he keeps shooting his mouth off I'll…"

Before he could finish, the main doors were opened by a pair of footmen and Tiberius entered with a determined look on his face. Jane trailed in behind him marching confidently, barely looking at Pierce as she passed. Everyone in the room was dressed in their formal hunting jackets, the predominant material being leather. Deciding to follow along with this tradition, Jane was simply stunning in a pair of form fitting black leather pants and a tight jacket.

"Give me your flask," Pierce moaned to MacDuff in defeat after she had passed by. She had fully transformed from the pretty but quiet maid he'd first met, into the beautiful senior member of the staff before him.

"Pay attention," MacDuff lectured, sitting back to listen to the proceedings.

"…As you can see there have been some changes from the last time we were in this room," Tiberius announced as he paced in the middle of the room. Rather than sit imperiously on the platform like Dr. Cleaver, he enjoyed getting in people's faces. "I'm not sure how much each of you knows about our current situation, so allow me to enlighten you. When the last hunt in Spain was taking place, Dr. Cleaver kidnapped Lord Lodge and tried to have him killed in an attempt to take power here at Ravenwood. However he miscalculated the strength of the Master of the Manor and was unsuccessful. When his treachery was discovered, Cleaver decided to flee the Manor and the Island rather than face his punishment. In order to cover his tracks he also managed to convince or coerce others to flee at the same time.

"The empty chairs that you see around the room belong to those who have fled in disgrace. As a consequence of these actions some changes have been made. Lord Lodge has appointed myself as the Master of the Hunt and Miss Piper as the Secretary of the Hunt. I will tell you now that the events of the past will not go unpunished. Miss Piper if you please."

Everyone looked to Jane as Tiberius motioned towards her. From below her desk Jane grabbed a bag and stood up, walking along the length of the room. As she passed certain chairs, she pulled out a solid black cloth roughly a foot square and placed it on the back. Most of those assembled looked on in bemused confusion; however Pierce quickly understood what they signified when a cloth was placed on the late Colonel Bufford's chair. When she finished Jane walked back to her desk and sat down.

"Unless you haven't guessed it, Miss Piper just placed death shrouds on the chairs of those traitors who have met a deserved end. I will not rest until the rest of the empty chairs have similar shrouds upon them. Those people who get in my way will receive a shroud of their own.

"Those of you who share in my disdain for the traitors and wish to help recapture them are welcome to join me. However I will find out if you're in league with Cleaver and if you try to aid him in anyway… Well you'll wish you received a simple death shroud.

"As of this moment the North Tower and all the portals within are locked and their use is strictly forbidden by those not approved by me. Some of you might feel upset at the idea of a former member of the staff ordering you around. Too bad. If you have a problem with the situation feel free to take it up with me, but I guarantee I'll win any argument you start. One way or another. I have been here longer than anyone in this room and I will be here long after you're all gone."

Tiberius let the thought sit in the air as he walked over to Jane's desk and had a sip of water. Usually a man whose iron glance spoke volumes, he found it strange to be speaking for such a long amount of time.

"As I've just said, the North Tower will be closed and no further excursions or hunts are planned," Tiberius continued his demeanour no less serious than before. "This however, does not mean that the island will be used as a replacement. Each member of the Hunt and their staff will have the same freedom to travel throughout the island as before. But there will be no leniency for any acts committed against the inhabitants of this island. The penalty for harming anyone will be severe. Are there any questions?"

The room was silent, no one was prepared for the firm message and hard tone that Tiberius had used. Under Dr. Cleaver, the members of the Hunt had been free to do as they pleased, when they pleased, in whatever method they pleased. They were the privileged few who lived without repercussions.

"No?" Tiberius looked around pleased. "Then this meeting is adjourned."

Tiberius walked over to Jane's desk and leaned over to speak with her, dismissing everyone gathered in the room. Pierce watched everyone leave in one's and two's, speaking quietly amongst themselves after the bombshell that had just been dropped. Pierce felt terrible and didn't feel like going anywhere, let alone standing up. He'd never been a big drinker and he now regretted the scotch he'd inhaled before the meeting. He leaned back in his comfortable chair and rubbed his temples, building up the nerve to stand up. After few moments he opened his eyes and Tiberius was standing in front of him.

"Nice speech," Pierce uttered tiredly. "I thought you really…"

But before he could continue Jane folded up the small notebook on her desk and slowly walked towards them. With more speed than he thought possible, Pierce found himself getting up from his chair and walking towards the door, leaving a confused pair in his wake.

"What was that all about?" Tiberius wondered aloud. "I hope Patrick's not sick, he looks terrible."

Jane shrugged with feigned incomprehension. She had a pretty good idea she was the reason he'd left, not some mysterious illness. She had conflicting feelings towards the Lord of the Brown Pack, and had no idea what to do about them. She really did care for him; sometimes she even thought she might love him. But her more practical side told her to ignore her feelings. They'd only known each other for a short time and she now had more important things to do than chase after romance.

Jane was desperate to succeed as the Secretary of the Hunt, and was equally desperate to prove she deserved the position. If she were to start a relationship with one of the members, especially one whose influence was on the rise like Lord Pierce, the word was bound to get out. She didn't want anyone thinking she'd seduced him into getting her the job. Besides she thought, he was still a member of the Hunt and she was still a member of the staff.

Despite the precedence set by Tiberius and his relationship with Kat, Jane wouldn't fool herself into thinking her situation was the same. Tiberius was the second most powerful person on the island and a legend of the Hunt. He had nothing left to prove and he didn't care what people said. But Jane didn't feel the same way, so she was inwardly relieved that Patrick decided to avoid her, hopefully making things easier for both of them.

"We'll inform the staff next," Tiberius said as he walked towards the exit. "Ensure everyone's gathered in the dining hall in thirty minutes. As soon as I'm done that I'm collecting Morgan and Dufresne to return to Luxembourg. I need to find out more about this potential mole. I'll need you to watch everyone while I'm gone. No overt investigations of course, but I want to know if anyone starts acting strange. I'll check the room outside the portal periodically, so leave me a note there if anything comes up."

Jane nodded and tried to push aside thoughts of Patrick Pierce as she set off to continue her work. With Tiberius gone, she was going to have a very busy time.

*

Pierce awoke in his luxurious four poster bed as the morning sun peeked through his bedroom curtains. Mercifully his head felt clear after some much needed rest and he quietly swore off alcohol. Which he knew wouldn't last very long.

After a quick shower and shave, Pierce walked across the hall into his dressing room, where he found his grey seventies suit waiting for him. He would be leaving the Manor with his team, heading back through the portal to hunt down Grigori Debochev.

As he put on the clothes and tied his straight black tie, Pierce felt as though he were donning a uniform or armour and heading into battle. His melancholy thoughts from the previous day were pushed to the back of his mind as he concentrated at the task at hand. After what they'd discovered from Leonardo, Hector, and the books from Debochev's study, his team realized the importance of their mission. It was no longer a simple matter of bringing back a stray in order to be chastised. Debochev had to be found to save all the people he was preying on. There were people being robbed of their savings and taken away from their homes. But most of all there were the countless girls being abused by this so-called holy man and his acolytes.

Pierce looked in the mirror after donning his suit jacket and was surprised by the hard faced man staring back at him. Since arriving at the Manor he had become a confident, powerful, and dangerous man with a purpose, no longer the aimless bureaucrat. Pierce liked this guy, but he also recognized the potential trap the man in the mirror could fall victim to. He had to ensure that he used his new found skills for a good purpose, lest he become the very people he was hunting.

"Be careful sir," Melrose offered from behind him, holding a bag of spare clothes. Pierce smiled at the genuine concern in his valet's voice and realized that he had surrounded himself with good people at the Manor. He knew that none of them would hesitate to tell him off if he started to stray from the positive path.

"Thanks Melrose," Piece accepted while he wrestled the bag from his valet. Despite his position in the Manor he still hated being waited on for everything. "I want you to keep an eye on Jane while I'm away. With all of us gone she'll need someone watching her back. I know she can look after herself, but I'd feel better knowing you're looking out for her."

"You can trust me sir. And if I might say, I'm sure she's just overwhelmed by her new position." Melrose reassured him cautiously. He knew how hard Jane's snub had affected Pierce and he didn't want his master thinking about anything but the job at hand.

"Whatever," Pierce muttered in annoyance. He hoped Melrose was right, but it didn't make him feel any better. He forced her from his mind once again and returned to business. "I'm going to go down and eat with the rest of them. Take care."

After a firm handshake, Pierce hefted the bag onto his shoulder and left Melrose to his duties. He quickly walked the familiar route from his rooms in one of the Manor's towers to the Brown Pack's lair on the ground level, passing few people as he went. He arrived at the heavy oak door within a few minutes and let himself in with his own key. He could smell the delicious sent of bacon and butter as he placed his bag on the foyer floor, entering the main room with a growling stomach.

"You've started without me!" Pierce observed with feigned indignation as he went to his place at the head of the table. Silver platters of food were spread along the middle of the table and he quickly heaped some of everything onto his plate. When no sarcastic comments emanated from the rest of the table, Pierce looked over to make sure Liam was with them. "Alright, I'm sorry about the leprechaun joke. I was a little under the weather yesterday."

"I'm not even that short," Liam defended as he chomped down on a piece of bacon.

"Sorry," Pierce repeated with smile, before returning to business. "Everyone packed and ready to go?"

"Aye," MacDuff replied, straightening an ugly tie with his right hand. They were all dressed in their seventies clothes from the Costume Department. The only one that didn't look ridiculous to Pierce was Kat. She was dressed once more in her vagabond outfit; sandals, jeans, and a yellow t-shirt.

"I've packed pistols for each of us, all police issue for our covers," Sean reported diligently. "Plus some shotguns and machine guns for good measure. We should be able to get anything else we want once we're there. It's America after all and weapons are plentiful."

"That should do," Pierce acknowledged, still not fully comfortable with guns.

"Speaking of weapons, did you pack that red bikini Kat?" Liam asked seriously before letting his smirk loose.

"If Tiberius hears you asking questions like that..." MacDuff warned.

"He's right," Kat continued playfully. "I don't think Ty has fully forgiven you for helping me buy that lace number, despite how much he liked it."

"Has Tiberius left for Luxembourg yet?" Pierce asked, unable to use the short version of the Master of the Hunt's name.

"He left last night," Kat confirmed.

"We'd better be leaving as well," MacDuff pronounced after piling his empty plate amongst the rest in the middle of the table. Everyone had filled themselves with the heavy breakfast and needed to get moving in order to avoid the urge for a nap.

After collecting their bags from the foyer and locking the door behind them, the Brown Pack made a curious group as they paraded down the halls and corridors of the Manor. Their determined and intense attitudes were in distinct contrast to their vintage clothing, making the few staff members they passed concentrate on not smiling or laughing. However the two guards watching the entrance to the North Tower were all business and nodded dutifully as Pierce led his team up to them.

The guard on the right looked over everyone assembled, verifying the faces against the list Tiberius had provided to them. They were all approved to travel beyond the portal, so he marched over to the Secretary's office and stuck his head inside after knocking. A few seconds later Jane appeared. Without saying anything she walked over to the door and opened it up, leading everyone across the footbridge to the North Tower.

Even though it was midday, the few windows that dotted the North Tower didn't provide enough light for the halls within. So the group passed rows of torches as they descended the circular stairwell in the middle of the tower. After going two levels down they walked down one of the door lined corridors, the sound of their footsteps echoing in the empty halls.

Jane finally stopped at door 5G301, the brass plate reflecting the flames of nearby torches. With little ceremony she handed the key over to Pierce, her hand lingering in his for a second longer than was necessary.

Before he could react, she turned and left the assembled group. A soft throat clearing from behind him made Pierce turn from watching Jane's departure to the door before him. Without fanfare he unlocked the door, pocketed the key and led them into the room beyond.

The room was empty apart from a circular opening in the floor that was actually another stone staircase. Everyone walked down it carefully, the torches providing dangerous shadows that obscured the stairs. Once at the bottom they were confronted by another door. This was the actual portal that would lead them to a small church crypt in San Diego.

Sean took four pistols from his bag and handed them around. The men were all portraying police of some sort or another, so they placed them in standard issue holsters. With a quick look at everyone with him, Pierce took a deep breath and opened the door, calmly walking along the stone passageway to a door on the other side. The short distance was covered in a few seconds.

Pierce turned the handle of the second door, and like previous times travelling through the portal was struck by the anticlimactic sensation. He was always prepared for it not to work and open up into a closet. But as before, he easily walked into a place and time far from his own.

The crypt was not very big, so everyone found themselves squeezing next to each other. Unlike the usual vision of a crypt this one was dry and dusty, owing to the lack of winters in San Diego. Sean was prepared as usual and had a flashlight out and working within seconds of passing the door. In order to avoid any unwanted attraction, they left the basement in ones and twos, hoping that it wasn't Sunday.

Pierce was relieved to see their luck was continuing, as the church was empty save for a few older women kneeling in a front pew. He walked out casually into a cloudy afternoon, the wind whipping dust and garbage along the sidewalk. He was the last one out the church, so he looked around to find the others. They were all lined up at the nearby bus stop, just another collection of random people waiting for the bus.

He knew that one of the buses that stopped there would take them to the local Greyhound station. But after the last bumpy journey crowded with sweaty people with seventies era ideas of hygiene, Pierce had made arrangements for future travel. They'd be going to L.A. in style.

"Guys I'm not going to let you take the loser cruiser," Pierce laughed as he approached the bus stop. "I've got us some alternate transport."

"What alternate transport?" MacDuff asked in surprise, not knowing anything about it. "When did you sort that out?"

"I started working on it about five minutes after getting off the Greyhound in Los Angeles last time," Pierce replied with a wink. "It'll be better than the bus, trust me. I just need Sean to come with me; the rest of you can hang out at the diner across the street."

"And do what?" Liam questioned. "We just ate breakfast."

"I don't know, blend in," Pierce offered with a laugh. "Have a cup of coffee, read the paper. We'll be back within the hour."

Pierce and Sean left their bags with the others and started walking down the sidewalk, watching for any cabs that might pass by. They only had to walk a block before one passed by that was on duty. Pierce flagged him down and jumped in when it stopped, yelling his destination over a blaring radio. The cabbie simply nodded and pounded on the gas, throwing Sean and Pierce into the dirty rear seat.

The taxi weaved through traffic with impressive accuracy, fighting through the morning traffic. Pierce was pretty sure that the cabbie wasn't trying to deliver them quickly; he just enjoyed speed and the challenge of avoiding collisions at the last moment. At one point Sean tried to start a conversation, but found himself breathless as he watched the back of a transport truck fill in the front windshield.

Whispering a silent prayer, Pierce paid the cabbie when he screeched to a halt on a dirty side street. When they got out he turned the radio up even louder and peeled off back towards the main road.

"You ok?" Pierce asked quietly, still slightly stunned from their brush with death.

"I think so," Sean replied without blinking.

"Alright then." They both shook their heads in order to put the ride behind them. The cabbie had dropped them off in a working class neighbourhood away from the coast. The back street they found themselves on ran behind a collection of rundown bungalows on one side and warehouses and workshops on the other. Spray painted garbage cans lined the street, providing the blustery wind a collection of rotten smells to deliver.

"This must be the place," Pierce decided after looking at a car filled yard in front of them. Since they were in the back, there were no street numbers. But the number of cars in various states of disrepair signalled it as the garage he was looking for.

"You've never been here?" Sean asked warily as they walked into the gravel lot.

"No, I bought some cars in L.A. and had them shipped down here," Pierce replied while looking around for someone to talk to. "They agreed to hold them and tweak them a bit for me."

"What do you mean tweak?"

"You'll see," Pierce winked, also eager to see how they turned out.

"Can I help you guys?" a voice called out as they got closer to the concrete building. A thin bearded man with greasy coveralls stood up from a crooked picnic table, curiously observing the two well dressed men walking towards him.

"You Joey?" Pierce asked casually, unable to read the name patch on the man's coverall's.

"Nope, he's inside," the mechanic answered before taking another drag from his smoke.

"I'm here to pick up two cars under the name Jones," Pierce told him, containing his disgust as he watched him spit onto the weed covered ground.

"We were wondering when you'd show up," the mechanic's nonchalant demeanour instantly changed as his eyes lit up and he tossed his smoke away. He jumped to the back door and held it open for Pierce and Sean. "You're going to love what we did for you Mr. Jones."

They followed him into the garage and were surprised to see that the space bared no resemblance to the vehicle graveyard out back. Pierce had been a little worried when he'd looked over the rust buckets in the lot, but now he was excited. There were three bays in operation with impressive hydraulic lifts holding up some expensive cars. Rows of lights along the ceiling displayed an organized and spotless garage floor.

The mechanic poked his head into the office and then wished them a good day before walking back to one of the cars being worked on. Within seconds a middle aged man in clean jeans and boots walked out. The name patch on his dark blue work shirt was evidence that he was the man they were looking for. His collection of rings, tattoos, and belt chains made Pierce confident he'd sent his cars to the right place.

"So you're Mr. Jones?" Joey smiled looking at Pierce. At first he seemed a little disappointed until he spotted the obvious bulge under his arm. He then looked at Sean and saw a similar bulge on the big Scotsman and his smile turned genuine. "You ready to see your cars brother?"

"You bet," Pierce replied, barely able to keep himself calm. One of the questions he'd asked Tiberius when he'd first arrived at the Manor was where the Manor's obvious wealth came from. Tiberius laughed as he reminded Pierce that they had access to almost any time in history, thereby able to basically print their own money. Seeing Pierce's confused face he explained that in a few hours they could travel back to ancient Rome, grab a vase, and then take it to an auction in 1950's Paris for period currency. He boasted that you couldn't go to any museum in the Western world without seeing a dozen artefacts the Manor had sold for cash. This had made Pierce think about all of the things he would love to get his hands on when he travelled through the portals. So when they emerged in 1970's California, Pierce knew that he'd be making at least two purchases.

"I've got to say you sent us two beauties," Joey continued as he led them out of the garage towards a second building with a single garage door. "We went to town on them, just like you asked; upgraded suspension, exhaust, big tires, and some serious engine mods. You looking to outrun some cops?"

"Not quite," Pierce laughed, flashing his FBI ID. "I want to make sure nobody can outrun me."

"You never said you were a cop," Joey objected, apparently not fond of the police.

"I'm not a cop," Pierce countered seriously. "I'm a Fed, I chase bank robbers, kidnappers, and terrorists. I don't give a damn if your parts are hot, if you drive too fast, or you want to have a few beers on the way to the bar. I leave that Mickey Mouse bullshit to cops."

"I like you brother," Joey brightened, opening the door to the second garage for them. "I hope you like your cars."

"Holy shit!" Sean exclaimed when Joey flipped the lights on.

Pierce couldn't even utter a single word. A grin had been slowly growing on his face since they arrived at the garage, but now it was a full blown smile that started to hurt his face.

"You're welcome," Joey nodded, seeing the look of sheer delight and love spread across Pierce's face.

Chapter 14

The Luxembourg Casino might not have been Monte Carlo, but it still provided the wealthy of Europe a place to lose their money. But due to Luxembourg's place as a financial hub, many of the gamblers were bankers and not the idle rich. So they were not as eager to bet big on chance, making the stakes much lower than what the classical décor suggested.

The warm crème and gold colours within were a nice contrast to the cold rain clouds that had shifted over the small European country during the night. Tiberius removed his rain coat and handed it over to the young lady at the coat check, taking in the rest of the entrance while Dufresne did the same. It was still early in the evening, making the large building seem empty with only the real die hard gamblers anchored to their seats. Thankfully the wretched pinging of slot machines could barely be heard, so Tiberius figured they must be at the farther end of the casino. Usually they were at the front door, trying to bait the casual gambler early. But this was a higher class establishment whose main targets were the blackjack and roulette players.

"Meet you at the middle bar in thirty minutes," Tiberius said, taking a look at his watch.

"Have you been here before?" Dufresne asked curiously, unable to see the bar from where they stood..

"No, but every casino has a bar in the middle."

They split up and headed towards the gaming tables with pictures of the unknown assassin in their hands. After returning to the Manor, Tiberius had the film from his camera developed, which included the scene of the *accident* and close up shots of the victim.

But that wasn't the only evidence they'd brought back with them. The napkin with the poison that had killed Zeidt had been given to Elena Sirinova to work on and there were also the contents of the assassin's pockets. One of the scraps of paper had been a receipt from the Luxembourg Casino.

Tiberius didn't want to question the cashiers right away, since they were less likely to assist him behind their steel cages. Instead he wanted to see if he could get anything from the dealers first, since they'd at least be friendlier and hopefully more talkative. He looked over the floor and saw a couple of tables that were empty; the dealer's patiently waiting to unburden some players of their chips.

"Eight thousand in chips please," Tiberius asked in french as he sat at one of the empty tables, placing 8 one thousand francs bills on the table. The dealer replaced them with eight chips after giving the bills a cursory look. Tiberius put the first chip on the table and waited for his cards to be dealt. A quick glance told him that he had two face cards, so he signalled that he would stick with them. The dealer hit after showing thirteen, turning over a ten and busting. Tiberius left his winnings on the table and played again, but this time losing when the dealer hit blackjack.

"21, sorry sir," the dealer offered amiably as he collected the chips on the table.

"C'est rien," Tiberius shrugged, pulling out the picture and showing it to the dealer. "Has this man ever been here?"

The dealer looked hard at the picture and then shook his head with disappointment. Tiberius thanked him for his time, collected his chips, and then moved to another table. His luck was about the same at the next table and two more after that. He was only down four thousands francs, but no one seemed to recognize the man in the photo.

"Anything?" Tiberius asked after sitting down at a marble topped table in the middle of the casino. Dufresne shook his head as he sat down beside him, having also come up empty. They placed orders for Scotch with the waitress and even showed the photo to her. She returned with their drinks but with no recollection of the man in the picture.

"I didn't think we'd find anything quickly," Dufresne allowed realistically.

"Niether did I," Tiberius concurred. Asking the dealers had been a way to provoke more information from a better source. When Dufresne looked at him quizzically, Tiberius merely took a sip of his fifteen year old amber gold. "Unless I'm mistaken, we're about to be accosted by the casino heavies."

Before Dufresne could say anything two men in identical blazers approached their table. The one on the left was thin with a shrewd face and slicked back hair, his companion was a hulk of a man barely able to fit into his jacket.

"Can I help you gentlemen?" The thin man asked with a suspicious glare. "There have been some complaints of you harassing some of the casino employees."

"I'd hardly call it harassing," Dufresne countered good naturedly.

"Call it what you like, you're no longer welcome here. Those drinks are on the house, so drink them and then get out."

"I'm afraid we haven't finished conducting our business yet," Tiberius disagreed, sipping his drink slowly. "But if you're buying, we'll take another round."

"This isn't a joke," the thin man warned, glaring at them.

"Indeed it isn't," Tiberius allowed, setting the empty glass down. "But we'll decide when we leave."

"You'll leave when I throw you out," the large man threatened.

"Which is in thirty seconds," the thin man finished.

"I don't think so," Tiberius looked both men in the eye, his steely gaze boring into both.

"Really why is that?" the big man challenged, not swift enough to take note of the powerful man facing him. His thin partner had remained silent, becoming concerned by the pair at the table.

"Because if you touch me two things will happen," Tiberius lectured, his voice calm but hard. "First you will end up with one or more broken bones."

"Oh yeah, what about the second?" the big man scoffed, too stupid to keep quiet.

"Second is that I tear this place apart on some trumped up charge and your bosses blame you two," Tiberius finished, slowly opening his Interpol ID and placing it on the table. "I'm surprised; you both seem like the type that would spot a policeman from a mile away. Unlucky for you, you didn't. All you managed to do was seriously piss off that policeman by threatening him with bodily harm."

"Wait…" the thin man replied holding his hands up, unsure what else to say. Luckily for him further words were not necessary.

"Shut up," Tiberius ordered quickly. "Get your chief of security down here immediately and I'll try to forget all about your stupidity."

The two security men scampered away with their proverbial tails between their legs and were quickly replaced by a much smarter looking man in a perfectly tailored Armani suit. Despite his unthreatening demeanour, Tiberius could instantly tell that this man could be ruthless if the situation required.

"I apologize for my men," the head of security offered after introducing himself. When Tiberius offered him a seat at their table, he thanked him and sat down. "You see we thought you might have been debt collectors and we have a certain responsibility to our customers."

"So one of your employees recognized the photo?" Dufresne observed quickly.

"Sorry, no. I should have said potential customers," he corrected before continuing with feigned dismay. "Some of our employees thought he might have looked familiar, however I'm sad to say they didn't recognize him."

"That is too bad," Tiberius agreed coldly.

"We have a very good rapport with the local police," he continued without reacting to Tiberius' comment. "They usually come and see me first when they have questions. That way I can make arrangements in order to avoid situations like this."

"Well you're here now," Tiberius smiled, mimicking the expression of the man across the table. He pulled out the photo of their inquiry and placed it on the table. "We're searching for anyone that may have information about this man. We know that he was here last Thursday and we need to question anyone who came into contact with him."

"What has he done?" the Head of Security asked without even glancing at the photo.

"I'm not at liberty to say."

"Gentlemen," he shrugged with open arms, his smile becoming smugger. "You have questioned the employees and have come up with nothing. I understand you have a job to do, but I have one as well. I can't have you disrupting the patrons haphazardly and without a warrant…"

He trailed off, leaning back into his chair with satisfaction. He'd been dealing with police his entire adult life and was used to their methods. He knew they were all mostly lazy and the slightest inconvenience would stop them.

"That's fair. Dufresne how long do you think before the judge signs that warrant we submitted?" Tiberius asked as he also leaned back into his chair serenely.

"Probably another hour," Dufresne replied instantly, despite being caught off guard by the question.

"So we'll just relax here until it arrives, along with about thirty other officers," Tiberius outlined lazily, before turning very serious. "I hope you don't have any plans for the rest of the week, because if I'm forced to bother a judge with a warrant for a few quick questions, I'm going to get my money's worth. I will tear this place apart and find out every little secret you're trying to hide. I'm talking about financial ledgers, payroll lists, and any other physical clues you might be hiding. You have any weapons here?"

"Perhaps," the Head of Security muttered doubtfully, unsure where the questioning was going.

"Of course you do," Tiberius carried on, enjoying himself. "That big baboon had a gun on a shoulder holster. So I'm going to collect every weapon you have here and run all the serial numbers and ballistics. I'm willing to bet that most are going to be dicey at best and potentially used in some unsolved crimes. Guess what happens if I'm right?"

"But you can't..." he gulped, suddenly fearful of challenge.

"Of course I can, but more importantly I'm willing to do it," Tiberius replied with a wolfish grin. "I'm not one of the local police that you've bribed to look the other way and I don't care how many tourists or employees are kept out of this place. I came here to informally ask some questions to avoid too much trouble. But you've chosen to do things the hard way."

"What do you need?" he asked with a renewed helpful attitude. "I'm sure we can help out with finding this man."

"Oh we've already found him," Dufresne piped in. "He was killed yesterday."

"Under questionable circumstances, so we need help tracking down people he came into contact with," Tiberius repeated his initial request. "You will take Inspector Dufresne to your security room and show him all the video from last Thursday. Meanwhile I will continue to prowl your halls with this photo."

The Head of Security knew an order when he heard one, and nodded obediently when Tiberius finished. He didn't want any cops digging around the casino, since it would be his neck on the line if he let them find anything. But if he could get them out with the little amount of info they were looking for, then he'd be fine.

Tiberius watched as the two men got up from the table and walked towards a discreet door on the other side of the bar. He hoped that there would be some video evidence of their assassin meeting someone, because he didn't think his canvassing of the employees would yield anything.

Without very much enthusiasm he decided to try his luck with the cashiers now that Interpol's presence at the casino was no longer a secret. He walked past some gaming tables and approached one of the cashier booths. A young woman was sitting behind the caged window, with obvious boredom at the lack of customers.

"Good evening," Tiberius began while he removed his ID and showed it to her. Immediately her eyes sprang to life with the possibility of something new and exciting. "Can you tell me if you've seen this man here?"

She stared at the photo for a few minutes with hopeful concentration, but no matter how much she wanted to help, the face was unknown to her. Tiberius thanked her anyway and left in search of the other cashier stations. They were littered through the casino floor in order to make it easier for people to deposit their money.

Two more cashiers yielded the same negative response and Tiberius was building himself up to approach the one nearest the slot machines. The constant mechanical noise of the dreadful machines drove him crazy and he couldn't risk losing focus. Luckily however he was saved from the entire ordeal when one of the casino security guards approached him.

"Monsieur L'Inspecteur?"

"Oui," Tiberius answered.

"They are ready for you in the video room. Please follow me."

Tiberius nodded, grateful for a reprieve from the binging and flashing lights. He was also hopeful that Dufresne had uncovered something useful. He'd been worried that the casino didn't have any recording devices hooked up to their television monitor's. VHS machines that allowed the easy taping and re-viewing of video were still pretty new and not yet widely used.

"What have you got?" he asked as the guard held the video room door open for him. There were four rows of workstations in the room, with a giant map of the casino on the wall. The map had a little light and label where each camera was located. Each workstation had access to each camera and could pull it up with an easy key command. Tiberius knew that someone like Pierce would have felt like he was working in the Stone Age with these antiquated systems. However Tiberius was much older and was grateful for what he could get.

"From what we know, our subject cashed out ten thousand francs worth of chips at 11:30 Thursday night," Dufresne began with the information they'd gleaned from the crumpled receipt. "So we were able to pick up his movements from the cashier's box at the front of the Casino at that time."

"Before the cashier's box he had a drink at the bar with a blonde woman in a very tight dress," one of the techs observed from his work station. He had three monitors running and Tiberius and Dufresne were crowded behind him watching the images. Tiberius had to clear his throat to get the tech to move from the shot of the woman, hoping to curtail any fantasy the young man might be trying to create. "Sorry. They stayed there for two drinks, about thirty minutes. Before that your suspect was at the blackjack table alone."

"Where was the woman?" Tiberius asked, watching the assassin play blackjack on the left hand screen. He was one of three people playing at that table and he wasn't talking to anyone. It felt a little odd seeing the man up close and alive. He was young, handsome, and well dressed with parted black hair and a five o'clock shadow.

"She seems to have been wandering the casino floor by herself," Dufresne replied, having already seen the boring replay. "I think she just wanted a free drink from him."

"Maybe," Tiberius conceded doubtfully. There was something about the scene he'd witnessed that made his sixth sense twitch. "Where did he go before the black jack table?"

"I'll show you," the tech offered, expertly switching between screens as he rewound and fast forwarded the tapes. He was able to show the assassin's progress through the casino from when he entered at eight o'clock by following him with the different cameras. Apart from the woman at the bar, he didn't really talk to anyone beyond a few words.

"Wait a second, go back to the craps table," Tiberius ordered, once again getting the nagging feeling he'd seen something important. He watched their suspect move with lightning speed as the tech fast forwarded the images, stopping once he reached the craps table.

"What are we looking for?" Dufresne asked as he stared at the screen, seeing the same images as before.

"It's the same woman," Tiberius pointed out as they watched the woman from the bar walk slowly over to the craps table and immediately drape her shoulder over the assassin's shoulder.

"Probably looking for a free drink," the tech suggested as he watched the woman cheer on the assassin's winning toss of the dice. "There's a lot of that down there."

"I think it's something more," Tiberius countered as he stared at the screen. The woman seemed to be really enthusiastic about the game, at one point drawing the attention of everyone at the table when she leaned down to throw the dice. The camera angle was from the back, but he was pretty sure her cleavage was on full display to the rest of the table. Again this made him suspicious. "Wait, rewind this again, just before she gets the dice from our guy."

The tech did as he was told and Tiberius had to wave off the inquiring look from his partner. All of the woman's jumping and gyrating automatically drew the attention of anyone watching the scene, so Tiberius decided to watch everyone else at the table instead,

"There," he pointed at the screen after the second review. "Look at the man beside our target, look what he does."

The tech rewound and replayed the scene a third time as they all leaned in a little closer to watch. The man beside their assassin was a heavy set man with a dark beard and thick black glasses who had a small stack of chips in front of him. He didn't speak to anyone and even appeared to be a little bored with the whole game. Once the woman got into her act he decided to leave the table without playing.

"You didn't see it?" Tiberius questioned them after he got the tech to stop the tape.

"Nothing," offered Dufresne and the tech in confused unison.

"Watch again, but this time I'll control the buttons." He replayed it from the time the woman approached the table, pausing at it suddenly as she leaned over and threw the dice. "Look at the mystery man, he's dropping something into the pocket of our suspect. We didn't see it the first few times because the human eye is drawn to movement and the male eye is drawn to attractive female movement."

"Holy shit," whispered the tech in appreciation of Tiberius' skills, but mixed with a little embarrassment for having missed it so many times. "How did you see that?"

"The woman at the table was just too excited for the amount of money being bet, especially since it wasn't hers. That made me look beyond her to the others at the table and what they were doing."

"I can't tell what he passed," Dufresne said squinting at the screen even closer than before. "Some paper maybe."

"We'll find out," Tiberius answered with determination before turning to the tech. "Trace the girl back in the tape to the time she enters. I'm willing to bet that she comes in a few minutes before the guy with the glasses."

The tech nodded and began rewinded the different tapes, switching between camera's as they followed the path of the woman. They watched her enter the casino at nine o'clock, minutes after the man in the glasses dropped off a jacket at the coat check. They then followed the man as he wandered the casino floor, eventually playing some roulette before reaching the craps table. After the craps table he went to the washroom and then left the casino alone.

"You know, this looks a lot like a…" the tech started after watching all the video.

"Like a pro job," the head of security finished from the wall behind them where he'd been leaning silently during the entire process.

"Exactly," Tiberius concurred, slightly more impressed with the man. "Those two were working as a team to pass some information to our suspect. They came in separately and scoped the place out first, probably checking your guards and anyone looking suspicious. They watched our suspect from a distance for almost an hour before moving in. She distracted everyone while he made the drop. That's some pretty serious tradecraft."

"What do you think we're dealing with?" the head of security asked with a hint of concern as he looked at the screen with the man in glasses on it.

"It doesn't appear like the casino was the target," Tiberius allowed, noting a strange look on his face. "It's too early to say, but I'm going to need your full assistance to get to the bottom of this."

"You've got it."

Tiberius was confident that his first assessment of the chief of security as a greasy con man with criminal ties was correct. However he realized that the man truly took pride in his position and wanted to maintain the security of the casino. He also realized that he was hiding something.

"I'm going to need a copy of the tape where the pass was made for our labs. I'll also need photos made of the two new subjects from the video. We'll take those tonight. I would like you to interview the staff about all three of our suspects; if they recognize any of them, what they said, what they did, etcetera. I'm not really expecting anything, but you never know."

"No problem," the head of security agreed as he ushered them out of the video room. "Have a seat at the bar and I'll bring the video and photos over as soon as the tech is done making copies."

They walked down a series of corridors in the casino's employees section, finally coming to a door that led to the gaming floor. They returned to the bar and sat back down at their original seats. The casino was gradually getting busier, so they had to wait a few minutes to place their orders with the waitress.

"What do you think?" Dufresne asked after she returned with a pair of scotches.

"I think we've just found a lead, but I'm not sure where it's heading," Tiberius conceded tiredly. "I'm willing to bet that the information passed to our guy was the order to hit Zeidt. The question is, who ordered it and why?"

They both thought silently as they drank their drinks. Tiberius was still not convinced that Zeidt's death wasn't linked to the Manor, even though the possibility seemed to be growing. The silence was broken as the head of security approached their table.

"I've got everything you asked for," he said, placing an envelope on the table.

"How about something we didn't ask for," Tiberius challenged perceptively, but without an overt threat. "Have a seat."

"I don't understand."

"I think you do," Tiberius began, waving the waitress over for another round of drinks. "I think that you recognized the man in the glasses and you're concerned by his presence here. But I also think that you wouldn't have told us about him."

The waitress returned and passed out their drinks, placing the new ones on paper napkins before departing.

The whole time the head of security sat facing the gambling crowd, looking at neither man directly.

"I thought as much," Tiberius accepted quietly, recognizing the concern in the man once more. "Who is he?"

"I can't tell you who he is," he replied simply before swallowing his whole drink and leaving them.

"Should we push him for answers?" Dufresne asked as he watched the head of security walk over to one of the floor managers.

"We don't need to," Tiberius replied slightly impressed. Despite sitting at the table with the man, Tiberius almost missed him place a note in his napkin. As smoothly as he could, he picked up the napkin and glanced in it briefly before passing it across the table. "Things just got more complicated."

Dufresne looked at the small paper square and nodded. In neat block letters the word STASI was printed out in blue ink. Apparently their new suspect was an officer in the East German secret police.

Chapter 15

Pierce screeched to a halt at the red light, the HEMI engine of his gleaming black 1969 Dodge Charger rumbling like thunder. He looked to his right as Sean pulled up beside him slightly less violently in an equally magnificent black 1967 Pontiac GTO hardtop.

After paying Joey for his impressive work, both had eagerly grabbed the keys and peeled out of the garage lot, tearing down the road as fast as safety allowed. They were retracing their way back to the diner across from the church where the others were waiting, but ended up taking a few detours to prolong the short journey.

Despite the glorious sound of eight cylinders firing in beautiful harmony, Pierce decided to try the radio. Scrolling across the dial he finally found the recognizable sounds of Led Zeppelin amid the static. Turning it up, he couldn't contain his joy as the music seemed to meld perfectly with the rumble under the hood.

The sound of another revving engine made Pierce look to Sean beside him, where the GTO was twitching with anticipation for the green light. Smiling, Pierce decided that he hadn't bought this car to poke around town in. So he also began revving his engine, concentrating completely on the light above. Like a starter's gun, the green light triggered a thunderous noise as both muscle cars shot off down the road. They screamed down the street eliciting looks from the few pedestrians on the sidewalks.

They were finally forced to slow down as they approached traffic ahead, Sean reluctantly pulling in behind Pierce in order to take the next left. They maintained a more orderly speed as they approached the diner, pulling up a block before it. Sean got out of his car after they stopped and fetched the others from within the diner.

"What the hell?!" shouted Liam as he lugged two duffle bags towards the cars. "Lord Pierce, you are a genius!"

"Aye lad," MacDuff nodded with an equal amount of admiration. "This is much better than the bloody Greyhound."

"They're just a of couple cars," challenged Kat as the men inspected every inch of them. "What's the big deal?"

"These are two of the giants in car history," Pierce explained enthusiastically. "I've dreamed of owning them ever since I knew about cars. I mean, they're classics. Well not right now they aren't, but they will be."

"You really think we'll be believable as cops in these cars," Liam pointed out as he slammed the trunk shut after depositing the bags.

"Well they haven't built any red Ford Torino's with a white stripe down the side yet, so they'll have to do," Pierce chuckled, referencing Starsky's ridiculous cop car from the late 1970' tv show.

"Fair point," Liam accepted graciously. "I'm just glad you refrained from painting the Charger orange with a confederate flag on the top."

"Ha, ha," Pierce laughed hollowly. "Alright let's get on the road. MacDuff and Kat, you're with me in the Charger. Liam, you and Sean are in the GTO."

"Shotgun!" Liam shouted as he ran towards the GTO.

"Idiot," Sean muttered as he shook his head and opened the driver's side door.

The two cars snaked their way through the streets of San Diego, eventually turning on to Route 101 and heading north. Route 101 was one of the oldest roadways in the West, running along the Pacific Coast from San Diego all the way up to Seattle in Washington State. The day remained cloudy as they drove the scenic route that followed the Pacific Ocean. The wind was still very strong, creating impressive white capped waves on the water to their left. The traffic was fairly light, with the roads sparsely filled with local traffic. Most drivers heading north to Los Angeles used the interstate that ran up California's interior. So both drivers kept their lead feet firmly on the gas pedals, tearing along the blacktop in the straights and screeching around the many corners.

"Duffy this here's the Foolish Fenian, you got your ears on, com' on back," crackeled the CB radio in the Charger as they slowed through a small seaside town. Pierce grinned as MacDuff shook his head and stared at the radio.

"Here I thought we'd get a break," he observed, finally grabbing the mic and then speaking into it. "Go for Duffy."

"Hey there Duffy good buddy," Liam responded, his amusement seeping through the speaker. "Me and

Tripwire are starting to feel the grumbles and wondered when we'd stop. How are you doin' up there with Swordsman and Miss Scarlet? Over."

"Happy as clams Fenian, I think we're going to keep the hammer down until we get to Angel City," MacDuff replied with a faint smile, deciding to indulge his inner trucker.

"Ten-four on that Duffy, we'll be hugging your bumper as we boogie down the road. Fenian out."

"What was that all about?" Kat asked from the back seat.

"Just Liam being himself," MacDuff explained with a shake of the head. Despite usually acting exasperated by Liam's antics, he knew that most of it was an act and he realized the benefit of having a jokester around. Missions beyond the portals could become stressful, bordering on the traumatic, and having someone around to help lighten the mood kept everyone calm and focused.

"I thought he was joking when he said one of his favourite movies was *Smokey and the Bandit*," Pierce laughed as he stepped on the gas, the Charger leaving the small town in its wake.

The modifications that Joey's crew made to both cars made them specimens of engineering and a thrill to drive. The new suspensions and wide wheels made the big cars take the winding curves of the Pacific Highway like race cars as they weaved along the coast. When the few straight sections appeared the drivers were able to let their modified engines run loose, like thoroughbreds being let out of the gates at the Kentucky Derby.

Pierce was glad he'd also had Joey install performance brakes and steering in the cars, otherwise they probably would have ended up in the ocean a few times. The longer he drove the car, the more comfortable he became taking it to the very edge of safety.

By evening the small convoy reached the hip beach cities that make up the southern edge of Los Angeles. The traffic increased and the drivers had to be watchful for pedestrians as they drove along the busy streets, forced to slow down to the relief of their passengers.

"Tripwire this is Swordsman, over," Pierce called into the CB mic as they reached a set of lights and stopped.

"Go ahead Swordsman," Sean replied in the car behind him.

"I think we'll take a pass on going home and go straight to Leon's place, but I don't know its twenty."

"No problem Swordsman, step aside and I'll show you the way."

"10-4 Tripwire, out," Pierce slid the mic back into its position, struggling to contain his enjoyment of the situation. Here he was driving around in the 1970's in a 1969 Charger, talking on a CB like Burt Reynolds. It didn't get much better than this.

"Fun isn't it?" MacDuff asked, watching Pierce intently.

"It kind of is," Pierce acknowldeged.

"Just remember why we're here lad."

"Don't worry, I know," Pierce replied turning serious as he watched Sean pass him on the left. "I'm just as eager to track down that Russian bastard as I was to drive this beast."

Pierce followed the GTO through the palm lined streets of Southern Los Angeles, the street lights offering the only upbeat colour to the dodgy part of the city. High walls and barbed wire dominated the local shops and warehouses they passed.

A loud roar above made everyone crane their necks to look up through the front windshield, eventually spotting a Boeing passenger plane rising steeply above them. They were stopped at another red light and the road they were on passed directly underneath the flight line for LAX. They could see a runway directly to their left and Kat cringed as another plane took off, heading directly for them. She shut her eyes as it approached, only able to crack them open when she heard the plane lift off above them.

They didn't drive too far from the airport after the light turned green, taking the next right. The road was like many they'd passed, filled with rough looking shops and warehouses. Pierce recognized Leon's beige sedan as they slowed down in front of a dark building inside a chain linked fence. It was only two stories tall, with a few small windows by a steel door. A larger garage door was further down the front of the building, with only a faded sign above it to add character.

Liam jumped out of the GTO and unlocked the front gate and then ran to the building. He disappeared for a few seconds before the garage door opened up, a faint amount of light peeking into the lot beyond. Pierce followed Sean into the warehouse, pulling up beside him once they were fully inside.

Liam flicked some switches after the garage door squealed shut, lighting the space with harsh white fluorescent bulbs. The smell of the cars exhaust's mingled with that of oil and charcoal. There was also the faint smell of something metallic that nobody could really place until Sean yelled out.

"Sir! You've got to see this."

He was the only one beside the cars along the north end of the warehouse, where industrial metal shelving lined the walls. The shelving was underneath a steel mezzanine that overlooked the warehouse floor. But as they approached, everyone realized that it wasn't shelving, they were metal cages.

"What the fuck?!" Pierce swore as he looked over the barbaric scene. There were three metal cages lined up along the walls, each one six feet square and eight feet tall reaching the grated floor of the mezzanine above. Chains and straps lined the cage walls and ceilings, with blood spattered on the concrete walls like some kind of monstrous surrealist painting.

"So that's why it stinks like iron in here," MacDuff confirmed, his face as hard as granite.

"I also found the source of the charcoal smell," Liam offered with no hint of his usual demeanour. "The bastard was branding them."

He pointed towards a small steel garbage can in the corner by one of the windows. Lined up beside it were a collection of wrought iron pokers. With growing anger they all spread out and took stock of the warehouse, observing the full extent of the sick man they'd already captured. There were stained torture devices of an industrial nature within the warehouse; chains, pliers, blowtorches, and the like.

Pierce could feel the evil that had been committed within the seemingly benign building and had to work hard to control himself. His first reaction was that Tiberius should have tortured and executed the fucker in the Manor cells. Made to feel what he had made countless others feel in these steel cells. But he immediately regretted these thoughts, ashamed that he could want such harm done on another human being, no matter how detestable they were.

His whole reason for remaining at the Manor had been to make sure that good conscientious people like those surrounding him had control of the power that resided within it. Despite the years employed at the Manor, he knew his men were genuinely decent and never relished inflicting pain on others. That was not say they had never done it, for their hands were just as bloody as the rest. Pierce knew that he himself was included in the same category, having killed or maimed five men since arriving at the Manor. But like his comrades, he hadn't enjoyed any of it and resorted to violence as a last option.

Unwilling to remain in the nightmarish warehouse, they all retreated into the office space that made up the other half of the building. Leon had converted it into a makeshift apartment, with a kitchenette and table at the far end near the washroom. The tile floor was scuffed and worn but seemed fairly clean, which also went for the neutral beige walls. All the furniture had the unmistakeable look of coming from a second hand store, but seemed to be clean and sturdy.

"I'm going to go grab some food," Liam offered eager to leave the building and just as eager to drive one of the muscle cars. "We passed a burger joint a few blocks back, is everyone good with that?"

Everyone nodded with mixed enthusiasm as he caught the keys to the GTO Sean threw to him.

"Wait, I'll go with you," Kat spoke up, bounding towards the door to the warehouse.

"Sean, go open the gate for them and check Leon's car for the matchbook while you're at it," Pierce instructed, stopping the other two from leaving. "Have a look around before signalling them to leave. We want to make sure Leon's contact doesn't spot us or think anything's wrong."

Sean nodded and then snuck out the back door into the dark alley while Liam and Kat got in the GTO. Within a few seconds he whistled the all clear and MacDuff opened the garage door, watching the GTO leave with a slight cringe.

"I know," Pierce acknowledge the silent rebuke. "It's not exactly the most conspicuous of cars."

"It lacks a certain stealth," MacDuff agreed, closing the garage door after Sean stepped through it.

"No Matchbook," Sean reported back inside the office. "I told Liam to park down the street when he comes back. That way we can watch out for whoever puts it in the car and then immediately follow them."

"Good thinking." Pierce stood behind one of the kitchen chairs, gripping the back until his knuckles turned white. "We're going to track down every single person that's involved with this sick scheme and make sure they pay for it. I don't know how we'll do it, but this won't go unpunished."

While they waited for the other two to come back, Sean pulled out some binoculars and other observation equipment and handed it out to set up surveillance on Leon's car on the street. Leon said he didn't know how long it took for the messenger to drop off the matchbook. Pierce had been sceptical about this statement, but now realized Leon had been too occupied with diversions that made his skin crawl and wouldn't have been watching for the messenger.

*

"Here's the next batch of files you wanted," Logan announced as he walked up the stairs into the Secretary of the Hunt's office. The circular iron staircase ascended from a group of offices below that were occupied by the Secretary's staff.

"Thanks," Jane murmured as she flipped a page in an opened file. The desk she was sitting at was a large masculine piece of furniture that the last occupant of the office used to compensate for his shortcomings. The entire office had yet to be redecorated and Jane felt that the entire room oozed with failed attempts to project power. Statues of naked women were in the corners and weapons adorned the walls, things Jane was sure Drummond had had no idea how to use properly.

"I still can't get over this place," Logan observed as he turned and looked out the large windows that made up one of the walls. The windows provided a spectacular view of the North Tower, the entrance to the Raven's Vale, and an imposing mountain range beyond. "I'm not going to lie, but I thought you were messing with me when we went through that door back in Copenhagen."

"You handled yourself fairly well," Jane smiled in recollection of the wide eyed soldier who stumbled after looking out the windows of the North Tower.

"I was pretty sure I'd been drugged when we walked across that bridge and I saw those mountains instead of a city."

"Well that's because you were drugged," Jane offered sweetly before turning back to her work.

"What?!"

"It was just a mild sedative to help you adjust to the change," she replied while scribbling a note on a sheet of paper, not bothering to look up. "Don't be a baby."

"Whatever," Logan grumbled as he took a seat across the table from her. "So what are we looking for?"

"These are the files of all the Hunt Members who are still at the Manor," Jane pointed towards the piles on her side of the table. "The files that you brought up belong to their staff; valets, maids, Hounds, and so forth. Everything that Lord Lodge, Cleaver, and Drummond compiled is in them. We need to filter through the files and look for possible clues that could lead us to the wizard."

Before leaving for Luxembourg a second time, Tiberius called Jane into his room and gave her this research assignment. Unwilling to discount the possibility of a mole, he wanted her to gather some preliminary information on possible suspects. He also didn't want word to spread of a possible mole in the Manor, so he told her to pick a code word.

Jane realized that this could be another significant step for her. Right now Tiberius wasn't really convinced of a mole and had no real evidence to support the claim. So Jane wasn't on the hook to produce anything significant. But if she could dig something up, then her value would become more apparent. She also realized that by conducting the background research, she would set the foundation for future investigations. From what she noted and presented, she could lead those with power either towards or away from potential suspects.

"So I'm looking for clues and anything suspicious in the files?" Logan asked with a hint of sarcasm.

"Yes, anything out of the ordinary," Jane confirmed with a nod.

"Do you realize how ridiculous that sounds to me?" Logan laughed as he picked up three folders. "This guy's a Viking, this one's a Greek priestess, and this last guy fought at the Battle of Borodino! There's nothing ordinary about any of this."

"I suppose I've become accustomed to the peculiar nature of the Manor," Jane allowed. "I agree that you fill find a motley collection of individuals in those files and their presence together in one place seemingly impossible."

"Just a bit."

"In time it will become normal for you as well," Jane continued, feeling slightly strange giving a lecture. "Forget about who they were and what they did. I doubt it will have any impact. Instead go to the most recent parts of the files, that's where we'll find our clues."

"You really think there's a mo… sorry, wizard here?" Logan inquired, catching himself in time.

"Tiberius is sceptical about the idea," Jane answered thoughtfully, remembering his demeanour as he'd related the incident in Luxembourg. "The timing of Zeidt's demise seems to be a coincidence. However when it comes to Dr. Cleaver, I'm fully prepared to believe that he could have left a high placed wizard behind."

"What is he, some kind of criminal mastermind?"

"Yes."

"Oh," Logan lamely conceded as he turned to look at the stack of files. Research wasn't really his thing, he'd much rather be given a target and told to capture it. But a part of him realized that he'd not only been given a new life, but the chance to make a new self. Apparently he'd have the time to learn all of the things he wanted to learn and the opportunity to grow beyond the weapon toting soldier he'd always been.

When he first walked the halls of Ravenwood Manor he'd been intimidated by it, not a common feeling for a battle hardened Army Ranger. The sheer size and wealth of the building was astounding and made him question his presence there. But then he was brought to the Hall of Hounds and presented with a familiar scene. He walked in to the smoke filled riot of drinkers, gamblers, and fighters with a sense of homecoming. It was just like any off base bar he'd been to, except better in every way. So if the rest of them were able to thrive in this place, he thought, so can I.

They ploughed through the files, the scratching of pencils on notepads the only thing breaking the silence. A steward brought up some coffee and sandwiches at some point, which the pair absently consumed as they read through the volumes of notes. The office slowly turned dark around them as the sun set, leaving only their two desk lamps to light the space.

"What time is it?" Logan finally asked as his eyes tried to focus on the large grandfather clock in the corner. He stretched in place, sore from being hunched over a desk all day, another feeling he wasn't used to.

"Close to ten I think," Jane yawned then stretched herself. Apart from also feeling stiff she was hungry. The sight of the dried sandwiches and the cold coffee made her flinch, so she suggested they walk down to the staff dining room. Logan eagerly agreed as his stomach began to grumble.

They tidied up their work spaces and closed the files they were reviewing, marking where they left off. Jane then locked their notes in her desk, leaving once she was satisfied that if anyone snooped into the room they wouldn't discover what she and Logan were working on.

The staff spaces within the lower levels of the Manor were fairly quiet this time of night, with the odd person finishing some last minute chores or duties in preparation of the next day. Thankfully the staff dining room was equally devoid of activity apart from a pair of footmen playing cards in one corner and three of the housemaids enjoying a final cup of tea by the door.

"Can I get you something ma'am," inquired one of the young kitchen staff who had seen Jane and Logan enter. The Secretary of the Hunt was considered one of the four top staff positions, along with the Butler, the Kitchen Manager and the Estate Manager. The four ran all aspects of Ravenwood and were treated with deference by the staff and professional respect by the Hunt members.

"We'll have some wine and whatever is warm," Jane ordered, not the slightest bit embarrassed at being waited on. She truly enjoyed the perks of her new position, though she promised herself not to become a petty tyrant like Drummond.

Within seconds the young woman returned with a large tray filled with bowls of rustic chicken stew, fresh bread with butter, and bottles of wine. She served it all out and left after Jane surveyed it with appreciative delight.

"So what did you discover?" Jane asked after taking a few quick spoonfuls of the hearty and delicious stew.

"Honestly? I have no idea," Logan conceded as he poured them some wine. "There are references to all kinds of places and names I don't really understand. Some of it seems like it's written in code."

"I found the same thing," Jane agreed, turning quiet as the two footmen got up and left the room. They both nodded respectfully to her as they passed and Jane continued after they left. "I was worried that the files would be almost empty. But it's just the opposite; Drummond has the files overflowing with information. Most of it rambling garbage."

"What did you expect?" Logan shrugged as he finished his bowl of stew. "It's not like he was going to write: *Met with Lord Cleaver and Lord X today in my office and decided that Lord X would stay and be Cleaver's mole.*"

"Wait, you just gave me an idea," Jane exclaimed brightly as a thought popped into her mind. "Maybe we're going about this all wrong."

"What do you mean?"

"We keep looking for clues as to who could be a wizard, based on Drummond's notes and Lord Lodges background info," Jane began, slowly outlining her idea. "Instead we should be looking at who we already know to be in league with Cleaver. We review their files and then track their movements."

"But that won't tell use who the wizard is," Logan countered, feeling slightly foolish repeating the codeword.

"Not directly, but it will provide us the where."

"Where?"

"Yes, where," Jane repeated excitedly. "To organize the mass exodus, Cleaver would have had to meet with those involved. Organized means face to face meetings because Cleaver would never trust written notes, since they leave a paper trail of evidence. So he had to meet with conspirators somewhere."

"But that could be anywhere, this building is huge," Logan observed, himself having only seen a portion of it.

"Cleaver always conducted his private business away from the Manor," Jane explained. "He said there were too many eyes and ears in this place. So we have to go through the files of the traitors and track their movements based on the notes. We then cross reference that with our list of suspects and see who was present at the same time."

"That's ingenious!" Logan exclaimed, following the logic of the plan. He raised his wine glass and joined Jane in a toast. "To finding the wizard."

"It's still going to take a long time," Jane conceded sensibly after they drank their wine. "And there's no guarantee it will actually work. Chances are that he met them all separately, so we'll never be able to discover a group meeting. But at least it's a start."

"It's not just a start, it's a trail," Logan smiled happily linking his previous skills with his new life. "If there's a trail, then there's something further ahead to hunt."

Chapter 16

A life spent amid the rotting corpses of battle made Tiberius almost immune to the sights and smells of the morgue. There were three covered bodies in the dimly lit tiled basement, all in various states of examination. The strong scent of industrial cleaner mixed with that of the bodies themselves created a stink that all rookie police officers dreaded.

Tiberius, Dufresne, and Sergeant Lafleur were all old hands and regarded the bodies with impassive professionalism. However the same could not be said for Lafleur's boss. Upon discovering that Interpol was involved with the hit and run case, the young Inspector had decided to join them for the coroner's findings. His immaculate tailored suit matched his carefully combed hair, creating the impression of a man intent on rising high by appearance as much as skill.

However his rise through the police had apparently not included many trips to the morgue. He kept fidgeting with his hands and shooting awkward glances at the sheet covered forms on the examination tables. He stopped momentarily when the coroner walked into the room with his assistant in tow.

"If I knew there would have been such a turnout I would have charged admission," the coroner joked as he handed his notes to his assistant and moved to the middle table.

"This is Inspector Tiber and Inspector Dufresne from Interpol," Sgt. Lafleur offered the introductions as the coroner removed the sheet from the body.

"Gentlemen," the coroner nodded, immediately noting the experienced look in their eyes. He usually enjoyed making cops squirm from the sight of dead bodies, but he realized these two weren't affected.

"And this is Inspector Midoux," Lafleur continued, gesturing to his boss. "You may have met before."

"You don't look familiar," the coroner said, looking thoughtfully before shooting a quick smile. "Ah yes, Midoux. The washroom is still in the same place if you need it."

Midoux immediately reacted with a flushed face displaying his anger and embarrassment at being mocked in front of his subordinate and the two impressive Interpol officers.

"What can you tell us George?" Lafleur asked the coroner, enjoying seeing the Inspector's discomfort but needing answers more.

"It's as I initially suspected, cause of death was due to blunt force trauma to the skull," he reported pointing to the deceased. The area of impact was very clear to everyone surrounding the table. "There were also some broken bones along his right side, all corresponding with being broadsided by a moving vehicle. Even if he had been wearing a helmet, he probably would have succumbed to internal bleeding before reaching an operating table."

"Well that seems very straight forward," Lafleur agreed, having had little doubt as to the cause of death after seeing the scene of the accident firsthand. Despite the presence of the Interpol officers at the scene, this case would be wrapped up fairly quickly.

"Indeed, which is more than I can say for his neighbour," the coroner admitted wearily.

"His neighbour?" Tiberius asked, speaking for the first time. He could tell the coroner wanted to talk about another case and he hoped it was about the other dead body they'd encountered in Luxembourg.

"Yes, this gentleman here," he said pointing to the stainless steel table behind him. He motioned to his assistant who promptly removed the sheet of the second body. "He apparently dropped dead outside of a café blocks from our accident victim. In fact they died minutes apart."

"You don't know the cause of death yet?" Tiberius asked with what he hoped was mild curiosity. He looked down and recognized the face of Josef Zeidt immediately.

"Nothing definite. If I had to bet I would say he'd been poisoned, but the lab hasn't been able to provide me with a substance yet," the coroner explained looking over the body. "I can't dispel the idea of a heart attack or natural causes, but he seemed to be in exceptional health."

"Wait a second sir," Dufresne interrupted, approaching the table from the back wall he'd been holding up. "That face looks familiar."

"What do you mean?" Inspector Midoux asked, happily looking at the man from Interpol rather than the body.

"I think you're right," Tiberius agreed after slowly studying Zeidt. "He could be the Banker."

"Who's the Banker?" Midoux asked.

"The photo on file is probably a few years old, but he looks the same," Dufresne concurred, ignoring Midoux's question.

"This changes everything." The look of concern on Tiberius' face was clear to everyone and they all stood silent for a few moments. "Who's in charge of the investigation on this victim?"

"I am," Midoux spoke up with similar concern. "What's this all about?"

"Not here," Tiberius uttered seriously before turning to the coroner. "Thank you Doctor for your assistance."

Turning away from the bodies and the questioning look on the coroner's face, Tiberius led the group out of the morgue. Unwilling to return to the police station, Tiberius hoped that a secluded café would provide the right amount of intrigue he wanted to convey. Sergeant Lafleur led them to such a spot after Tiberius asked if he knew of a quiet place for them to talk.

It was still early for the lunch crowd, so the four men had the small family run café to themselves as they sat down in a corner by the window. Despite the large window and the rows of lights dangling from the ceiling, it was dark and moody inside. Tiberius could imagine it as a place where literary snobs huddled together and listened to bad poetry. Without being prompted a waiter deposited four cups of coffee on the table and this time Tiberius scrutinized the server. He was not in the habit of making mistakes twice.

"Gentlemen, I have not been completely forthcoming with all that we know about the incidents that occurred two days ago," Tiberius began with both

Luxembourgish policemen hanging on his every word. "Due to security I could not divulge everything. I have since spoken with my superiors and they granted me the approval to dispense with what information I see fit. In light of what we just discovered in the morgue, the time has come to do just that.

"My men and I were tracking the man who was hit by the car after a tip that he was responsible for the killing of an Italian policeman. We believe he's a burgeoning contract killer, but we're unsure how many people he may have targeted. Sadly he evaded our surveillance for a few hours and when we finally found him it was under the car at the scene of the accident."

"That was bad luck," Midoux nodded soberly. "At least he got what was coming to him."

"Except that it wasn't because of luck that he was hit," Lafleur pointed out shrewdly. "It must have been on purpose."

"Indeed," Tiberius concurred, trying to not discourage Midoux completely. He'd need him later as a pliable ally. "I had my doubts about it being an accident at the scene, but now I'm convinced. The resurfacing of the Banker sealed it."

"So who is he?" Midoux repeated his question from the morgue.

"The Banker was one of the most effective operatives with the French DGSE working against the Soviets," Tiberius explained in hushed voice. "He received his name because of his talent with figures and money. He used these talents to disrupt countless Soviet operations throughout Western Europe by tracking down and sometimes removing their source of funds."

"He's a spy?" Midoux reacted with shock and excitement.

"He was a spy," Tiberius continued, trying to convey the seriousness of the situation. "He caused so much trouble for the KGB, GRU and every other East Bloc security service that his identity was hidden and he became only known as the Banker. He soon disappeared and went underground, leaving the service without a word. Some said he had been killed; other's that he'd been turned by the Soviets. But it was discovered that he'd taken a cut from all the funds his section had seized, presumably a large value."

"I wonder what he was doing here?" Lafleur offered the question to no one in particular.

"The consensus at Interpol was that he'd turned his skills towards less legal activities," Dufresne finally joined in. "But the man's a ghost, so there's no trace of his involvement in any crimes. That being said, the list of potential enemies could be very large."

"Which brings us back to our deceased contract killer," Tiberius said after looking out the window. "I have to apologise, but I lifted a note from his pocket at the scene."

The sergeant shot him a dark look but didn't say anything and the Inspector was too thrilled by the tale of espionage to care about the flaunting of police procedure.

"I figured it would be waved off as an auto accident and that any evidence on the victim wouldn't be looked into too deeply. However the disappearance of the driver led me to believe it was not a simple accident. When I spoke with Sgt. Lafleur and discovered he shared my doubts it was too late to bring him into my confidence, as I'd already taken the note." Tiberius was glad to see the dark look on Lafleur's face lighten as he delivered his explanation. "The note was in fact a receipt from the Casino for a few hundred Francs paid out by the cashier.

Dufresne and I went to the Casino last night with the victim's photo and tried to find anyone who knew the man or could identify him."

"What did you find out," Midoux asked eagerly. "Who is he?"

"We still don't have a name," Tiberius explained calmly. "But we do have a new lead. Casino security was able to provide us with their video surveillance from the night he'd been there. At the craps table he was slipped a note of some sort during a commotion. We believe that the note provided the assassin with his target. But the method that the note was passed was what made us suspicious, it had been meticulously planned and carried off. When we asked if anyone recognized the man who passed the note, we came up blank. That is until I pressed the head of security."

"Good idea," Lafleur commented with a nod. "That gangster knows just about every crook in the country."

"So what did he say, who is he?" Midoux asked expectantly.

"He was pretty shaken and wouldn't give us a name," Tiberius replied slowly, building the tension around the table. "Instead he left a note under his glass with a single word printed out on it. STASI."

The reveal was anticlimactic, with no one really reacting to the news. Tiberius couldn't tell if the policemen were either to stunned or too ignorant by the news. But eventually Lafleur let out a low whistle while looking extremely uncomfortable.

Midoux reacted little slower, but eventually a small smirk broke out across his face despite trying to look serious. Tiberius was sure the young ambitious policeman was thinking of the rewards that would come his way if he could play a part in resolving this intrigue while assisting Interpol.

"Gentlemen, right now we're stuck with more questions than answers," Tiberius announced as he raised his hand and began counting on his fingers. "First, is the man from the casino actually a member of the Stasi? Second, did he get our assassin to kill the Banker? If so, for what purpose? Fourth, who killed the assassin and why?

"At this stage I think it would be better that we tackle these questions in manner that Napoleon would accept, divide and conquer. I suggest that Dufresne and myself look into this Stasi character and discover his identity and motives. With no offence meant towards the Luxembourg Gendarmerie, I doubt you have the resources for intricate counter espionage work."

Tiberius was rewarded with grudging acceptance from both policemen. Although proud of their abilities, both were also aware of their limitations and wanted to stick with more routine police work.

"We'll go back to the car accident and try and track down the driver," Midoux offered confidently. He needed to show these men that he could be useful. "Anything you need from us, don't hesitate to ask. I'll have one the clerks at the station ready in case you need any files or documents tracked down."

"That's very kind of you," Tiberius allowed happily. "Have her get the files of all the diplomats from the East German Embassy for me. We might get lucky and he might be covered as one of them."

With a preliminary plan of attack agreed upon, Lafleur and Midoux returned to the police station to continue work on tracking down the driver of the car.

Tiberius and Dufresne meanwhile ordered some lunch with some more coffee and eased back into their chairs.

"That went better than I thought," Dufresne admitted as the fresh coffee was set down in front of them and the other cups collected. "They didn't even seem phased when you told them you'd looted their crime scene."

"I can't blame them," Tiberius shrugged as he took a sip of coffee. "Every cop secretly wants to play cloak and dagger games. What do you think the chances are of the guy from the casino actually being a member of the Stasi?"

"You mean the head of security was playing us the same we played them with Zeidt?"

"Exactly. Like I said cops love to track down spies," Tiberius agreed. "What better way to get rid of us than to make our suspect an East German spy? But somehow I think he was telling us the truth. He was scared and realized he was in over his head."

They stopped talking when the waiter brought out their lunch, soup and ham sandwiches that looked deliciously fresh. The café began to fill up and they ate in silence, enjoying the people watching through the window.

"I wonder how Morgan is getting on," Dufresne mused contently after the waiter removed their empty dishes.

"He's probably found us a new lead," Tiberius hoped after throwing some bills on the table. "If he hasn't been arrested or shot."

*

"This sandwich was good, but I could really go for a stack of pancakes," Pierce confided as he scrunched up the paper his BLT had been wrapped in. They were parked in a dusty lot across for a small diner that appeared to be doing a good days business despite it's less than appealing exterior.

Not long after midnight in the early hours of the morning, Pierce and his group had observed a man in work clothes casually walk over to Leon's car and briefly open the door. Within seconds he continued walking down the street as if he'd never stopped and placed a cryptic message within the beige sedan. When he reached the end of the block he jumped into a car waiting at the corner.

Sean and Liam watched the exchange in the GTO across the street, ready to follow whoever made the drop. Ready for action they pulled out and followed their new target at a safe distance when it started driving away. As they trailed this new blue sedan through the empty streets of South L.A. MacDuff radioed them on the CB, saying that the guy had indeed left the matchbook. He then gave them the location of the meet and wished them good luck.

The address on the matchbook led the other three to small diner outside of Bakersfield, where they parked Leon's car in the parking lot. Pierce realized that they couldn't do anything to alarm the man they were waiting for, so Kat agreed to go back in the trunk in case he searched it first.

The sun was just starting to rise, but Pierce could tell it was going to be clearer and warmer than the day before. The land beyond the empty intersection was as close to the desert as he had ever been. Small trees dotted an otherwise dusty brown expanse of land, with mountains just visible in the distance. The coastal winds they'd experienced the day before had disappeared as they passed into the California interior and Pierce knew he'd miss them as he rolled down his window.

"I'm glad you remembered to toss in a few water bottles for her," Pierce observed as he drank some coffee from a Styrofoam cup.

"I'm just glad that bastard Leon was decent enough to put some ventilation holes in the trunk," MacDuff grimaced in reply. "Even so, it's going to get mighty uncomfortable in there for her."

"She's a trooper."

MacDuff nodded in agreement and then grabbed Pierce's arm, directing him to the diner parking lot. A beige sedan the twin of Leon's pulled in and stopped right beside it. While MacDuff watched their target casually get out and head to the diner, Pierce busily snapped photos through a telephoto lens.

"He looks like a goon," Pierce said after lowering the camera to his lap. MacDuff was silent as he continued his vigil on the car and the diner. Pierce meanwhile turned his attention to their surroundings, making sure they weren't being spied on.

But nothing happened along the quiet stretch of road until MacDuff once more grabbed his arm twenty minutes later. The messenger exited the diner and lit a cigarette in the parking lot. Pierce thought he was either very confident or very ignorant, as he approached Leon's car without even shooting a glance around the area. He calmly opened the door and slid behind the wheel, crouching down momentarily to pick up the keys MacDuff had left on the floor mat.

Pierce started the Charger and pulled out after their target was well down the road heading north. There were no other cars on the road, so Pierce had to stay almost a kilometer behind him in order to avoid arousing suspicion. They didn't know how well trained Grigori's agents were, so they had to assume they'd be able to pick out a tail on an empty stretch of road. But following the beige sedan proved easy even at the extreme distance. The road they travelled on was boringly straight and empty, with the odd side road branching off every few kilometers.

A repetitive scene of sand, shrubs, and sky followed the Dodge Charger as it rumbled along the empty blacktop. Road signs and mile markers provided welcome signs of life to an otherwise vacant landscape. As they drove north an increase in vegetation altered the desert-like atmosphere but did nothing to change the monotony. Patchworks of green fields and orchards flew past them, offering only a new colour to ignore.

"So what was William Wallace like?" Pierce asked, breaking the silence an hour into their long drive. "My dad's last name was originally Wallace before he changed it, so we might be distantly related."

"Wallace? He was a soldier of his time," MacDuff answered enigmatically.

"Which means?"

"He liked to fight, brawl, drink, whore, and generally cause mischief," MacDuff explained as he watched the car ahead through his binoculars. "I was probably no more than 16 or 17 when I first saw him. I was in a large group of pikemen at the battle of Falkirk and he rode past us before the fighting started. He was rumoured to be a giant, but he was no bigger than me."

"You were at Falkirk?" Pierce questioned, realising how little he knew of his men's pasts.

"Aye, a bloody day it was too," MacDuff answered solemnly, lowering the binoculars but staring straight ahead. "There we were, a bunch of Scottish hooligans armed with long pointy sticks facing the English Army. We braced ourselves for a cavalry charge, but it never came. Instead their Welsh bowman opened fire on us, raining down a hail of arrows. I was one of the lucky few with a shield strapped to my back, but most weren't and our ranks were decimated. The English then sent their troops in to mop up. I managed to escape by following a creek."

"Sounds like the movie."

"Ach, bloody Braveheart," MacDuff spat with contempt. "We didn't go running around in plaid blankets with blue painted faces. Plus the idea of him with the English Princess, it's laughable. The man was no saint and no military genius, I should know. After Falkirk I joined other survivors and met up with Wallace. He took thirty of us to France looking for help, money, women, booze, anything really."

"So…"

"We found as much as we could handle of the latter, but none of the former," MacDuff smiled in recollection. "Then after pissing off some members of the French court we returned home. We parted ways after reaching Scotland and a year later Wallace was captured, then tortured and executed.

"I still had the fire of revolt in my belly and sought out the next man that could help me feed it. I found him and then followed him for almost ten years, Robert the Bruce King of Scotland."

"That's right, you said you fought for him at the Battle of Bannockburn," Pierce recalled, now fully into the story.

"Aye, I did," MacDuff confirmed as he raised the binoculars once again. He remained silent, straining to see in the distance before quickly ordering Pierce to stop the car.

"What is it?!" Pierce asked breathlessly after their car skidded to a stop on the gravel shoulder.

"The target stopped his car and is..." MacDuff trailed off as he concentrated on the scene in the distance. "...and he's relieving himself on the side of the road."

"Classy."

"Wait a second," MacDuff whispered seriously. "He's going to the trunk and opening it."

"What's he doing?" Pierce demanded with concern as he shifted the car back into gear, ready to close the distance in an instant. "Can you see if Kat's ok?"

"She's fine. He's got a pistol out, but I don't think he's going to do anything. Oh," MucDuff then dropped the binoculars down with a hint of embarrassment. "It appears that she also had to relieve herself."

"Well that doesn't surprise me," Pierce allowed after a few calming breaths. "She's probably put a big dent in the water we packed for her and she's not one to stand on ceremony. It's probably not the first time she's had to squat behind a bush."

"Hmph."

"Fine you want to talk about something else?" Pierce asked seeing MacDuff uncomfortable with the current topic. "So what was the Bruce like?"

"The Bruce was a man who grabbed history by the throat," MacDuff replied reverently. "As I said I followed him for almost ten years and the entire time he was focused on one thing, becoming the King of an independent Scotland. Even after a series of defeats at the hands of both English and Scottish enemies, he refused to give up. But he was also a great military mind who learned from his mistakes and successes."

"But I though he only fought that one battle at Bannockburn," Pierce challenged as he pulled back onto the road after seeing their target continue driving with Kat now sitting in the front.

"And you call yourself Scottish," MacDuff swore with a shake of his head. "That was merely the culmination of years of fighting and hardship. The Bruce was a nobleman raised in the art of feudal warfare, which meant that two armies faced each other, exchanged pleasantries and then fought until one side retired. The nobles would be on horseback and let the skirmishers fight it out until they became tired and then charged into the fray and cleaned things up. Either that or they would charge down some poor collection of archers with no armour.

"But that kind of fighting doesn't work in the highlands and it sure as hell doesn't work against a bigger and better armed enemy. So the Bruce devised new tactics and stopped thinking of himself as a knight. We turned to guerrilla warfare, strategically jumping from castle to castle and town to town eliminating and harrying our enemies. With each encounter our tactics improved and our strength increased. A lesson I'll remember for the rest of my life."

With that he fell silent and Pierce took the cue and silently concentrated on driving. He'd been so engrossed in MacDuff's story that he hadn't noticed how close they were to the mountains. In the distance he watched as their target took a left and headed directly towards the rolling peaks.

He followed and soon they were driving out of the San Joaquin Valley and into the mountains. The beige sedan was clearly not kept in great shape and didn't have half the horsepower of the Charger, so Pierce had to slow down considerably as they followed the road rising towards a pass in the mountain.

The winding road of the mountain pass provided a much more interesting drive, however it also created more of a challenge. With all the blind corners, there was a chance of either losing their target or getting too close. Neither man in the black muscle car took their eyes of the road as they followed; missing the majestic mountain scenes they were passing.

But by mid afternoon they were able to sit back in relief as they descended into the Salinas Valley. A lush verdant expanse filled the valley in front of them, with straight roads cutting through the endless fields. They renewed their acquaintance with their old friend Route 101 as they followed the beige sedan. An increase in traffic meant that they were able to get a little closer to their target without arousing too much suspicion, allowing them to see two distinct heads through the rear windshield.

"Where the hell is he taking her?" Pierce wondered aloud, feeling uncomfortable as the chase continued.

Chapter 17

Jane awoke to a warm sensation upon her face and she smiled as she opened her eyes to a sun filled morning. She loved her new room and continued to appreciate the perks of her new position. As the Secretary of the Hunt, she had to be accessible to the Hunt Members at all times. This meant that staying in her old room in the staff quarters was no longer possible. Although she'd spent many years in the small comfortable room below, she didn't miss it for a second. She'd had a wardrobe, a small desk, and a single bed wedged into the room with only a small window for natural light.

But now she had three rooms all to herself two corridors down from her office. However unlike her office, these rooms had not been handed down from Percival Drummond, which meant that they were actually nicely decorated. Silk floral prints covered the walls, complementing the faded white princess furniture perfectly. The bedroom was spacious and connected to an equally sized sitting room similarly decorated. She even had her own bathroom with a separate tub and shower!

Forcing herself out of bed, Jane knew that her new rooms came with responsibility and she couldn't lounge around all morning in the soft sheets and thick duvet. Slipping out of bed she padded to her bathroom and had a quick shower before preparing for the day.

Having spent her entire adult life as a maid at the Manor, Jane had little experience with make-up or other beauty products. It wasn't that the staff were discouraged from using them, they simply didn't have the time to apply them in the mornings. But now Jane could set her own timetable and used it to enhance her already beautiful features with all kinds of new products. Melrose had once again come to her rescue, offering her some discarded items collected from the various ladies maids at the Manor.

Finished at her vanity, she moved to her closet and began grabbing clothes for the day. She sorted through a few outfits before settling on a black leather skirt, a silk shirt and a dark but feminine blazer. Inspecting herself in the mirror she nodded appreciatively and headed towards the door.

Not being a fan of breakfast, she skipped the dining hall and went straight to her office. She and Logan were still trying to find links between the members who had fled the Manor and those who had remained. They had worked late into the night, desperate to make some progress. But they finally had to stop when their eyes could no longer focus on the documents in front of them, the letters fading into a jumbled mess.

Jane reached her office without passing anyone but the two men guarding the North Tower. It was still locked up and under guard despite no attempts to access the portals within. After nodding to the guards she opened the door to her office and was greeted by the sweet smell of coffee. Her assistant was standing with a coffee tray eagerly pouring her a cup, which she accepted gratefully.

"Will there be anything else ma'am?" he asked after taking a step back.

"Nothing this morning, Logan and I will once again be working alone and don't want any interruptions," she ordered. The assistant nodded dutifully and then turned for the stairs, good enough at his job to leave the coffee tray. Jane watched his progress to the spiral staircase in the corner and was suddenly shocked to see someone else was in her office.

A series of wooden tables had been set up along the windows and a man was hunched over them, poring over something of importance. Jane quickly recognized Logan when he straightened up, so she walked over to him with curiosity.

"What are you doing here so early?" She inquired after taking a sip of her coffee.

"I can't seem to sleep past the crack of dawn anymore," he shrugged in response. "Must be the Army training. Anyway, this problem kept bothering me and I decided to start working on it again."

"Well you've certainly been busy," Jane agreed looking at the line of tables. There were ten identical maps of the island laid out, with different coloured pins stuck in each of them. "What is all this?"

"I did what you said and started reviewing the files of everyone who had fled the Manor, looking for meeting places. But I couldn't keep it all straight in my head, there's just too much info. Even sorting the different reports into piles was no help, since it will take way too long to see any connections. Then I remembered the old sand tables we used in the Army. Lots of guys could never remember specific orders or coordinates printed out on paper. So instead the smarter officers would show everything on a map or a mock-up. I'm a visual guy so I decided to do the same."

"So what exactly am I looking at?" Jane asked as she looked over the maps with their multi-coloured pins strewn about in a seemingly random pattern.

"Ok, so each map consists of a specific month going back from the date they all left the Manor," Logan began explaining, pointing to labels he'd written out beneath each map. "I've flagged all the pins with the pack colour of each person, so the white pins for the white pack, gold pins for the gold pack, and so on."

"What do these numbers mean?" Jane picked up one of the pins and could see a small number 2 written on it.

"The numbers designate which member of the pack the pin represents," he answered. "It's been my experience that people always focus on the officer, but never look at the soldiers beneath him. But they're the ones actually running things and the ones who know what's going on. I bet it's the same thing here, so I'm tracking all the members of a pack. The flags with 1 on it represent the Hunt member, number 2 the pack whip, and so forth down the line."

"Good thinking," Jane approved, slightly surprised by Logan's ingenuity and perception. She'd been around the Manor long enough to know the truth of his statement. Some of the Hunt member would be completely lost without their packs.

"Thanks," Logan smiled with confidence. When they began this wide search he'd been tentative and slightly uninterested. The idea of sorting through documents in search of a possible mole was not his idea of an exciting challenge. He would have much rather been on the team sent to hunt down any mole that was discovered. But as they progressed through the files, Logan found himself intrigued by the problem and suddenly driven to find a lead. So much so that he'd devised the map system he and Jane were currently looking at. He was discovering that he enjoyed working out his mind as much as his body.

"So we go through the files and put a pin on the map anywhere someone is mentioned being?" Jane continued as she took a closer look at the pins already in place.

"Exactly. Hopefully we'll be able to see a pattern of where the traitors gathered. From there we go through the files of those people still here and see if they went to the same place. It's not exactly proof, but I have a feeling this place doesn't really have a courtroom."

"No, but we do have a judge, jury, and executioner," Jane observed firmly.

With renewed energy they both returned to the large desk and tackled the remaining files. The sound of shuffling paper and furious scribbling soon filled the office as their research followed a more directed path. Names, dates, and locations seemed to jump out at each of them as they scanned through the files.

They spent the entire morning passing each other in excited silence as they took their notes from the desk to the tables with the maps. Here they picked up handfuls of coloured pins and carefully placed them within the many maps that lined the tables. Once all of their pins were placed, they rushed back to the desk and began making notes from the next file. They continued at this steady pace even as the number of flags on the maps began to increase, neither of them wasting any time trying to decipher a pattern prematurely. They both knew that the maps had to be fully populated to be of any use to them.

Jane's assistant brought up a tray of sandwiches and some drinks for them after noon, receiving an automatic thank you for his trouble. After watching their rotation from the desk and the maps, he set the tray down in between, realizing it would probably be the only way either of them would notice it. Only after watching his theory proven did the assistant descend back towards the offices on the floor below.

The rays of the setting sun began to pierce through the office windows when Jane slammed the final file shut, shaking Logan from a brief daze. He had to squint past the light as he watched her walk over to the tables and begin placing the last set of pins on the maps. Like a cat he stood up and stretched, soaking up the warmth of the golden glow filling the space.

"Alright let's have a look at what we've got," Jane announced after placing the last pin. She began by trying to find any large groupings, but after inspecting all ten maps she realized that the largest number in any one place was never more than six. Plus those six never consisted of more than four packs.

"I'm not sure this is going to work, I can't see any pattern," Logan admitted after spending ten minutes poring over the maps. The pins seemed to spread along the maps in random, with neither the colours nor numbers on the pins offering any kind of clue. "You'd think that they would have met together more than this, even by chance if nothing else."

Jane barely heard Logan's comment; she was too focused on the task before here. She was trying to employ the skills Lord Lodge at taught her when approaching a problem.

"I think the absence of a pattern, is a pattern in itself," Jane finally uttered without looking up. She could feel an answer floating around in her mind as she looked at the maps, but it hadn't yet taken shape fully.

"What is that supposed to mean?" Logan asked, wondering if they were looking at the same thing. All he could see was a wasted day of tedious work.

"It looks as though someone went through extra pains to ensure none of the conspirators were ever together in the same place," Jane explained going from one map to the next. "I agree that many of them should have been in the same place by chance. But instead there's never more than a few together at any given time. That looks planned to me and reeks of Dr. Cleaver's attention to detail."

"Even if that's true, this was still a waste of time," Logan shook his head. He was disappointed that his idea hadn't produced the results they'd been looking at. Although the work had been tedious, he'd been surprised at how excited he'd been by the chase for clues. "Say we go through the files of potential wizards, jeez that sounds stupid. Can't we use the real name when we're alone?"

"No," Jane dismissed immediately. "Cleaver wasn't merely being paranoid in believing these walls have eyes and ears. Knowledge is power here and we can't afford to have anyone find out what we're doing. We keep using the word wizard."

"Fine," Logan deferred rolling his eyes. "Like I was saying, none of the conspirators were ever in the same place together. So even if we found a potential wizard that had visited one of these groups, it wouldn't prove anything. I bet it wouldn't even narrow the numbers down."

"Let's not give up on our little project just yet," Jane cautioned. She felt like they were getting closer to an answer and they just needed to keep looking. "What have we discovered so far?"

"The maps show that effort was put into concealing the meetings of the conspirators," Logan began, more comfortable summarising the problem than solving it. "So the group was never together in one place. Second…"

"Wait a second," Jane interrupted with a waved hand. She began pacing quickly back and forth along the map tables and a pattern was starting to slowly emerge. "You're wrong."

"What?! I'm not wrong," Logan countered, shooting a questioning look at his new boss. She looked like she was coming unglued with all the pacing and staring. "Are you looking at the same thing I am? None of the packs were together at the same time and at the same place."

"But that's not what you said," Jane smiled as she finally saw what she'd been looking for. The solution was suddenly crystal clear and she was almost mad at herself for not seeing it sooner. This must be how Lord Lodge feels, she thought seeing the look of confusion on Logan's face. Lord Lodge always seemed to be two steps ahead of anyone, quickly deducing solutions of seemingly impossible problems with ease.

"I think I know what I said."

"No, the first time you said that the group was never together in the same place," Jane replied quickly. "But that's not entirely accurate and you corrected it when you repeated yourself. They *were* all in the same place, just not at the same time."

"What?"

"Look," Jane pointed, running down to the first map. "There is a pattern if you look at this location. How many packs visited this spot?"

"Three," Logan answered, still unsure what Jane was getting at. He followed her to the next map.

"Same location the next month, how many packs this time?"

"Four this time, but none from the month before," he confirmed, slowly realizing the point.

"And the same place for the month after that?" Jane asked confidently, seeing the truth of the situation dawn on her helper.

"Three different packs again," Logan replied. "I assume that this same pattern continues on the rest of the maps?"

"Yes it does," Jane smiled in triumph. "When you look at that one location on all ten maps you will find that every pack that fled the Manor met Dr. Cleaver there. There are two other locations on the maps that are the same. There's no chance that this is a coincidence."

"Holy shit," Logan murmured in astonishment before returning Jane's smile. "It worked!"

"Good job, we make a pretty good team," Jane praised as she walked over to her desk and pulled out a black bottle with a raven etched on the front. "I think this calls for a little celebration."

"Sounds good to me," Logan agreed as he turned his attention to the three locations on the maps. "So what are these places anyway?"

"I don't really remember what the locations actually were," Jane confessed as she filled two tumblers. "I was concentrating on the pin groupings. What are the names?"

"The first is Harrow's End," Logan called out. "It's on the far east coast of the Island."

"Well that's actually a nice spot," Jane explained as she walked over and handed him a glass. They clinked them together and each took a well earned drink. "There's a large Greek style pavilion there and a really nice beach.

The Hunt members use it during the summer months when the weather is nicer. What's the second?"

"Umm, the Crows Nest," he confirmed after re-reading the strange name on the map.

"I'm very familiar with that place," Jane scowled remembering her last visit to the place. Along with Lord Lodge, she had been imprisoned there by Dr. Cleaver in his bid to take power. "It's basically a Viking stronghold perched on a mountain cliff."

"Sounds intense," Logan offered appreciatively. He wondered if actual Vikings had built the place and still lived there or if someone had simply used their architectural style. From what little he had learned about the island he wouldn't have been surprised either way.

"It is," Jane confirmed with a little apprehension. They'd have to visit all three locations in case there were any clues left behind, but she'd try and save the Crows Nest for last. Although she would take pleasure in returning to the place of her imprisonment in the capacity of her new position, she'd rather avoid it altogether. "What about the third location?"

"Right, it's south of here at the edged of the giant lake," Logan replied after looking back down at the map. "Loch Dhu Castle."

"Loch Dhu Castle," Jane repeated in a whisper. The prospect of going to the Crows Nest didn't seem so bad after hearing the last location.

*

"Did you come alone?" challenged a voice from within the darkened warehouse door. The derelict brick building sat along a quiet stretch of railroad track near the West German border. The distant sound of cars travelling on a nearby highway was the only sound filling the quiet night.

"As agreed, but I see you didn't," Morgan replied as he saw the red glow of a cigarette from a second floor window.

"Host's prerogative," countered the owner's voice as he walked out into the dimly lit yard. A single streetlight on the far side of the road provided the only source of light in the midnight gloom. "You a cop?"

"Of course I'm a cop," Morgan responded with tired sarcasm. "You?"

"Myself as well," chuckled the man before motioning for his compatriot to exit the warehouse. "Louis knows all the cops in the country."

"Sounds like a heavy dating schedule," Morgan observed. "How do you find the time for business?"

"Shut up asshole!" Louis exclaimed walking out of the warehouse, fumbling with a pistol in his waistband before pulling it out and pointing it at Morgan's face.

"We were also supposed to come unarmed," Morgan shook his head with disappointment, completely ignoring the threat. "Let me guess, host's prerogative."

"You catch on very quick," came the shrugged response. "Louis do you recognize him?"

"No, I've never seen him before."

"Good, so put the gun away," his boss ordered, staring at him until he complied. He then turned back to Morgan and offered a friendly smile as an apology. But there was no friendliness within the dark calculating eyes. "You can call my Guy. What is it you want, Mr.?"

"Really? We're going to do the name thing?" Morgan asked with cocky exasperation. "I was led to believe you were pros. But you're taking names and this guy has his gun so far down his pants that he'll blow his junk off the next time he coughs."

"I like you," Guy replied after a moment's pause. He pulled out a piece of gum and began methodically chewing it as he studied Morgan with interest. His business suit, overcoat, and polished shoes belied a dangerous and cunning criminal mind. "So Mr. X, what do you want?"

"I need a taxi," Morgan replied simply, pulling out a cigarette and lighting it with a silver zippo.

"So go to the train station," Guy offered with feigned disinterest.

"I need a taxi that's willing to cross international borders," Morgan reiterated. "And I need a driver that doesn't ask too many questions."

"The cargo?"

"The package is roughly four cubic feet."

"Destination?"

"Berlin."

"East or West?"

"East," Morgan answered calmly despite the momentary look of surprise on Guy's face. "Is that a problem?"

"Not at all," Guy chomped away. "It only means the cost goes up. I'm assuming you received my name as someone who gets things into East Germany. That is true, however Berlin is a slightly different story. There's more scrutiny there, more armed men on both sides, but much more danger on the Eastern side. For that reason I subcontract any work in East Berlin to one of my contacts. He's good, but he doesn't come cheap."

"Who is he?" Morgan asked.

"Now Mr. X, didn't you just criticize me for using names?" Guy rebuked playfully.

"I meant his background," Morgan clarified, although he was pretty sure Guy was just trying to get a rise out of him and watching his reaction. So he decided to keep playing it cool and not act out of character. "If I'm paying extra, I'd like to know what I'm paying for."

"I suppose that's fair," Guy conceded, deciding on how much to say. "He's a member of the East German Security Service who has branched out into other avenues. There are rumblings within the regime and many aren't sure how much longer the workers' paradise of the Eastern Bloc will last. So he's started setting up contacts and raising money for the time when the people tear down the wall and storm Stasi headquarters."

"Very smart," Morgan nodded as he flipped his cigarette in the air towards the empty road. "I appreciate a practical man. So how much will this delivery cost me?"

"You pay in dollars?"

"Of course."

"I think this will cost you fifty thousand, plus any extra bribes that are incurred," Guy replied after doing some mental arithmetic.

"I'll agree to the fifty thousand, but any bribes will have to come out of that amount," Morgan negotiated with practised ease. "How am I to know how much the bribe was? I doubt your contact will get a receipt for his bribe to substantiate the reimbursement."

"I suppose not," Guy laughed imagining the situation. "Fifty thousand firm is acceptable. Half now and half on delivery."

"Here you go," Morgan pulled out a thick envelope and held it out to Guy, who stood motionless for a few moments. Morgan knew his hesitation was probably due to the illegal transaction they were about to complete. Without any money changing hands, he still had plausible deniability and could argue his way out of any charges. But once the money was in hand it would be a different story. "What you don't trust me? The delivery instructions are printed inside the envelope, along with ways of contacting me if the need arises."

With his hands remaining in his jacket pockets, Guy nodded Louis towards Morgan to grab the envelope. Louis did his part and snatched the envelope from his hands, quickly retreating behind his boss as he opened the envelope.

"It's all here," he reported after doing a quick count. "Can I kill him now?"

"By all means," Guy smiled as he turned back towards the warehouse. "I'm sorry Mr. X, but I don't know you and twenty five grand for doing nothing is too good a deal to pass up. I have no intention of incurring the wrath of the Stasi by smuggling into East Berlin."

"What?!" Morgan exclaimed with mock confusion. He'd been prepared for a double cross and had a plan on how to deal with it. He knew Guy's type and was pretty sure he wouldn't attack him directly, that was what Louis was for. So he ignored Guy's departing form and lunged towards Louis without hesitating.

The gun was indeed wedged into Louis' pants very tightly and he once again had trouble pulling it out in time. The barrel hadn't even passed his belt when Morgan kicked his hand, creating a loud boom from Louis' crotch as the gun fired through his pants.

Louis immediately doubled over in pain as the fiery gunpowder singed his legs. Miraculously the bullet harmlessly shot through his pants and thudded into the ground. But he had no time to appreciate his luck before Morgan knocked him out with a heavy punch from above.

Then in one fluid motion Morgan spun around towards Guy, pulling a pistol hidden in the small of his back.

The initial action and gunshot had surprised Guy momentarily, but he reacted quickly pulling his own gun out in time to face the one Morgan was pointing towards him. They both stared into gun barrels and then into each other's dark eyes. Both men had nerves of steel and weren't about to back down.

"I thought we agreed to come unarmed," Guy offered lightly as he looked at Morgan's pistol. A life in the grey criminal world had put Guy in contact with all sorts of fiends, so he knew a killer when he faced one. This impressive stranger in front of him was certainly a killer; his eyes were clear and focused, his hand steady, and there was just a hint of a smirk on his face. Guy felt a small shiver run down his spine and had a hard time realizing what the foreign feeling was at first. But he quickly registered it as fear, something he hadn't felt in a long time. Unwilling to feel it any further he decided to capitulate and lowered his weapon. "Perhaps I was a little hasty."

"Just a little," Morgan confirmed coldly. He then looked down at Louis prone form, a small plume of smoke rising from the hole in his pants. "You need to surround yourself with better company. Now you pay the price for your error in judgement."

"Wait!" Guy implored dropping his gun and raising his hands. "How about I do the job for half? You keep the money and we take the envelope, completing the instructions inside."

"Sorry, you had your chance," Morgan replied pulling the hammer back on his pistol, the threatening metallic click ringing out ominously. "For some reason I just don't trust you."

But instead of a shot ringing out, sirens and shouting erupted all around them. The bright lights of multiple vehicles filled the abandoned lot as a rush of footsteps echoed along the paved road. Morgan and Guy were soon surrounded by armed policemen, ordering them to drop their weapons and drop to the ground.

"You set me up you bastard," Morgan uttered angrily through gritted teeth. He dropped his pistol and slowly lowered himself down to a familiar position with his hands above his head.

"It wasn't me," Guy countered with an equal amount of anger.

"Well, well well, you're slipping Renard," observed a plainclothes policeman as the two men on the ground were being handcuffed by the uniformed officers. He looked over the scene with reserved satisfaction before continuing. "I've been looking forward to this for a long time."

Chapter 18

Morgan looked around and thought it was the nicest interrogation room he'd ever been in. To be fair, some of the interrogation rooms he'd occupied had actually been used by the Spanish Inquisition. But this one was clean, the lights were not too intense, and it didn't smell like an industrial cleaner plant. Usually the smell was overpowering so that it seemed like the room had just been cleaned out after a bloody beating. The sound of a key in the door got Morgan's attention and he looked over as it opened and Tiberius walked in with a young well dressed man behind him.

"Did he buy it?" Tiberius asked immediately, not bothering to sit down.

"I think so," Morgan confirmed positively. "I'm pretty sure he thought I was going to kill him, and cops aren't supposed to do that."

"You're a policeman?" the young man asked, surprised at the instant friendliness of the Inspector from Interpol and the man they'd just arrested.

"Sorry, I forgot about introductions," Tiberius apologised. "Inspector Midoux of the Luxembourg Gendarmerie meet Detective Sergeant Morgan on loan from Scotland Yard. He's in deep cover here on the continent."

"A pleaure," Midoux offered graciously, simply happy to be surrounded by yet another representative of a prestigious law enforcement agency.

"We observed your signal before moving in, the thrown cigarette," Tiberius continued Morgan's debrief, ignoring Midoux. "So he confirmed a Stasi contact?"

"Indeed, fairly quickly in fact," Morgan answered, reverting to his native accent for the sake of his new role. "He didn't provide a name, but he will if you push him."

"I agree, good work," Tiberius allowed, finally joining them at the table. "Midoux, any leads on the hit and run driver?"

"None," he responded dispiritedly, upset that he didn't seem to be doing anything to help. "The car was wiped clean, no prints, not even from any of the workers at the car rental agency. He fled before any eye witnesses could get a good look at him. We're still looking, but I'm not very confident anything new will emerge. It looks like this agent is our only lead."

"Well that at least gives us an important clue," Tiberius allowed thoughtfully, raising Midoux's spirits. "We can rule out an accident. A car wiped clean of fingerprints points to a professional hit."

"So what's the plan sir?" Morgan asked.

"Dufresne is currently grilling Louis in the room next door," Tiberius began, his plan already formulated. "We're going to send you back in with Guy to the holding cell to ruffle his feathers."

"The Strasbourg treatment?" Morgan smiled, remembering one of their more clever ploys. He would go into the room and claim Louis was an informant after watching him released by the police.

"Exactly," Tiberius confirmed. "We will then pull Guy in and try and turn him before his lawyer shows up and tells him to keep quiet."

"Well let's get moving then," Morgan inhaled, raising his arms up at Midoux. "The silver bracelets if you please. And make sure your men aren't too gentle about it."

Morgan's direction was followed and he was unceremoniously dragged and then thrown into a bright holding cell in the basement of the station. One of the burly policemen bent down and removed the handcuffs, eliciting a wince from Morgan as he twisted his wrists in the process.

When the cell door closed, Morgan slowly pulled himself up onto a wooden bench that ran the length of the cell. He rubbed his wrists and then stretched his back, finally noticing Guy sitting on the far side.

"Don't say a fucking word to me," Morgan threatened, shooting his fellow inmate with a dark look. "You can save your breath. I know you're an informant, so I'm not going to say a thing and you'll have nothing to report to your friends upstairs."

"What?!" Guy exclaimed with shock. He was still trying to process how he'd ended up in custody, knowing he must have been set up.

"Don't play dumb with me, I saw you're buddy upstairs," Morgan began, baiting the hook. "When they brought me back down here I passed him in the hall. Somebody must have screwed up, because he was being led to the door and not the interrogation room."

"But that's impossible," Guy muttered with obvious confusion. "He couldn't possibly be an informant, I would have found out."

"Sure," Morgan retorted sarcastically. "You better hope they lock me up, because if I get out I'm spreading the word about you. Nobody will want to work with a rat."

"I'm no informant," Guy replied indignantly, his anger raising. "My record speaks for itself and I don't have to explain myself to some insignificant nobody. And if you plan on lying about me, you'll find it very hard with no tongue and dead on a slab!"

"Fine you may be clean," Morgan allowed calmly, not showing any fear from Guy's threat. "But Louis is definitely a rat. I bet they were just waiting to gather enough info on you before bringing you in. Just ask yourself how much he knows about your business."

"He would be implicating himself as well," Guy shook his head slowly, realizing the potential fallout if this stranger was right.

"Not if he's got immunity as an informant."

Their conversation was cut short when the two large policemen returned to the cell and pointed towards Guy. He got up slowly and walked towards the cell door, failing to hide his obvious trepidation. If Louis was truly working for the police, than he'd be facing some damning charges that would be almost impossible to deny.

He was led upstairs with the same rough handling and seated in the same interrogation room, his hands remaining manacled. Like Morgan, Guy had seen many interrogation rooms and unknowingly agreed with his assessment of its condition.

"Jean-Guy L'Oiselle, we meet again," Inspector Midoux exclaimed has he walked through the door, immediately followed by Tiberius. As before, Midoux sat down directly across from the prisoner, while Tiberius stood by the corner and stared.

"I want my lawyer," Guy responded automatically.

"I thought you might," Midoux acknowledged happily. Although not a skilled investigator, Tiberius was discovering that the young policeman's talent lay in being personable and persuasive. "But I think we could save you some money by delaying that phone call for a moment."

"I demand to see my lawyer," Guy repeated.

"I don't deny you might need him," Midoux smiled as he leaned back in his chair. "But I'd rather talk to you for a few minutes first and save you a few hundred dollars in legal fees. How about it?"

"I'm not saying anything, but I'll listen to you for a few minutes."

"I think that's acceptable," Midoux nodded, leaning forward and opening a file on his desk. "Your associate Louis is next door throwing you under the bus, telling us all kinds of things. I for one would like nothing better than to charge you with some of the minor offences his testimony could offer. However things have become slightly more complicated."

True to his word Guy sat silently, nodding for Midoux to continue as the officer paused for a moment.

"You have ended up in the middle of some real international intrigue, by luck more than design I imagine," Midoux continued, returning to the file before him. "There are two paths open for you because of this."

"What do you mean?" Guy asked, unable to stay silent.

"The man you were arrested with is known as Le Renard, one of the most wanted men in Europe," Tiberius explained from the back of the room. His voice was quiet and intense, making Guy worried. "We can say that you played a part in his capture and we let you go…"

"Or we say that you were one of his accomplices and you both get deported to one of the wretched prisons that are dying to hold him. The choice is yours," Midoux offered plainly, letting the threat hang in the air between them. "Like I said, I don't think you need a lawyer to advise you on this one."

"How do I know you'll keep your word?" Guy challenged as he adjusted the handcuffs on his wrists. "The answer is that I don't. Not unless I have a signed deal delivered to my lawyer."

"I'm afraid our deal is only available as long as the lawyer stays out," Tiberius countered as he walked towards the table. "The truth is you don't have a choice. You demand your lawyer, you go to prison. You lie to us, you go to prison. You tell us the truth but we just lied to you, you go to prison. So you might as well tell us the truth and hope that we keep our word, because that's the only way you stay out of prison. Understand?"

Tiberius delivered this with a cold and menacing tone he'd used many times over his long life. He found it the perfect way to effectively threaten men who thought they were tough. He knew that if you were too loud and angry, they'd only match your attitude. But if you chose the opposite method and tried to be persuasive and nice, they would distrust you immediately.

"So how does this work?" Guy finally accepted after a thoughtful pause.

"To close the loop on the Renard case, we need the name of the East Berlin contact," Midoux explained pulling out a sheet from the file. "You identify a photo, give us a name and coordinates, and then you walk out of here. The accusations of your friend Louis are ignored as the rantings of a dissatisfied employee."

"Do you recognize this man?" Tiberius demanded as he took the photo from the file and placed it in front of Guy.

After staring at the photo for thirty seconds, Guy took a few breaths and then nodded. He closed his eyes as he fought to control the mixture of emotions he was feeling. For the first time in his life he'd helped the police, not something he wanted known. But on the other hand he'd hopefully just avoided a long prison term.

"Who is he?"

"He goes by the name Hans Blick," Guy offered wearily, tired from the long night and unused to the feeling of informing on others. "He's a disaffected member of the Stasi, working in Western Europe as a journalist attached to the embassy. He's been pretty active in the last year, raising money and getting contacts. He knows his days as an operative are numbered, so he's getting ready to become self-employed. Not a very good communist is he?"

Guy's attempts at a joke fell on deaf ears as both Midoux and Tiberius tried to remain calm. They both felt that Guy was telling them the truth, but more importantly it fit with their investigation. They'd gone through the employee files at the East German embassy and came up empty. But as a journalist attached there, his files were not included.

"What was the Renard trying to move into Berlin?" Midoux asked to keep the interview moving.

"He didn't say and I didn't ask," Guy answered truthfully before giving them the dimensions Morgan had provided.

"How do you get in touch with Herr Blick?"

"There's a park that runs along the outside of the old city that I use to walk my dog," Guy continued, ignoring the smirking look from Midoux. "I always stop at a specific park bench for a break. If I want to meet Blick, I put a mark on the bench with a piece of chalk. He then sends me the meeting location in the next day's classifieds, an advert for a meeting of the LKA Society."

"Classic trade craft," Tiberius observed acknowledging the ring of truth in it. An operative like Blick would use all of the skills he'd been taught, whether for official business or otherwise. "Mr. L'Oiselle, you're going to set a meeting for us. You're going to go to Herr Blick with the Renard's smuggling request."

"With you swooping in and arresting us at the meeting?" Guy scoffed angrily. "No chance. He'll know it was me that set him up and double crossing the Stasi would be a death sentence."

"Relax, that's not the plan," Midoux reassured him calmly. "We'll observe the location of the meeting and trail him after you're done. Any arrest would come well afterwards and not be associated with your dealings."

"I don't really have a choice do I?" Guy lamented, feeling deflated at his loss of control.

"No you don't," Tiberius smiled for the first time. They were making progress and he could feel them closing in on those responsible for ordering Zeidt's death. Hans Blick had almost definitely passed the information on Zeidt to the assassin, but he was probably not the one behind it. Blick was the perfect middle man and Tiberius wondered who was on the other side. Was it the mole, the Stasi, or some other criminal element?

*

The evening sun was glinting off the shimmering water of Monterey Bay, whitecaps dotting the nautical expanse. Surfers and beachgoers scampered along the beach below like ants, soaking up the last remnants of the day. To Pierce it was finally the classic California scene he'd expected when they first emerged from the portal.

The Charger was parked on a makeshift lookout on a winding road amongst the mansions overlooking the bay. They'd followed the beige sedan to the coast, finally watching it pull into a large waterfront estate perched at the base of the hill. It was a massive Spanish Colonial house, complete with white adobe walls and a red tiled roof. As they passed the house, Pierce noticed houses up above them on the hill and followed the road as it snaked up towards them. They eventually found a spot that provided a decent observation point of the mansion below.

"Can you see the car?" Pierce asked as he lifted up the camera with the telescopic lens. He swept the grounds, picking out the main house and a few out buildings.

"I can't see it," MacDuff reported from behind his binoculars. "But he could have parked in either of the house's garages, or one of the sheds behind. They're all big enough for a car to fit inside and they all have garage doors. Hell, even the boathouse has a garage door on the side."

"I don't like it," Pierce muttered anxiously. He'd put Kat into a dangerous position and he didn't like the fact that she was now on her own. He hadn't felt this way as they trailed the beige sedan across California, since they were right behind it the entire time and ready to offer a rescue at a moment's notice. But the house and grounds below them were so big, that it would take a long time to search the entire place.

"Stay calm, everything is alright," MacDuff advised confidently. "They know nothing of our involvement and won't be suspicious. In fact their security seems to have worked against them. With no face to face meetings, they haven't discovered the break in their chain yet."

"Fair enough, but I still don't like it."

As dusk fell they watched the mansion's driveway slowly fill up with cars. There appeared to be some kind of party happening, they counted an increasing number of headlights turning past the gates as darkness enveloped the affluent neighbourhood.

"We should go down there," Pierce stated as it became too dark for them to observe anything from their perch.

"We need to be patient lad," MacDuff countered. "If we go down there flashing our badges, there's no telling what will happen."

"Who said anything about badges? We're just two more people at a party. Look at all the cars, there must be close to a hundred people there. We go down, ask a few innocent questions, have a look around, and then come back."

"It's usually not that easy," MacDuff sighed, remembering just how new Lord Pierce was to their work. He knew fake ID's and guns could offer an inflated sense of security and protection. But all it took was for some wealthy or connected person to call their bluff and they'd be in a lot of trouble. None of their covers would hold up to prolonged scrutiny.

"We've got to do something," Pierce objected forcefully. "Kat's down there right now and we have no idea what's going on. We're in the dark up here, figuratively and literally."

"Fine," MacDuff finally acquiesced. "But we keep it low key."

"Obviously," Pierce agreed, wincing slightly as their muscle car rumbled to life. Although it was painted black, the Dodge Charger was not the most subtle of cars.

Pierce turned around and drove the car back down the road towards the party. They stopped to let a long Cadillac turn in first when they reached the driveway, following it in. The mansion grounds were much more chaotic than they'd appreciated from the lookout above; cars were parked haphazardly on the driveway and lawns, music filtered out from the house, and pockets of partygoers lounged about smoking and drinking. They needn't have worried about any attention their car might draw, as they past numerous flamboyant and significantly more expensive cars.

After parking near the road, the pair made their way to the house amidst the upbeat tones of either a Rod Stewart or Elton John song. Pierce had to work hard keeping a straight face as they passed the other guests. Bell bottoms, leisure suits, and miniskirts made from every pattern imaginable adorned the animated partiers. Pierce had always been dubious that the movies he'd watched that took place in the 1970's had been authentic. The actor's had always acted and dressed in such an outlandish fashion, that he presumed it was an exaggerated version of reality. But now he wasn't so sure.

The front door was open, so they just walked in and found themselves amidst a crush of sounds and bodies in the front foyer. A haze of smoke hung in the air and Pierce immediately recognized the scent from his days in a college dorm. As they waded deeper in to the chaos, they noticed that everyone had a drink in one hand and a smoke of some kind in the other. There were rooms and hallways on either side of the foyer and different music seemed to seep in from both directions, creating a confusing but entertaining mixture of sounds among the drone of conversation.

MacDuff pointed to the left and Pierce nodded, following the larger man as he ploughed through the crowd. They soon found themselves in a quieter sitting room filled with ugly floral patterned furniture. There was a small bar set up in the corner and both men made themselves a drink in order to fit in. No one in the room seemed to pay attention to them, too caught up in their own conversations.

Pierce's attention was immediately drawn to a group of books lining the mantle of the room's fireplace. They all shared the same style, but more importantly the same name. The author's name was Cedric Holloway, but Pierce didn't recognize it or the titles of the books.

"So how do you know Ced?" asked a vapid voice from behind Pierce, startling him slightly. He turned around and looked into a pair of seemingly empty blue eyes through a cloud of smoke. MacDuff had vanished and had been replaced by a tall lanky brunette with long straight hair. She was wearing a tight pair of brown striped pants with a silk floral shirt that was tied up to show her midriff. Pierce didn't know how to respond, so he simply shrugged and took a sip of his drink.

"Good, I thought you might have been a fan," she accepted quickly. "They're always so boring."

"I've never even heard of his books," Pierce replied truthfully.

"Perfect, you'll fit right in," she said happily. "I doubt anyone here reads his books, he just throws really good parties."

"What are they about anyway?"

"Oh I don't know," she shrugged ignorantly. "Detectives, or police, or something boring. Nothing that expands your mind."

"Right," Pierce concurred half-heartedly, looking around the room to see where MacDuff was.

"You want some blow?" she asked next, tired of talking about books.

"Um, maybe later," he replied spotting MacDuff walking out of the room. He followed him as slowly as possible snaking his way to a door at the end of the room. He held his breath as he walked between a pair by the door smoking like chimneys.

The door led to the dining room that mercifully had high a ceiling, allowing the smoke to gather amongst the open beamed rafters. A long table ran the length of the room and seemed to be the central point for drug consumption at the party. Almost all of the seats were taken with people doing every kind of drug Pierce knew about, and a few that were new to him. Although there was no line up, every time someone finished their hit and stood up, they were quickly replaced by someone else.

Pierce had never witnessed anything close to this and the scene made his skin crawl. He felt like he was in a waiting room for cancer patients, knowing that most of the people sitting around him would end up dying prematurely.

"You want some man?" asked a long haired man sitting at the table in front of Pierce. Lines of white powder were spaced evenly on the polished wood.

"Um, maybe later."

Variations of these scenes played out as Pierce and MacDuff casually searched the house. Alcohol, tobacco, and drugs were being consumed in vast quantities, creating a Dionysian atmosphere. Everyone was simply living for the moment and trying to enjoy themselves as much as possible, regardless of any consequences.

The second level of the mansion was less chaotic, but no less festive. Cries of ecstasy emanated from many of the rooms they passed, some with multiple voices. Pierce was reticent to look into the rooms, unwilling to be accused of being a voyeur. But MacDuff argued that Kat could be in one of the rooms being abused, and he quickly lost his reticence. However all they found were moving masses of naked parts, with none of the participants the least bit shy of being discovered. Both men even received invites after looking in to a few rooms.

So it was with quiet relief when they opened the door at the end of the hall and found it to be empty. Needing a break from the bedlam beyond, they entered what appeared to be an office or a library. The only light in the room came from a single desk lamp and a bright moon peeking through the windows. Bookcases lined the walls, with a collection of mismatched chairs placed on a carpet in the middle of the room. The large desk in front of the windows dominated the space and was clearly used. Books and sheets of paper were stacked on the top, surrounding an old typewriter.

"Hello?"

Pierce almost jumped out of his skin when he heard the voice and watched a figure appear like magic from in front of a massive curtain by the window.

"Sorry for the intrusion," MacDuff replied quickly, seemingly expecting the appearance of the man in the room.

He was dressed in a much more conservative fashion than anyone else at the party, looking like the idyllic college professor. He looked over the two intruders through a pair of reading glasses perched on the end of his nose, assessing them lazily.

"You don't seem like Caroline's usual friends," he allowed pointing towards the windows. Pierce walked over and looked through them onto the front of the estate. There were people and cars strewn about the front lawns, both making loud obnoxious noise.

"We're not," Pierce replied, the answer seemingly satisfying the man enough for him to refill their glasses with a bottle from the desk. "You're Cedric Holloway, aren't you?"

"That's right," he sighed, looking back over the destruction of his property. With a pained look on his face he eventually turned from the window and walked to the middle of the room, collapsing on one of the chairs. "Would you gentlemen care to join me?"

Shooting a quick glance at each other, Pierce and MacDuff sat down beside the melancholy man. Pierce couldn't tell if he was drunk or just slowed by ennui. It was probably a combination of both, but either way he might be able to provide them with some information.

"You're a writer aren't you?" Pierce asked remembering the books from the sitting room.

"Yes, and an unsuccessful one at that."

"Really?" MacDuff uttered with confusion.

"Most assuredly," he confirmed with a drink. "Don't let the house fool you, it didn't come from my royalties. Caroline's from a rich family and she's responsible for everything you see around here. She was in a rebellious stage when we met, still in the afterglow of Woodstock. She probably thought it was romantically bohemian to get involved with an impoverished author. Luckily for her, she received her inheritance before the reality of our situation set in."

He drained the rest of his glass and wobbled over to the desk and brought back the bottle, filling his glass and offering it to his visitors. When they declined, he merely shrugged and continued drinking.

"What kind of books do you write?" MacDuff asked with genuine curiosity.

"I write the Detective Strongman mysteries," Holloway replied with little enthusiasm. "Don't feel bad for not knowing about them, few people do. He's a modern day take on the hard nose private eyes of the thirties and forties."

"Sounds interesting enough."

"I suppose. You can judge for yourself," he offered pointing to the bookcase behind him. "There's copies of my books up there, feel free to take any of them."

MacDuff nodded and walked over to the book case, thumbing through the volumes carefully. Pierce noticed the hint of delight on the author's face at having someone show interest in his work.

"How would you like to help out on a real mystery?" Pierce inquired, trying a slightly direct approach after seeing Holloway's changing demeanour.

"What?" he replied with some confusion. "Are you two detectives or something?"

"Or something," MacDuff intoned from the bookcase.

"We're trying to track down a missing girl," Pierce lied, trying to avoid revealing their identities. He didn't believe Cedric Holloway had anything to do with Debochev or his despicable activities. He still wasn't sure why the beige sedan had pulled into this estate, but he was pretty sure it wasn't to hand Kat over to him. "We tracked the car of a potential witness here, but we don't know who the driver is. Then we lost him in all of the confusion."

The point was emphasised when the door to the room opened and the loud noise of the party below barged in. A petite blonde in a ridiculously flashy outfit soon followed, only adding to the intrusion.

"Cedric, you're ignoring our guests," she reproached him coldly before realizing he wasn't alone. Her attitude changed in an instant and she shot the two other men with a sweet smile. "Hello, I don't think we've met. I'm Caroline Holloway. Are you friends of Cedric's?"

"No they're detectives and they're looking for someone," Cedric answered for them, clearly happy at being a step ahead of his wife.

"Oh," Was all she could muster, her eyes drifting downwards as she thought about the activities taking place below. But her cautious attitude disappeared quickly as she realized that if these men were police they would have already broken up the party. "If you're looking for someone to answer your questions you should ask me. Cedric wouldn't know anything, shut up in this dreary office all day long."

"We just have a few pictures we'd like you to take a look at," Pierce carried on, taking the snapshots of Debochev and his remaining two men from his jacket pocket. "Have either of you seen these men?"

He passed the photos to Cedric first who studied them with great intensity, clearly hoping to be of assistance. But when nothing came to him he dejectedly handed them to his wife. She was about to do the same thing, eager to show up her husband, but instead she offered only a passing glance after looking at the first photo.

"I'm afraid we've never seen these men before," she stated coldly. "What detective agency did you say you were from?"

"We didn't," MacDuff replied offhandedly, hoping to avoid the question.

"Gentlemen, this is a private party and I don't want you annoying my guests. It would be best if you left."

"But Caroline, they're looking for a missing girl," Cedric implored. "Surely we should help them out any way we can."

The wife's face blanched a shade after hearing the reason for their appearance at her house and she immediately became less than welcoming. "Cedric, I'm not about to let these two ruffians without credentials ruin my party! You will both have to leave."

"I'm afraid it's not that simple Mrs. Holloway," Pierce objected calmly, pulling his ID from his jacket pocket. "I'm afraid we weren't completely honest with your husband, we're not really detectives. I'm agent Gunn and this is Agent Bruce, FBI."

He flipped open the ID, flashing the gold badge like he'd seen on TV and the movies. The couple's reaction to this statement was as different as they were from each other. Cedric almost grinned with delight at having legitimate federal agents investigating a mystery at his own home. Caroline meanwhile suddenly looked like a trapped animal, her eyes wide and looking for an escape.

At that moment the loud screech of tires and the sound of metal smashing together rang out from the front of the house. MacDuff rushed to the window that looked out over the front lawn and driveway. Pierce was quick to join him, confident he'd see the taillights of the beige sedan speeding away.

Chapter 19

A blue car had smashed into a station wagon parked on the lawn that blocked the path that led to the boathouse. At first Pierce looked on with curiosity as two men tried to clamber out of the wreck. Glad that he'd been wrong about the beige sedan, he assumed they were just two more drunk party goers late to the party. But that thought quickly dissipated when they pulled out pistols and started firing towards the front gate.

"It's the car from Los Angeles!" MacDuff exclaimed at the same time Pierce recognized it from Leon's warehouse. One of the men from the car had been the messenger that dropped the matchbook in Leon's car. Suddenly Pierce had a pretty good idea who they were firing at. He took off for the stairs, ignoring their hosts who were still stuck to their seats in fright.

Pierce and MacDuff took the stairs down two at a time, barrelling through the crowd in the foyer who were fleeing from the sounds of gunshots. They emerged through the front door in time to see the black Pontiac GTO come screaming though the gate and skid across the lawn, finally coming to a halt behind some other parked cars. Pierce wasn't sure if this was a planned move, but he was glad for it when he watched a large Lincoln get hit by flying bullets instead of his car.

"Federal Agents!" MacDuff bellowed as he pulled out his pistol and ran behind a golden Ford near the front door. He received a few shots in his direction for his trouble, but it provided enough of a break from Sean and Liam to run from their car and get within firing distance.

Hearing screams behind him, Pierce turned and pulled out his own ID and ordered those nearby to get down. So far none of the shots had come into the house, but that wouldn't last long. The loud crack of a rifle brought Pierce's attention back to the front of the house, worried that his men were now facing more than a pair of pistols. But his concern was unfounded as he watched both Sean and Liam pop up from behind a bullet riddled car holding M-16 machine guns. With similar cracks he watched them take down the men from the blue car as they tried to flee from its protection.

As the echo from their two shots died away, all that could be heard was the lamenting voice and twangy guitar of Waylon Jennings from one of the record players within the house.

With weapons raised, the members of the Brown Pack cautiously converged on the blue car from different angles. There were two bodies lying in a crumpled mess on the grass, both shot through the chest. Sean bent down to check for a pulse, but found none.

"What the hell was that all about?!" Pierce demanded of his two men whose unceremonious arrival still had his adrenaline pumping.

"They…" Sean began to explain, but was cut short when the windshield of the station wagon beside them exploded from a poorly aimed shotgun blast.

Without another word they all jumped over the hood of the car and took cover behind it. A few more shots rang out, quickly followed by another booming shotgun blast.

"Where are they?" Pierce shouted as he crouched behind the cars wheel.

"I see them," Liam answered calmly, aiming his machine gun at them from underneath the car. "They're in the trees between us and that big shed."

"You keep their attention and we'll flank them," Sean offered, nodding to Pierce.

Liam took a few shots at the trees to keep their heads down while Sean and Pierce retreated back to the front door of the mansion. Once inside Pierce led them towards the back of the house amid the screams of the guest still taking cover. Both men identified themselves and instructed those they passed to stay down. They emerged from the kitchen into the dark back yard, wary of any potential ambush.

They skirted along the side of the house, staying in the shadows while they looked for targets. Luckily the pool was behind them, so they didn't have to worry about mistakenly shooting a bystander in a bathing suit.

When shots rang out again, they were able to see the muzzle flashes from two guns in a stand of trees twenty yards in front of them. Keeping low, they approached from the shadows, with Pierce almost tripping over a prone body by a shrub. It was another gunman, but luckily he was too dead to shoot at them.

With quick breathes, Pierce carefully crept closer to the remaining gunmen. He could feel his pulse racing and his grip tight on his pistol. He was enraged that despite his best efforts, they were once again in a fight that had claimed lives. He felt as though death was following him around, staying close no matter how hard he tried to lose him.

Pierce signalled to Sean that he wanted to take them alive, unwilling to simply shoot them in the back. Sean nodded he understood and aimed at the farther man while Pierce trained his sights on the nearest one.

"Fedeal Agents!" "US Marshals!" They both shouted at the same time, shocking the two men in front of them. The farthest gunman spun around and aimed his shotgun at them, firing into the air in his haste. Sean took him down with a shot of his own before he could reload. But the second gunman dropped his gun immediately, shouting a plea as he watched his former associate go down.

Sean then pointed his rifle towards the front of the house, lowering it once MacDuff answered his challenge. All four found themselves once again standing over a dead body, Pierce taking little solace that they had taken one alive.

"Why were you shooting at us?!" Pierce demanded of their new prisoner, watching him hesitate with fear. When Pierce repeated the question he merely shook his head from side to side.

The sound of approaching sirens filled the air as police cars sped towards the mansion by the ocean. Pierce felt as though they were running out of time and couldn't shake the feeling he was missing something. Losing his patience he nodded to Liam, who grabbed the prisoner and pointed his gun to the man's head.

"You see this badge?" Pierce inquired coldly, flipping open his ID. "You just fired on Federal Agents, so when those police show up and find your dead body, there will be no investigation. Which means you'll have to be dead before they show up. Sounds like you've got about a minute. Why were you shooting at us?"

"They told me to!" he blurted out immediately, trying to point towards the boathouse behind him.

Before he heard another word, Pierce was off like a shot running across the grounds towards the boathouse, MacDuff close behind. He immediately realised the nagging feeling he'd been having and cursed himself for being too slow to act. Driving around with a kidnapped girl in a car was very risky and offered too many opportunities for something to go wrong. A boat however offered a more controlled method of transportation and was much more discrete.

They reached the boathouse without incident, breathing hard as they took positions on each side of the door. With a heavy boot, MacDuff kicked the door down and then followed Pierce in.

"Shit!" Pierce screamed with frustration. The boathouse was empty except for an empty beige sedan. Thinking of Kat being spirited away on a boat out of their protection made him feel sick and he found himself leaning against the rough wooden wall. His body suddenly felt limp as the adrenaline seeped away and their failure hit him.

"Pull yourself together lad, the police are on their way," MacDuff observed from the boathouse doorway. Flashing red and white lights filled the front of the house and loud voices were calling to each other. They both dropped their weapons and then pulled out their ID's, waiting for the police to barge through.

"Hands up!" yelled two policemen as they ran into the boathouse, immediately feeling foolish. "You guys with the Marshal's?"

"That's right," Pierce concurred as the policemen inspected their badges. "Agents Bruce and Gunn, FBI."

"You're going to want to see my Lieutenant sir, he's out front."

"Fine. In the meantime, seal this building off, that car is evidence," Pierce ordered as he and MacDuff picked up their weapons. They walked to the front of the house, passing groups of police and medics grouped around the dead gunmen. They saw Sean and Liam standing beside an unmarked police car by the front door, the owner yelling into a radio. Seeing them approach the man slammed the mic down and got out of the front seat.

"Let me guess, two more feds?" he called out with exasperation. "What the hell happened here?"

"We were following a group of fugitives in two cars," Pierce explained, leaning against the car. "That blue one that's all shot up and a beige one in the boat house. The beige one got here first and Agent Bruce and myself searched the party for them. We were questioning the home owners when the blue car crashed the party, soon followed by the Marshals. The suspects opened fire on the Marshals when they tried to apprehend them. Sadly we were only able to take one of them alive."

"So you got all of them? Why did they come here?"

Pierce flashed a look at Sean before he could answer, unsure how much he wanted to tell this policeman. If they left out Kat and boat, the case in the eyes of this cop would be closed. But if they told him about Kat and the Boat, things might become more complicated and escalate beyond their control. He might try and call the coastguard or their fictional boss at the FBI. Although the extra manpower would be useful at this stage, he wasn't willing to compromise their mission.

"That's right, we've identified all five of the fugitives we were chasing," Pierce finally confirmed. "They probably came here by chance. Saw the big party going on and thought they could steal a new car."

"Speaking of this party," the lieutenant sighed looking back at the mansion. "It seems I'm going to have my hands full with everything in there. I'd be grateful if I could wipe my hands of those dead bodies and the prisoner."

"No problem," Pierce smiled, offering his hand to the clearly flustered cop. "We were in there briefly, that's going to be a headache to clear up. Would you be able to have the homeowner's placed in a room and have one of your men watch them until we get there. I just have a few questions for them and then we'll get out of your hair."

"You got it. Thanks," the Lieutenant shook his hand quickly before turning to some of his own men that were waiting patiently.

"We'll grab the prisoner and find somewhere quiet to take him," Sean said as they all huddled together.

"There must be a seedy motel around here where they don't ask questions," Liam offered. "That should scare some information out of him."

"Good thinking," Pierce acknowledged. "Squeeze him for all he's worth, he must know something that will help us find Kat. And Liam…"

"Ya boss?"

"No torture, things have already gotten out of hand."

"Yes sir," he agreed. "What are you guys going to do?"

"We're going to go in and have a little chat with Mrs. Caroline fucking Holloway and find out why she lied about not knowing Debochev and his men."

*

The skies were dark and threatened rain as Jane, Logan, and Melrose rode along the edge of Black Lake. The wind had picked up and was showering them with spray as the waves crashed against the shore.

Despite having grown up on the island, Jane had never been to Loch Dhu Castle, so she had talked Melrose into being her guide. She knew she could trust his discretion and loyalty to Lord Lodge. It had been as Lord Lodge's servant that he'd first been to Loch Dhu Castle, accompanying his old master on a tour of the island

Eager to leave the confines of the office after days of research, both Jane and Logan decided to check out the meeting places they'd discovered. Neither of them were expecting to find anything profound, but they hoped they might stumble across a clue of some sort. If nothing else, walking in the steps of the conspirators might offer an insight into their actions.

"Holy shit," Logan muttered breathlessly as they rounded a corner of the road and Loch Dhu finally came into view. "That's one honest to god castle."

Seemingly rising from the waves of Black Lake, the castle's grey stone walls stood solidly amid the chaotic water surrounding it. Two towers sat atop the square building, providing any inhabitants a clear view of someone approaching. As they rode closer Jane spotted a stone causeway that went from the shore to the castle's island, a set of gates protecting both sides.

"I hope there isn't anyone guarding this place," Logan pointed out. "Because we'll need a lot more than my rifle to assault this place successfully."

"It should be empty," Jane hoped, trying to sound confident. "Dr. Cleaver used this place as his private retreat. I didn't even know it existed until recently. I found the key to it in his things, so it should be locked up."

"So what's the deal with this place Melrose?" Logan asked their guide, his curiosity not satisfied.

"Cleaver had it built shortly after taking his position as Master of the Hunt," Melrose explained evenly, recalling his last visit to the island castle. "Lord Lodge allowed him to have it, as he viewed it as a potential trap for him."

"What do you mean?"

"Lord Lodge thought it better to know where Cleaver would retreat to if they ever clashed," he continued without emotion. "Although it didn't end up working that way. This was the first place Tiberius and his men searched after discovering Cleaver's disappearance, but it was empty."

"It was a good plan," Jane defended, accepting the logic behind the idea.

"You're right," Logan agreed, surveying the land around them. "Sure it looks impregnable, but that just makes it easier to cut off. Lord Lodge would have been able to keep tabs on anyone within that castle with only a handful of observers. Nobody would have been able to escape once they were inside."

Everyone agreed with this sentiment as they pulled up to the gate that guarded the entrance to the causeway. Running roughly one hundred yards across the water to the island, it was just wide enough for two people on horseback to ride beside each other. Any large exodus trying to break through a siege would have been easily cut down before they could reach shore. Alternatively, Jane realized, her small group would be exposed for a dangerous period as they themselves crossed.

The sturdy iron gate sat within a large turreted stone archway, blessedly devoid of any guards. Everyone descended from their horses and Jane pulled the large key from her backpack. Unlike a standard castle gate, this one was actually in two parts like a double door with a lock and handles in the middle. She tentatively inserted the key into the lock and turned it until a sharp click rang out. With little effort the gate swung open, the hinges well greased despite their old appearance.

After riding since dawn, the small group gratefully remained dismounted as they led their horses across the stone causeway. The cobblestones beneath their feet were wet from the waves, forcing them to concentrate on their footsteps rather than the imposing fortress they approached. Without any accidents they reached the other end and the second gate opened for them just as easily as the first. There was a small open stable by the gate where they tied up their horses, surprised to see food and water still laid out.

Melrose led them across a small dirt courtyard to a set of stairs that led up to the front door. Built in the same fashion as the main door of the Manor, this one yielded to Jane's key with similar ease and they quickly found themselves standing in a dark entrance hall.

Logan whistled in surprise as he looked around, the noise echoing in the seemingly empty building. He'd been posted to an army base in Scotland for a year as part of an exchange and had toured some of the historic buildings. Most of the castles he'd seen had been crumbling relics, with only a few maintained in their original condition. Walking within them he'd felt like he was going back in time until the crush of other tourists ruined it. But now the feeling was much more profound and he truly felt like they'd travelled back in time.

He pulled out some flashlights from his backpack and passed them to the others, while he turned on the light at the end of his modern rifle. The building seemed empty, but he wasn't willing to bet his life on it.

"Let's split up and have a look at this place," Jane suggested as she looked at her watch. "If we're quick enough we should be able to get back to the Manor by nightfall."

"No way, I've seen way too many scary movies to go along with that plan," Logan shook his head seriously, but received confused looks from the other two. Remembering that they weren't familiar with horror movies he decided to explain. "When people search old abandoned buildings they always split up. But when that happens they're always picked off one by one by the killer."

"What killer?" Melrose asked.

"There's always a killer, or an alien, or some kind of murderous animal. Listen, we stick together and go room by room until the castle is clear."

"Well you're the expert," Jane conceded.

With the tactics decided, Logan led the group from room to room as they slowly checked out the building. They started on the ground floor and worked their way up, not finding a door to any basement. Although some of the paintings, tapestries, and weapons that filled the walls were impressive, their search provided few clues as to any potential conspiracies that were plotted within. Despite its warlike façade, the castle was actually quite civilized within. There was a dining room, a library, and a music room. The rest of the rooms were devoted to personal quarters, the kitchen, and staff spaces.

"Nothing," Jane cursed as they finished looking at the top floor. It was taken up exclusively by one large bedroom that probably belonged to Cleaver. But none of the drawers from the desk or cabinets provided any potential clues. None of the rooms had provided even a scrap of evidence; no notebooks, maps, or anything suspicious.

The sound of the howling wind outside had been present during their search, but now they could hear heavy rain pelting the windows and walls. The impending storm had moved in fast and Jane realized that they would have to stay the night rather than brave the elements.

Dejectedly, the three searchers descended the single staircase that ran down the heart of the building and headed for the kitchen. A giant cast iron woodstove sat in the middle of the room and would provide warmth against the damp stone.

Logan fired it up effortlessly, finding ample wood and kindling in the storage room. He also found a few lanterns that he lit with a lighter from his pack. The kitchen immediately became more welcoming and the heat from the stove brightened everyone's spirits. The mood became even better when Melrose emerged from the storage room with two dusty bottles under his arm. With practised ease he uncorked the bottles and gave them each a sniff, nodding in appreciation.

"You two enjoy while I prepare dinner," Melrose instructed as he poured the red liquid into three glasses.

"So what's on the menu?" Logan asked after accepting the glass.

"Beef stew, apparently," Melores replied sceptically as he took two cans of food from his backpack and poured them into a pot he'd scrounged. The contents fell into the pot with an unappetising plop. But as it heated up, the stew filled the room with a delicious smell that made them all realize how hungry they were.

Before too long the stew was ladled into three bowls and passed along the table. Melrose then pulled out a bag of rolls he'd taken from the baker at the Manor, passing them around as Logan refilled the wine glasses. Famished they attacked their food without speaking to one another, pausing only long enough to drink their wine.

"How have you found the transition Logan?" Melrose inquired after they had all pushed their empty bowls into the middle of the table.

"Good I guess, but it probably hasn't all sunk in yet," Logan admitted. "I mean none of this seems possible; a hidden island, portals through time, people centuries old. But this castle is real and this wine is real, so I don't know."

"I suppose it must be very mystifying," Melrose acknowledged. "Myself, I've lived on the island my entire life and don't know anything different."

"How long has that been?"

"Over fifty years," Melrose answered truthfully.

"That's crazy, you don't look much older than me."

Melrose merely shrugged in response, not sure what else to say.

"I wonder if the fountain of youth is on this island," Logan mused to himself, eyeing his wine glass. He then looked at his companions and saw they were intrigued by his statement. "There's a legend about a fountain of youth, the water providing long life to whoever drinks from it. It was rumoured to be in Florida, where I'm from, during the days of exploration. One explorer, Ponce de Leon is even thought to have found it during his travels."

Melrose and Logan continued talking into the night, sharing stories and experiences as both tried to learn about each other's worlds. Jane chimed in every once in a while, but her mind was elsewhere. She was disappointed at having found nothing and she was missing her warm bed. She didn't know when Tiberius would return and she had wanted to present him with something more than a few maps.

She also found herself wishing Patrick was with her in this search. She missed his calming influence and the safety she felt in his presence. Jane knew that his mission was just as important, but she felt that if he were with her they would have discovered something important. But a part of her rebelled at these thoughts for their weakness. She'd long prided her independence, never needing to rely on anyone. Even when she'd sided with Lord Lodge over Dr. Cleaver, she had done it on her own terms and not out of need for protection.

These duelling feelings made her unsure on how to deal with Patrick and probably led to her trying to ignore the situation completely. It had been easy when she was preparing for her mission to recruit Logan, she'd been too busy to really think about him. But after her return she'd tried hard to ignore her mixed feelings for the Lord of the Brown Pack, resulting in her cold business-like demeanour during their few brief encounters. Jane actually felt a twinge of guilt, recalling his confused and pained expression from her nonchalance.

"One more bottle," Logan called out as he emptied the second bottle of wine, bringing Jane back to the present.

"Yes sir," Melrose saluted after draining his own glass, heading back to the storage room.

"Don't call me sir, I work for a living," Logan called after him, chuckling as he heard a loud noise. "You ok in there? You haven't drunk nearly enough to be falling over."

"Uh, Miss Piper, Logan," Melrose replied excitedly after a brief pause. "You had better come in here."

Jane and Logan shot each other a questioning look and then got up from the table. Reverting to his training, Logan grabbed the rifle leaning against the table beside him and followed Jane into the storage room.

They both stopped with wide eyed surprise as they found Melrose standing in front of an open passage door where the wine rack had been. A staircase descended into darkness below.

"I tried to grab one of the bottles and it didn't budge," Melrose reported, unable to contain his joy. "So I gave it a stronger pull and woosh, the wine rack slid backwards."

Chapter 20

"Hans is one canny character," Dufresne observed as he watched the Stasi officer check the surrounding street before unlocking the door to his house. They'd been trailing Hans Blick for days after his meeting with Guy at a small café. True to his word, the gangster had met with Herr Blick and proposed his smuggling deal without tipping off the German operative that Interpol was on to him.

"He was probably trained at Moscow Center by the KGB," Tiberius surmised from the other side of the empty apartment. Inspector Midoux had obtained keys to an empty apartment for use as an observation post and makeshift headquarters. "He does all the right things to avoid detection. Sadly for him it's too late."

"How do you want to proceed?" Morgan asked as he calmly sharpened a blade.

"I think we should confront him as soon as possible," Tiberius decided, standing up and pacing the room. "We're not here to build a case against him, so continuing to watch him has little added value. We shock him and then put the questions to him, forcefully if necessary."

"What if he clams up?" Dufresne challenged behind his binoculars.

"He won't," Tiberius guessed. "I doubt he wanted Zeidt killed and merely acted on someone else's behalf. Depending on what his job is with East German Intelligence, he would have contacts for the kind of guys who carry out dirty jobs."

"But what if the hit was sanctioned by the East Germans?"

"Then I'd say the chances of Zeidt being killed because of his knowledge of a mole at the Manor would be slim and our job is done."

"Right."

They watched the house in shifts throughout the rest of the day, but seeing very little through Blick's closed blinds. By late-afternoon Tiberius heard Morgan offer a small exclamation from the window, signalling that Blick was once again on the move. Dufresne was already on the street ready to follow their target.

Tiberius moved to the window and hefted his own set of binoculars and watched as Blick sauntered down the street towards a corner store. He went into it, emerging a moment later with a coffee, carefully watching the few occupants on the street. Seemingly satisfied, he continued his route around the corner and out of sight.

"I've got him," Dufresne announced over the radio in the room. "Heading towards the park."

The last few days they'd followed Hans Blick to the same park, watching him put chalk marks on benches and meeting people seemingly at random. Tiberius had some experience with intelligence operations and the park looked like Blick's place of business. To the casual observer he would be just another middle aged man out for a daily stroll, completely harmless and easily forgotten. But now that he'd been identified as a foreign intelligence officer, his actions were being scrutinized and the park was no longer the safe zone he thought it was.

"I'll be heading over then," Morgan smiled, collecting a series of weapons from a nearby table. He placed a small pistol in an ankle holster, a knife in his jacket and a silenced pistol in the small of his back.

"Remember, don't kill him, just scare him," Tiberius reminded him. "I'll be right behind him in case he tries to make a run for it."

Morgan nodded solemnly, knowing his boss trusted him and that it was just nerves making him nag. He walked out of the apartment and glided down the few flights of stairs to the front foyer. The day was growing cool as the sun began to set and Morgan was glad it would soon be dark.

Unlike most people, Morgan was completely at home in the dark. He didn't know if it was because he'd be born before the advent of electricity, or the fact that he'd grown up inside the dark confines of sailing ships. But what he did know was that he'd come to see darkness as another tool to be used to his advantage.

Within a few minutes he walked around the block and was approaching Blick's house from the back. A small street snaked its way behind the row of houses, small gardens and parking spaces running along it. Morgan already knew which house belonged to Blick, recognizing it from an earlier reconnaissance. A small Volkswagen sat in the gravel parking space behind the house and Morgan leaned down to let out the air of the driver's side tires just as a precaution.

The back door yielded to his collection of tiny tools and he was careful to replace a small wooden wedge in the door frame. It was obviously a warning sign for Blick if he came in through the back, signalling that someone had broken in. Morgan was pretty sure there would be more telltale signs within the house, but he didn't bother looking for them. Once inside, it would be too late for Herr Hans.

From their observations, Blick seemed to spend most of his time in the front room, his shadow moving against the drawn curtains. Morgan found the space was a sitting room converted into an office with a large desk and a pair of chairs on the other side. An electric typewriter was prominently placed on the desk, no doubt used to prepare articles to fulfill his cover as a journalist. A collection of filing cabinets were lined against the far wall with a wingback chair wedged between them in the corner. Morgan removed a stack of newspapers from the chair and pulled his pistol out as he sat down. The chair was actually quite comfortable as he leaned back and waited for his prey to enter.

As the room became black with nightfall Morgan was in no danger of falling asleep on the comfortable chair. He was energized with the feeling of the hunt, all of his senses fully alert. He loved the thrill of the chase and the anticipation of the catch, the kill merely being something he did under certain circumstances. He didn't enjoy killing people and remembered the faces of all of the ones he had. But he also knew that most of those had deserved their end.

"He's coming," rasped the short message in Morgan's earpiece, making him slow his breathing. A few moments later he heard a key in the lock and the door slid open, footsteps echoing along the front hall. A nearby streetlight shined a sliver of light through the sitting room curtains, allowing Blick to cross to his desk without turning on any lights.

Morgan couldn't help but smile as he watched his target remove his jacket with a heavy sigh and throw it over one of the chairs, finally sitting in his own with a thump. He was completely oblivious to Morgan's presence in his house, which would only make the next step that much sweeter.

"Mein Gott!" Blick exclaimed clutching his chest with shock after he flicked his desk lamp on and observed Morgan sitting casually in the far chair. The look of shock turned to disbelief and confusion as he tried to figure out what was happening.

"Guten tag Herr Blick," Morgan whispered coldly, his dark eyes betraying no emotion. Morgan was fairly sure Blick had come across enough killers to realize the severity of his situation without being told.

"What are you doing in my house?" he challenged weakly fumbling with his desk drawer.

"You've been a naughty boy Hans," Morgan replied without any hint of humour. "Don't bother with the gun in that drawer, you'll find it rather useless without the bullets."

Blick hesitated for a moment before he looked at the silenced pistol on Morgan's lap. With a mixture of fear and frustration he slammed the desk drawer shut.

"What do you want? Who sent you?!"

"I did," announced a firm voice from the sitting room doorway. Blick looked over in shock as his sanctum had been invaded by not one, but two thoroughly dangerous looking men.

"Who are you?" Blick asked hesitantly, still unsure what the reason for their presence was.

"Someone you'd don't want to make an enemy of."

"That doesn't answ…" Blick began weakly before being cut off by a mincing glare from Tiberius.

"I'm going to tell you a story and you're not going to speak until I tell you, nod if you understand"

Blick nodded once, still confused by what was going on.

"This man was killed by a waiter who laced his drink with poison at a café," Tiberius began, placing the photo of Zeidt on the desk followed by a few more. "This is the waiter who fled the scene and was hit by a car and killed moments later. This last photo is you meeting this assassin at the casino, passing him a note by the craps table."

"But I…"

Blick's protestation was cut short when the side of his chair exploded as a bullet slammed into it, sending the padding into the air. He looked over in horror as Morgan sat with the smoking gun, still sitting on his lap.

"That's your first warning, do you understand?" Tiberius repeated, content when Blick's head bobbed up and down enthusiastically. "Did that note contain instructions to kill the man in the first picture?"

Blick made a small jerking nod, his eyes locked on the gun sitting on Morgan's lap. In all the years he'd worked in the intelligence business, he'd never had his cover blown before. Without it he felt naked and powerless, too concerned with his well being to make any denials or to try and develop a new story.

"Why was he targeted? Who wanted him killed?" When Blick didn't react Tiberius snapped his finger, drawing the man's attention back from the gun. As Blick hesitated over an answer, Tiberius realized he couldn't nod a reply. "You may speak now."

"I was instructed to terminate him from my superiors in Berlin," Blick finally offered, his anxious voice becoming more accented than before.

"Why?"

"Apparently he was a member of an emerging fascist group intent on conducting counter revolutionary activities in East Germany," he rhymed off quickly.

It sounded like a party line to Tiberius and he wasn't fooled in the least. But he wasn't sure if it was Blick or his superiors that had constructed it.

"Herr Blick, I had hoped that we could do this in a civilized manner, however you're not leaving me much choice," Tiberius trailed off nodding to Morgan. Flashing his first smile, Morgan stood up and placed his pistol on the nearest filing cabinet. He then removed the knife from his jacket, flicking it open with menace.

"But I'm telling you the truth!" Blick exclaimed upon seeing the glinting blade and imagining the worst. He'd seen violent interrogations before and was not brave enough to want to experience one. "The man in the photo was accessing funds stored in a numbered swiss bank account."

"So?"

"After the war the Russians put together a list of known and suspected Nazi sympathisers and collaborators," Blick explained quickly, knowing he'd only have one chance. "Through this work they were able to identify numbered bank accounts that held ill-gotten Nazi loot. But many of the owners were unknown and inaccessible. So they put a watch on these accounts, ready to pounce when any funds were withdrawn."

"Go on," Tiberius instructed as the Stasi officer paused.

"The KGB lost interest in the whole activity over the years and we've taken over the vigil. Some time ago a contact of ours at one of the banks reported activity on an account on our list. A quick investigation led us to this banker in Luxembourg and I was ordered to facilitate a resolution."

Part of the story rang true to Tiberius as he listened to Hans Blick. The man was definitely scared enough to avoid telling any outright lies and didn't have enough time to manufacture the story. He also knew that Zeidt probably had access to old Swiss accounts that he would have managed during the war. He could have easily discovered which owners were dead and decided to use their money to continue his lavish lifestyle. But there was one part that didn't add up and was nagging Tiberius.

Josef Zeidt, though a soulless and self-centered human being, was not a Nazi. He hadn't been at their height of power and was probably even less so with their demise. The man worshipped money and had no time for theoretical politics. So Tiberius wasn't convinced with the explanation that Zeidt was trying to fund neo-fascists.

"That's a nice story, but I don't believe you," Tiberius frowned with feigned dismay, nodding at Morgan who was lurking beside Blick.

"That's the truth!" Blick pleaded desperately.

"What are you leaving out?" Tiberius demanded, sure there was more to the story. "How were you able to trace the withdrawal to this man?"

"Through some informants," he replied vaguely, before succumbing to Tiberius' impatient glare. "I received a tip that money from a Nazi account was going to be withdrawn and I made a deal to share the funds. They said he was using the money to finance neo-nazis and that they'd help me stop him if we split the amount he took out."

"Who contacted you?"

"They didn't use any names, but they said they were his business partners," Blick continued warily. "They found out what he was trying to do and wanted to stop him, having lost family to the Nazi's. I received details on the man and which bank would be used."

"How did you plan on keeping the money after informing your superiors in Berlin," Tiberius challenged, not completely convinced. "Millions in Nazi gold would certainly be grabbed up swiftly."

"They didn't know about the money," Hans disclosed looking down at his hands. "I requested approval to eliminate the man and left the bank transfer out. They agreed after hearing of his plans to support neo-nazis."

"So there was no secret list of bank accounts, no contact at the bank, and probably no neo-nazi movement being supported?" Tiberius summed up, seeing the truth. "This was all a way to make some money and cover your ass from your bosses, wasn't it? It was just you and these business men trying to steal some money."

Suddenly the whole scenario made sense and Tiberius understood the probable sequence of events. When Cleaver threatened Zeidt to leave the Manor, he travelled to this time and place in order to make use of funds he'd squirreled away in his numbered bank accounts. He planned on living out the rest of his life here, but someone discovered his plan and devised one of their own. The list of suspects that could have known about Zeidt's financial situation was pretty short.

Suddenly Tiberius felt an icy ball of doubt in his stomach as he recalled his meeting with Zeidt. The banker must have discovered the plot against him, forcing him to make contact with the Manor. Rather than get his own hands dirty, he had planned on using Tiberius to get rid of his enemies.

He'd sat at the café with that flattering smile, offering up his men as an exchange to stay in Luxembourg. It hadn't just been a sign of goodwill, it had been a matter of survival. They were the only ones who would have known about Zeidt's activities and had probably helped him make his financial arrangements upon exiting the portal. But they'd acted quicker than Zeidt thought possible, the assassin striking with deadly efficiency.

"What are you going to do to me?" Blick uttered, breaking the silence.

"That depends on how helpful you are," Tiberius replied, eyeing him coldly. "In a few minutes the Luxembourg Gendarmerie will be here to arrest you for espionage. Until then you have three choices.

"One, you can answer my next few questions truthfully. In which case I will make sure that you end up traded for another Western agent being held by the Stasi.

"Two, you can remain silent and refuse to answer my questions. I will accept your decision but will make no effort to help you and you will probably be imprisoned for life.

"Three, you can lie to my questions and try to be clever. In that case you will be charged with espionage, smuggling, and other criminal activities. You will then be sent back to East Germany and I will make sure your superiors discover all the crimes you've committed in the name of capitalism. I wonder how they will react to that news."

The threat hung in the air as Blick struggled to maintain his composure. He'd worked hard to accumulate a decent amount of wealth in order to start a new life. Now he saw it crumbling around him and there was only one option left open for him.

"What would you like to know?"

"I need the contact information for your informants. You will tell my associate here their names, addresses, secret codes, everything," Tiberius ordered, relieved to see the look of utter submission on Blick's face as he nodded once again. While he disclosed what he knew to Morgan, Tiberius took a quick walk through the house. He wasn't really looking for anything, merely needing some time to think.

Every time he took a step towards discovering the truth about the presence of a mole at the Manor, another step seemed to emerge. He'd hoped that Zeidt had made some enemies since arriving and that they'd ordered his death. For a moment he'd felt relieved when Blick had said that the Stasi had been behind Zeidt's assassin, but the moment passed as he quickly saw the lie.

From everything Blick said there was a chance that this still had nothing to do with a mole. Zeidt's men might simply have been greedy and distrustful of their leader, conspiring with a crooked agent to achieve their goals. But there was also the chance that they were more devoted to Dr. Cleaver than Zeidt and decided to steal his money and have him killed because he might give up the name of the mole.

Both scenarios were possible and Tiberius wouldn't be comfortable until he had all three men in custody in front of him. He knew all three well and would be able to get whatever information he wanted out of them. But first he had to find them.

*

"Sorry for the disturbance Mrs Holloway," Pierce apologised as he led MacDuff back into Cedric Holloway's study. "It appears some gun toting kidnappers and federal fugitives decided to crash your party."

"Thank goodness you were here," she exclaimed behind a tear stained face. "I can't imagine what would have happened if you hadn't been here."

"Can't you?"

"Now what's that supposed to mean?" she countered angrily. "I don't like your tone. My father is friends with the Governor, so if you and your…"

Pierce sat quietly as she rambled on with threats and demands, barely registering what she was saying. He knew she was involved with Debochev somehow, but he wasn't sure how. He'd have to be careful questioning her. Threats probably wouldn't get him too far and any use of force made his skin crawl. He suddenly had a thought that brought a smile to his face. He would try the Columbo technique and see where he got.

"You're right of course, you couldn't possibly be a part of this," Pierce finally admitted after she finished her frenetic diatribe. "But I'd be really grateful if you could both have another look at these photos. My boss is a real stickler for this kind of thing."

MacDuff leaned over and passed the photos around again, but received the same responses as before.

"Are you sure you've never seen them before?" Pierce prodded hopefully. "Maybe while you were driving, at a party, somewhere else?"

"No, never," she confirmed impatiently.

"Any idea why they might have come here?" Pierce asked, trying to look as confused as possible.

"I have no idea," Caroline Holloway answered quickly.

"Maybe they saw the party and thought it would be a good place to disappear, blend in," Cedric Holloway offered helpfully, smiling when Pierce nodded.

"That is a possibility."

"They drive by, see the crowd and try to ditch their car," MacDuff agreed, following Pierce's lead. "With all the people they probably thought they could even swap cars."

"But that doesn't account for the two separate cars arriving at the same party," Pierce frowned as he tapped a pencil against his notebook. "I must have forgotten to tell you. The reason we were here in the first place is that we followed a suspicious car to your house."

"They could have been coming to the party, some of Caroline's friends are pretty suspicious characters," Cedric laughed at his own joke, but was quickly silenced by a frosty look from his wife.

"Obviously the men from the two cars were working together," Caroline continued, shifting her gaze to Pierce. "The first car you followed found the party and then telephoned their friends to join them here."

"That makes sense," Pierce agreed with momentary relief before frowning once again. "But then why did they go to the boathouse?"

"What do you mean?" Cedric asked with renewed interest.

"The second car crashed into a station wagon out front," MacDuff summarised. "But the car we followed was found in the boathouse."

"Do you own a boat Mr. Holloway?" Pierce asked.

"Heavens no," his wife answered for him, happily attempting to humiliate him. "Poor Cedric hasn't the stomach for boats. He practically gets seasick by just looking at the ocean."

"Well then what could they possibly want with your boathouse?" Pierce replied with another tap of his notebook.

"I don't think either one of us has ever been in the boathouse. We've never owned a boat, it simply came with the house. We locked it up and have never been in there since."

A knock on the door brought Pierce's attention away from the couple and he nodded at MacDuff to answer it. The Scotsman marched over to the door and spoke with one of the policeman for a second before receiving an envelope. He closed the door and brought the envelope over to Pierce, telling him it held the pictures they'd requested inside. The crime scene technicians had worked their magic getting photos of the dead men outside developed so quickly.

"These are the men we, ah, apprehended tonight," Pierce explained as he pulled the photo's out of the envelope and handed them around. "Do these men look familiar to you?"

Again the couple stared at them and shook their heads in ignorance, but this time Pierce could tell the wife's reaction was more honest.

"Well I had to ask, we won't take up any more of your time," Pierce thanked them, much to the wife's relief and the husband's dismay. Pierce followed MacDuff to the door after the photos were collected, only to stop halfway across the room. He shuffled back around to face them, a cunning smile breaking out across his face. "Ah, actually there's just one more thing."

Chapter 21

"How is it that one of the men we killed was found with a key to the boathouse in his pocket if neither of you have ever seen him before," Pierce asked pointedly as he walked back towards the couple who had stood up to follow them out.

Caroline opened her mouth to reply, but nothing came out as she looked at Pierce's stern face. She then fell back onto her chair as he returned and placed the photos back on the table.

"I believe that you've never seen these men before," Pierce acknowledged as he pointed at the group of men they'd killed that evening. "But I know you're lying to me about the other three."

Cedric Holloway looked at his wife in shock while she simply stared defiantly at a space between Pierce and MacDuff.

"Mr. Holloway, where is the boat house key regularly stored?" Pierce asked, placing a photo of the boathouse key on the table between them. It was a small brass key with a wooden anchor keychain.

"In the mudroom cabinet, hanging on a clothes hook," he answered thoughtfully, picturing its location.

"Shut up!" Caroline exclaimed through gritted teeth, seething at her husband's continued assistance. "This place was a madhouse; those men could have come in and taken a key without anyone noticing."

"They just happened to find the very key they needed in an obscure storage location in an unknown house?" Pierce laughed hollowly. "I think they chose this house specifically and knew exactly where the key was stored."

"But how?" Cedric asked, trying to follow what was happening.

"You're wife told one of these three men, who in turn told these goons," Pierce explained, seeing the truth of the statement in Caroline's reaction.

"But why?"

"That's a good question Mr. Holloway, one that only your wife can answer," he replied, his steely gaze never leaving her. "However I'll give it a try and we'll see how close I get. I believe that this house, and more specifically your boathouse, is used as a stopping point for an inter-state kidnapping ring."

"That's preposterous!" Caroline Holloway shrieked before clamming up once again.

"We tracked a car that we know had been used to abduct a young woman from Los Angeles a few days ago. She was transferred between cars in Bakersfield and we followed that car to your house. It now sits in the boathouse, with the girl gone but the driver dead on the lawn."

"The second car that appeared was also involved with the initial kidnapping," MacDuff lied, not wanting to get into too many details.

"I believe that the girl was loaded onto a boat that docked here and whisked her away to join others like her," Pierce continued calmly, staring straight at Caroline. "They probably went north and that means the ultimate destination is Oregon, Washington, or Canada. Do you know what that means?"

"It means that this is a Federal case," MacDuff chimed in when no one else spoke.

"Exactly," Pierce confirmed. "The penalty is much greater and the case is well out of the control of your Daddy's pal the Governor. The crime scene techs are scouring the boathouse as we speak and they're going to find evidence of multiple women being there. I'm then going to have them search the house. What are the odds we're going to find more evidence in your basement?"

"Betting odds I'd wager," MacDuff smiled.

"You might be able to wrangle out of the drug charges heading your way from that party downstairs. But you're sure as hell not walking away from a federal kidnapping charge," Pierce threatened, finally turning up the volume of the interrogation. "And if you don't tell us where that boat is heading, you're going to be stuck with the entire jail bill."

"But those girls weren't kidnapped," Caroline finally muttered as she stared at the photos on the table. "Master Gladius wouldn't do that, he doesn't need to."

"Master Gladius?" Pierce asked. Caroline Holloway wordlessly pointed towards the photo of Debochev on the table.

"Master Gladius, leader of the Holy Order of the Glorious Light," she rhymed off almost reverently. "The girls were all for him, but they weren't kidnapped. They needed salvation and awakening that only he could provide. He is a holy man who would never stoop to kidnapping."

"What a load of..." MacDuff scoffed, rolling his eyes in disbelief.

"It's the truth!" she pleaded.

"Calm down Mrs. Holloway," Pierce instructed, worried that she'd lost her control. The rich woman's carefully constructed mask of snobbish indifference was cracking and he still had more questions. So he decided to change his approach from confrontational to one of support. "I believe you and this is all some kind of misunderstanding. But I'm going to need your help to prove it. I need to know where to find Master Gladius."

"Why should I help you?"

"Because I trust you and I don't want anyone getting hurt."

"What do you mean?" she uttered behind wide eyes.

"If you tell us where he is, then I'll know that you're telling us the truth," Pierce explained softly. "In that case only two of us will go and see Master Gladius to make sure these girls are truly there for, uh, enlightenment. We won't arrest anyone or cause any trouble."

"And if I refuse to tell you?"

"We're the FBI," Pierce stated proudly. "We'll find him without your help, but then we'll know you were hiding something. In that case I will organize an entire platoon of heavily armed agents and we will storm his compound. We will arrest everyone, along with yourself, and slowly investigate the whole affair."

"But what if someone gets shot or even killed?"

"That will be on your head, not mine," Pierce retorted. "I gave you a chance for a peaceful resolution and you ignored it."

Pierce watched as an inner battle raged in her mind, trying to figure out the right decision. Finally she seemed to completely deflate on the chair, collapsing in on herself as she sunk down. With a few rigid nods she signalled her desire to help.

Still shocked by everything that had occurred, Cedric Holloway stood up from his seat and walked over to a wooden sideboard. With a shaking hand he poured a large drink, not offering one to anyone else in the room.

Mrs. Holloway slowly stood up from her chair and motioned for Pierce to follow her out of the room. Two police officers were still outside the door and Pierce signalled one of the men to follow him. She led them along the upstairs hall to the other side of the mansion ignorant of all of the activity going on beyond the balcony below. Uniformed officers, detectives, and crime scene techs scurried about the ground floor collecting evidence. Most of the party goers were gone, either sent home or sent to jail.

Pierce followed her into what appeared to be the master bedroom that would offer a magnificent view of the ocean during the day. A large waterbed sat in the middle of the room and Pierce smiled at the woman's obvious attempt to keep her sea sick husband out of her bed.

Carefully opening a jewellery chest, Caroline Holloway pulled out a folded up piece of paper from beneath a collection of pearl necklaces. With lowered eyes she passed the paper over to Pierce before sitting on the edge of her bed, slowly bobbing as the water shifted beneath her.

Pierce immediately recognized it as a section of road map as he unfolded the paper, the various coloured lines criss-crossing a section of coast. A thick red line was traced along the middle of the map; starting on an interstate and ending in a secluded bay. Also jumping out at him were the thick black letters spanning the map O-R-E-G-O-N.

"I appreciate your help Mrs. Holloway," Pierce offered as he folded the map back up and placed it in his suit pocket. "I'll do everything in my power to help you avoid any formal charges."

"Thank you," she beamed him a smile, her face much more sweet than the shrewd look he saw in her eyes.

After returning her smile Pierce retreated from the bedroom, shaking his head with wonder and dismay. She really thought she'd tricked him into believing she was an innocent bystander in the entire affair. But he wasn't fooled by the act. He knew she was probably up to her head with the scheme to kidnap girls for Debochev's evil desires. It probably excited her to be a part of something dangerous and mystical, a break from her carefully planned life.

"Agent Gunn," called out a familiar voice and Pierce looked over to the police lieutenant walking up the staircase. "The marshals left with the prisoner. They were going to take him to the jail, but it's at capacity with all the drug charges I've laid. So they took him to a local Motel, the El Lobo, thought you'd like to know."

"Thanks," Pierce accepted as he tried to figure out how to broach his next request. He hoped the cop standing beside him had an ambitious streak. "I imagine this is going to be a big headache you weren't looking for. A mansion full of the rich and influential, a myriad of drug charges and potential lawsuits..."

"No kidding," he agreed with a disheartened nod. "And the worst part is that most of them will walk. The city doesn't have the means or the time to prosecute this mess."

"I think I can make it up to you," Pierce offered conspiratorially. "My case is closed here and I'll be leaving town with the Marshal's. Another case is waiting for me. But I uncovered something that you could work and take credit for."

"What's that?" he asked suspiciously.

"We interviewed the homeowners as a matter of routine," Pierce began, pulling the Lieutenant aside as few technicians passed them. "Somehow they thought I was here about something else and ended up divulging some interesting information; a potential kidnapping ring."

"The husband?"

"The wife," Pierce corrected with a raised eyebrow. "When I asked them about the boathouse she became defensive and then broke down. Apparently some girls have been kept in the boathouse and the basement. I'd have the tech's tear both apart and compare evidence against any lost children notices."

"Son of a bitch," the cop swore, sharing his profession's disgust at kidnappers.

"The husband seems clean, but that woman is one devious bitch," Pierce summed up, feeling his own anger rising. "Don't quote me on this but charge the shit out of her."

"What about you?"

"What about me?" Pierce asked innocently. "I've got enough on my plate without opening a new file. We showed up and either killed or captured the fugitives and then left. Your diligence in collecting evidence of drug use turned up the link to the kidnappings. This is a career building case, just keep me out of it."

"Deal," smiled the Lieutenant shooting his hand out. Pierce grabbed it and they shook hands warmly.

"Agent Gunn? I think we're all done here," reported MacDuff as he walked up.

"You're right," Pierce nodded to his associate before once more turning to the cop. "Give her hell."

*

The Royal Luxembourg Hotel straddled the edge of the old city and the parks that surrounded the north. It was one of the most prestigious hotels in the city, offering fine dining and excellent service. The staff also offered their guests a certain amount of anonymity that the rich and famous often desired. The lengths they would go to maintain this were finite however, when faced with a police warrant.

After handing Hans Blick over to Inspector Midoux, Tiberius had decided to share some of the information he had gained. He told the young officer that Blick was an admitted agent of the East German Stasi and that it was the Germans who had ordered the death of the Banker. Believing in Zeidt's fictional history as a shadowy international figure, Midoux easily swallowed the lie.

He then shared the false identities of Zeidt's three pack members, who Morgan had tracked to the hotel. He told the Inspector that they were Stasi Agents, a hit squad that was in place to take out the Banker if the assassin had failed. He further offered his truthful opinion that one of them had probably been behind the wheel of the car that had killed the assassin.

Eager to help, Midoux had used his charm and persuasive skills to obtain permission to set up surveillance on the hotel and the three suspects. There were observers with tech gear and an armed response team watching the hotel around the clock, much more than Tiberius could have organized alone.

"Looks like another batch of escorts have finally left," observed someone from the surveillance team as a group of women walked out the front door. They were the same women that the team had watched through the hotel room windows of their targets.

"Surely they'll go to sleep soon," offered a second tech behind a yawn, surprised and little jealous of their targets' vigour.

Tiberius felt a little helpless in the observation post as he stood at the back wall overseeing things. These were all Midoux's men and he had to take a back seat. Deciding to check in on his own men, he silently left the room and strode down the empty hallway beyond.

The police were using an office building across the street, closing off an entire floor due to an "electrical problem". The mirrored windows provided them with a clear view into the target's suite without the possibility of counter detection.

"Those guys always were pigs," Dufresne commented after Tiberius asked them how things were progressing. His two men were positioned on the roof of the office building, Morgan behind his sniper rifle and Dufresne as his spotter.

"Not really keeping a low profile," seconded Morgan as he rolled onto his side and stretched his arms and fingers.

"Hopefully they think everything is over and they'll become complacent," Tiberius offered, not really believing it. There was something bothering him about the current situation. Members of the Black Tower Hunt Club and their deadly assistants were in the practice of staying in the shadows and not drawing attention to themselves. It was for this reason that they had survived throughout the centuries without anyone ever noticing. There weren't even any crackpot conspiracy theorists spouting conjectures about their existence. So why were these men living it up like rock stars in a reputable and well known hotel?

"Sir," Dufresne announced with a hint of worry from behind his spotter's scope.

Tiberius shook the thoughts of doubt from his head and looked over to the Frenchman. Dufresne merely pointed down to the street, where a handful of armed policeman were swarming towards the door of the hotel. Inspector Midoux was among them and Tiberius was furious.

"What the hell is he doing?!" he growled to no one in particular, pulling out a radio from his pocket. "Midoux? This is Inspector Tiber, what is going on?"

"We're going to take them now," came the crackled response, Midoux's young enthusiastic voice recognizable over the radio. "They'll be asleep soon and won't be prepared for us."

"Wait, we don't have enough intel!" Tiberius urged.

"Now's our chance, out."

Tiberius wanted to throw the radio onto the street in frustration. He knew exactly what was happening. The young ambitious policeman was eager to apprehend some foreign secret agents before any of his superiors arrived to steal the glory. The young man saw this as his opportunity for advancement and didn't care about the consequences.

"Dufresne, get over there and make sure they don't fuck this all up," Tiberius ordered angrily. "Those are just normal cops, not tactical troops and they have no idea what kind of men are in that room."

"Yes sir," Dufresne nodded, rolling up and taking off towards the rooftop stairwell at a jog.

"What are you going to do?" Morgan asked as he once again took his position behind the sniper scope.

"I'm going to go back to down to the ops center," Tiberius replied thoughtfully. "Someone will have to be ready to take charge when this goes to shit."

"Sounds good," Morgan chuckled before jerking his head down. "Down!"

Years of experience made Tiberius' body react to the command before he fully processed what was going on. But the echo of gunfire quickly made him realize the situation. From his belly he looked over to Morgan whose head was lowered as bits of concrete exploded in front of him.

"I think they've spotted us," he laughed, seemingly only happy when in a gunfight.

"Shit they're walking into a trap," Tiberius swore as he scrambled towards the stairwell door. He reached it without incident and began descending the stairs two at a time. Breathlessly he ran into the makeshift operations center, a businessman's office crammed with radios and people. "What's going on over there?!"

"There's one gunman shooting out of the hotel window," reported one of the observers at the window. "He's shifted his fire from your man on the roof to some of the police cars that have just shown up on the street."

"Where's Midoux right now?"

"Sir, they're on the same floor right now and are about to assault the room," reported another man with a headset beside a radio.

"Tell him to wait," Tiberius commanded, trying to slow things down.

"No response."

"Keep trying," Tiberius uttered between curses.

"I've got eyes on one of the targets," Morgan's voice came over the radio in Tiberius' hands. "No ID yet, his face is hidden. Execute?"

"Wing him," Tiberius immediately responded. "We need them alive."

"Acknowledged." A second later a loud shot rang out from above them, the sound of the higher caliber weapon unmistakable. "One target is down."

"Lots of gunfire and yelling now, I think they've breached," reported a third man holding a parabolic microphone. He had a large pair of padded headphones attached to it and was using it to listen in on the room across the street.

"Dufresne, what's going on?" Tiberius yelled into the radio in his hand. It took a few moments before a crackled reply came through.

"We're pinned down in the hallway," he responded breathlessly. "They've got some heavy weapons in there and some of the cops are already down. Wait they're going in again..."

The radio then cut out amongst the cacophony of gunfire and shouting.

"What's going on over there?" Tiberius pleaded, frustrated at feeling so powerless.

"I think it's over," Morgan announced over the radio moments later. "I see uniforms walking around the room."

"Confirmed," one of the observers concurred.

"Sir, Inspector Midoux for you," announced the radio operator, passing the mic to Tiberius.

"Midoux, report," Tibnerius ordered angrily.

"Suspects are all down," he said tiredly from the other end. "We...we need some ambulances here. Casulaties..."

"Hang on, they're on the way," Tiberius reassured him despite the rage he felt within. He needed those men alive! Calming down he ordered one of the men to get some ambulances to the scene and to inform their headquarters of what had happened. "I'm going across the street to sort this mess out."

"Morgan, Dufresne, you both still with me?" he asked over the radio as he walked down the stairwell to the ground floor. They both confirmed quickly, giving Tiberius a sliver of relief. "Dufrense, ID the bodies and make sure they're dead. Morgan, get to the car and get ready to leave. If they're truly dead then I want us out of here quickly. We can't get involved with the enormous investigation that this fiasco is going to create. Too many questions and too much scrutiny."

The sound of sirens filled the street as Tiberius emerged from the office building and walked across the street. The blinking lights of the emergency vehicles seemed impossibly numerous as they reflected off the neighbouring buildings. Looking up at the hotel, he could clearly see wisps of smoke escaping the embattled hotel room.

"Sir, there's a problem," Dufresne reported hesitantly over the radio. "These men aren't them."

"What? That doesn't make any sense," Tiberius reacted with confusion, stopping in the middle of the street. "We observed them in that room. Wait, something's not right..."

Tiberius' mind suddenly switched into overdrive and he was suddenly overcome by a swirling mess of thoughts and images. Their surveillance of the men at the hotel had been too easy and the targets had been too indiscrete. Hounds of the Manor would never act like that. And then there was the gunman who had suddenly started shooting at Morgan on the rooftop. Plus there was the presence of the heavy weapons in the hotel room. Walking around with machine guns in Europe was a real risk. None of it made any sense unless they had been watching the whole thing and had been waiting for the assault. Tiberius couldn't help but think that if that were true than this whole operation had been a set-up…

"Dufresne are you sure?"

"I've known Zeidt's men for a long time, of course I'm sure," he replied with a hint of annoyance seeping through.

"Get the hell out of there!" Tiberius yelled at the radio as an icy feeling ran up his spine. "Get everyone out of …!"

Before he could finish a large spout of flames shot out of the hotel window, raining down bodies, glass, and debris onto the ground below. The explosion echoed throughout the street and was soon followed by sounds of shrieks and screams. Smoke billowed out of the hotel window and fire alarms soon joined the nightmarish orchestra.

"Dufresne!" Tiebrius screamed as he sprinted towards the sidewalk where some of the bodies had landed. A wave of relief flooded over him when his trusted friend was not among the doomed men.

The sound of screeching tires brought Tiberius' attention from the ravaged scene to the back of the hotel. The ramp for the parking garage was there and he got close enough to see a black BMW crash through the gate and veer on to the road. Without thinking he drew his pistol and began firing at the car. The rear window shattered before he ran out of bullets, quickly speeding out of view.

Seething with fury Tiberius was about to chase after the car on foot when he heard a car pull up beside him. Morgan was behind the wheel of a powerful Mercedes sedan and yelled at him to get in. Ripping the door open, Tiberius jumped in and was barely sitting before they off in pursuit.

Morgan deftly changed gears while accelerating, concentrating on the swerving vehicle ahead. Watching it speed through an intersection as the light changed, he stomped on the gas determined to follow. They dashed through the intersection amid the honking complaints of their fellow drivers, missing a pedestrian by mere feet.

The tight winding streets of Luxembourg City slowly became wider and more open as they drove away from the center of town. With fewer cars surrounding them, the more powerful Mercedes was easily able to close the gap with the fleeing vehicle ahead.

"Want me to ram him off the road?" Morgan asked with a devilish grin, his two hands clamped on the wheel.

"You read my mind," Tiberius yelled over the roaring engine.

Dodging the odd car between them, Morgan slowly approached the other car, waiting for the perfect opportunity. He wanted to nudge the back corner in such a way to veer them off the road, but without flipping them or driving them into a building. They still wanted the bastards alive.

"What the hell are they doing up there?" Morgan wondered aloud as they passed a small Peugot. Bodies seemed to be moving around in the back seat of the car ahead.

"I think one of them just moved into the back seat," Tiberius offered as he squinted through the windshield. "Oh Shit!"

Two bright flashes suddenly filled the blown out back window of the BMW as Zeidt's men began firing at them. Luckily Morgan reacted seconds before they began shooting and had already swerved out of the way, the bullets slamming harmlessly into the pavement. Needing a release for his emotions, Tiberius shifted in his seat and shoved his own pistol out the window and began firing back.

Despite Morgan's skilled driving, some of the bullets were starting to hit home, glancing off the sides and the hood. He backed off slightly, putting some space between them.

"I can't hit anything with this thing," Tiberius swore as he reloaded pistol once again.

"I've been telling people that for years."

"Shut up and drive."

"Have a look in the back seat," Morgan offered, still concentrating on the road.

Tiberius leaned back between the seats and noticed a duffle bag for the first time. Opening it he instantly grinned upon seeing a collection of weapons. He eagerly pulled out a sawed off shotgun and two uzi submachine guns, grabbing extra ammo for both.

"Hold on!" Morgan exclaimed and Tiberius had just enough time to look up as they approached a traffic circle at full speed. The BMW was skidding around the opposite side, trying to take the road on the left. They had cut off a delivery truck, stopping it in the middle of the road and blocking any pursuit. So Morgan decided to cut the corner and go through the circle in the opposite direction.

Cars honked and swerved as the Mercedes barrelled past them head on, jumping over a curb as they took the road on the left. Morgan was starting to feel the intensity of the chase take its toll on his body. His muscles were stiff and his head was pounding from staring out the window, unwilling to blink unless necessary

The road they turned on to was a two lane side road with even less traffic. Taking the opportunity from the absence of any innocent bystanders, Tiberius leaned out of the window and began peppering the BMW with his Uzi. He quickly emptied the magazine, leaving the trunk pock marked with bullet holes. He didn't actually want to hit any of them, lest they be killed before he could question them.

With renewed determination Morgan pulled their car up behind the BMW, slamming into the back bumper and making it swerve. But their driver was also experienced in high speed chases and he righted the car before it veered off the road.

"They must be out of ammo," Tiberius reasoned from the absence of return fire. Morgan kept bumping in to them but the enemy guns remained silent. Putting the Uzi down, Tiberius decided to try something new and grabbed the sawed off shotgun.

Immediately understanding what his leader had in mind, Morgan once again stomped on the accelerator and brought the Mercedes in close. When no shots rang out he pulled up beside them, finally seeing the familiar faces of their prey.

The two cars slammed into each other as they barrelled down the empty stretch of road, the clean air of the countryside doused with the acrid stink of gunpowder and brunt rubber. As the cars separated Tiberius pulled out the shotgun and pointed it at the driver, screaming at him to stop. But out of the corner of his eye he watched as one of the passengers in the back pointed his own weapon. Tiberius shifted his aim and fired into the back of the car at the same time as the other shooter fired, filling the space between the cars with smoke.

Unprepared for Tiberius' change in target, the shooter in the back of the BMW had cringed as he pulled the trigger. This had thrown off his aim and he ended up shooting out the tire of the Mercedes instead of putting a bullet in the head of the Master of the Hunt.

Dropping the expended shotgun, Tiberius grabbed the dash as the Mercedes started to swerve wildly. Morgan tried to maintain control as they skidded into the ditch, but the speed and the damage to the car made it impossible. Both men braced for impact as they felt the car start to flip over.

Chapter 22

Tiberius felt a powerful hand grasp his shoulder, pulling him out of the fog that enshrouded his mind. Blinking through bleary eyes he slowly focused on Morgan's concerned face in front of him. He slowly tried to take stock of any injuries he might have suffered, finally feeling relief when none drew his attention.

Their car was on its side in the ditch, the front grille fully planted in the murky water. Having put his seat belt on before he started the pursuit, Morgan had emerged from the crash unscathed and was now helping his boss out of the car.

Crawling out of the opened door onto the gravel shoulder, Tiberius immediately started assessing the situation. A wave of relief washed over him as he saw that the BMW was similarly positioned in the opposite ditch. Luckily they hadn't been able to escape.

"What's the damage?" he asked nodding towards the other car.

"One of the guys in the backseat is dead," Morgan reported, having checked out the car already. "The rest have fled to the north."

"Who was it?"

"Not sure," he replied grimly. "He took the full brunt from both barrels of your shotgun."

"Damn. The last two we take alive," Tiberius ordered.

"We can try but I don't think they're going to come peacefully," Morgan observed, pulling out some more weapons from the duffle bag. He passed a pistol and an uzi over to Tiberius and then took the same for himself before throwing the bag over his shoulder.

They walked over to the BMW, checking it over for a second time. The man in the backseat was totally disfigured from the shotgun blast. Not surprisingly the shot had dealt damage to the entire vehicle and Tiberius quickly noticed drops of blood along the side of the road.

There wasn't enough blood to show signs of their quarry bleeding out, but there was enough for two skilled trackers like Tiberius and Morgan to easily follow. Rather than continue down the road, the trail of blood led towards the field on the other side of the ditch. This late in the farming season the field was barren, providing a full view of the surroundings. Within seconds of searching, both men could clearly see a pair of figures climbing over a fence in the distance.

"What the hell are they up to?" Tiberius muttered as they jumped over the ditch and continued the chase across the field. There were a few stands of trees beyond the field, but nothing to hide or get lost in. The entire area was mostly rolling pastureland.

Speeding up their pace, both men quickly reached the fence and cleared it easily. Their prey was still visible in the distance, seemingly unconcerned with hiding or making a final stand.

"We're missing something," Morgan allowed as they closed the gap to within a few hundered meters. "We've passed a few really good spots for an ambush already. At this pace they're going to run out of energy before getting away."

At that moment everything became clear as the throbbing hum of a small airplane sounded in the distance. Within moments the large birdlike shape appeared from the south and descended to the ground beyond their view.

Speeding up the chase, they crested a small hill and could clearly see a small airport in the distance. It was nothing more than a strip of flat grass, a pair of metal hangars, and a small control tower. But there were at least five single engine airplanes sitting in the open.

"Are they going to hijack a plane?" Morgan wondered aloud as he watched the two figures reach the airport.

"It was probably a part of their plan all along," Tiberius answered with a mixture of annoyance and appreciation.

They slowed to an easy jog as they reached the airport, suddenly diving for cover behind a bush as a shot rang out. It wasn't directed at them, but they still peered carefully over their cover to see what was going on. After a quick scan of the area provided no clue, they slowly crept towards the control tower.

It was nothing more than a one story temporary building with a small second floor tower jutting out of the side. There were a few windows, but they were able to approach the building from a blind spot.

"Please monsieur, I cannot take you up in your condition. You need a hospital," pleaded an unfamiliar voice from within the building.

"Shut up and prep the plane or the next shot is through your kneecap," rebuked the familiar voice of Ashford, Zeidt's right hand man and leader of the Gold Pack.

Peeking up through one of the windows, Tiberius could see Ashford holding two men at gunpoint. One was dressed as a pilot and held a small flight bag in his hand. The other man wore an ugly cardigan over a crumpled shirt and was probably the flight controller. Ashford had a gash across his forehead and was holding his left hand closely against his body.

Sensing an opportunity, Tiberius led Morgan to the back door of the building and crept below the windows. When they reached the door Tiberius instructed Morgan to watch out for the other gunman while they confronted Ashford. Nodding Morgan reached up and swung the door open for Tiberius, who silently entered the room.

The look of surprise on the controller's face made Ashford turn his head around, but he kept his gun trained on the pilot. He was angry but not surprised to see Tiberius walk in with a pistol aimed at his head.

"He's right Ashford, you need a doctor," Tiberius calmly stated as he walked in. Morgan soon followed him in and went to the front door.

"Not another step closer!"

"Relax, I just want to ask you a few questions," he replied coolly.

"You're here to kill me!"

"Calm down. If I were here to kill you Morgan would have put a bullet in your brain before you realized we were here."

The truth of the statement made Ashford hesitate. He was still obviously shaken and probably going into shock from the car accident as the adrenaline wore off.

"Why did you want Zeidt killed?" Tiberius asked simply.

"You wouldn't understand."

"Try me."

"He was going to throw us all under the bus," Ashford began, his breathing becoming ragged as his anger rose. "That bastard never lifted a finger the entire time he was at the Manor. I planned and led every hunt while he went in search of warm beds and good food. All he cared about was himself and his damned money. We didn't want to leave the Manor with him, but he told us Lord Cleaver demanded it."

"Cleaver is a traitor and you all committed treason by following him," Tiberius spat, momentarily losing his cool.

"Lord Cleaver is a great man of great vision."

"He's a dead man," Tiberius scowled before returning to the matter at hand. "Why did you search out Hans Blick?"

"We found out Lord Zeidt was planning on taking out all of the money he had stashed away in numbered accounts. But he had no intention of sharing it with us! We'd served him for decades and how did he repay us? By taking us away from the Manor to serve him like slaves. He knew we couldn't go back, so we had no other choice."

"You have a choice now," Tiberius offered calmly. "Let these people go and come back to the Manor with us. You'll be questioned, but you have my word you won't be harmed."

"We can't go back," Ashford shook his head wildly. "If we double cross Lord Cleaver we're as good as dead. Look what happened to Lord Zeidt."

"Wait, what do you mean?" Tiberius asked immediately, the pronouncement not matching with his previous statement. "Did Cleaver instruct you to kill Zeidt?"

A momentary hesitation in Ashford's response was all Tiberius needed. Either Cleaver knew Zeidt would betray him, or he was in contact with the Gold Pack and discovered the Swiss banker's treachery. In any case it led credence to Zeidt's assertion of a mole in the Manor.

"We knew we could never return to the Manor, Lord Cleaver said as much," Ashford answered after finding his voice. "The money was our reward and would set us up to live the rest of our lives."

"We can change that," Tiberius declared, feeling sympathy for the man facing him. Although they came from different backgrounds and centuries, there was a kinship amongst the Hounds of the Manor. They had all been turned into killing machines destined to serve at the pleasure of others, with little chance of altering their fate.

"I think it's too late for that," he coughed, red spittle running down his chin. Without any warning he dropped to the floor, his gun banging loudly on the tiled floor. Tiberius dropped his own weapon and rushed over to the dying man, the signs all too familiar.

The gash on his head wasn't bleeding any longer, but Tiberius was pretty sure Ashford was bleeding internally. The car crash must have injured him more than he realized and the race to the airport would have only worsened things.

"You can die with honour Ashford," Tiberius offered, gripping the man's hand tightly. "Is there a mole at the Manor? Do you know who it is?"

Ashford stared straight at him for a second before give two jerking nods. Tiberius felt a mixture of elation and disappointment at finding out the truth. He was glad to finally have Zeidt's assertion corroborated, but he was worried where it might lead.

"Who is it? Tell me the name."

But all that he received in response was a big smile, Ashford's teeth stained red with his blood. The smile stayed plastered on his face as his eyes rolled back into his head and his body went limp.

"No! Who is it! Wake up and tell me damn you!" Tiberius yelled, shaking Ashford's body angrily.

The sound of an airplane taxiing past the building made Tiberius' head snap back up to the window. Morgan was squinting out the window, but couldn't make out the pilot of the small plane.

"If you're down here, who's allowing that plane to take off?" Tiberius questioned the flight controller.

"I don't know, I'm the only one on duty," he mumbled with confusion, still shaken from the standoff he'd just witnessed.

"It's got to be whoever's left," Morgan guessed with only one last member of the Gold Pack at large.

Realizing the truth Tiberius leapt up from the floor and charged out the front door, Morgan quickly following him. The plane was picking up speed and was well beyond the range of their guns by the time they started shooting. As it slowly took off, a man in dirty overalls rushed up beside them waving his hands.

"What's the matter?" Tiberius asked him as he reached them out of breath.

"The gas monsieur," he wheezed, not used to running. "I hadn't refilled it after it landed. The tank is almost empty."

As soon as he spoke those words the engine of the plane started to sputter as it tried to climb higher. After a few loud knocks the engine became silent and the three men on the flight line looked on in horror as the plane keeled over and plummeted to the ground. It met the ground in an instant, crumpling upon impact with no fuel to cause a real explosion.

Tiberius dejectedly walked back to the control tower, thrusting his pistol into his jacket pocket. He walked directly over to Ashford's body and searched it for any clues, but coming up empty.

"What's this all about?" the flight controller finally asked, still shaken from everything that had happened.

"Call the police and tell them what happened," Tiberius instructed after showing his Interpol ID. "We'll need to borrow your car. You can pick it up at the main police station."

The keys were handed over without protest and Tiberius and Morgan were soon heading back to Luxembourg City. They turned on to the main road where they passed the two cars that were still in the ditch. A police car was already at the scene and a flustered Gendarme quickly waved them through.

"What about Dufresne?" Morgan finally asked, voicing the thought that had been in the back of both their minds.

"We'll check and see where they took the casualties," Tiberius answered grimly, knowing that there would be many of them. "And then we'll see if that idiot Midoux is still alive."

*

The stairs of the secret passageway circled downwards, the stone slick from the cool damp air. Logan led the way down with the light on his rifle illuminating the way. Jane and Melrose followed close behind, stepping carefully to avoid falling into each other. After a dizzying descent that seemed to go on forever, the group finally emerged into a large dark room.

"This is really creepy," Logan observed as he moved his light across the large space. The ceiling vaulted high above them, held up by sturdy square columns. The floor was made of smooth stone slabs, but the walls were seemingly carved out of the ground like a cave. The air was thick, moist, and deathly still.

Melrose spotted some torches on the columns and started lighting them, satisfied that they were alone. The flickering flames of the torches soon sprang to life, creating menacing shadows that seemed to move about.

A large table sat in the middle of the room surrounded by multiple chairs. The furniture was all gothic and black, with clawed feet and pointed edges. Papers were scattered and piled along the table at random, a potential treasure trove of information.

"Thank God for wine," Jane beamed as she catalogued the contents of the table. "Alright everyone, take a section of table and let's start going through this stuff."

"What are we looking for?" Melrose asked as he went to the far side and peered at a stack of books.

"Anything that seems suspicious," Jane replied with a shrug. "Look for Lords and Ladies names, anyone that could be assisting Cleaver."

With the directions given, they all pulled up a chair and started going through the various papers, books, scrolls, and maps. But it didn't take long for them to notice that the seemingly rich sources of information were useless. The papers were mostly blank, with a few containing simple doodles. The maps around the table were general in nature and had no markings on them. The books might have been useful, but none of the group could decipher their connection to one another. They were all from the Manor library and were devoid of any notes of underlined passages.

After an hour of searching and cataloguing the contents of the table, they all slouched back in their chairs with defeat. Not one piece of useful information had been found.

"I really thought we would find something here," Jane observed wearily. "The conspirators must have met here, it's the perfect place."

"It does have a certain evil lair quality about it," Logan agreed while leaning his chair backwards. But the round feet of the chair on the damp floor made it start to slip backwards, forcing him to thrust forward in order to keep from falling. He managed to stay up, but knocked over a pile of papers in the process.

"Here let me help you," Jane offered as Logan started picking them up from the floor. Some had floated under the table and Jane was pretty sure Logan was too big to get underneath without contorting himself into an uncomfortable shape. She quickly collected the sheets of paper and was about to back out from under the table when something caught her eye.

Further back than the rest of the papers and wedged under one of the legs, was a sheet of half burnt paper. Jane would have ordinarily dismissed it as garbage, but they were desperate for any kind of clue. So she pulled it out gently, careful to keep it intact.

"What have you found Miss Piper?" Melrose asked as she slowly rose from the floor and placed the paper gently on the table.

"I'm not sure," she replied, too enraptured by it to reprimand Melrose for his formality.

"What does it say?" Logan asked after returning a handful of papers back to the table.

"It appears to be a conversation written on paper," she said while studying intently. "There are two distinct sets of hand writing that alternate. Wait, I think we have something. *Mornignstar is essential to our Plans*, says the first writer. The second writer responds with, *I understand and will endeavour to make Morningstar available*."

"What is Morningstar?" Logan asked quizzically. "A code for something?"

"Or someone," Jane offered amid a growing smile. "They go back and forth on little things until near the end. *Morningstar might be hard to use*, says the second writer, *is there another contact in 1940?* At least that's what it looks like, there's some smudging between some of the words."

"Then what does it say?" Melrose pressed energetically.

"*I need Morningstar for this to work*, the first writer replies and is then followed up by the second writer, *it is done, Morningstar is under our control*," Jane spoke eagerly and then had to look closer at the paper.

"What is it?" Logan inquired leaning over her shoulder.

"The last entry is hard to read," she replied without looking up. "It doesn't look like English."

"That's because it's not," Logan confirmed staring at the paper. He recognised the words immediately, history being one of his few good subjects. "It says *Seig Heil!*"

"What's that supposed to mean?" Jane asked nonplussed by the words. Melrose was equally confused by them.

"It means that either Morningstar or the second writer is a Nazi," Logan spat with distaste. But he quickly calmed himself and thought back at the endless files he'd gone through with Jane. It had been a rogue's gallery of seemingly evil men and women. "And if that's the case we now have a better idea of who the, I still feel stupid saying this, who the wizard is."

"Lord Schell," Jane grimaced, quick to understand Logan's reasoning. Schell was the only member of the Hunt with a Nazi past. He was either the second writer and used his old salute, or it had been written in reference to him.

"Is that possible?" Melrose asked quietly. "Lord Lodge and Tiberius seemed so confident in his loyalty."

"I know, they've even sent him to track down some of the escapees through the portals," Jane confirmed.

"But his name was one of the few that we came up with during our research," Logan offered logically. "We didn't give it much credence before. But now?"

"Now he goes to the top of the list," Jane replied confidently. "But we keep it quiet and we don't do anything rash until Tiberius returns. We don't know who else is in on this and if we go tearing into his room looking for evidence we could ruin everything."

With nothing left to discover or discuss, Jane led the way back up the treacherous staircase and they were all soon back in the familiar surroundings of the castle's kitchen. The storm was still raging outside and they were all too keyed up from their discovery to sleep, so they returned to their seats around the small table. Melrose had grabbed a bottle of wine as they passed through the cellar, and began working on the cork.

"Lord Schell, I can hardly believe it," Melrose sighed as he poured drinks for the others. "He always seemed so disinterested playing games of intrigue, simply enjoying the pleasures the Manor had to offer."

"Sounds like a good cover to me," Logan observed thoughtfully. "Nobody takes the harmless ones seriously."

"Hmm," Jane murmured as she swirled her glass of wine, staring at it intently.

"What is it?"

"Oh nothing," she recovered quickly, taking a drink and then setting the glass down and returning to the conversation.

"Well this discovery has got me thinking," Logan began has they got back on track. "We didn't really suspect Lord Schell until we found this paper, which was a stroke of unbelievable luck."

"So?" Jane inquired.

"So if Dr. Cleaver is as devious as you say, then I think we've cast our net too small," Logan continued haltingly, nervous on how to breach his point. "I think we need to look at Lord Pierce as another possible accomplice."

"What?!" exclaimed Melrose and Jane in surprised unison.

"Hear me out…"

"No, it's preposterous," Melrose declared with a fire in his eyes. "I have been with him every day since his arrival at the Manor and it's impossible."

"An arrival that was used to thwart Dr. Cleaver I might add," Jane added with equal force. "He would never work with someone like Cleaver. He's a good man. Loyal, just, honourable, and kind."

"Listen I read the file about his arrival," Logan carried on with determination. "I just think it's a coincidence that he shows up just when all this stuff happens. Maybe it's in my head."

"Well it is," Jane rebuked, feeling the flush on her cheeks. "He can't be the mole."

"Wizard," Logan corrected with a smile.

"Shut up," Jane countered with annoyance before breaking into a smile. The rest joined her and the mood lightened considerably.

But behind her smile, Jane's thoughts once more returned to Patrick and she was worried for him. He was once again on the frontlines, chasing down dangerous people who would not blink at the idea of shedding his blood. Due to her busy schedule and the ongoing investigation she'd been able to ignore her feelings and thoughts for the Lord of the Brown Pack. But Logan's accusations brought him back to the forefront of her mind. She suddenly felt guilty for her dismissive tone towards him the last few times they'd met.

Jane had had many admirers in her life, but he was the first one whom she felt the same way towards and it was unsettling. She was worried that by lowering her guard towards him, she would start to do the same towards others. But she couldn't risk doing that if she wanted to succeed as the Hunt Secretary.

Inwardly she whispered a short prayer for Patrick's well being, hoping he would return. She really didn't know what she'd do when that day came, but she wanted it to happen anyway.

Chapter 23

"Do you want to talk about it?"

"What?" Pierce asked absently while he concentrated on driving along the straight interstate.

"You know, about being dumped," Liam offered casually as he thumped his fingers along the door. "I don't really have experience on the receiving end of that kind of thing, but I can try and help."

"Why did I have to choose heads?" Pierce lamented quietly, ignoring his co-pilot.

After leaving the Holloway's mansion, the Brown Pack had met up at a small motel outside of Monterey. The time had been used to gain some much needed rest and to sweat out some more answers from their new prisoner. He turned out to be a reformed junky who had little info on Debochev's plans, merely acting as a driver.

Unwilling to harm him outright, Pierce was still not willing to completely forgive the man for his past sins. Instead he decided to let the man decide his own fate. After the lengthy interrogation, Pierce had MacDuff give him a wad of cash and send him on his way. When the others questioned him, Pierce told them that there were two possible outcomes that could happen and he was willing to live with both. Either the man would use the money to change his life around and become a contributing member of society or he would revert to his old ways and use the money to buy so much drugs that he would probably overdose.

They woke early the next morning and ate breakfast together in the diner attached to the motel. While they waited for the check, MacDuff voiced his desire to drive the GTO and took the keys from Sean. This meant that each driver had to choose a new riding partner. To make things fair MacDuff grabbed a quarter from the table and flipped it in the air, telling Pierce to pick heads or tails. The winner would then be able to choose who he drove with.

"Maybe she's just playing hard to get," Liam observed without being asked. "Girls play that game with me all the time. They love being chased. All you have to do is stay after them and wear them down."

"I really don't want to talk about it," Pierce replied gruffly.

He didn't want to talk about it because he was too busy thinking about it. They were a few hours outside of San Francisco, heading north on Interstate 5. It ran the length of the interior of California into Oregon in a very straight and unexciting line. This meant that the driving was easy and Pierce found his mind stuck on one topic.

He felt a mixture of feelings towards Jane and was overwhelmed by it. He'd never felt like this towards someone before and didn't really know how to process these new emotions. On one hand he felt a mixture of desire and physical attraction to her. But on the other he felt scorned and depressed by her current avoidance of him. He was also angry that she wouldn't talk to him. He could tell that something was bothering her, but she wouldn't let him in to help. It was infuriating and devastating at the same time.

"Sir, you want to ease up on the steering wheel?" Liam cut in, breaking past Pierce's inner dialogue. "It's already dead, so strangling it won't help."

Pierce looked down and saw his fists clenched around the wheel so tight his knuckles were white. With an embarrassed smile he leaned back in his seat and tried to drive as a casually as he could, one hand on the wheel.

"I knew this girl Moira back in the old country," Liam began despite Patrick's audible sigh. "She used to give me the darkest stare when we'd pass each other in the village. But when we found ourselves alone it was a different story altogether."

"What, you forced yourself upon her?"

"Very funny, do you want to hear the story or not?" Liam laughed.

"Not really."

"When we were together, Moira was as fiery as her long red locks," Liam smiled in recollection, undeterred by his audience's lack of interest. "It was all I could do to keep her from ripping my buttons off as she attacked my shirt. What a fine rose she was."

"So why did she ignore you in public?" Pierce asked despite himself, too bored with the driving to fully ignore the Irishman.

"She was Protestant and I was Catholic, she didn't have much of a choice really," Liam shrugged. "She would have been shunned by her people and possibly attacked by mine."

"So how the hell does that help my problem?" Pierce exclaimed with exasperation

"I don't know, there are some similarities," he offered smiling. "Listen I just tell the stories, what you do with them is up to you."

"Fenian this is Tripwire, you got your ears on?" crackled Sean's voice in a decent southern accent from the CB radio.

"Roge-O Tripwire my old son, come'on back," Liam replied after picking up the mic.

"We're just about bingo for go-juice back here, y'all want to stop at the next station, over?"

"Thank God," Pierce breathed, happy for a break. Maybe he'd be able to flip MacDuff again.

"That's a big 10-4 on the go-juice, out," Liam clicked off the mic and shoved it back onto the holder. "These things are grand, we should get some for the Manor."

After ten minutes of blessedly quiet driving, Pierce spotted a gas station sign ahead and eagerly rumbled in beside the pumps as they arrived. The GTO pulled in on the other side and everyone stepped out to stretch as a skinny teenage attendant ran out to fill them up.

They were just outside of the town of Redding, with the flat fertile farmlands of the valley behind them and the rolling Cascade Foothills before them. From here on out the road would become more treacherous, much like their mission. The border to Oregon was not much further down the road and every inch they travelled brought them closer to Debochev and rescuing Kat.

Despite his annoyingly flippant attitude, Pierce didn't have the heart to try and trade Liam to MacDuff when they finished gassing the cars. But it didn't seem to matter because Liam, like the rest of them, began putting on his game face as they continued their journey. Pierce planned on driving as far as Astoria that day, a small town on the Pacific Coast that sat at the mouth of the giant Columbia

River. From the map they'd taken from Mrs. Holloway, Debochev's camp was on the other side of the river. They would stay there for the night and then take a ferry across the next day.

"You don't think she was just using you, do you?" Liam broke the silence as their black Dodge Charger crossed the Oregon border.

"No way," Pierce replied automatically before shooting Liam a curious look. "Wait, what do you mean?"

"Well it's no secret around the Manor she's an ambitious little... lady," Liam informed him, watering down some of the sentiment floating around. "After all, you did put a good word in for her with Lord Lodge."

"Hey we all did, remember," Pierce corrected him. "Or have you forgotten what she did in Marseille? She definitely saved my life and probably the rest of you hooligans on top of that."

"Now wait a second, I had everything under control," Liam countered before quickly laughing at himself. "That's fair; it was a pretty tight spot."

"Besides, she didn't need that good word from us," Pierce continued his defense of Jane, needing to hear the words from his own mouth. "She helped Lord Lodge escape from the Crow's Nest."

"How very convenient," Liam offered conspiratorially.

Pierce decided to ignore him and concentrate on the road. He was pretty sure Liam was just winding him up to make conversation. But the truth of the matter was that he'd already had these thoughts about Jane.

After arriving at the Manor he'd personally heard her conspire with Dr. Cleaver and believed they were allies. It seemed like a strange coincidence that she ended up being locked away with Lord Lodge and eventually gaining his confidence. A more cynical person would immediately say it smelt of a set-up. But he trusted Lord Lodge's judgement and he trusted her. But what if she were in fact the mole Tiberius was looking for? What if she had never stopped working for Dr. Cleaver?

*

The normally sedate hospital was a flurry of activity with the obvious increase in security adding to the dark mood. The lobby was full of silent policeman frustrated at being powerless as their comrades were under the surgical knives in the operating rooms beyond. Their silence was in stark contrast to the distraught ramblings and rhythmic sobbing of the victims' families that were slowly arriving.

Tiberius and Morgan were immediately scrutinized when they arrived at the hospital and their Interpol ID's did nothing to soften the reception. Luckily a member from the observation team recognized Tiberius and intervened on their behalf. But before they could start their search for their missing comrade a doctor grabbed Tiberius and led him towards one of the many beds that was set up in the emergency ward.

Apparently he had not walked away from their small car accident unscathed and a nurse began cleaning and dressing a small wound on his forehead. Noting the existing scar on Tiberius' brow, she didn't bother giving him any post care instructions. She gave Morgan a once over and then walked off when she was satisfied with his seemingly acceptable condition.

"I'm glad to see you in one piece," Sgt. Lafleur exclaimed as he walked up to Tiberius' bed. He then looked around in disappointment. "What a mess."

"Midoux?" Tiberius inquired, still angry with the brash young Inspector. But his feelings soon changed when Lafleur shook his head solemnly.

"To his credit he led the final group into the hotel room and survived the encounter, only to be killed by the blast."

"I told him to wait," Tiberius growled, just as angry with himself. He'd gotten the police involved and was partially to blame for the carnage surrounding him. There were another five police officers in various states of injury in his ward. But he knew the more serious cases were in the operating rooms, or the morgue.

"He was young, brash, and eager to prove himself," Lafleur shrugged, having already dealt with his feelings for the Inspector. "But I think I have some good news for you."

"Dufresne?" Morgan asked immediately, the concern for his friend clear across his face.

"I believe he is here and in stable condition," he nodded eagerly. "One of my men said that they found a civilian in the hotel room. I imagine they simply saw his clothing and didn't look for an ID. There was a lot going on."

"Completely understandable," Tiberius waved the thought aside. "Take us to him."

Standing up too quickly, Tiberius wavered for a second and Morgan stepped up and steadied him. His body was completely drained of the adrenaline that had carried him through the car chase and the confrontation at the airport.

They walked slowly through the ward, the clean smell of sanitation products overwhelming their nostrils as it combated invisible germs and microbes from the wounded. They passed by a few recognizable faces, but most of the men were from the assault force that initially attacked the hotel room. Lafleur led them into a room with four beds, three of them with heavily sedated men out of surgery. A quick glance did not reveal Dufresne as one of them.

"Where is he?" Tiberius asked with concern.

"I don't understand this is the room number I was given," Lafleur double checked, looking just as perplexed. "The empty bed must be his, maybe he's in the washroom."

As Morgan checked it, a nurse walked in with a tray and clipboard. Lafleur asked her about the whereabouts of the occupant of the fourth bed. But she looked just as confused as the rest of them.

"He was here a few moments ago," she informed them. "He couldn't have gotten very far."

"I will have my men search the hospital," Lafleur offered energetically. Tiberius was about to take him up on his offer, but stopped when he caught a look from Morgan beside the empty bed.

"I'm sure everything is all right," Tiberius calmed him. "In fact I'm feeling a little tired and will return to my own bed. I'll come back later and see him, as I'm sure you have much better things to do."

"That's true," Lafleur acknowledged before shaking his hand. "I'll check up on you again soon sir; it's been a pleasure working with you."

"And you."

Morgan then led Tiberius out of the room and headed back towards his bed as Lafleur took off in the opposite direction.

"So what is it?" Tiberius demanded once they were alone.

"It's time to leave," Morgan announced seriously. "Dufrense left a mark on his bed, a dot within a circle. He's gone home."

"He's returned to the portal," Tiberius concurred nodding, knowing the meaning of the symbol they had all used many times.

With renewed energy the two men casually walked past the small groups of people in the lobby and emerged onto the street as dusk fell. The street lights were slowly flickering on as people journeyed home beneath them. They walked across the street to where their borrowed car was parked, Morgan getting in behind the wheel.

Remembering the deal they made with the car's owner, Morgan headed towards the main police station. Traffic was blessedly light as they navigated the narrow confusing streets of Luxembourg City, eventually finding their destination. Morgan thumped the car up onto the curb in front of the building and both men calmly got out and walked down the street.

Tiberius began feeling better as they walked, which relived Morgan as they began descending the steep road down to the Grund where the portal was located. The uneven cobblestones were treacherous to even the most surefooted at the best of times. But at night they could send the unwary to the bottom of the valley in a messy heap.

The small little enclave sitting in the shadow of Luxembourg City was just as they'd last left it, with the small restaurants and shops catering to the few residents and tourists. They were a block from the cottage that housed the portal when they heard a familiar whistle pierce the night air.

"I should have known," Tiberius exclaimed, rushing over to the small pub patio they'd previously drank at.

Dufresne was sitting at one of the tables with three drinks in front of him and a wide smile plastered across his face.

"And here we were worried about you," Morgan smiled, eyeing the beer with appreciation. Dufresne just smiled and stood up, embracing his brothers in arms enthusiastically.

"What the hell happened in there?" Tiberius finally asked as they all sat down and had a well deserved drink.

"What a mess," Dufresne lamented as he recalled the scene from the hotel, unknowingly repeating Sgt. Lafleur's earlier feelings. "You should have seen the hallway outside the room. They were waiting for the police and started firing as they ran down the hall. By the time I got there the gunmen had retreated into the room and Midoux was organizing the last assault."

"That idiot," Tiberius growled again. "Him and his inexperienced assault team must have alerted them as they crossed the street."

"Well he tried to make up for the mistake by leading the final assault into the room," Dufresne continued shuddering slightly. "In fact it reminded me of Normandy and the room to room fighting on D-Day and the days afterwards."

"How did they do it?" Morgan asked, ever the student of tactics. "Flashbang grenade through the door and then stormed in after?"

"Pretty much," Dufresne nodded. "With no vest and a tiny pistol, I decided to hang back. Luckily for Midoux one of the gunmen had his arm almost blown completely off. Your handiwork?"

Morgan nodded, but did not smile or relish the action. He'd done what needed to be done.

"When we last spoke you said it wasn't them," Tiberius cut in, remembering their last words over the radio.

"Shit I almost forgot," Dufresne replied with shock. "It wasn't the Gold Pack in the hotel. Christ, they could be anywhere now!"

"Relax, it's been taken care of," Tiberius announced solemnly. "They must have planted doubles in the hotel room and then escaped to the parking garage. After the explosion we saw them try and make their getaway."

"So what happened?"

"We chased them out into the country," Morgan answered between sips of his drink. "Both of our cars ended up in the ditch by a field. One died there while Ashford and Ian tried to reach a local airfield."

"We caught up with them there," Tiberius continued soberly. "Ashford soon died from wounds suffered in the car crash and then Ian took off in a plane with no gas."

"Death seems to follow us doesn't it?" Dufresne observed quietly, taking no pleasure in the demise of his fellow colleagues.

"Indeed it does," Tiberius concurred, having thought the same thing before.

"Speaking of which, how did you escape death's icy grip?" Morgan inquired.

"From the size of the blast, you should be in pieces now if you had been in the room when that bomb exploded," Tiberius reasoned in wonder.

"As soon as I saw it wasn't them I got the same feeling you probably did," Dufresne began, recalling their last conversation on the radio. "Luckily the last man I checked out was by the bathroom. Even before you shouted a warning I ducked inside and fell into the bathtub. It shielded me from most of the blast, so all I received were a few cuts and bruises and a massive headache."

"Close one," Morgan whistled in appreciation. "I'm glad you're ok."

"Thanks," Dufresne acknowledged happily before his face grew dark once more. "Wait a second! If they're all dead, then we failed to discover if Zeidt's theories were correct. This whole thing has been for nothing."

"I wouldn't say that," Tiberius countered with a hard and clever look. "First we tracked down traitors of the Manor that could have played havoc with the timeline. Second Ashford basically confirmed Zeidt's claim."

"Well, who is it?" Dufresne asked with exasperation.

"He didn't say," Tiberius replied as stoically as he could. "But he confirmed there was a mole at the Manor, but he died before he could give a name."

"Well I suppose that's something," Dufresne conceded with little enthusiasm.

"I think it is," Tiberius allowed with slightly more optimism. "When I asked him who it was, he just gave me a big smile. He probably could have answered, but it was his last little jab at me."

"So what does that tell us?"

"It tells us that whoever the mole is, it's not one of the servants," Tiberius concluded firmly. "Whoever the mole is, it's someone well placed in the Manor and someone we probably don't expect."

Chapter 24

The fog from the Columbia River created an eerie and solitary feeling as it enveloped the morning ferry. The small vessel plied its way across the wide mouth of the river, doggedly progressing against the strong current. The unseen shore in the distance reinforced the sense of the unknown that awaited them on the other side.

Huddled beside the wheel house, the four men dropped their coins in the captain's collection tin. He was an old grizzled seaman, whose craggy features reassured the men that he probably knew every inch of the river and would not be troubled by mere fog.

"So we're in agreement then?" Pierce asked the men surrounding him. They all had their jacket collars turned up against the rain, but clearly nodded at the question. Sitting in the motel the night before they had discussed the situation they faced.

They knew very little about Debochev's compound and even less about how many people would be there. Pierce assumed that many of them would be innocent followers of the fake holy man. But he also figured that there would be just as many that resembled the men they'd fought at the Holloway mansion.

The map made it look like the compound was by one of the river's inlets, which made using a boat for transporting the women make sense. Therefore Liam and Sean would charter a boat once they crossed and approach the compound from the water. Meanwhile Pierce and MacDuff would drive as close to the compound as they dared and approach on foot through the forest.

With the plan agreed upon the group split in two and returned to their respective cars. Engines were turned on to provide some respite from the cold damp morning they'd been standing in.

With frightening speed the far shore suddenly sprang to view through the thick fog and Pierce started to brace himself for impact. But their belief in the wily old captain's ability was not misplaced, as he came up alongside the pier and docked without any noticeable issues. His young first mate quickly tied them up and the ramp was dropped, allowing the two muscle cars to rumble off and continue their journey.

"So what did he say about her?" Sean asked as he followed the Dodge Charger off the pier and onto the main road.

"Not very much," Liam conceded with a shrug. "And I was being very sympathetic to his cause."

"I bet you were."

"I was," Liam countered evenly. "I even told him about Moira."

"I'm sure that helped," Sean rolled his eyes. "Every guy that's been dumped wants to hear about another couple who couldn't keep their hands off each other. Very sympathetic."

"I see what you mean," Liam conceded thoughtfully. "But that wasn't really the point I had tried to make."

"What was the point, that woman do all sorts of things that don't make sense?"

"Very funny," Liam groused as he squinted out the window. "Wait, there's the place the motel owner said we could find a boat."

The road passed by a small rocky cove where a log cabin sat amongst towering pine trees by the river. There were two fishing boats moored out in the river, bobbing with the tide. The dark smoke from the cabin's chimney signalled that someone was at home, or at least nearby.

Sean carefully drove the car up the gravel drive, avoiding the deepest of the potholes as they appeared. A faded blue pick-up truck was parked beside the cabin, the tailgate speckled with rust and mud. He finally stopped a safe distance from the house, hoping to appear non-threatening. The motel owner had had a small smile on his face when he directed them here, making both men unsure what to expect.

Liam followed Sean's lead as they slowly got out of the car, keeping the doors open in case they needed a quick getaway. When no one appeared on the front porch, they decided to go up and knock on the door.

They made it to the stairs when they both saw a shape bent over a small rowboat near the shore. Sensing it was the owner of the other two vessels; they ignored the cabin and made their way over to him.

"Morning," Liam opened happily.

"Yup," came the grumbled reply after a thick cough. Both men were surprised when he stood up and turned towards them. Instead of another grizzled seaman with a grey beard, a young man of no more than twenty five stared back at them. He had distant blue eyes and two days' worth of stubble covering a scar on his chin. "Can I help you?"

"One of the motel owners over in Astoria said we should see you about a charter," Sean replied, surprised by the young man's courteous voice.

"Oh sure, no problem," he replied casually, his eyes displaying his boredom. "You guys want to go fishing?"

"Hunting," Liam countered, pulling out his Marshall's badge. "US Deputy Marshall's Mick and Donald. We're tracking down some escaped fugitives and need a boat."

The young sailor's bored look suddenly sprang to life at the mention of action. He jumped up right away and threw the bits of rope he'd been playing with to the ground. He motioned for them to stay there as he took off into the cabin. He re-emerged a few seconds later with a dark blue jacket and a hunting rifle on his shoulder.

"All we need is a driver," Sean cautioned as he joined them. He was worried by the enthusiasm of the young man and didn't need a glory hound with them.

"I understand sir," he said confidently. "But I believe in being prepared. It's the only reason I made it home in one piece last year."

"Were you in the Navy?" Sean asked, eyeing the dark pea coat appreciatively.

"Yes sir, Bosn's Mate First Class Lukas," he answered with practiced cadence. "I did a tour on patrol boats in the Mekong over in 'Nam."

"Well that's good enough for us," Liam smiled, sensing a kindred spirit. "Your boats any good?"

"They might not look like much," Lukas answered with a quick smile. "But they've been modified a bit. But don't tell the Coast Guard. You guys ready to go?"

They were already dressed for their excursion, but needed to get more firepower from the trunk of the car. Liam ran over to the car and came back with a green duffle bag that Lukas eyed curiously for a moment. But without another word he led them down to the rocky shore where another wooden rowboat was tied up. They climbed in and Lukas pushed them out, jumping in at the last second without getting his feet wet.

Liam took up the wooden oars and rowed them out into the river while Lukas steered them towards the closer of the two ships. It was a nondescript thirty foot fishing trawler with a small cabin close to the bow and a big deck at the stern. They all boarded easily and went into the wheelhouse together.

"So where are we headed?" Lukas asked while he started up the engine and made his pre sail checks.

"The men we're after are on a ship that we think is bound for this inlet here," Sean announced over the roar of the diesel engine as he pulled out the map. They had bought it at the motel and duplicated the markings from the original.

"What are they driving?"

"We don't really know," Sean admitted, having never seen the boat. None of them had been able to catch a glimpse of it during the shootout at the Holloway mansion. "My guess is a thirty to forty foot yacht, with at least a few cabins. They're using the boat to transfer kidnapped women to the site off the inlet."

"Fuckers," the sailor spat as he switched on a small winch that pulled up the anchor. The boat immediately started to drift as the anchor lifted from the riverbed, but he didn't rush to start until the anchor was firmly in place. Without a second glance at the map, Lukas increased the throttle and slowly moved out into the main part of the river.

The Columbia River is a massive moving body of water and is more like a sea near the mouth where it empties into the Pacific Ocean. As such it is a major shipping lane for the American Northwest, with cargo ships dotting the vast watery expanse.

Lukas easily navigated past the large steel behemoths and the numerous small crafts as they headed towards their destination. The morning fog was lifting, but the wind had picked up and they all huddled in the wheelhouse to stay out of the freezing spray.

"So how're you doing back in the world?" Liam asked cautiously, having some previous experience with Vietnam vets.

"Honestly? Not too good," Lukas replied while keeping his eyes glued to the water. "I was energized when I got off the plane. I knew so many good guys that didn't make it home like me. But nothing was like I remembered it. I got a job on a ship but only lasted a few weeks before getting into a fight. For the next few months it was the same thing, I just bounced from ship to ship."

"That's a good way to get a bad name for yourself," Liam grimaced sympathetically.

"Yeah, no kidding," Lukas nodded sadly. "The shipping community's not that big and soon I couldn't get a job with anyone. But I was actually fine with that, I couldn't deal with all the people anyway. So I found the cabin on the river and got myself two boats with the last of my money. I charter a bit, fish a bit, but barely make ends meet. But at least it's quiet."

"But quiet's not enough is it?" Liam prodded cautiously and received a raised eyebrow in return. "I saw you light up with the possibility of action. Why don't you re-enlist."

"No chance," Lukas laughed hollowly. "You might not be able to tell from the look of me, but I barely made it out of that hell hole alive. There's no way I'm going back."

After his pronouncement they all remained silent as the fishing trawler made its ponderous progress up the river. But it didn't take too long for them to approach the opening of the bay that marked their destination. The wind had picked up and was creating white capped waves on the river.

"It should be calmer once we get inside the bay," Lukas announced as the ship took a hard bounce off a wave. "It looks like a storm is moving in."

Sean nodded and reached down to open up the duffle bag, pulling out two flak jackets from the top. Handing one to Liam, they both put them on, the silver Marshal star clear on their chests. He then bent down and started pulling out the tools of their trade.

"Whoa, that's a lot of guns," Lukas announced, sneaking a peak at their opened bag.

"These guys are really dangerous," Sean replied coolly. "We've already been in one shoot out with them."

Once they entered the bay, the wind died down enough for Sean and Liam to brave the weather beyond the wheelhouse. They could tell that this was the ideal place to set up a secretive compound. There were no buildings in sight and no nautical traffic to speak of. Massive pines and evergreens crowded the shoreline and receded into the hills beyond as a large green forest. Without the map they would have never found this place.

A loud crash brought their attention from the shore in front of them to the river behind. Thick dark storm clouds were rushing in from the ocean like the wings of a huge demonic beast. Hard rain and lightning would soon follow and make life on the water completely miserable.

"Hey guys!" Lukas called out from the wheelhouse, bringing the other two back forward from the stern deck. He was holding binoculars up to his face with one hand while the other steered the boat. "I think we've got company, might be your guys."

Sean took the offered binoculars and looked for himself. A large motor yacht was speeding towards them, cutting through the small waves of the inlet. He could see one man on the fly bridge, but no one else.

"Everyone stay cool, we're just a bunch of fishermen taking refuge from the storm," Sean instructed calmly.

"Well then you better cover those vests up," Lukas pointed out, motioning to the silver badges.

They threw on a pair of plaid jackets and went out to the back deck to play with some netting. Within a minute the other boat was upon them, speeding by first before turning back around. Sean picked out two other men at the stern of the ship, bringing the total up to three. That they could see.

"I don't see any weapons on them," Liam whispered as he played with some netting covering his machine gun.

"Me neither, but I think it's them," Sean allowed carefully. "Lukas, slow the boat right down and we'll see what they want."

The other boat came up behind them, but slower this time. It pulled up alongside the fishing boat and matched pace.

"You guys need some help?" called out the stern voice of a big man at the back of the boat.

"No thanks we're good," Lukas replied easily. "Just looking for a place to anchor and ride out the storm."

"What are you guys fishing?" the man asked suspiciously as the two boats almost touched.

"Nothing right now," Lukas laughed before pointing back towards Sean and Liam. "We ripped some of our nets and with this storm…"

They were close enough now that Sean could clearly make out the three other men on the boat. None looked familiar, but he could tell they were goons and bullies. Exactly the type Debochev would gather around him. They all had obvious bulges under their jackets and he hoped they couldn't spot his weapons.

"Well I wouldn't go too much further in the bay, there's lots of underwater logs if you don't know a safe path," the driver of the other boat announced from above them. He was just as suspicious as the other two, but had a better perch to observe the fishing boat from. He eyed them carefully, but seemed to eventually make up his mind that they were harmless.

Tensions were high on the fishing trawler as they waited for the other boat to leave. Luckily all three men were used high stress situations and were able to appear calm during the intense scrutiny. They could have easily taken all three men out, but they didn't know who else was on the boat. Sean and Liam were both worried that the girls were still onboard under guard and they weren't prepared to endanger them by shooting first.

"What the hell are we stopped for!" yelled the voice of a fourth man as the cabin door of the motor yacht crashed open. He stumbled out onto the small deck and stared at the fishing boat in frustration first. But as his eyes locked on Sean and then switched to Liam, his look quickly turned to one of surprised recognition and then hatred.

"Down!" Sean yelled towards Lukas as he and Liam bent down simultaneously for their hidden weapons.

*

Pierce parked the Charger on a dirt track off a back road as close to the map reference as they dared. Despite the crashing of the trees as they slammed against each other in the storm, the noise of the Hemi engine was just too distinctive to risk discovery.

As they donned their rain jackets and shrugged into their packs, Pierce could feel the anxiety of the situation creeping into him. It became worse as he picked up his rifle and loaded it. They were about to go into the woods to hunt down people and there was a good chance that some of them would be injured or even killed.

He remembered railing at Tiberius and Lord Lodge about the utter repulsiveness of hunting people. He still felt that way, but he now found himself doing exactly the same thing. The hypocrisy of it was not lost on him and he felt sick from it. He was following MacDuff into the woods with loaded weapons, intent on hunting down fellow human beings. But the fact that they were kidnappers and abusers of women made Pierce realize how naïve he must have sounded before. Debochev and his men were prefect candidates for the heavy handed tactics of the Manor.

"This needs to be done lad," MacDuff offered solemnly as he watched Pierce catch up to him under a tall pine tree. He could see the conflicted feelings across the younger man's face.

"I know Duffy," Pierce replied quietly. "I just feel like a hypocrite. What are the odds Debochev and his men lower their weapons when we show up?"

"Slim to none," MacDuff answered coldly. "But that's why I brought this guy along."

He lifted up a simple looking rifle and patted it gently. Pierce stared at it in confusion before realizing that it was a tranquilizer gun. Pierce immediately felt better, the idea of tranquilizing some of the more innocent followers was more appealing than the alternative.

"Very sneaky," Pierce approved, motioning MacDuff to continue leading the way through the dark woods.

The wind began to pick up even more as they walked, but thankfully the thick forest of towering trees created a canopy to shield them from the rain. The ground was also thankfully devoid of too much shrubbery, making their progress easier. The terrain was hilly and crisscrossed with small ravines, creating a myriad of possible ambush locations.

The echo of a shot rang out, quickly followed by more, making Pierce and MacDuff drop to the ground immediately. But the Scotsman already knew that the sounds were from far away and not aimed at them. The sounds stopped as quickly as they began and the two men looked at each other with concern.

"Sean and Liam?" Pierce worried aloud.

"Probably," MacDuff nodded. "Let's get going."

They got up and quickened their pace through the forest, MacDuff constantly checking his compass against the map. They eventually came to a road and stopped behind a tree above a ditch, watching for traffic. After five minutes of nothing but solitary road they sprinted across and continued their journey.

Cresting a small hill, a collection of buildings in a little valley sprang into view through the thick foliage. There was a large timber hall with smaller cabins surrounding it, and a few other buildings beyond. The wind and rain was picking up and they could see white clad figures scurrying amongst the buildings.

"I don't know how much use that gun is going to be in this storm," Pierce called out over the wind. "You might end up shooting the wrong person."

MacDuff shrugged and then led them down towards the compound, crouching low and weaving through the trees. Their diligent approach paid off when they heard some coughing from a nearby tree. Stopping and slowly kneeling against the ground, they watched as a guard desperately tried to light a cigarette in the storm. Without hesitating MacDuff raised the tranquilizer gun up and aimed at the figure.

The pop from the gun was inaudible against the creaking of the tress and the dart hit home in an instant. The guard reached for his arm in surprise before falling to the ground in a heap. When he didn't move again Pierce and MacDuff scurried over to the drugged body.

"I can't believe you actually hit him," Pierce observed proudly, fingering the dart on the guards left arm.

"I was aiming for his right arm," MacDuff responded sheepishly, as he checked the guard over. He was dressed in various shades of brown that seemed monkish, apart from the pistol, in his waistband.

"I wonder how many more of these guys are around here," Pierce thought as he tied the guard's hands and feet. "And are they here to keep people out or keep the others in?"

"Probably both…"

Before MacDuff could continue speaking, a loud explosion erupted from beyond the compound, coming from the waterfront. The few remaining people out in the compound suddenly stopped and stared in the direction of the explosion. Those in white quickly hurried in doors, while those in brown ran towards the sound with weapons in hand.

"Let's go," Pierce ordered with determination. He hoped that his men weren't injured in the explosion, but the element of surprise seemed lost so there was no point in waiting.

He ran down the small hill towards the nearest cabin, keeping low as he dodged around trees. The cabins were positioned in a makeshift circle with all of the doors pointing inwards. It reminded Pierce of a summer camp he'd once attended and he quickly realized that that's what this place must have been in an earlier life.

MacDuff was right behind him and peered over his shoulder into the cabin. It appeared to be empty, so they opened the window and began to climb in. The window wasn't big, but it was close to the ground and they made it in without too much difficulty.

The memories of summers long ago flooded into Pierce's mind as he looked over the cabin. Wooden bunk beds with chests at the ends lined the walls, with utilitarian furniture placed wherever there was space. The only difference was the smell. Instead of the sweaty stink of young boys, this cabin was filled with the sweet fragrance of flowers and incense.

Shaking these thoughts aside Pierce followed MacDuff up to the front door and peered out the window beside it. No longer a flurry of activity, the inner compound was now devoid of people or movement. The wind continued to howl and the rain was falling in earnest, making a ruckus on the cabin's tin roof.

"What do you think Patrick?" MacDuff asked, turning towards his leader as more gunshots rang out from the direction of the explosion.

"I think I won't be able to live with myself if we don't head towards the water and make sure Sean and Liam are ok."

"Aye you're right," MacDuff nodded before carefully opening the cabin door. He sprinted out and Pierce was right behind him, ignoring the big hall to their left.

The wind and rain was almost blinding as the storm raged around them. Branches cracked above their heads and fell to the ground, mimicking the random thunder and lightning. The sound of gunfire increased as they approached the shore.

A small sandy beach stretched from the tree line to the water, where the smoking wreckage of a yacht smouldered. Approaching from behind, Pierce and MacDuff spotted six men taking cover behind trees, randomly shooting pistols towards the beach. They were shooting at a derelict looking fishing boat that kept approaching the beach, firing, and then turning away.

"What the hell are they doing?" Pierce nudged MacDuff as they watched the cycle repeat itself again.

"They're being smart," MacDuff smiled appreciatively. "They know these goons only have pistols and can't hit a thing with them. So they keep coming close, but still out of range to get them to fire. They'll probably be running out of ammunition soon."

"How come they haven't hit any of them? Our guys have M-16 machine guns with greater distance," Pierce challenged despite admiring the tactics.

"It's true they're both master marksmen," MacDuff finished eyeing Pierce closely. "Maybe you're wearing off on the lads. They probably could have picked off at least half of these idiots, but they might be trying to take them alive instead."

"Maybe," Pierce conceded doubtfully, the visibility from the water to the treeline was pretty bad. "How about we even things up a little, see if we can scare them into submission?"

"Agreed, but be ready to find cover if it doesn't work," MacDuff instructed.

After a moment's pause Pierce and MacDuff jumped out from behind one of the tress and each fired a warning shot over the brown shirted men in front of them. They announced themselves as Federal Agents and yelled at them to get down. One unfortunate man raised his weapon towards MacDuff, but received a shot in the chest for his efforts.

Seeing the dangerous looking men behind them with automatic rifles yelling FBI, the remainder quickly dropped to the ground and put their hands on their heads. Apparently they were used to the position and knew what to do.

"Gentlemen, this weapon has a thirty round magazine," MacDuff called out as he approached the men splayed out on the ground. "For those of you who can count that leaves twenty eight bullets left, more than enough for you to join your friend. So stay calm and don't move."

Pierce shrugged out of his back pack and pulled out lengths of rope and carefully approached the first man on the ground. He leaned down and grabbed the dropped weapon, throwing it aside before tying him up. He continued through the group repeating the process each time. He was finishing up with the last one when a familiar voice called out.

"Just like the FBI to swoop in when the work is done and take credit," Liam called out as he marched up the beach.

"Good to see you gentlemen finally decided to disembark from your pleasure cruise," MacDuff retorted before lowering his weapon to shake hands with the new arrivals. Despite being separated for only a short time, everyone was relieved to see each other unharmed. He then nodded towards the young lanky man with the rifle in his hands. "Who's this?"

"This here's our old grizzled sea dog, Cap'n Lukas," Liam replied, giving him a slap on the back. "He got us out a tight spot back there."

"You in the service?" MacDuff asked shrewdly, giving him a quick appraisal.

"Yes sir, the Navy. I drove patrol boats over there." MacDuff merely nodded before returning his attention to the prisoners

Pierce looked over at the smoking wreckage on the beach and figured things must have got pretty intense. The second boat was beached up on the sand, but the bullet holes in the sides and the wheelhouse were obvious from this distance.

"What now?" Sean asked between shivering teeth. The storm was still in full force and everyone was soaked to the bone.

With everyone together and unharmed, the next step was to find some shelter. Pierce led them back towards the main compound where they all crowded into the cabin he and MacDuff had previously broken into. The bunk beds were all solid and bolted to the floor, so the prisoners were tied to the legs. Lukas was given the job of guarding them as the rest huddled up.

"One of these pieces of filth said that there should only be four or five more guards left," MacDuff began suspiciously.

"I assume they've locked themselves up in the great hall after all those fireworks," Pierce reasoned.

"That's a good bet," Sean agreed as he dried his hair with a towel he'd found.

"Well it's dark enough out we can probably sneak up close to the building," Pierce thought aloud, before shaking his head with dismay. "But we can't risk running in guns blazing. We saw a lot of people in white robes running around before. It's a good bet that they're innocent victims in all this and could get caught in the crossfire."

"Don't forget the girls," Sean reminded them. "Kat and the others are in there and could be used as hostages."

"Well we can't wait them out," Tiberius pronounced from the window. "Madmen like these will have stocked an enormous amount of supplies and will be able to wait us out."

"So then what do we do?" Pierce challenged angrily. "You're supposed to be the pros; you must have dealt with something like this before."

"Well we could pull a Budapest," Liam finally offered with a smile.

"I knew you'd mention that one," Sean swore, hanging his head down. "It barely worked that time and I spent two months in the hospital."

"Wait what happened in Budapest?"

"Lord Pierce," Liam whispered to make sure the others didn't hear. "You're going to love it."

Chapter 25

The smell of sweat and urine filled the dark and damp room as Kat groggily opened her eyes and vainly tried to focus on the surrounding space. When this proved too difficult, she raised her hand to her face and was finally able to focus on her flexing fingers. With this small victory she shifted her gaze along her body, stopping at her feet. After a few seconds concentration she watched her toes wiggle and then laid back down, exhausted from this small exertion.

After taking a few deep breathes, Kat propped herself up again and started to look around the room, slowly becoming sickened as forms started to take shape in front of her. Initially believing the soft hum was coming from her head, she suddenly realized that it was in fact the soft sleeping noises of at least ten other girls in the room. They were all splayed out on thin mattresses haphazardly strewn across the room. Some of the girls were cuddled up against each other in an attempt to keep warm.

The room itself began to present itself to her the longer she looked around. It was a small rectangle with rough timber walls and a pair of small windows high up on the walls. A single door on her right appeared to be the only way out.

Kat laid back down again and concentrated on her breathing. She could tell she had been drugged, she'd felt the same way after receiving a dose from Leon back in LA. She kept from panicking by trying to remember what had happened to her. Thinking hard she remembered being in a car and then seeing a big building full of lights and sounds. But no more images popped into her mind, just the feeling of floating or rocking.

While she lay there thinking, some of the other girls started to wake up around her. Apparently they weren't all new, as a few sat up easily and walked over to the far wall and removed white robes that hung there on nails. Their movements were slow, methodical, and devoid of any emotion. Her sister Maddie used to sleep walk in the middle of the night and Kat used to follow her to make sure she didn't hurt herself. It had been an unsettling sight then, but seeing someone do it while awake made her shiver anxiously. Eventually the rest of the girls got up and grabbed their robes, except for Kat and two others.

"Here, these holy robes are for you," a young blond girl intoned quietly as she handed Kat one of the hung robes. "They are a gift from the Master and will keep you safe."

"Safe from what?" Kat asked as she rose slowly to her feet and slid the robe around her. It was soft and cotton, with faint designs in gold thread near the sleeves and collar.

But the girl didn't respond, merely dropping the rest of the robes at the feet of the other new girls who were slowly waking. They reacted less calmly than Kat as they took in their surroundings, their eyes wide in terror and bodies shaking in fright.

"You're ok, just breathe," Kat soothed them after walking over and rubbing their backs gently. She handed them each their robe and helped them to their feet. Deep down she was just as scared as them, but her life experiences made it much easier to deal with the shock. It also helped that she knew that four thoroughly dangerous men were looking for her.

The metallic sound of a lock being opened brought her attention to the door and she squinted as it opened and revealed a bright light from beyond. But no one entered the small room, instead the other girls mindlessly walked out in a slow line.

"Follow the others and do what they do," Kat instructed the other two as she nudged them to the departing line. "It will be alright."

Joining the back of the line, Kat followed the others into a bright hallway and then up a flight of squeaky wooden stairs. The group emerged into another long hallway, with doors flanking both sides. Kat could see a large man in Brown leading the procession and watched carefully as he pulled out a key ring to unlock a door at the end of the hallway. They continued following him until they entered a large bright hall with an open beamed ceiling and lots of windows. Blinking through the brightness, Kat was surprised to discover it was actually a very grey day as her eyes adjusted.

Enormous green trees filled most of the windows, but a few offered a view of dark water in the distance. Dark clouds were in the horizon and she felt this to be an ominous sign.

"The Brides of the Master," announced the man in brown solemnly as he directed them to a long table.

"The Brides of the Master," repeated numerous voices in the same tone.

Too distracted by the windows and figuring out where she was, Kat was surprised by the voices and suddenly looked up in shock. There were four other long tables in the hall, each with ten to twelve people standing around them. They were all dressed in similar white or brown robes and watched the progression of the women with rapt attention as they lined up around their own table.

It was laid out for a meal, with bowls, spoons, and cups evenly spaced out. Kat stood behind one place setting and looked over the other tables as she waited to see what would happen next. Unlike the women around her table, many of the others didn't seem to be in the same kind of trance. Some of them were absently looking out the windows while others whispered quietly to their neighbour.

"The Master has blessed this food," called out a new voice from behind Kat. "May it energize us and brings us closer to the glorious light."

"The glorious light," repeated the congregation with various levels of enthusiasm before sitting on the bench seats that lined the tables.

More white robed members with aprons emerged from behind a door at the far end of the room carrying platters and large bowls. The other tables received two of each and quickly started serving themselves. However Kat was surprised when those with the aprons began serving those around her table individually.

Breakfast consisted of oatmeal, bread, and fruit, with tea to drink. Growing up in Rivermead, Kat was used to such simple meals and was grateful for the much needed nourishment. Everyone seemed to share the same opinion because there was little chatter during the meal.

The sky outside the hall was turning very dark and the wind picked up by the time the brides were led back down into their basement accommodations. But instead of the cramped sleeping room, they were ushered into a much larger room next to it. Again they were locked inside with a loud metallic click after the door was shut.

Although conditions were better in this room, Kat could still tell it was a cell. There were three windows instead of two, but they were all too small for even her small frame to fit through. Wooden chairs and tables filled the room, with only a few threadbare carpets to offer any kind of warmth.

After the door closed the girls divided themselves up automatically while the three initiates stared at each other. Three of the girls sat on chairs by the door, while the others went to the tables and pulled out baskets from below.

"What happens now?" Kat asked one of the girls who was busily emptying her basket. She pulled out brown fabric, scissors, spools of thread, and a small box.

"We busy ourselves with outfitting the Master's brave Acolytes," she replied absently as she started working.

"What about them?" Kat then asked pointing to the girls by the door. They simply stared straight ahead with the faint hint of a smile on their faces.

"They wait to unburden the souls of the Acolytes," she replied serenely. "We've been blessed by the Master and our touch helps purify them."

"Right," Kat offered sceptically, the sarcasm in her voice not even registered by the other girl. Deciding to play along, she pulled out a basket from under the table and started going through it. She found all kinds of useful things inside, setting them on the table like she was preparing for surgery.

The scissors were fairly sharp, so she put them aside as her first weapon. The cloth was rough, but too fragile to tie someone up with. She watched as the other girls layered pieces of the cloth to make it more durable. However she realized it could still be used to gag someone effectively. Needing another weapon, Kat went through the basket more thoroughly. The only thing that she could possibly think of was to use the thread as a garrotte to strangle someone from behind. But it was too thin and would probably snap. Seemingly stuck, she watched one of the girls toss her braided hair to the side. She suddenly smiled from the stroke of genius and began working.

The morning passed by quietly and Kat ignored those around her as she worked on her weapons and planned an escape. She busily braided three lengths of thread, repeating the process three times. These three newly braided lengths were then braided again, to create a thin but stronger length. As she finished her concentration was pulled away by a sudden raucous.

One of the new girls was pounding on the door in tears, screaming to be let out and threatening to call the police. The other new girl was huddled on a chair in the corner, her eyes closed and lips moving as she muttered something to herself.

Before Kat could get up and stop the wailing girl, the door flew open and a tall bearded man in the brown Acolytes clothing walked in. He took one look at the new girl and smiled cruelly. He lazily grabbed her with his big hands and pulled her out of the room, slamming the door behind him and blocking out the girl's screams.

Kat looked around angrily as none of the other girls even batted an eye at what had happened. Those at the table continued working and those by the door almost seemed disappointed that they hadn't been taken.

"I'll be damned if any of those bastards are going to pull me out of here screaming," Kat promised as she finished work on her homemade rope. It wasn't as thick as she would have liked, but she knew it would work. "And I'm not going to wait to be rescued like some damsel in distress."

Despite the situation she now found herself in, Kat realized she felt empowered from not feeling scared. She then looked over at the other new girl cowering in the corner and wanted her to feel the same way.

"Take a few deep breaths it's going to be alright," she instructed her after walking over to the corner with her basket of goodies. She gently touched her face and turned it so that they could look each other in the eye. "What's your name?"

"Cindy," the girl sobbed, before steadying herself with a few deep breaths.

"OK Cindy, I don't know about you but I didn't come her by choice," Kat began quietly, receiving a nod in reply. "That's what I thought. I'm getting out of here before they turn me into a zombie. You want to join me?"

Kat watched intently as thoughts of freedom fought with those of the repercussions of being caught within the girls head. With the battle won, Cindy finally nodded and then wiped away her tears.

"Good girl," Kat congratulated her. "These guys aren't that tough, just a bunch of bullies. Do you know how to beat bullies?"

"No," Cindy gulped despite her growing confidence.

"You stand up to them," Kat declared with the fire once more in her eyes. "You show them you won't be intimidated and they lose their power. Now there are two of us and only one guard, so we have the advantage."

"What do you want me to do?"

"I just need you to cause a distraction," Kat replied intensely. "Then leave the rest to me."

*

Kat was back at the work table when the door finally opened again and the guard dragged the new girl in. He dropped her unceremoniously on the floor and then left after shooting a yearning glance at the girls sitting by the door.

Cindy immediately left her spot in the corner and crouched by the girl's side. She had no visible bruises or marks on her, but Kat knew they were there. She watched as her young protégé helped the other new girl, gently stroking her hair and whispering to her. After a few minutes Cindy nodded at Kat, who casually stood up and moved to the end of the table.

"Help! Somebody help!" Cindy screamed out through the door. "She's stopped breathing!"

She had to repeat this a few more times before Kat could hear footsteps on the stairs beyond the door. Quietly but swiftly, Kat moved from the table and stood beside the door trying to look as innocent as possible.

The door slammed open and the guard barged in like a snarling beast. But his look immediately turned to one of shock and horror. The girl he'd just violently raped was lying on the floor, possibly dead. But more importantly to him, he'd robbed the Master of his chance with the new girl. He dropped down beside her with concern, checking for a pulse or signs of life.

Before he dropped down Kat pulled out her makeshift rope from the sleeve of her robe and wrapped it around both her hands. As soon as the guard was on his knees, Kat ran up behind him, looping the rope around his neck and pulled back as hard as she could. She then placed her knee on his back and pulled even harder.

The shock of the attack made the guard gasp in surprise, only making the garrotte more effecting. When he tried to yell something, Cindy ran up and shoved a piece of the brown cloth into his mouth. After another minute's struggle the guard fell face down with a loud thump.

The other girls simply sat in shock, unable to process what had just happened. Kat had been a little afraid that they'd be so brainwashed that they might turn on her. But instead they did nothing.

"Cindy, watch the door," Kat instructed after letting go of the rope, ignoring the bright red marks it had left on her hands. She bent down and made sure the guard had no pulse. Satisfied by its absence, she was too pumped full of adrenaline to fully realize she'd just taken a human life. Instead she pulled out the key ring from the guards pocket and then found something just as useful. A revolver.

Kat then went over to the new girl who was by now propped up on her elbows, staring at the body with a mixture of horror and triumph. She helped the girl up and led her to the stairs where Cindy gratefully grabbed her.

The door at the top of the stairs was open, so Kat could hear a storm raging above them. Hard rain pelted the hall, the wind howled through the windows, and thunder rumbled randomly. But as they reached the stairs, a loud explosion broke through the cacophony of noises. Then a spattering of smaller explosions sounded.

"That's gunfire," Kat smiled knowingly, her escape plans suddenly more realistic. However this didn't make the other girls nearly as optimistic and they almost looked back longingly for the cell. "We're going to go up the stairs and see what's happening. Stay behind and be as quiet as possible. If the guards show up, don't run away."

"But I thought we were escaping?" Cindy asked with slight confusion.

"We are escaping, but we're also being rescued," Kat replied, further confusing the others. But they still followed her up the stairs, quietly as possible.

When Kat reached the top she quietly scurried to the open door at the end of the hallway, breathing easier after seeing the dining hall was empty. As the others followed her up, she realized she didn't know where anything else was and didn't want to be dragging the other two around as she blindly walked around. Needing a place for them to hide, Kat looked around quickly until her eyes fell on the kitchen door. Scampering across the empty hall, they found the kitchen similarly empty.

"Go hide in there until I come back," Kat instructed them, pointing to a large pantry by a wooden prep table. They looked scared but nodded anyway.

Retracing her steps back out to the dining hall, Kat observed a door that led outside and then a few mystery doors. A quick look out of the many windows told her that she wouldn't find anything useful out in the storm. Plus with Lord Pierce and the others probably here, she didn't want to get caught in any potential crossfire.

With that option removed, Kat turned to the opposite wall and looked at a hallway and a door about ten feet beside it. Going with her gut she headed towards the hallway entrance, staying close to the wall as she approached. The storm outside made listening for signs of anyone else almost impossible; she'd have to look around the corner to see if the hallway was occupied.

The sudden eruption of more gunfire made Kat's heart jump into her throat as she peeked around the corner. Thankfully it was empty, because she just stood there frozen in shock. The gunfire was much closer than before, but she wasn't willing to go hide in the kitchen pantry.

The hallway wasn't very long and only had a single closet door along the way. But as she neared the other end, she could hear murmuring voices. Quietly gliding along the wall, she snuck up to the edge and carefully peered around the corner.

"The time has come children! The apocalypse is upon us and we must journey towards the light!" exclaimed a deranged looking man in white robes standing on an alter. He had long greasy hair seemingly plastered to his head and a long scraggily beard. But it was his eyes that really drew Kat's attention. The photo she'd seen of Lord Debochev did not do him justice. His eyes were powerful, wild, and hypnotizing.

"The light!" shouted out the mass of similarly white robbed people standing in front of the alter. They all stood in front of chairs that had something placed on them.

"I have reached the light and brought its power back to you, creating the water of light!" he continued, raising a silver goblet above his head. Everyone reached back to their chairs and grabbed a cup that was placed there, diligently holding it in front of them.

"The water of light!" they all repeated enthusiastically.

"Everyone stop!" Kat screamed out, surprising herself by the outburst. MacDuff had given her a book about cults before they had set out on this mission and she suddenly realized what she was witnessing. Despite the fact that this cult was part of a human smuggling ring, she knew that many of them were also innocent victims.

Her outburst caught some of the congregations' attention, even Debochev glanced at her. But despite the brief look of irritation on his face, he continued the ritual.

"The power of the water will brighten our inner light and allow us to shed these imperfect bodies."

"Don't drink it!" Kat pleaded helplessly.

But no one heeded her call, blindly following Debochev's lead and drinking from their glasses. Everyone finished it in one big gulp, smiling as they set the glasses back down behind them.

"You idiots, it was poison!"

"Pay no attention to my bride," Debochev proclaimed as some of the congregation looked back at her. "She has not yet been purified and does not yet carry the light within her."

"You're full of shit and no holy man," Kat countered, marching up to the alter. Despite the enormous odds against her, she couldn't help but challenge the demonic man before her.

"He is the Master of the Light," objected a middle aged man with glasses, placing himself between her and Debochev.

"He's a fraud and he just signed your death certificates."

"She's crazed, Acolytes seize her!" Debochev ordered.

Kat had been so preoccupied by the ceremony she hadn't noticed the four brown cloaked men by the far wall looking out the windows. They'd been busy watching something outside, but they now ran towards her. Reacting without thinking, Kat raised her pistol and fired a shot in Debochev's direction before retreating back towards the hallway.

Screams erupted behind her as she made her escape. She turned to look behind her, hoping to see Debochev's prone body. But instead she saw two of the Acolytes right on her heals with pistols in hand.

"Stop!" one of them ordered, but Kat had no intention of complying. Instead she aimed the pistol behind her and blindly fired another shot.

Two shots rang out in response, slamming into the walls on either side of her and sending wood chips flying into the air. Kat didn't want to stop but those had been warning shots and the next ones wouldn't miss. Reaching the dining hall, Kat slowed to a stop and dropped the pistol on the floor, feeling defeated.

"Good girl," taunted one of the Acolytes as they approached her from behind. "Looks like someone needs to be taught a lesson."

"Yeah, you need to be purified," chuckled the second menacingly.

Kat heard the distinct sound of a zipper being undone as steps sounded behind her. Deciding she would face her tormenters rather than cower like they wanted, she spun around defiantly.

"One chance to change your minds about this and let me go," Kat proclaimed with renewed determination as she saw what was behind her.

"Oh I don't think so," the second Acolyte laughed as he reached into his pants.

"You had your chance," Kat shrugged, taking a small step backwards.

"Federal Agents you pieces of shit," Pierce growled as he shoved the barrel of his rifle into the back of the head of the first Acolyte. "Drop your weapons."

"Or try and make a run for it so I can put a bullet in your brain," Liam continued, his own rifle up against the second Acolyte's head.

Kat breathed with relief at the presence of her friends. Both men had been against the wall beside the hallway entrance when she'd run past into the dinning hall. She didn't know how things would have ended up if they hadn't been there.

"Staying out of trouble I see," Pierce observed as they shoved the Acolytes against the wall and began searching them. After kicking their pistols away, Liam began tying the men up.

"I'm fine, but there's a bunch of girls here that are in trouble," Kat replied, the concern clear in her voice.

"After we deal with Debochev," Pierce nodded.

"I can't just leave them," Kat pleaded, looking back at the kitchen and then the stairs to the basement below.

"I'll take care of the women," Liam offered with a quick smile.

"What about these pieces of trash?"

"No problem, they're tied up and unconscious," Liam replied, cracking each of them in the back of the head with the butt of rifle. Both tumbled to the floor and didn't move, but none of them bent down to see if they were alright.

Kat started to explain about the two girls in the kitchen, but a loud crash from beyond the hallway stopped her immediately. Before she could wonder what had happened, gunfire erupted from the same direction.

"Patrick! Get in here!" bellowed MacDuff's familiar voice and Pierce took off down the hall with his rifle at the ready.

Chapter 26

Expecting to run into a shoot out, Pierce was relieved when no one shot at him as he ran into the main hall. But his relief instantly turned to horror as he looked around the makeshift shrine. His mouth went dry and he felt a knot in his throat as he lowered his rifle in shock.

Forty to fifty white robed bodies lay strewn about the floor like broken dolls in a child's playroom. Their lifeless eyes stared at the ceiling and trickles of blood stained their lips and cheeks. Pierce wanted to be sick at the massive loss of life.

He walked among the bodies and immediately saw the glasses. Some were still sitting innocently on chairs, while others accompanied the bodies on the ground. Pierce knew about cults and easily recognized the signs of a mass suicide, but the reality was something completely different.

"Sir, we were able to capture two more of the guards," Sean reported near the front door, his face slightly cut.

Pierce walked over and looked down at the brown clothed Acolytes with even more disdain than the previous two he'd just left. They were both face down on the ground with their hands tied behind their back.

"Sean, take them outside and put them with the rest," Pierce instructed looking out to the small open space between the hall and the cabins. "And thank Lukas for me, his help was appreciated."

Knowing that the remaining guards were holed up in the main hall, the team had used a diversion to keep their attention. Lukas had given each of the captured guards a broom handle and had them turn over tables out in the open. The idea was for the guards inside to believe their comrades were actually more police officers setting up a barricade. It allowed Pierce and the others to sneak up to the hall unnoticed. Pierce and Liam went in the back by the kitchen while MacDuff and Sean climbed up onto the roof.

Luckily the storm had masked the noises of the intruders to the guards inside and total surprise had been achieved. The only issue had been when MacDuff and Sean rappelled into the main hall from the roof. MacDuff had crashed through the front door with no problems, but Sean had gone through one of the windows. The shattered glass had cut his face, but Sean didn't feel too bad, since it was much better than what had happened to him the first time in Budapest.

"I forget you've never lived through a massive battle or a plague," MacDuff consoled his leader, seeing the bleak look on Pierce's face. They were walking amongst the bodies looking for Debochev and his last remaining Hound. The other one had been on the motor yacht and Sean confirmed that he'd died in the shootout before the boat exploded.

"Why would he do this?" Pierce wondered aloud, aimlessly walking amongst the corpses. "Is he really deranged or is this part of his plan?"

"I can't say," MacDuff frowned as he climbed up on the altar. He bent down and began examining the floor around him. "But despite his claims, the bastard isn't immortal."

"What do you mean?"

MacDuff stood up and raised two of his fingers, the red tinge of blood clearly on the tips. When he pointed to the floor Pierce's mood lighten as he saw a trail of blood heading towards the back door.

"Let's go get the fucker," Pierce breathed, hefting his rifle once again. MacDuff merely nodded with the same determination and went to the back door, opening it carefully.

Wind and rain greeted them as the door opened, blinding both of them momentarily. Undeterred by the storm they walked out into it, ignoring the wet and cold. While MacDuff looked for the trail, Pierce scanned the area around them.

The forest sprang up twenty feet from the building, the towering trees reaching impossibly high into the sky. The only thing Pierce could see through the enormous trunks was a building with a green tin roof.

"The trail's washed away in this rain," MacDuff exclaimed after finally standing up.

"Let's check out that building then," Pierce offered, pointing to the structure in the distance. "I think it's one of the maintenance buildings we saw from the hill."

"Good idea, they might have a vehicle there," MacDuff nodded as he looked around for himself. Satisfied, he ran across the clearing and took cover behind a tree. Pierce was right behind him and crouched behind the tree next to him.

They slowly progressed towards the building, their rifles raised as they went from tree to tree. The whistling wind offered them no telltale signs of where their quarry was, but it also gave them the same advantage. Despite the rain seemingly coming down sideways, they both noticed it lighten as they walked below the green arbour canopy.

"What's the matter?" Pierce whispered to MacDuff as the Scotsman seemed to stop mid step.

"I thought I heard something,"

"Are you sure? I can barely hear you," Pierce asked cautiously.

"No I'm not sure, but this is a decent place for an ambush…"

Both men dropped to the ground instinctively as a bullet tore into a tree trunk inches from Pierce's head. They rolled backwards to a fallen tree, raising their rifles and shooting back in response.

"I hate guns!" Pierce yelled as he emptied the magazine of his rifle. Neither could see the other shooter, but they could tell his general direction.

"It's got to be Carlos," MacDuff reasoned, naming Debochev's last remaining Hound. "He's taken up a position between the Main Hall and the other building. Probably stalling us to let Debochev escape."

"Just like you would do for me?" Pierce smiled as he reloaded his weapon.

"No my Lord," MacDuff smiled back. "You should know by now that I'm too good to allow you to need a getaway."

"I'll have to remember that," Pierce laughed hollowly as a bullet slammed into the tree beside him. "Debochev is mine, you take care of his trash."

Nodding, MacDuff rose up and provided covering fire as Pierce scurried off to the right. Like before, he crouched between the tress, taking a circuitous route towards the building. It was located in a clearing and the rain became harder as he approached it.

There was a pair of open garage doors on the side, along with a regular door that was closed. Taking a few deep breathes Pierce sprinted towards the side of the building, reaching it without incident.

Initially happy at not being shot at, Pierce suddenly worried that the reason might be that Debochev had already escaped. Although it would only result in extending the chase, Pierce wanted to it to end now. Taking another breath to steady himself, Pierce raised his rifle and slowly approached the closest garage door.

Peeking inside, Pierce could only see a derelict tractor, some rusty machinery, and piles of wood. Feeling disappointed he walked in to the building quickly, too late in realizing he wasn't alone.

A shovel descended upon Pierce with surprising speed, his trained fencing footwork the only thing allowing him to avoid being crushed. However the brunt of the blow fell upon his rifle and it slammed to the ground with a crack.

Shrieking at the top of his lungs, the deranged Russian hefted the shovel once again and swung it at Pierce's head. He dodged it easily, but he was shocked by the other man's appearance. He'd only seen Debochev a handful of times at the Manor, usually from a distance. But up close he was just as frightening as Colonel Bufford had been. Luckily he wasn't nearly as skilled at fighting.

"You've robbed me of paradise!" he screamed, slowly raising the shovel again.

"You're insane!" Pierce yelled back. "You just committed mass murder!"

"I rid those poor souls of their mortal bonds," Debochev laughed in response.

"You can't believe that," Pierce challenged him, seeing a devious glint in his eyes.

"Of course I don't," he smiled devilishly as he raised the shovel once again.

Pierce had hoped that the messiah complex was for real, since it might explain his actions better. But instead of facing a madman with no understanding of reality, Pierce was looking into the eyes of a true psychopath.

"You sick son of a bitch," Pierce swore as he backed away. He still had a knife and a pistol in his jacket, but he wanted to bring the bastard back alive. Death would be too good for someone like Debochev and he was sick of seeing dead people. "You're coming back to the Manor with me."

"Never!" he yelled back, taking another wild swing that Pierce avoided. "This place is perfect; lonely, sad, bored, and simple people everywhere. They're all looking for someone to believe in and I'll give it to them. Me!"

"If you think you're getting out of here, then you're more insane than I thought," Pierce shouted back over the wailing wind just beyond the door. The garage was shaking from the storm and the metal tools hanging on the walls clanked and rattled, creating a strange symphony of noise. "After what you did to those people, we'll never let you leave."

"They did that to themselves," Debochev countered, dragging the shovel towards Pierce. "No one put a gun to their head and made them drink."

Pierce didn't expect that argument and was momentarily speechless. He didn't know what a judge would say to that, but he knew what he thought. It was bullshit. They had been brainwashed and he had held a figurative gun to their head.

"What about the girls you kidnapped and locked up?" Pierce reminded him angrily. "They had guns to their heads and we know all about it. We captured Leon and he told us everything he knew. Then we followed the rest of your lackeys here."

"Those girls were all homeless or unwanted," Debochev smirked as he once again lifted the shovel. "Nobody missed them and they proved much more useful here with me. They helped ease the burdens of a great man, instead of wasting away on drugs at the beach. And once the bomb goes off in the main hall, no one will even know they were here."

Pierce suddenly looked back out the door with concern. Everyone had probably taken shelter in the Main hall from the storm and were now in danger. It explained why Debochev had been so eager to perform the Mass suicide once Pierce and his men had arrived. He was trying to erase all the evidence against him.

But Pierce's momentary lapse in attention gave the Russian the opening he had been waiting for. As soon as Pierce looked out the garage door, the shovel flew across and slammed into his shoulder. A shot of pain went up his side as he fell against a pile of wood, knocking a gas can over at the same time.

"I'm going to kill you and burn your body," Debochev sneered as he got closer, eyeing the gas can and the wood. Pulling a lighter from his pocket, he lit it and threw it over Pierce's head onto the wood pile. Flames immediately erupted, forcing Pierce to crawl one handed away from the growing heat.

Pierce couldn't feel his left arm as he backed away, watching helplessly as the shovel was once more raised into the air above him.

*

He would later say it was a lucky and desperate shot, but Pierce was being modest. With a distance of less than ten feet, he had struck exactly where he wanted to.

As he crawled backwards against the floor, the forgotten pistol in his pocket fell out and hit his hand. Without thinking, Pierce raised the gun and fired a well aimed shot at the shovel. It mercifully hit its target and sent the metal tool flying backwards out of his attacker's hands.

Struggling to his feet, rage started to well up within Pierce as he pointed the gun at Debochev's head. The Russian's confidence evaporated immediately as his eyes focused on the barrel of the gun.

"You're coming back to the Manor to answer for everything you've done," Pierce commanded through gritted teeth. "For those poor trusting souls inside, for the helpless women you tormented, for your treachery to the Manor, and for one more important thing."

"What else could there be?" Debochev challenged defiantly, almost taking pleasure in hearing his crimes being rhymed back to him.

"It might seem inconsequential against everything else you've done, but it will have the biggest impact on what remains of your life," Pierce replied seriously. "You had Leon try and kidnap the wrong girl and then you locked her up in your little dungeon."

"I told you, those girls were all homeless drifters, why should one make more of a difference over the others?"

"Because one of them wasn't a homeless drifter, she was our spy," Pierce replied, seething at the thought of Kat in the basement cell.

"So, you used some of the girls as well then," Debochev laughed uneasily. "Not my fault."

"She came with us through the portal," Pierce countered before a smile broke out across his face. "But more importantly, she's Tiberius' lover and you tried to kidnap, rape, and torture her."

"Wait... but that's... impossible," he croaked with confusion, the fear suddenly clear in his voice. He was so scared that his thick Russian accent remerged.

Debochev, like most of the members of the Black Tower Hunt Club, feared and respected Tiberius. He was an imposing figure that had lived longer than the rest of them, Lord Lodge's loyal servant. But he was more than that; a powerful and vicious warrior, a devious and efficient spy, an inspiring and courageous leader, and more. But he was also a product of his environment, and the dark ages always seemed to be just beneath his honourable veneer. At his core, the members of the Manor knew he was an eye for an eye kind of man and left forgiveness to God and his master.

"What do you think Tiberius is going to do to you? Even if I were to let you go, do you think there's anywhere on this planet or any time in history where you'll be able to hide from him? Tiberius will find you and when he does, you're going to wish you had drunk the same thing as your followers back there. You kidnapped his woman, you fucking moron!"

"But how could I know?" he pleaded, backing away.

"That's not going to matter, you're the only one left," Pierce shrugged, lowering the pistol. "Leon cut a deal, Yves died on the boat, and MacDuff probably put a bullet in Carlos' head. Tiberius is going to take his vengeance out on somebody and like I said, you're the last one left."

"But…"

"But what? Is it finally sinking in that your little parlour tricks, fancy incantations, and weird stare won't get you out of this?" Pierce continued berating him. He hoped he could break him down and bring him back without any further violence. "You managed to make a mortal enemy out of the guy some say mentored Vlad the Impaler. Fucking Dracula! I'm not sure that it's even true, could be just gossip. But we both know Tiberius and I don't think it's far fetched. Do you?"

He merely gulped and looked from the fire to the open garage door and then back at Pierce.

"You want to make a run for it? Be my guest, I won't stop you," Pierce offered calmly, lowering his gun. "But I also won't stop Tiberius from tearing you apart when he finds you. However there's another option. You come back to the Manor with me and I promise that he won't touch you. Lord Lodge gave me his word that anyone who returned of their free will would receive amnesty from any retribution."

"I won't be paraded around like a caged beast!" Debochev yelled wildly, his eyes almost glazed over with fear. "I won't spend eternity in a cell when I am destined for greatness!"

Without any further preamble, Debochev ran past Pierce and jumped into the fire he'd just started. The gasoline had ignited the enormous pile of dry wood with great speed and the flames were almost licking the roof of the garage.

Pierce turned with stunned surprise as he watched Debochev's body consumed by the fire, his crazed screams joining with the wind to create a thoroughly hideous noise. Unable to stand the sound any longer Pierce slowly raised his pistol to put the man out of his misery, but the screaming stopped before he could pull the trigger.

"Thank God!" exclaimed MacDuff's breathless highland voice from behind Pierce. "I heard the screams and feared the worst."

"He just jumped into the fire Duffy," Pierce stammered, still staring at it with disbelief. "Who does that?"

"A crazy man that's who," MacDuff replied confidently.

"Where's Carlos?" Pierce asked after sadly turning away from the blaze.

"He's back at the camp with the others," MacDuff answered. "He's got a small wound but nothing too serious. He'll make it back to the portal."

"Wait, the camp!" Pierce exclaimed, panicking as he remembered what Debochev had said. "There's a bomb in the main hall!"

"Shit," MacDuff swore, immediately taking off towards the camp with Pierce right behind him.

The storm was losing its strength and they could easily see the roofs of the other buildings through the forest as they started running through the trees. Zigzagging around the large trunks, both hoped that the bomb would malfunction or that the timer was optimistically set.

They learned this wasn't the case as the main hall exploded into flames, the eruption sending debris in all directions.

"No, no ,no," Pierce whispered as he came to a halt behind MacDuff. They both stood staring helplessly at the burning rubble, unsure what to do. Seeing the immensity of the wreckage, the chance of any survivors seemed pretty slim.

"Wait do you hear that?" MacDuff whispered, holding up a hand.

Pierce stared at him for a second in confusion before he started to hear the faint sound of voices on the wind. They were coming from the beach and both men immediately started sprinting in that direction.

A wave of relief washed over them both as they reached the beach and saw it crowded with people. Thugs in brown clothing were tied together and sitting in groups and girls in white robes were huddled together under thick wool blankets.

"Ha! I knew my Lord Debochev would escape," called out Carlos as he saw Pierce and MacDuff approach alone.

"That maniac threw himself into a blazing fire and burnt to death," Pierce corrected as he walked past him, not even bothering to look at the prisoner.

"So what happens now?" Lukas asked as he walked back for the shoreline where his boat was grounded. He had checked it for bullet holes and deemed it seaworthy.

"Thanks for all your help Lukas," Pierce nodded, extending his hand to the sailor. "We couldn't have saved these girls and apprehended these criminals without your help. But you're not done helping yet. We're out of radio range, so we need to load all these people up and then take them out of here to the local authorities."

"Umm, about the local authorities…"

"What's the matter?" Pierce asked.

"It's like this sir," Liam began, coming to his new friend's aid. "Mr. Lukas is not exactly one of their most liked individuals and then there's the issue of one of the guards…"

"What about one of the guards?"

"I shot one," Lukas replied without hesitation, but with obvious unease. "He went to go after one of the girls when they were brought out and I shot him before he could reach her."

"You did the right thing," MacDuff shrugged; disappointed that he hadn't pulled the trigger.

"I know, but I'm not a cop like you guys," Lukas countered.

"When we commandeered your boat we deputized you," Liam suggested to the others.

"I don't think it works like that," Pierce shook his head. Inwardly he was glad of this new situation. The idea of dropping a boatload of kidnapped girls and their kidnappers at the local sheriff's office was not conducive to keeping a low profile and would have created unwanted attention to him and his men. "I've got a better idea. Lukas, load the girls on your boat and take them back to your cabin. The marshals will go with you and contact someone to pick them up. We'll stay with the prisoners until the local authorities come and investigate the explosion."

Everyone nodded in agreement and began helping the girls onto the fishing boat. The storm had all but past, so the wind was no longer whipping the water into white capped waves. Within a few minutes the boat was full and backing into the bay.

"These men aren't with the FBI!" Carlos yelled as Pierce and MacDuff turned back to the prisoners on the beach. "They can't arrest us."

"He's right," MacDuff shrugged, pulling out his pistol and passing it to Pierce.

"Yeah, none of you guys are under arrest," Pierce agreed as he accepted the pistol and checked the bullets. "How many bullets do you have left?"

"Around ten," MacDuff guessed as he looked in the magazine from his rifle before reloading it. "You?"

"Six in this one and five in the other," Pierce replied, hefting a revolver in each hand. The initial pain from being hit with the shovel had worn off and he could stiffly flex his left hand. "That makes almost two bullets for each of them."

"Sounds good to me," MacDuff nodded sagely. "I hate loose ends."

Chapter 27

"I don't believe it," Tiberius disagreed, unable to shake his head as a nurse stitched it up. "Lord Schell was recruited specifically by Lord Lodge to be our ally."

"I don't like it anymore than you, but it's the best lead we've found," Jane allowed with frustration. "We've been over the files and nothing is else is popping out."

"Who's we?"

"Logan and I, that's all," Jane replied.

"Hmm," Tiberius hummed, seemingly lost in thought for second before coming out of it. "How's your recruit doing then?"

"He's actually adapting better than I thought," Jane conceded truthfully. She was finding herself becoming more and more dependant on him. He was a diligent assistant, a thoughtful sounding board, and a menacing attack dog.

"That's not surprising, I've run into Special Forces guys like him before," Tiberius smiled in recollection. "They thrive on challenges and like nothing better than overcoming them."

"He's outside if you'd like to meet him."

"In a second," Tiberius delayed, thanking the nurse as she finished up. She nodded politely and then left the room after collecting her equipment. "Have you heard any word from Lord Pierce and his men?"

"Nothing yet," Jane replied uneasily despite trying to appear unconcerned. She knew that tracking down Debochev could take a long time and hoped that nothing was wrong. In truth she was worried for Patrick and wanted him to get back safely. But she still didn't know what she'd do when that time came. However the look on Tiberius' tired face made her suddenly realize that he hadn't asked the question out of professional curiosity. Kat was with Pierce and he was worried about her. "I'm sure they're fine."

"I know and I'm glad it's Debochev they're chasing," Tiberius continued, erasing the concern from his face and once more looking like the powerful CEO he had become. "He's not as dangerous as some of the others that escaped."

"Speaking of which, I'm afraid Lord Lodge hasn't come up with anything new," Jane reported haltingly with her eyes on the ground. She hesitated for a second as she decided on how to proceed before finally making a decision and looking up. "Tiberius, I'm worried about Victor. He's not the man I remember from before. The man who tutored me at the Crow's Nest and engineered our escape isn't there anymore."

"You've been in to see him?"

"Only a few times," Jane nodded, closing her eyes as she remembered each time. "But he'll only see Melrose regularly. I might be crossing a line, but he needs help. He's been worse each time I've seen him and I can't see it getting any better. He's up and down, speaking in riddles so quickly I can barely understand him. Or he says nothing at all, staring into the fire as he puffs a thick cloud of smoke around him from his filthy pipe."

"He'll be fine," Tiberius reassured her, partially trying to convince himself of his own growing fears. "I've seen him like this before and it won't last, it never does. His failure in predicting Cleaver's actions shook him, but he'll regain that confidence and return as the great man we know."

"I hope you're right, because I found this and it's not reassuring," Jane allowed, pulling a small leather pouch from beside her. She handed it over to Tiberius who immediately recognized it for what it was. But to make the point, Jane opened the pouch to reveal a collection of syringes and liquid filled bottles.

"Have you shown this to anyone else?" Tiberius whispered as he snatched the pouch and shoved it into one of his desk drawers. When Jane shook her head he let out a slow breathe. "Good, things are at a very precarious time at the Manor right now. Everyones confidence in Lord Lodge is the only thing keeping things together."

"That's not entirely true," Jane corrected him gently. "Their confidence in you has also made a big difference."

"Their fear of me doesn't hurt either," Tiberius allowed before moving on. "But Lord Lodge is our leader and ultimately the one people look to. If we're going to remedy this situation, we're going to need him back in form. Between being kidnapped by Cleaver and locking himself away, people haven't seen him walking the halls in a long time. I'm worried about what will happen if he doesn't re-immerge like his old self soon."

They both sat in silence as the possibilities hung above them, each one worse than the last. Jane had worked hard to get to where she was and had no intention of losing her position now.

"Well let's see this new recruit," Tiberius finally ordered after the short pause. Jane nodded and went to the door, waving him in.

"Lord Tiberius, this is Staff Sergeant Logan, retired," Jane smiled as they both stood in front of Tiberius' desk.

"Actually I'm dead," Logan corrected, still amused by the fact.

"Indeed, well take a seat both of you," Tiberius replied coldly. Leaning back in his chair, Tiberius silently eyed the new recruit before turning his gaze towards the recruiter. "Let me begin by saying this isn't a meet and great. This file on my desk contains a significant amount of information on you and I helped put a large part of it together. This also isn't an interview as that would suggest you can walk away if we're not impressed by what we see. You will stay with us here, one way or another."

Reverting to his life as a soldier, Logan maintained a rigid posture and didn't react to any of the speech.

"So the question remains, what will you do with this opportunity?" Tiberius continued as he straightened up and leaned forward. They stared at each other for a solid minute, neither man willing to look away. Eventually Tiberius smiled knowingly and leaned back into his chair, seemingly satisfied. "Jane tells me that you agree with her views on Schell, that he's the mole."

"Wizard," Logan corrected as he felt the tension in the air recede.

"What?"

"Sorry I thought that's what we were calling them," Logan apologised, quickly shooting Jane a sarcastic smile.

"I thought if the word mole got out it could be just as harmful even if it weren't true," Jane explained. "So we're using the word wizard instead, like a code word."

"Yes I understand," Tiberius nodded patiently.

"As to your question I agree with Ms. Piper's view on Schell," Logan answered confidently. "But we're not saying he's the wizard. Just that he's the best lead we've found."

"You've seen his file, what do you think?" Tiberius challenged him. There were many men like Logan at the Manor, good with a gun and following orders. But fewer that could think for themselves.

"You're asking me if I think a Nazi could be a bad guy?" Logan replied sarcastically. "But then again from what I've seen and read, everyone here is a bad guy."

"Very good," Tiberius smiled at his astute observation before reverting to his serious demeanour. "Now please answer the question."

"Honestly? I don't know," Logan finally offered. "I've never met him so you both might have a better read on the guy. But from what I've read he's not a risk taker and being a mole is one hell of a risk. You end up with enemies on both sides and eventually mistrusted by both. He's met with Cleaver a bunch of times at locations that we believe were used to coordinate their plans. It could be a coincidence or it could be a red herring."

"So what do you suggest we do?"

"We need more than a torn note from a castle basement," Logan observed quickly. "I'd search his rooms and anywhere else he might have hidden possible clues."

"We can do it very quietly," Jane agreed, voicing a plan she'd been building in her head. "We send his valet on an errand somewhere on the island and tell him that Lord Schell's rooms will be cleaned in his absence. I know which members of the staff we can use for the cleaning who are more discreet. That will give us the time and opportunity to conduct a search."

"Very well, I'll let you organize it," Tiberius nodded thoughtfully. "Inform me when the preparations have been made. I don't want you to rush things, but we need to finish the search before Schell and his men return from their mission."

Jane and Logan took this final instruction as their dismissal and left the office without a further word.

After the door closed Tiberius stood up and walked over to his bookshelf and pulled down on one of the books. Halfway out of its place, the book stopped and released a latch to a secret compartment filled with bottles and glasses. Tiberius poured himself a drink and returned to his desk. With a tired sigh he drank half of his drink and set the glass down on the desk. He then opened one of the drawers and pulled out the leather pouch.

He'd been serving Lord Lodge long enough to know that his mentor was an occasional user of cocaine. He wasn't an addict, merely using it when a bout of ennui due to boredom enveloped him. But this time it was different and Tiberius was worried. Drugs should have been the last thing on Lodge's mind as he tackled the mystery of Cleaver's treachery and future plans. This was the type of challenge that he craved, something to test his immense mental prowess.

Finishing his drink, Tiberius stood up and grabbed the leather pouch angrily. He wasn't about to sit back and let his mentor and best friend fall apart before his eyes. The downward spiral had to end and he was the only one who could pull Victor Lodge out of it. He opened the secret passage that led to Lord Lodge's office, taking a deep breathe before marching into the darkness.

*

"The Great Lord Pierce spares the lives of some worthless scum," Carlos taunted as he followed behind MacDuff. His hands were tied together with a long length of rope and the Scotsman held the other end, dragging the prisoner roughly through the woods. "You think that was mercy back there, not putting a bullet in their heads? It was weakness."

Pierce was walking behind him and trying his best to ignore their new prisoner. They'd scared the guards on the beach with the threat of death, but decided to leave them there. Waiting for the authorities to show up and then handing them over was impossible. Again it would have led to too many questions, even with their fake credentials. So instead he decided to leave them on the beach until someone investigating the explosion found them.

But as they walked, even that decision seemed flawed to Pierce. Debochev had picked the location of his compound well. It was secluded with no neighbours and no busy local roads. There was every possibility that no one noticed the explosion in the storm.

"My Lord Debochev was a great man, a holy man," Carlos continued, turning his head to leer back at Pierce. "Others could see that and they flocked to him, look at how many became his followers in such a short time. He was decisive and strong."

"He was a lunatic and a predator," MacDuff countered, yanking the rope and making Carlos stumble into a tree.

"He was a tool of God, a Saint," Carlos continued without missing a beat. "Not appreciated in his own time, he'll be revered in years to come."

"He's a pile of ash that no one will remember after you're dead," Pierce finally responded tiredly. He was exhausted from the chase and the frantic last few hours. "He was a coward who chose to kill himself rather than come back and face the music."

"That's not true!" Carlos exclaimed defiantly.

"He wasn't a holy man," Pierce replied as they approached the small road where they'd parked the car. "He was a shyster, a con man, and a psychopath. Gregori Debochev was nothing more than a phony with a bag full of tricks spouting ridiculous sayings which weren't even his. We found a book in his study from some other lunatic, full of lines about following the light and shit like that."

"How dare you!" Carlos yelled, his eyes growing wild by the accusation.

"MacDuff, I'm tired of this idiot and this conversation," Pierce breathed with exasperation.

Without missing a beat MacDuff pulled out the tranquilizer gun and shot a dart into Carlos' side, dropping him within seconds. Luckily they had reached the car, so they only had to carry him a few yards before unceremoniously throwing him into the trunk.

"Let's get out of here in case someone actually did hear that explosion," Pierce offered as he sat behind the wheel of the Dodge Charger. He smiled as it rumbled to life and skidded down the road. He would miss this car, but had already planned a way to put it in storage so that he could pick it up whenever he went through some of the other portals. Sadly there was no way to actually get it through a portal, and no real roads on the island to drive it on even if he could.

It was completely dark by the time they reached the main road and they had yet to see any emergency vehicles of any kind. Although Pierce believed that the men they'd left on the beach deserved to be punished, starving to death in the harsh elements was not what he had in mind.

"We'll make an anonymous tip from Lukas' cottage," MacDuff offered, reading Pierce's frowning face perfectly. Pierce merely nodded as he drove, glad that he and MacDuff were on the same page.

Within half an hour Lukas' cottage came into view and Pierce slowly parked beside the Pontiac GTO. Despite driving slow to avoid any attention, they were probably well ahead of the fishing boat. Even though he knew the waters, Lukas would still have to go slow to avoid any potential accidents.

"I'm starving, let's see if Lukas has any food," MacDuff thought aloud as he walked towards the cabin. After checking the trunk, Pierce decided to join him, his stomach suddenly feeling angry with its emptiness.

"Well it's a little bit spartan isn't it," Pierce observed as he followed MacDuff in through the front door.

The log cabin was small from the outside, but seemed smaller once inside. It was a single room with a woodstove in the middle. A cot was shoved against the far wall with an army surplus sleeping bag on it. What could be generously described as a kitchen was by the front door, consisting of a small fridge and a mismatched table with two chairs.

"It must be grocery day," MacDuff sighed as he checked the fridge and small cupboard. "Doesn't look like things are going too well for our new friend."

"We'll slip him some cash for helping us out," Pierce suggested optimistically as he looked around.

"I've seen this before," MacDuff replied sadly. "The lad doesn't need money, he needs a purpose."

"I know what you're thinking Duffy," Pierce allowed as he sat down at the kitchen table. "But aren't there rules to this kind of thing."

"With all due respect sir, bugger the rules."

"Well I guess that's what we've been doing lately," Pierce agreed with a smile. "What with all of our helping others and not killing everyone we come across. I keep going on about how things need to change. I guess it's time to put my money where my mouth is."

MacDuff just nodded and joined him at the table. It was beside a large window that provided a great view of the Columbia River during the day. However at night they could only see the twinkling lights of the stars and ships passing by.

Eventually a set of lights began to approach rather than continue past and they got up to welcome the new arrivals. Rather than mooring the fishing boat at its regular location out in the river, Lukas brought it right up on the beach.

"You made good time," MacDuff called out as he approached the boat.

"Well the girls were getting cold," Lukas replied as he helped one over the side into MacDuffs large arms.

"And even I couldn't keep them all warm," Liam winked, handing another one down to Pierce.

The boat was quickly emptied, Kat and Sean ushering the girls into the cabin and the warm embrace of the woodstove. The rest of the men shoved the fishing boat back out into the river for Lukas to moor it properly.

"Sir, I've been thinking about Lukas," Liam began as they watched him jump in the small rowboat and return to shore.

"He doesn't seem like your type," Pierce observed with a grin, unable to help himself.

"Very funny, but I'm serious."

"Well it's about time," MacDuff pointed out. "Don't worry lad, we're well ahead of you."

"Good."

Kat and Sean rejoined them from the cabin just as Lukas was tying his rowboat up at the rickety dock. He stared at the group for a second before lazily walking up to them.

"I put a call in to the State Police," Sean reported. "They'll go check out what's left of the camp and make sure the men on the beach are apprehended. They're also sending a car here for the girls."

"Good," Pierce nodded, stifling a yawn. "How are the girls doing?"

"They're still really shook up and are worried about the Master," Kat offered, shaking her head incomprehensibly. "But the two girls that were with me are looking after them. They've got good heads on their shoulders."

"Who are you guys?" Lukas finally interrupted, unable to remain quiet any longer. "You're not with the FBI or the Marshals."

"Why do you say that?"

"Let's just say I've had enough run-ins with the cops to smell a pig a mile away," Lukas challenged them seriously. "And none of you smell like bacon.

"We're part of a special task force..." Pierce began before Lukas held his hand up and cut him off.

"Save it, I think I deserve some answers," he said angrily. "I just witnessed some crazy shit and even killed a man. Apparently the cops are coming to my place, where a collection of kidnapped girls are being held. But I don't really care about any of that, I just want the truth."

"Fine," Pierce offered with a sigh. "We're not the police; we work for an international security company."

"Like mercenaries?"

"Something like that," Pierce allowed with a quick nod. "We go places were the authorities can't or won't go. The man we were after was beyond the power of the police and had to be stopped. We were commissioned to rescue the girls and stop him, one way or the other."

"There's more to it than that," Lukas observed shrewdly.

"Obviously," Pierce replied simply, turning towards the cars and leading the rest there. Kat squeezed into the back seat of the Charger, with MacDuff and Pierce sliding into the front seats and slamming the doors shut.

"So what do I tell the cops when they show up?!" Lukas yelled over the sound of the HEMI engine as it roared to life.

"Don't tell them anything!" Pierce yelled back before driving away.

"Shit!" Lukas swore before he noticed that the GTO was still parked there. Sean was already in the front seat, but Liam was standing by the open driver's door.

"Are you coming or what?" Liam asked seriously pointing to the back seat of the car.

"Huh?"

"You didn't think we were going to just leave you here after you helped us out did you?" Liam smiled as the fisherman slowly approached the car. He hesitated for a second by the door, taking a look back at his cabin and the fishing boats. Then with a look of relief and determination, he climbed into the back.

"So what have I gotten myself into?" Lukas asked after Liam got in and started the car.

"How long is it from here to San Diego?" Liam replied as he put the car into gear and slowly drove to the end of the driveway.

"I don't know twenty hours," Lukas shrugged.

"That might give us enough time to explain," Liam smiled as he stomped on the gas peddle and rocketed the GTO down the road.